D0021397

HOME FREE

H·O·M·E
F·R·E·E

ELIZABETH FORSYTHE HAILEY

Delacorte Press

Published by
Delacorte Press
Bantam Doubleday Dell Publishing Group, Inc.
666 Fifth Avenue
New York, New York 10103

Library of Congress Cataloging in Publication Data

Hailey, Elizabeth Forsythe.
    Home free : a novel / by Elizabeth Forsythe Hailey.
      p.   cm.
    ISBN 0-385-29914-1 (hc) ISBN 0-385-30399-8 (Large-print ed.) I. Title.
  PS3558.A327H6   1991
  813'.54—dc20   90-40454
                                                            CIP

Book design by Barbara Cohen Aronica

Manufactured in the United States of America
Published simultaneously in Canada

February 1991

10   9   8   7   6   5   4   3   2   1
RRH

For Carole Baron,
who willed this book into being
and who has provided me and my books a home

HOME
FREE

ONE

"Promise me, Kate, that you won't let this ruin Christmas."

Cliff's voice sounded as if it were coming across a vast distance. If she had been holding a phone, Kate would have told him to hang up and dial again, to try for a better connection. But he was standing across the front hall. "Please, Kate, try to believe me, I didn't mean to tell you now, with Nina on her way home."

Kate moved to the window. Outside on the curving, tree-sheltered street, a battered station wagon at least ten years old sputtered to a stop. It looked the way she felt.

"At least talk to me." Cliff's voice reached across the room, pleading for a response, any response, but his feet remained rooted in the doorway, waiting for her to release him.

Instinctively Kate put her hand to her throat. The muscles felt paralyzed—just like the dream she had at least once a month in which she was calling for help but making no sound. She turned back toward Cliff. He was studying her now as if she were

1

an actress about to play the crucial scene in a film he was directing. She looked away. It made her profoundly uncomfortable to be on the receiving end of the kind of attention he usually reserved for his work.

The sound of an engine turning over but refusing to start drew her attention back to the street. A tall, lean man, who looked younger than Kate but moved as if he had weights tied to his arms and legs, slowly opened the door of the old station wagon.

"Poor man," she murmured as he raised the hood and bent anxiously over the engine. Even at a distance she could sense that his fate somehow depended on getting his car to start.

"What?" Cliff asked, hearing the promise of forgiveness in the sudden softening of her voice.

"You'd better get started for the airport," Kate said without looking at him. In the past she had always tried to give Cliff the response he wanted—but there was no longer any reason to say anything she didn't mean. She was surprised to discover how much her newfound silence could disconcert him. Finally he slammed the front door and left the house.

Kate watched as he walked to the garage and backed his green Jaguar down the driveway. The car had not left the garage in his absence—until Kate drove it to the airport last night to meet him. She had started it once a week and let the motor run a few minutes to keep the battery working, but the car was too important to Cliff for her to risk driving it.

Cliff shifted gears and sped down the street. Amazing how much men still enjoyed shifting gears, Kate thought.

Cliff had bought a Jaguar when his first film proved a box-office bonanza and had replaced it with a newer one with each succeeding hit. This car was ten years old—but behind the wheel Cliff was still a success. Kate often wished he could drive it to the dinner table and into bed. It might have made all the difference.

Still numb from their conversation, Kate looked around their living room as if it were a hotel she was entering for the first time. Suddenly furniture with which she had lived on intimate terms for years seemed alien and impersonal, and she stood motionless at the window, waiting to be shown to her room.

A clap of thunder broke into her thoughts. As the rain began, the owner of the old station wagon took refuge in his car. Kate could swear she saw him bow his head in prayer before he turned the key in the ignition. "Come on, start," she whispered under her breath. She felt a surge of gratitude when the motor caught—as if her will still retained some power. At least one life had averted disaster, for the moment anyway. But before she could take any comfort from the thought, the car coughed—a death rattle—and gave up the ghost.

Kate stood frozen at the window, her eyes riveted on the street, as the man rested his head against the steering wheel and began to sob. "Don't look," Cliff used to shout when they'd pass an accident on the highway. But Kate always felt compelled to try to understand what had happened. "Why? Why do you do it?" Cliff would say later, holding her in his arms, trying to erase with his physical presence the images she could not forget. "You can't do anything to help, so why do you torment yourself by looking?"

She waited for the man to lift his head, wipe his eyes, and try again. But all life and hope seemed to have left his body. She felt trapped in a freeze-frame. This was no highway accident she could speed past.

Kate stood watching at the window, praying for the man to make some move that would release her from sharing in his fate. But he remained with his head on the wheel—a statue of silent despair. Finally, as if bowing to the inevitable, Kate walked slowly to her front door and opened it. Still no movement from the man in the car.

Cautiously she moved down the flower-guarded path that led from her house to the street. Only when she reached the stalled car did she realize she was soaking wet. It had never even occurred to her to look for an umbrella or put on a raincoat.

This is what happens to us, she reflected, knocking on the car window to attract the man's attention. We sit inside our safe, comfortable houses and feel inviolate. We forget that once we step outside, we get wet, just like everybody else.

The expression on the man's face as he turned to look at Kate cut into her consciousness. Every feature seemed to humble itself in apology for inflicting his presence on a street where he had not earned the right to come to a stop. "Do you mind opening your door?" she called through the window, which she saw now was badly cracked. "I'm getting soaked."

Reluctantly the man opened the door on the passenger side and motioned for her to climb in beside him. What am I doing? she asked herself as she lowered her body onto the exposed springs of the worn front seat. All her life she had followed the rules—obeyed her mother, honored her husband—and now suddenly here she was, sitting beside a strange man in his car, the kind of man she would have done her best to avoid if she had passed him in a parking lot.

"Never get into a car with someone you don't know," her mother had said to her over and over before finally allowing her to walk to school alone when she was ten. And now, at forty-five, Kate was defying every cautious instinct that had shaped the first half of her life. But what did she have to show for forty-five years of playing it safe?

Suddenly Kate screamed as a furry form lunged at her from behind. "Down, Homer," shouted the man. "Get into the back."

Kate turned around to see a huge red Irish setter retreat to the back of the station wagon and lie down obediently on a blanket that he clearly recognized as his bed.

"I didn't realize it was raining," Kate said, taking the scarf from around her neck to dry her hair.

"This happens to be the only roof I've got," the man muttered. "It's not much—but at least it was dry under here before you climbed in."

"Are you living in this car?" Kate asked, astonished.

"Got a better idea?"

Kate wished she were back in her house with the door locked, but she couldn't just leave him without some kind of explanation. "I saw you from my house trying to get your car started. I thought maybe there was something I could do to help."

"Not unless you've got another green Jag like the one that just came shooting out of your driveway. Who was that man?"

"My husband."

"He almost took my rear fender with him. I never saw a man in such a hurry to leave home."

Kate put her hands in front of her face but could not prevent a low moan from escaping her mouth.

The man turned toward her in alarm. "You didn't come out here to be sick in my car, did you? That's all I need."

Kate opened the car door. "I shouldn't have bothered you. I'm sorry."

Ignoring her, the man closed his eyes and leaned his head back against the seat. Whimpering, Homer began to lick his face.

Kate saw how strikingly handsome he could be—separated from his circumstances. His dark hair fell in shaggy locks over his high forehead. A stubble of beard could not disguise the high cheekbones and the strong set of his jaw.

"Are you all right?" she asked as he continued to lie there with his eyes closed.

"I feel like I'm about to faint," he said.

"Come into the house," Kate said before she thought. "At least it's warm in there. And I could fix you something to eat."

He turned to look at her for the first time, searching her face for a hidden motive. "If I rang the doorbell of any house on this street and asked for help, I'd get the door slammed in my face— that's if anyone was brave enough to open it to me in the first place."

"Maybe it's the fact you didn't come to the door," Kate said slowly. "My daughter gets furious if she sees me open the door to a stranger. She says I'm living in the past, refusing to recognize how dangerous the world has become."

"She's right," he agreed. "So why are you willing to let me inside your house?"

"If I don't, what will you do?" Kate asked.

"I don't know."

"Then we don't have a choice, do we?"

The rain was coming down steadily now. "We'll have to make a dash for it," Kate said and started toward her front door at a run. The sound of Homer barking frantically made her turn around. The man had fallen to his knees beside the car door. He was clinging desperately to the handle, trying to get to his feet, while Homer circled him, barking an alarm.

Kate ran back to the car. "Put your arm around my shoulder," she said. "I'll help you into the house." Then she turned to the growling dog. "It's all right, Homer. You can come with us."

The dog pressed close to his master, as if trying to provide support, until they were inside the house. Only then did he lie down on the rug in front of the fire.

Kate guided the man to the couch. "Why don't you stretch out here while I heat up some soup?"

The man looked down at his torn, stained jeans and shook his head. He crossed to the fire and knelt on the rug beside his dog. "That fire feels good. I'll be fine right here."

Suddenly Kate saw that he was shivering. "You've got to get out of those wet clothes," she said. "I don't mean to insult you, but would you like to take a bath while I fix something to eat?"

He smiled broadly. "Insult me? You've just said a word I fall asleep dreaming about."

As Kate led him up the stairs and through the master bedroom, headlines flashed through her mind: "Housewife Assaulted by Vagrant." But there was something so vulnerable about this man—she could still see the child within him. "This is my husband's bathroom," she said, opening the door. "Help yourself to anything you need—shampoo, shaving cream, razor . . ."

The man turned to her with a curious stare. "Are you sure he won't mind?"

Kate smiled brightly. "Oh, I'm quite sure he will."

He shrugged. "I don't know what to say. We've gone way beyond thank-you." And he closed the bathroom door behind him.

Kate found herself humming under her breath as she moved into the huge walk-in closet that separated the two bathrooms, hers and Cliff's. "I hope we never have separate bedrooms," Cliff had said when he brought her to this house as a bride twenty-five years ago, "but this marriage will have a better chance if we have separate bathrooms." Kate grimaced. Apparently separate bathrooms had not been the answer to the question "Can this marriage be saved?"

Taking off her own wet clothes, Kate felt strangely comforted by the sound of running water. With Nina away at school and Cliff on location, it had been weeks—months—since anyone besides herself had turned on the shower. As she reached for a pair of slacks and a sweater, she thought she heard someone calling her name. She stopped to listen, then realized the man was just singing in the shower.

She imagined him standing under the running water, feeling really clean for the first time in weeks. Suddenly there was quiet as the water was turned off and the singing stopped. Kate could almost see him standing there, the water dripping off his shoulders, catching sight of his reflection in the full-length mirror opposite the shower. Stripped of his shabby clothes, he would be able to see the man he still was.

Clothes! She had to find something for him to wear. Kate began ransacking Cliff's side of the closet, grabbing trousers, shirts, and sweaters from the neatly hung, color-coordinated rows.

She emerged from the closet, her arms piled high, just as the bathroom door opened. Enveloped in a cloud of steam, the man stepped in front of her wearing only a towel around his waist. He was taller than she had realized and his body was lean and hard. Kate could not help staring at his well-built frame. This was not the man she had helped into her living room.

"I hated to put on my clothes just yet," he said. "They're so wet."

"Of course," Kate said, anxious to keep this new man from disappearing into his old self. "There's a robe hanging behind the bathroom door."

"Must have missed it," he said, turning quickly back into the bathroom.

7

Kate sank onto the bed, dropping the pile of clothes she was holding in her arms onto the comforter, as the man emerged from the bathroom, wrapped in Cliff's thick white terrycloth robe. She tried to concentrate on his bare feet sinking into the carpet as she collected her thoughts.

"I'm sorry. I guess my feet are still wet," he said, following her gaze to the path his feet had imprinted.

"My husband is about your size," she said quickly. "Take any of these clothes that fit."

"Won't he miss them?"

"I doubt it. I haven't seen any of these things leave the closet in over a year. He just can't be bothered to give anything away." She stood slowly. "I'll go fix lunch while you get dressed."

Standing in front of the stove heating a pot of homemade vegetable soup, Kate thought in what a happy mood she had awakened that morning.

She had been in the kitchen basting the turkey for Christmas Eve dinner when Cliff finally came downstairs.

"Happy holidays, darling," she said, putting her arms around his neck. "It's so good to have you home."

"It's just Christmas Eve," he said as he disentangled himself from her embrace. "Can't you hold the holiday cheer till tomorrow?"

Kate stared at the basting bulb in her hand. A giant tear was forming at the end. She quickly turned her attention back to the turkey, squeezing the bulb mercilessly. "I started celebrating when you came home last night," she said, still bending over the turkey.

"I know." Cliff poured himself a cup of coffee. "I'm sorry I was too tired to join you. That was a lovely late supper you had waiting."

Kate ached for him to take her in his arms. A month away and he had barely brushed her cheek at the airport last night. Once they were home, he had gone straight upstairs. By the time she had put away the unopened bottle of champagne, the smoked salmon and caviar, he was asleep in their bed. His suitcase lay open on the floor, a trail of clothes marking his path from the bathroom to the bed. The room was dark, except for a flickering, voiceless image of Ingrid Bergman that filled the television screen. A slender wire channeled the dialogue directly into Cliff's ear. Last night, like so many nights in their marriage, the last voice he heard had a husky Swedish accent.

"What was it like—being back in Canada?" Kate asked finally, abandoning hope of an embrace.

Cliff looked up from the mail she had carefully stacked for him in his absence. "If I'd been treated like that thirty years ago, I might never have left—a welcoming ceremony from the mayor, interviews every day during lunch, TV chat shows, people asking for my autograph in restaurants . . ."

"Hail the conquering hero," said Kate. "No wonder you didn't have time to write."

"I never have time to write letters when I'm on location, Kate. You remember what it's like."

Kate moved behind him so he couldn't see her face—on the off chance he might look up from his mail. She wished she could hide what she was feeling—it was the only reason she had ever wanted to be able to act.

Cliff used to say that Kate was the first person he ever directed. He taught her to dance and to walk across the room with a dancer's grace, to speak but also, and even more important, to listen and to ask questions.

To outsiders, to friends, even to her own mother, Kate had been transformed by marriage into a radiantly assured woman whose warmth and kindness drew other people into her presence and whose husband, it was clear to all, continued to adore her.

So why was she standing behind him, nervously massaging his shoulders and wondering what the future held for her?

"Please, Kate, I'm trying to drink my coffee," Cliff said irritably, shuffling envelopes in front of him. "And I've got to deal with this mail before I go back."

"When are you coming home to me, Cliff?" The words were out of her mouth before she could stop them. "Do you realize you haven't even given me a proper kiss?"

"I'm sorry, Kate." He reached for her hand and held it to his lips. "I've never done this before, you know. Come home in the middle of a shoot. Especially one I've been thrown into like this —with no time to prepare. Maybe it was a mistake. I just wanted to come home for Christmas. To spend it with you and Nina."

"And I wanted you home. Don't pay any attention to the way I've been acting. I just missed you so much. I wish I'd come with you to Toronto, but it all happened so fast." She slipped into his arms without allowing herself to consider whether she'd be welcome and pressed her lips against his mouth, closing her eyes so she wouldn't have to look into his.

He stood up abruptly. "Damn it, Kate, I've been a bastard."

Her heart pounding with fear, Kate followed him into the living room. He stood in front of the fireplace, his back to her, staring at the three hand-sewn stockings hanging from the mantel. "I haven't even had time to buy you a Christmas present."

"I'm so glad," Kate said with relief. "Because I know just what I want."

"Wonderful," said Cliff. "Where do I go to get it? I'll stop on my way to the airport."

"You don't have to stop anywhere. I've already made the reservation. Just pay for the ticket when you get to the airport."

"What ticket?"

"To Toronto. Tomorrow. On the flight with you."

"Don't force my hand, Kate. Can't we just get through Christmas—for Nina's sake."

"For Nina's sake? Are you telling me you only came home for Nina? What about me? What about us?" Suddenly Kate reached for the stockings and ripped them from the mantel. "It's ridiculous to fill a stocking for a child who's in her first year of law school. And I'm sick of pretending to be surprised by presents I've bought for myself."

Cliff moved to her and took her in his arms. All night she had longed for his touch. Now at last he was holding her and she felt nothing. "We have to talk, Kate. I wanted to wait till Christmas was behind us—I know how much you always enjoy the holidays."

So there was something wrong after all. Kate was not just imagining the distance that continued to separate them—even in the same room. "Whatever it is, Cliff, you have to tell me," she said, suddenly calm. "You're no good at keeping things from me. You never have been." She paused. "Thank God."

He sat heavily on the couch and put his head in his hands. "I'm not sure I can get through this," he said in a whisper. "Living with it is one thing, but talking about it . . ."

Her knees trembling, she sat down beside him. What terrible secret was causing Cliff so much pain? Not cancer! Her heart stopped at the thought. Please, God, no. She reached for his hand. "Whatever it is, darling, we can lick it. But you have to let me help you. Stop trying to spare me. I'm stronger than you think. Now tell me what's wrong. Have you seen a doctor?"

That was the last question she remembered asking. A torrent of words began to pour from Cliff, but none of them made sense to her. If only he hadn't gone to Canada, he kept saying. She listened attentively, trying to comprehend. If Cliff had contracted some terrible disease, what difference did going to Canada make?

"I just want you to know I didn't make the first move," he said finally. Kate could tell from the way Cliff was looking at her that he was trying to make an important point, but she felt as if she were listening to a record played at the wrong speed. Words were coming out of his mouth, but all she was hearing was noise. She put her hands over her ears.

"I'm going upstairs," she said, standing abruptly. "I didn't sleep very well last night. I kept dreaming you didn't come home after all. I would run from gate to gate, meeting flight after flight . . ."

"Damn it, Kate," Cliff said. "I didn't want to talk about any of this till after Christmas. But you drove me to it. You can't run away now. Sit down and listen to what I have to say."

As he talked, Kate's mind kept focusing on the only reality she could accept—Cliff was dying of cancer. She would devote herself to him, canceling all commitments of her own, staying at his side around the clock. At last she would be able to repay in some small measure what he had done for her by marrying her and providing her with a life beyond anything she had been able to imagine as a young girl. "I'll take care of you, darling, I promise," she whispered, frozen with the fear of losing him. "I won't let you die."

"So you see, you can't come to Canada now." His voice cut through her grief.

"No, of course not," she said quickly. "We're staying here so you can get well."

"She wouldn't move in with me until I'd told you. Until everything was out in the open," he continued, his words steamrolling through her consciousness, clearing a path through the forest of speculation where she had been taking refuge. There was no longer any place for her to hide.

"She?" The word was forced out of her against her will. Kate could feel the pressure rising from the pit of her stomach, pushing against her throat as she spoke. "Who is *she*?"

"The name won't mean anything to you."

"None of it means anything to me." A roar came from deep inside her. "But I need a name." Kate was burning with anger. Before it consumed her, she had to direct it outward, somehow find a focus—something, or someone, more real, more human, more flawed than just a "she." "She" was every other woman in the world. "She" was everything Kate was not.

Cliff was being very patient and careful with her now, telling the story simply as if she were a child. And at first Kate found herself listening, fascinated.

Wenda Stone. Her name was Wenda Stone. Kate repeated it under her breath, trying to make the name into a tangible presence—something with weight and texture to replace the elusive "she" that taunted her with her own inadequacy.

Cliff had met Wenda thirty years ago—at college in Toronto. Something in Kate surrendered when she heard the word "college." College represented a charmed time in the lives of those who could afford it—a four-year reprieve from the unrelenting dailyness of adult life.

Kate had gotten a job waiting tables in the Universal commissary the week after she graduated from North Hollywood High School. Her mother couldn't afford to send her to college and she had never known her father. He had been killed in the last year of World War II, just before she was born. He had met her mother while he was stationed in Long Beach and they had gotten married just before he shipped out to the South Pacific. The letter she wrote telling him she was pregnant was returned unopened along with the picture of her he carried with him and the rest of his things.

But having a father she had never met made it possible for Kate to shape his identity to suit her imagination. If she had had a father, she used to say to herself before she met Cliff, everything would have been different. She would have gone to college with her friends.

"Look, this isn't any easier for me than it is for you, you know." Cliff's voice interrupted her thoughts and Kate realized she was crying.

"Oh, I think it is." She laughed bitterly. There was a long pause and she realized Cliff was going to leave the room, leave the house, leave her life, if she didn't stop him with questions. "So what went wrong between you and Wenda Stone? In the beginning, I mean?"

"I thought she understood about the life I wanted—in the theater. But while I was working in repertory, she married someone else. A banker."

"I see. Wenda didn't think you were good enough for her so you came to Hollywood and found someone who didn't think she was good enough for you."

"You're wrong."

"You're damned right I'm wrong. You're the one who's not good enough for me. But you and Wenda deserve each other. What did she do? See your picture in the paper and come to your hotel to tell you what a mistake she'd made marrying the banker, not waiting for you? Especially now that you're a famous Hollywood director."

"I didn't think it would hurt to see her. She was part of my past."

"And now your past has stolen my future. What's going to happen to me?"

The kindness in Cliff's voice dissolved all Kate's defenses. It had been a long time since he had spoken to her with such tenderness. "You have the house and I'll keep enough in your housekeeping account to cover your expenses. I'm afraid that's the best I can do for now. I'm rather short of cash."

"I don't want your money. Not without you!"

Anxious to extricate himself, Cliff looked at his watch. "Nina's plane will be landing in another hour. If I don't leave now, I won't be there to meet her."

Kate stood hesitantly on the stairs. "I may not be here when you get back."

Cliff opened the front door. "I no longer have the right to ask you to do anything for me. But think of Nina. She almost didn't come home at all—she has so much work. Can't we forget ourselves and make this a merry Christmas for her sake?"

"Can you do that? Forget everything you've just told me and pretend we're still a happy family?"

"Just for one night. Nina leaves tomorrow afternoon. Think of the pressure she's under. Please, Kate, I never meant for any of this to happen. But it doesn't have anything to do with Nina. It's between us. As angry as you are at me, I know how much you love our daughter. You don't want to hurt her any more than I do. Whatever mistakes we've made with our lives, we've been the best possible parents. Don't destroy that."

"How dare you? The only mistake I made with my life was not going to Toronto with you in the first place."

The waste. That was what haunted her now, as she moved around the spacious country kitchen that they had remodeled with such care early in their marriage. She stared at the gleaming appliances around which her domestic life revolved, all of them in perfect working order. Only her marriage was beyond repair.

How dare Cliff not be happy in this house with me, she thought. She closed her eyes as images of their life together unreeled inside her head. Cliff had always been so good at character and motivation. If he had been given their marriage as a script to direct, he would not have allowed it to end like this.

Suddenly Kate felt something furry brush the back of her knees, shocking her into the present. "Homer," she said, stroking his silky back. "You must be hungry too." She took a package of ground meat from the refrigerator, crumbled it into a tinfoil pie pan, and put it on the floor. Homer ran to it eagerly.

Then she picked up the tray she had prepared with two bowls of soup and a platter of cheeses and started for the living room.

"Here. Let me carry that for you." A man she hardly recognized was coming down the stairs. He was wearing Cliff's clothes, but any resemblance ended there. This man owned his body whereas Cliff gave the impression he rented his, like a tuxedo no amount of alteration could make fit properly. The shower and shave had put some color back in his cheeks. Though Kate could see that he was younger than she was, there were lines in his face. His hands were large and capable as he took the tray from her, but the roughness of his skin betrayed a lifetime of exposure to the elements. "Where shall I take this?" he asked in a warm, deep voice.

"How about in the living room—in front of the fire?" Kate suggested. "I built it this morning before breakfast. It's a shame to waste a good fire."

The man set the tray on the floor and lowered himself onto the rug. She handed him a bowl of soup, then, kneeling beside him, took one for herself. As she started to eat, she noticed him looking at her hesitantly. "Would you rather be alone?" she asked. "My husband really preferred to eat by himself. It took me years to figure it out."

The man gave her a smile that seemed intended to erase the sense of neglect she had just revealed. "You don't know how much it means to me that you set two places on that tray," he said quietly, "that you're sharing a meal with me and not just giving a handout to someone in need—though God knows I qualify. I was just wondering if you'd mind if I said a blessing."

Kate put her bowl back on the tray, folded her hands, and bowed her head.

In a resonant, unhurried voice the man who had been faint with hunger on the street now spoke to God as if He were a caring friend. He thanked Him for renewing his strength and his faith by providing such a tangible expression of His love. The words seemed to flow spontaneously from his lips.

Kate marveled at the ease and eloquence with which he expressed himself. She was suddenly taken back to her child-hood. "My grandmother used to say grace before meals. But she always said the same words. I still remember them."

"You couldn't get away with that in my family." Finally, it seemed to Kate, the man had relaxed his guard. "My daddy taught us to talk to God like he was right there in the room. There were four kids. Every time we sat down at the table, he would call on one of us to bless the food we were about to eat, but there was never any order to it, so you never knew whose turn it was going to be. We used to complain, especially if we were called on two nights in a row, but Daddy would just lean back in his chair and laugh. He'd say he was preparing us for life—we had to learn early not to count on things to happen in any predictable order. Each of us was at all times totally and completely at the mercy of God."

"Amen," said Kate, surprised by the fervor of her response. "How about some more soup?" she asked, seeing that he had eaten everything she had put before him.

"Thank you." He followed her into the kitchen, carrying his bowl. Kate was struck by the dignity with which he accepted everything she offered him. She had never been very good at receiving—especially from Cliff. She had always felt so grateful for the way he had transformed her life—and at the core so unde-serving of his love. From the day he had asked her to marry him, she had dreaded the day he would leave her. Now it had finally arrived. She was almost relieved.

"Do you realize you haven't even told me your name?" Kate said as she refilled his bowl.

"I was waiting till you asked." His eyes weighed her with a

steady gaze, as if testing her capacity for compassion. "Once you can call a thing by name, you start to care what happens to it."

"My name is Kate," she said, accepting his challenge. That was the only name she was really sure of right now, she thought to herself. Her last name belonged to her husband.

"You can call me Ford," he responded. "I was born in one. Daddy was driving Mama to the hospital, but he didn't get there in time. My parents picked out names from the Bible for all their children. I was the oldest—and all set to be 'Peter,' you know, 'the rock'—in fact, it says 'Peter' on my birth certificate—but I grew up being called 'Ford' and I decided I liked it. A Ford is the only kind of car my family has ever owned. I bought mine the day my son was born—to bring him home from the hospital."

"A car seems to go along with giving birth in your family," Kate remarked with a smile.

"A Ford has never let our family down," he said. "I've had that car out there for ten years. If it gives out on me, I don't know where I'm going to turn."

"Where is your family now?" Kate asked gently.

"Downtown. In a shelter for wives and children who've been deserted."

"You deserted them?" Kate could not conceal her shock. She trusted her instincts about people—but this man was not what she thought.

"We were desperate. The places that take families—and there aren't that many—were full. So my wife had to pretend I'd walked out on them—which I might as well have, for all the good I'm doing them." He looked down at his bowl and, using a crust of bread, soaked up the last bit of soup. "I guess you're wondering how I got in this mess," he said as he carried his bowl into the kitchen and carefully washed it.

"You don't have to tell me," Kate hurried to assure him. "It must be hard to talk about it."

"Talking about it is easy."

There was nothing unusual in the story Ford began to tell. No point at which Kate could separate herself from the events which had overtaken him and say, "But of course, that's where he went wrong. I would never do that and so what happened to him could never happen to me."

He had been born on a farm in Iowa in a house his grandfather had built on land given to him by *his* grandfather. For five generations his family had made their living from the land—but for the past five years going further and further into debt. Ford was the only one of the four children who stayed on the farm. When it was repossessed, he and his family lost not only their livelihood but the roof over their heads.

Relatives took pity on them while he looked for work. But his neighbors were no better off than he was and every time he heard of a job opening, ten men were there ahead of him. Finally he packed his wife, Sunny, his son, Joe Wayne, and his daughter, Marvella, into the only shelter he still owned—his Ford station wagon—and headed west to look for work.

"How long have you been here?" Kate asked.

"Since the Fourth of July. We got to the ocean just as the fireworks started. We thought we'd reached the Promised Land." He sighed, then took a deep breath and continued his story. The trip across the country had been an adventure. They stopped at campgrounds along the highway, pitching a tent and cooking over an open fire. When they first arrived in Los Angeles, they slept on the beach, under the stars. But when summer ended and Ford was still without a steady job, the adventure started becoming desperate. He earned enough doing odd jobs to buy food but every week there were unforeseen expenses that cut into their meager savings—the car breaking down or one of the children getting sick. He had been told there was work in southern California, but he found no one willing to hire a man with no references, no experience, and, most important, no address.

When school started, Sunny said she'd had enough. They had to have help. Joe Wayne and Marvella needed an address so they could register for school. He drove them to the welfare office and they applied for shelter, only to be told there was no space available for families. Finally the woman took pity on them and, searching her files, found a vacancy in a shelter for women and children. "Don't go with them," she warned Ford. "This place is for women whose husbands have walked out on them."

"And maybe that's what I should have done," he said in a hoarse whisper. "I have to sneak in to see them—and every time I do I risk getting them thrown out. I know I should stay away, but they're all I've got. If I didn't have Homer here—some other living thing I can call by name—I'd be out of my mind by now."

He took a deep breath, summoning his strength, and looked out the window. "I think I'll give that engine another try—now that the rain has stopped."

"Where are you headed?" asked Kate as she walked with him to the car, Homer at their heels.

"I was on my way to the shopping center. Sometimes, if you stand outside the grocery store . . ."

"Yes, I know," Kate interrupted, sorry she had asked. "It's hard to push a full basket of groceries out that door without thinking about families who don't have enough to eat. They know what they're doing, those people who stand around with signs saying they're collecting for the homeless."

"I don't stand around panhandling," he said with a flash of anger. Kate felt uneasy at this show of temper and thought for the first time about his wife. It could not have been easy for her, even in the best of times, living with a man whose mood could change so quickly.

"I didn't mean to offend you," she said quickly. "I was just trying to explain that there are a lot of people like me, who feel sympathy for people like you—people who've lost their homes. We just don't know how to help."

"Christ," he said, getting into his car and slamming the door. He continued to mutter as he tried, without success, to start the engine. Kate stood helplessly on the sidewalk, straining to hear what he was saying. She wished she were back in her house with the door closed, but she was frozen in place. Like it or not, she knew his name now.

It was clear the car was not going to start, but Ford continued to stay at the wheel with the door closed and the window raised.

Kate walked toward the house without looking back. Suddenly she heard the car door slam. She turned around and saw Ford removing a sign on a stick. Holding it defiantly against his shoulder, he approached her. The sign read, "Help me feed my children. Give me a job."

Kate's eyes filled with tears. She imagined him standing in front of the supermarket holding the sign. Wordlessly, she held the front door open for him.

"I'm sorry for the way I sounded out there," he said tersely. "I didn't mean to scare you away."

"I wasn't running from you," she explained. "I was coming into the house to call the Auto Club."

"The Auto Club?" He looked confused.

"You know. To come look at your car, try to fix whatever is wrong with it."

"You'd do that for me?"

She shrugged. "It doesn't seem like much."

"Wait till the day your life depends on your car."

While Kate dialed the number, Ford walked over to the window, began to examine it. "An hour?" Kate said into the phone, looking helplessly at Ford. "Yes, I understand," she continued. "What choice do I have?" She hung up the phone with an apologetic glance at Ford. "It's the rain. It creates havoc in California. I'm sorry. I know you're anxious to be moving on."

"The thought of spending another hour in this house is hardly the worst thing that ever happened to me," Ford said with a smile. "If it wasn't for my wife and kids, I wouldn't care about going anywhere ever again. But I've got to find some work today, so I can bring them something tonight. They're counting on Christmas. I guess I am too." He paused. "These windows could use a paint job. I've got some sandpaper in my car. I could get started right away."

"I've got a better idea," said Kate, heading for the stairs. "Come with me."

She opened a closet in the hallway where boxes of old clothes were stored. "There used to be a Goodwill collection bin behind the grocery store," she said. "But a woman had a heart attack when she started to leave some clothes and saw a pair of eyes staring back at her. A man had been sleeping inside. She reported it to Goodwill and they came and took the bin away. So lately I've just been piling things in here."

"You'd be surprised at the places people find to sleep," Ford said. "You know those dumpsters in the parking lot? Late at night, when they're pretty sure the garbage trucks have stopped for the day, people climb into those. It's better than sleeping on the sidewalk. At least they've got a roof over their heads. Of course, they've got to be out by dawn. One man I heard about overslept and was almost buried alive in a load of garbage."

Trying to erase the image now engraved inside her head, Kate busied herself opening the boxes for Ford's inspection. "Take any of these things your family could use."

He smiled. "There's nothing you could give me that someone at that shelter couldn't put to good use." He took a pair of gloves from one of the boxes and began trying them on as he talked. "At least our two kids got off to a good start. They're strong and healthy. They'll get through this. But some of the little ones are going to be scarred for life. There are babies in that place wearing newspapers for diapers because their mothers have to choose between feeding them or clothing them."

Kate grimaced. "I think I could stand almost anything for myself. But it must be unbearable to see your children suffer and not be able to do anything about it."

Ford nodded, not trusting himself to speak.

Kate saw his thumb showing through a hole in the glove. Embarrassed, she reached for his hand and pulled off the glove. "Let me sew that up for you," she said quickly. She saw how rough and red his hands were, the skin cracked between the fingers. "Why don't you put these boxes in your car," she said, slipping the gloves in her pocket, "while I go upstairs and look in my closet, see if I can find something for your wife."

"I'd sure be grateful," he said. "She never gives a thought to herself. It would mean everything to me to be able to do something nice for her for Christmas."

He headed out the front door, carrying the boxes. Kate started for the stairs, then caught sight of the Christmas tree surrounded by the packages she had taken such pleasure in wrapping. One by one, she picked up the packages with Cliff's name and ripped off the tags. Then she took a box of unused tags from a drawer. She met Ford at the front door with an armful of brightly wrapped packages.

"For me?" he asked in surprise as she handed them to him.

"Read the tags."

He looked at her in disbelief. "My name is on every one of them. Where did they come from?"

"From under the tree. Merry Christmas."

"I don't understand," he said slowly. "You couldn't have bought them for me."

"I didn't know you when I bought them." Kate smiled. "But as luck would have it, you're the same size as my husband—and at the moment I like you a lot better."

"You're a beautiful woman," he said, his eyes embracing her.

"Thank you. That may be the nicest Christmas present I'll get this year."

He stood hesitantly at the door, not sure what was expected of him. "I guess I should take these packages to the car before you change your mind," he said with an awkward laugh.

"Would it be unfair to ask you to celebrate Christmas right now—with me?" The words were out of Kate's mouth before she could stop them. "I mean I'd love to see how everything looks on you." She hurried back into the living room. "Just wait till I turn on the Christmas tree lights."

When the Auto Club truck arrived, Ford was waiting by the front door, dressed in a new tweed sports coat, flannel trousers, striped shirt, and paisley tie.

"What do you want with this old wreck?" the serviceman asked as he opened the hood.

"Sentimental value," said Ford, smiling.

Kate was basting the turkey when Ford returned to the house to tell her good-bye. "He's finally gotten it started," he said. "So I'd better get to where I'm going before it cuts out on me again." He took out his car keys and removed a rabbit's foot from the chain. "I don't have any way to thank you," he said. "My daddy gave me this when I was a boy. I thought it had lost any power it had a long time ago, but it brought me to your door today, so maybe it will bring you the same kind of luck. Merry Christmas."

"Thank you," said Kate. "I'll put it on my key chain and think of you every time I start my car." She reached in her pocket and pulled out the mended gloves. "Here," she said. "I mended these for you. I didn't know they had a hole in them when I gave them to you."

"Don't apologize for anything. Not after all you've done for us," said Ford, holding out his hand.

As she took it, Kate said hurriedly, "About your wife . . ."

"What?" Ford dropped her hand, disoriented.

"I went through my closet just now. There are two more boxes of clothes by the front door—things I haven't been able to wear in years—one suit I never even wore at all. Maybe they'll fit her."

Ford smiled. "She'll make them fit. Sunny's good with a needle and thread." He continued to stand there, smiling at her, as if reluctant to break the connection. "I could start painting those windows any time you say," he said finally.

Kate shook her head. "I don't care what happens to this house. It has nothing to do with me." She started to put the turkey back in the oven, then suddenly stopped, choking back an angry sob. "I don't know why I'm putting myself through this tonight." She reached into the cupboard and found a top for the roasting pan. Covering the turkey, she said to Ford, "Take this to your family. I'd like to think of the four of you eating it."

"But what will you eat? You and your family?" he protested as she filled a picnic basket with containers of chestnut stuffing, cranberry sauce, and candied yams.

"That's a question none of us has ever had to face," Kate said. "It's about time we did."

TWO

Kate stood watching at the living room window as Ford's car sputtered its way down the street. I wish I'd given him the Christmas tree too, she thought. He could have tied it to the top of his car, decorations and all. The picture of a fully decorated tree making its way through town on top of the old car made her laugh and she began singing carols to herself as she arranged the few remaining packages—all tagged for Nina—under the tree.

There was nothing left for Cliff to open on Christmas morning. But he had already confessed he had brought home nothing for her—except the news that he no longer loved her. Examining her motives for her actions of the past hour, Kate had to question how much she had done out of sympathy for Ford and his plight and how much out of hurt pride and a desire for revenge against Cliff.

When Cliff returned home from the airport with Nina, he found Kate soaking in his bathtub. "What are you doing in here?"

he asked, hardly believing this territorial affront. "Don't tell me there's something wrong with the plumbing in your bathroom."

"I don't think so," said Kate, squeezing a giant sponge over her shoulders.

"Then why are you bathing in my tub?"

"I got in the habit while you were away," Kate lied, looking around to make sure there was no evidence of another man's having used the bathroom. "Your presence is so strong in here. It kept me from missing you so much." She climbed from the tub. "Shall I run a bath for you?"

"Stop this, Kate," he said brusquely, handing her a towel. "I've never asked you to wait on me. Don't you have any sense of who you are?"

"Who am I, Cliff—if I'm no longer your wife?"

"That's a question I've been wanting you to answer for a long time," he replied. "Now go say hello to Nina."

As Kate walked down the hallway to Nina's room, she tried to remember just when and how their roles had reversed and her daughter had become the authority figure in their relationship.

Five years ago, when Nina was a senior in high school, their tastes began to diverge in every area—clothes, food, and people. Kate noticed it first on Christmas morning when Nina unwrapped present after present, smiled a polite thank you, but left each item in its box. The next day she returned everything for credit.

With a few exceptions, the pattern was repeated every year. Kate would resolve with the New Year not to buy any more presents for Nina since there was so little chance of pleasing her. She would stand firm through her birthday in late June, when she and Cliff would take their daughter to dinner at the restaurant of her choice and over dessert—anything but a birthday cake—present her with a check enclosed in some small item like a purse or a picture frame. Kate had not been present at Nina's birth—she and Cliff had adopted her when she was just a baby—so it seemed appropriate somehow for Nina alone to decide exactly how she wanted to celebrate the anniversary of her arrival into the world.

But Christmas was different. It was a time of tradition—a collective celebration. As Kate walked through the stores, humming along with the carols coming through the speakers, she could not resist buying things she would have liked Nina to like. And this year, once again, the tree was surrounded with presents that Kate did not expect to see again after Christmas morning. Still, she could not restrain herself from trying to find some tangible expression of the love she found it increasingly difficult to express in words and impossible with physical gestures.

"Come in," Nina called as Kate knocked tentatively at her bedroom door. Kate was embarrassed to admit, even to herself, how relieved she was to see Nina talking on the phone. Kate could usually feel Nina stiffen at her approach, knowing she would have to submit to a hug. Tonight Kate just blew her a kiss from the doorway and closed the door again, leaving Nina to continue her conversation.

Kate wondered if it was Adam on the other end of the line. Probably—since Nina seemed to be doing most of the talking. Kate marveled at Adam's devotion. He had fallen in love with Nina their last year in high school and been desolate to leave her behind when his parents insisted he go east to college.

Those had been lean years for Cliff and Kate. His career as a director of feature films seemed to be behind him, and he had come to depend on episodic television to pay the bills. However, Nina seemed to understand their financial situation and offered no objection to living at home and going to UCLA. In fact she seemed almost to welcome the enforced separation from Adam so she could concentrate on her studies.

She had decided to become a lawyer—so she would have a power base, she told her mother pointedly, and no one would ever be able to take advantage of her. The unspoken message behind this goal was that she did not intend to end up like her mother, dependent on a man to provide not only her economic support but her purpose in life. Kate couldn't help admiring the ferocity of her daughter's ambition, even though it was forged in reaction to her own choices.

Nina was never without a part-time job and worked long

hours during the summer at a legal firm in Century City. She was determined to save enough money to send herself through law school and never again to be dependent on her parents for what she wanted to do, but to their proud surprise, she was awarded a scholarship to Harvard Law School. So this fall, just as Adam was returning to Los Angeles to begin his life as a journalist, Nina was crossing the country in the opposite direction.

Kate wondered how much longer Adam would allow Nina to set the terms for their relationship. She would not have been surprised if he had come home from his first year of college and confessed he had fallen in love with someone else—someone soft and yielding and eager to please. But he seemed welded to Nina's strong sense of who she was and what she wanted from life, as if her ambition could help him define his. Her fierce honesty, which Kate often found devastating, delighted him. She never spared his feelings, but beneath her candor and caustic wit he seemed to sense a core of need that so far only he had been able to fill.

"I've invited Adam for dinner. I hope you don't mind," Nina said as she entered the living room, her arms loaded with presents.

"I love having him here. You know that. I don't see much of him when you're away. I've missed him almost as much as I have you." She moved to Nina and stood behind her, watching her arrange packages under the tree.

"Everything under here is for me," said Nina with surprise. "It's a good thing I came home or you and Daddy wouldn't have had any Christmas at all."

There was nothing Kate wanted more at that moment than to take Nina in her arms and confess everything. But Kate resisted the impulse. There was some question in her own mind, however, about her motives. Was she being noble and unselfish, suppressing her own unhappiness for the sake of her daughter, or was she simply not ready to risk Nina's judgment? Would Nina be angry at her father for betraying her mother or would she feel that Kate somehow had it coming?

"The only thing about tonight is," Kate began slowly, kneeling in front of the fire, picking dog hairs left by Homer off the rug, "I'm not cooking dinner."

"Oh," said Nina, only briefly taken aback by this information. "Then we'll go out. But what are you and Daddy doing? I could swear he said you had a turkey roasting in the oven and people coming to dinner."

"I changed my mind," Kate said. "About the turkey, that is. Ruth and Henry will be here, as usual. They couldn't get through Christmas without us. I think it's the only time they ever regret not having children."

"I'm glad you're not going to all that trouble cooking a turkey. I wasn't planning to eat it anyway. I've given up meat."

"Why didn't you tell me?"

Nina shrugged. "It doesn't matter. I don't live here anymore. You shouldn't be planning your meals around me."

But it's only because of you that we're going through the motions of Christmas at all, Kate wanted to scream, but she stopped herself. She'd gotten this far. Somehow she would make it through the next twenty-four hours. "So what would you like to eat tonight?"

"I don't care. What were you planning to serve?"

It suddenly occurred to Kate how many hours of her life she had devoted to discussing what to have for dinner. "Nothing," she was amazed to hear herself say. "I thought we'd just sit around the fire and have drinks. I'm not cooking again for people who have more than enough to eat. They don't appreciate it."

"Good for you," Nina said with a surprised laugh. "I've been waiting twenty-two years for you to go on strike!" And with that she crossed to the fire and gave her mother a warm hug.

"Oh, darling," said Kate, daring to kiss her daughter for the first time since her return, "I'm so happy to have you home— even for just a day."

"By tomorrow night you'll be ready to get rid of me." Nina laughed.

Kate hugged her again. "Not now—just as I'm getting to know you. You have no idea how much I've missed you these past three months. I wasn't prepared for it myself. It's funny.

When you're here, I don't miss the child you used to be, but when you're away, I ache for you at all the ages you'll never be again. I miss the baby I used to sing to sleep, the little girl who came to me for help with her homework, the teenager looking at her face for endless hours in the mirror and wondering if anybody besides her parents would ever tell her she was beautiful."

To Kate's surprise Nina suddenly lay down in front of the fire and put her head in Kate's lap. "And all this time I thought you wanted me out of the house—so you could be alone with Daddy." Nina had closed her eyes, so she did not see the pain that filled her mother's face.

"How in the world could you think something as ridiculous as that?" Kate asked, stroking Nina's forehead and smoothing back her hair.

"Sometimes I'd see the way you were looking at me at the dinner table when I was talking to Daddy. A look of such envy."

Kate had to smile at the shrewdness of her daughter's observation. "I do envy the way you argue with him when you think he's wrong," she confessed. "And the way he listens to you. Whenever I start a sentence, I can feel his impatience for me to get to the end of it."

"He has a way of finishing your sentences for you," Nina agreed. "If you let him."

"But you never let him," Kate said.

"And you never *not* let him." Nina opened her eyes and stared up at her mother, ready to risk the sweetness of the moment if it could not survive this challenge.

"He brought you up to be his equal," Kate responded calmly. "But that's not what he wanted in a wife. At least I never thought it was."

"I could never marry a man who didn't think of me as his equal," Nina said firmly. "How could you?"

"You have no idea how it feels to be poor—and desperate for someone to come along and change your life. You never stop feeling grateful. Whatever happens with your father . . ." Kate took a long breath, thinking of what had happened just that morning, and found it difficult to continue. "Whatever happens," she whispered, more to herself than to Nina, "I'll always love him for daring to love someone who had nothing to give him in return."

"Nothing except a lifetime of looking after him." Nina suddenly got to her feet. "I can't listen to any more of this. Don't you see how unfair you're being—not just to yourself, but to him and most of all to me. Do you remember when I was little and you were trying to teach me good manners? You said I didn't have to remember what you told me, I should just watch you and remember what you did. So I did watch you—all through my childhood. I learned to stand when an older person came into the room and I wrote a thank-you note every time I got a present and I finally even figured out which butter plate to use. You taught me all that but you never taught me the one thing a mother owes a daughter—you never taught me how a woman can love a man without turning herself inside out for him. That's one example you never set for me and I don't know where else to turn for it. But I am desperate to learn it and if somebody doesn't teach me soon, I'm going to end up alone—terrified of trying to love anybody."

Nina suddenly began to sob. But when Kate moved to her, she turned and ran from the room. Kate followed her to the stairs —and saw Cliff coming down. Nina rushed past him and slammed the door to her bedroom.

"Christ, why did you have to tell her?" Cliff's face was frozen into an angry mask. "Don't you ever think of anybody but yourself?"

"Nina just accused me of doing the exact opposite."

"How did she take the news?"

"I told her nothing," Kate said wearily. "Your secret is still safe."

"Then why was she so upset?"

"Unfinished business. Mother-daughter stuff."

"Two women under one roof—it just never works, does it?" Cliff was expansive in his relief.

"Not when there's a man in the middle," Kate replied. "But

once you're out of the picture, I have a feeling Nina and I are going to get along a lot better."

"I hope so, Kate. I hate thinking my happiness is going to make you unhappy. I wish you could just let go."

"I'm trying, Cliff. I really am."

"That's my girl," Cliff said, kissing her the way she had seen him kiss difficult actresses on the set more times than she could remember, trying to cajole them into good behavior.

"No, Cliff, I'm not your girl. Not anymore."

"I just meant . . . well, I don't see any reason why we can't stay friends. Do you?"

"None whatsoever."

"Good." He sank into an armchair by the fire. "You don't know how worried I've been about telling you. I haven't been able to eat anything in days. My stomach has been tied in knots. But now that you're taking it so well, I'm getting my appetite back. In fact, I'm hungry. What time is dinner?"

"I have no idea," said Kate.

THREE

Ford was five miles from the shelter when his car ran out of gas. In his elation at getting the motor started again, he had forgotten to check the gas gauge. Swearing to himself, he pushed the car into a parking space. He put the turkey on the floor of the front seat and tied Homer in the back, safely out of range. He left the windows open a crack, thinking good luck to anyone desperate enough to steal this wreck.

Then he walked a block trying to get his bearings. There was no gas station in sight but in the distance he saw a building he thought he recognized. He walked closer. It was a clinic where he'd given blood. He checked his pockets. Barely enough to buy a tankful of gas.

Resolutely he walked into the clinic. He used to hate getting shots as a kid and he fainted the first time he had to give blood. But now that his blood was the only thing he owned that he could exchange for cash, the needle was no longer an enemy. He smiled at the thought of all the bodies in which his cells had found a home. Probably part of me is a bank president by now, he mused, rolling up his sleeve. Or maybe even a movie star.

Laughing aloud at the thought, he caught sight of himself in a mirror and hardly recognized the image that stared back at him —a haircut was the only thing that separated him from one of those successful men in magazine ads. He had never given a thought to his appearance when he was running the farm. His work was the measure of his worth. But now, admiring the broad-shouldered, clear-eyed man in the mirror, he remembered how the girls used to follow him around in high school. Even the nurse who was tying the tourniquet around his arm seemed to be treating him with unaccustomed deference. "Nice tie," she said, stroking the paisley silk appreciatively.

"Thanks," Ford replied, loosening it with his free hand and unfastening the top button of the dress shirt Kate had given him. He couldn't remember the last time he'd put on a tie. Probably his father's funeral. Imagine having to dress like this to go to work every day! He grimaced at the thought. Still, it was nice to own the kind of clothes that automatically earned respect. Only his old shoes, scuffed and split at the seams, betrayed him. But the nurse wasn't looking at his feet. He felt confidence growing in every cell, even as the blood left his body.

Usually he arrived at the clinic in a state of desperation, exhausted and weak with hunger. After donating blood, he would feel light-headed and dizzy. He would drink as much orange juice as they would give him, then lie down until they made him leave. Often he fell asleep and they would have to wake him to send him out into the street.

Today, however, he was anxious to be on the move. If only the employment office were open! Ford was certain he would come away with a job. But it was Christmas Eve and he had a turkey dinner in his car, waiting to be transported to his wife and children. He felt a surge of joy thinking how surprised they would be.

He stopped an attractive nurse to ask where the nearest gas station was located. She smiled and insisted on drawing him a map. To his amazement he realized she was flirting with him. It had been a long time since a woman had looked at him in that way. He felt his blood stirring. He couldn't remember how long it had been since he had slept with his wife.

No, that was a lie. He knew exactly. There had been a furtive scuffle on the bathroom floor on Thanksgiving—a month ago. But what happened between them that night had nothing to do with making love. He winced at the memory.

From the day Sunny had taken the children to the shelter, he had ceased to think of himself as a husband—or a father. On the nights he dared to risk eviction for all of them by staying overnight, he and Sunny shared the bed with their two children—the four of them sleeping huddled together like brothers and sisters. Even if he had wanted to make love to his wife, there was no place, no time, no way for them to be alone. But in his heart he was relieved. He didn't feel like a man in that place—and at least he was spared that final failure.

But today, as he thanked the nurse, he found himself admiring the roundness of her breasts under the stiff uniform. He longed for the touch of his wife, for the length of her body lying naked against his, the wordless comfort of her warm flesh. Somehow, he vowed, before the night was over, he would find a way for them to be together.

At first he didn't realize the man standing next to him was talking to him. "Would you like a lift to the gas station? It's on my way."

"Sure." Ford nodded his thanks. Poor fellow. He looked worse off than Ford. Unshaven, torn jeans, stained denim jacket. But it was the eyes that really betrayed his despair. Weary, without hope. Ford remembered having seen him here before. Another regular, selling the only thing he had left. "Look, if you're hungry," Ford said, "you can get a meal tonight at the mission downtown."

The man reached out and clapped Ford on the shoulder. Ford found himself backing away, ashamed to realize how much distance a bath and clean clothes could put between people.

"Thanks, pal," said the man, "but I've got someone waiting at home."

Suddenly the gulf widened but their positions were reversed. Home. This man who looked like more of a bum than Ford ever had was on his way home—where someone was waiting for him. Ford felt his eyes fill with tears. "Sorry," he said. "I didn't mean to insult you or anything. It's just that I usually come in here hungry myself."

"What about now? Are you hungry now?" the man asked, looking at Ford like a brother.

Ford shook his head. "I'm okay." As they crossed the street to the parking lot, he saw the man start to reach in his pocket, then change his mind, struggling to reconcile Ford's outer appearance with the desperation he had just revealed.

"I'm glad things are going better for you," he said finally, as he handed a ticket to the parking attendant.

Ford watched in astonishment as the attendant brought a gleaming Rolls-Royce to a careful stop. "Thank you, Sam," the man Ford had mistaken for a homeless, hungry bum said, handing the attendant a twenty-dollar bill. "Have yourself a merry little Christmas."

"It's going to be a bigger Christmas than I thought," Sam replied with a smile. "May your days be merry and bright too, Mr. Goodman. How's the new picture coming?"

"I saw a rough cut last night, Sam. I've got high hopes for it. As soon as we get it scored, I'll invite you to a screening."

"I'll look forward to that, Mr. Goodman. Thanks a lot. Happy New Year!"

Ford opened the door on the passenger side and gazed at the rich leather interior. If it hadn't been for the new clothes he was wearing, he would have been hesitant to climb inside. "I've never ridden in a Rolls," he said.

"Neither had I until I bought this one last year," the man replied. "I've often thought if worse came to worst, I could sell my house and live in it." He noticed the look Ford was giving him. "I guess that sounds strange to you."

Ford laughed. "I know just how you feel. As long as I've got wheels, I've got hope."

"Hope." The man repeated the word slowly, as if the sound could reveal its meaning. "I've learned to live without that."

"Sounds like you have everything you could want in the here and now," Ford said. "Hope is for folks who are banking on the future."

Mr. Goodman pulled into the station and told Ford he'd drive him back to his car with the gas. When they stopped in front of the battered station wagon, he looked at Ford in disbelief. "These are the wheels that give you hope?"

"They're the only ones I've got." Ford shrugged. "But what makes a man with a Rolls-Royce give up hope?"

"A year ago I wouldn't have traded places with any man alive," Goodman said with a wry smile. "I felt like the producer of my own life—all the elements had come together. I had a hit picture, my wife had just given birth to our first child—a boy we named for my father. We took him home to our new house on the beach. But it had been a difficult birth. They finally had to do a Caesarean. She lost a lot of blood, and she didn't seem to be able to recover. She just kept getting weaker and weaker. Six months ago she was diagnosed with AIDS—from a blood transfusion." He paused, then continued slowly. "I'll never forgive myself for not having given her my blood that day, but I was a wreck about what she was going through, and the hospital had plenty on hand. Money was rolling in from the picture. I assumed I could buy anything I needed. All my life I thought if I could just make enough money, I'd be able to take care of everyone I loved, to keep them safe. But here I am with a Rolls-Royce, a house at the beach, and a wife who's dying of AIDS. There's not much I can do for her—but at least I can come here as often as they'll let me and give my blood and try to keep what happened to her from happening to someone else."

"God bless you," said Ford, getting out of the Rolls with his can of gasoline. "I'll remember you in my prayers. And your wife."

"Thank you," said the man, offering Ford his hand. "Her name is Amy," he shouted as he drove away.

FOUR

"Let's drink a toast to Ruth and Henry," said Kate, reappearing from the kitchen with a bottle of champagne. "To your new life!"

"We're joining the ranks of the homeless," said Henry. "I wish Ruth were as excited about it as I am."

"I've never not had a home," said Ruth. "I'm terrified. And I'm going to miss my garden."

Kate looked at her friends as if she were seeing them for the first time. Had they always been so at odds with each other—or was their marriage only now beginning to strain at the seams, ready to split apart as hers had just done?

In the past Ruth and Henry had always tried to create the impression that their marriage was a romantic adventure. They had made a conscious decision to remain childless and unencumbered—they never even owned a pet—so they could devote themselves entirely to each other and to their life together.

In lieu of children, their house was the beneficiary of most of their time and energy. Ruth and Henry worked hard at house-holding—a term they used to imply a shared responsibility. "I am not a housewife and Henry is not a house husband," Ruth was in the habit of saying. "We're householders."

In a town that pegged people by what they did for a living, Henry called himself a writer but only because it was "as close to not working as I could get," he once confessed to Kate. He always seemed to be involved in some project "in development," but Kate could not recall ever seeing his name on a screen, large or small. Once Henry and Ruth had bought their house, he was only interested in making enough money to maintain and improve it and, between assignments, to travel. Without children to feed and clothe, educate and inoculate, they were free to go whenever and wherever they pleased.

Lately Henry had begun talking to real estate agents—and discovered to his astonishment that by selling their house they could make more money than he had earned in his entire career as a writer in Hollywood. "It's time to cash in our chips," he told Cliff and Kate. "It's a seller's market but it's not going to last. The bubble is bound to burst."

"But where will you live if you sell your house?" Cliff asked.

"That's the thing," Henry explained with mounting excitement. "We don't have to *live* anywhere—at least not for a while."

"But everybody has to have a home somewhere," Kate said, looking at Cliff.

"Not us," Henry insisted. "Don't you see, this is where we've been headed all along. We've planned our lives so we wouldn't be tied down. We never had children and I never signed a long-term contract with a studio. I never even wrote a pilot without making it clear I wouldn't be around if it got picked up for a series. Not that that's been a problem," he added with a laugh. "But we've always stayed clear of commitments that would keep us from doing exactly what we wanted to do. And now that we've proved we know how to play the game by making up our rules as we go along, we've finally been given a shot at the grand prize. We'll bank the money from the sale of our house and live on the interest. We won't settle anywhere, at least for a while, just move from place to place, staying till we get restless. We still have so much of the world left to see. And I'll be fifty on my next birthday. Half my life is already behind me."

Ruth had to laugh at that. "Henry told me the day we met he had every intention of living to be a hundred, and if I wasn't aiming for that kind of longevity, he wanted to know before he allowed himself to get seriously involved."

"So when do you leave?" Cliff asked, pouring himself another glass of champagne. Kate saw him glance at her and knew he was wondering when dinner would be ready. The only time she had made a move toward the kitchen since Ruth and Henry arrived over an hour ago was to bring out a bottle of champagne to toast their new life.

All this talk of home seemed to be making Cliff nervous. He was also drunk. He never could handle champagne, Kate thought. Especially on an empty stomach. However, no amount of champagne could blur the hard fact that once he left this house tomorrow, he'd be as homeless as Ruth and Henry. But without a windfall—and without a wife. Was he having second thoughts? Kate searched his face for an answer.

In the background she could hear Henry discussing their plans. They would travel first to Europe and try living in different countries, never signing a lease for longer than three months. And in between leases they would explore, renting a car, taking back roads, never knowing in the morning where they would be spending the night.

"What is it about men as they reach middle age?" Ruth asked. "Why do they feel compelled to change something in their lives—house, career, wife . . ."

"I know plenty of men who still have the same three they started out with," Cliff interrupted, clearly uncomfortable at the turn the conversation was taking.

"Who besides yourself?" Ruth asked.

"I wasn't counting myself," Cliff replied brusquely.

"Then you can be damn sure he's changed agents," Henry interjected with a laugh.

"Guilty," said Cliff, throwing up his hands in a gesture of

surrender. "Don't you think it's time to put dinner on the table?" He turned to Kate, taking charge of the conversation before it could backfire further.

"I have no intention of putting food in front of people who aren't really hungry," she replied calmly.

"I haven't eaten all day. I'm starving," he said. "And I'm sure I speak for everyone. It's after nine."

"Nina still hasn't gotten home," Kate reminded him. "She and Adam are doing some last-minute shopping."

"Then we'll eat without her," Cliff announced.

But Kate remained rooted to her chair. The strained silence that followed was broken by Nina as she entered from the kitchen and set a platter of food on the dining room table. Adam followed with more platters.

"What's all this?" asked Kate in surprise.

"This is supposed to be a holiday for everyone—even you." Nina crossed to her mother and gave her a hug. "We've brought home the best take-out food Beverly Hills has to offer. No one should have to cook on Christmas Eve."

Kate's eyes filled with tears. "Thank you, darling. This is the nicest Christmas present anyone has ever given me."

"What are we waiting for?" Cliff asked impatiently. "Grab a plate, everybody. Let's eat."

"I'd like to say something first." Kate moved to the head of the table.

"Can't it wait till we eat?" Cliff asked, with an apprehensive look at this woman whose actions were making less and less sense to him.

"No," she answered firmly.

"Please, Kate." His eyes were pleading. "You promised."

"Would you mind bowing your heads?" Kate continued. "I want to say a blessing for this food."

FIVE

Ford stood waiting at the elevator in the lobby of the old down-town hotel now serving as a temporary shelter for homeless women and children. He pushed the button again and started to look at his watch to see how long he'd been waiting, then he remembered—he'd hocked it the week before. "Lay not up for yourself treasures on earth," his father used to say. Ford smiled grimly, thinking how well he had carried out that instruction.

"You have about as much chance of seeing that elevator come down the shaft as you do of seeing Santa Claus come down the chimney tonight. It's stuck on the top floor," a clerk who had been sitting behind the front desk ever since Ford arrived finally called out to him. Ford had to restrain himself from punching the smug bastard in the mouth.

He walked over to the desk and demanded, "Why didn't you tell me sooner? You saw how long I've been standing here."

"I was busy. The paperwork doesn't stop just because it's

Christmas Eve. I've got to account to the higher-ups for everybody in here."

"Was anybody trapped in the elevator when it stopped?" Ford asked anxiously. "My wife—I mean I know some people who live on the top floor."

"No one has walked down those stairs to put in a missing person report." The clerk shrugged. "And we haven't had any complaints about noise, except the usual ones. The Jackson kids are at each other's throats and Mrs. Harris has been straddling the fire escape, cursing people below her on the sidewalk, threatening to jump, to kill herself and take a few of them along with her. God, I hate this job."

"Look, I've got to deliver some things," Ford said, pointing to the cardboard boxes of used clothes, the roasting pan, and the picnic basket.

"I suppose you're with one of those organizations that gets to feeling guilty around Christmas—and tries to make up for keeping your eyes closed the rest of the year. If only it were Christmas every day! But one good meal just gets the appetite going, makes people remember how it feels to eat regular. You'll wake up with an easy conscience in the morning but by evening the people you fed tonight will be hungrier than they were before you got here with your fancy basket."

"I'm just trying to do the best I can," Ford said, hoisting a box to his shoulder.

"At least you're here. I'll give you that. Most people in this city—in this country, for that matter—don't want to know about it."

"Will you give me a hand with some of this stuff?" Ford asked as he started toward the stairs, nodding at the boxes still stacked by the elevator.

"You've got to be kidding," said the clerk, going back to his paperwork. "I don't have to work off any guilt. I get my face rubbed in this every day. Besides, I'd probably die climbing the stairs to the top floor. I've got a weak heart—not to mention a weak stomach."

"Would you at least keep an eye on it till I come back down?" Ford asked wearily.

"Can't make any promises."

Ford wanted to grab the man by the collar and squeeze his throat till he cried for mercy. More than the hunger he had felt in the past months, more than the humiliation of failing as a husband and a father, it was the feeling of helpless rage in the face of indifference to his plight that he found the most difficult to ignore. But the safety of his family, fragile as it was in this place, depended on his swallowing yet again his anger and his pride.

"Then I'll have to get help from the outside," Ford muttered, setting down the boxes and stalking grimly to the door.

"Good luck," replied the clerk in a sardonic tone. "You've got more faith in the outside than I do."

Ford walked down the street to the corner where his car was parked. It was the first time he'd ever found a free park so close to the hotel. He hated wasting good luck on something as unimportant as a parking space, but with as much as he'd had to carry today, it was a blessing. He opened the car door. "Come on, Homer," he said. "You have as much right to sleep inside as I do."

Homer nearly knocked Ford down in his excitement at being allowed to accompany him. He ran in frenzied circles around Ford's legs, barking joyously. "Homer, you always think where you're going will be better than where you've been," Ford said, reaching down to pat the dog's head as he pushed open the door to the hotel. "I wish I could feel the same."

"Hey, no pets allowed in here," the clerk shouted as Ford headed toward the stairs with Homer at his heels.

"Pet? You didn't see any pet come through here. That dog works for me." Without waiting for a reply, Ford began carrying the boxes to the first floor landing. Homer bounded up the stairs after him. Ford stacked the boxes in a corner and picked up the roasting pan and the picnic hamper. "Now sit, Homer," he ordered. "Stay here and don't let anybody lay a hand on these till I get back."

Whimpering with frustration at not being allowed to follow his master (and whatever he was carrying that was sending out such food-promising odors), Homer stood reluctant guard over the boxes whose faint smells hinted at nothing more interesting than strangers.

By the time he reached the top floor, Ford was weak with exhaustion but he managed to call out a cheerful "Merry Christmas."

"Ford, is that you?" A thin, once-pretty blonde, wearing blue jeans and a faded sweatshirt, opened the door with a cry of relief.

"You're gonna think it's Santa Claus when you see what I've brought," he said, brushing her hollow cheeks with his lips, wishing he could put the color back in them. "How's my sunshine?"

"I thought I smelled turkey," Sunny said, taking the roasting pan from him and setting it on the bed. "But then I told myself I had to be dreaming." Ignoring his outstretched arms, she gave him a hard stare. "You look so handsome, Ford. Where did you get all those new clothes?"

"Same place I got the turkey," he replied. "I'll tell you all about it while we eat."

"What's in there?" asked Joe Wayne, eying the hamper. A solemn ten-year-old, he had learned in the past year not to ask too many questions for fear of getting answers he didn't want to hear. But the mood of happy surprise his father brought with him into the room made him bold.

"You'll see soon enough," Ford said, giving him a hug.

Marvella, a six-year-old miniature of her mother but with round cheeks and trusting eyes, threw her arms around his neck and began covering his face with kisses. "Mama said she didn't think Santa Claus would be able to find us here."

"She just didn't want to get your hopes up, honey. But sometimes there are miracles."

Sunny took four tinfoil pie pans from a rusty metal cabinet and placed them on the bed beside the turkey. "You know what I thought we were going to be eating for Christmas dinner?" She held up a can of pork and beans. "This is all we had left."

"You haven't seen anything yet," said Ford, opening the picnic hamper. "Put away those pie plates, Sunny." While the children watched in amazement, he removed four china plates, silverware, and cloth napkins from separate compartments inside the hamper.

Sunny picked up a plate with great care and ran her fingers around the smooth rim. "I never thought I'd eat off a real plate again."

"What else is in there?" Joe Wayne asked, trying to control his excitement. With his father away so much of the time, he had to act like the man of the family. Sometimes it was hard to remember how much fun he used to have last year, when he was just nine.

"I'm not sure myself, son. Why don't you take things out one at a time and let us guess."

"Oh, boy," cried Joe Wayne, opening the first container. "My favorite."

"Must be yams," said Sunny. "Last Christmas you ate the whole pan while I was looking for the marshmallows to put on top."

"Don't eat them all up tonight, Joe Wayne, please," Marvella begged. "I like yams as much as you do."

The sound of barking was heard in the distance. "I almost forgot about Homer," Ford said. "He's guarding some boxes at the bottom of the stairs. Joe Wayne, why don't you go down and see what he's got."

But Marvella was already out the door, headed for the stairs, calling, "Homer, we hear you. We're coming!"

"She can't go down there alone," Sunny cried in alarm. "Go get her, Ford. You don't know what goes on inside this building."

The fear in Sunny's voice was something Ford had not heard before. "Come on back, Marvella," he called. "You help your mama spread out our dinner. Joe Wayne and I'll go down and get the boxes."

He brushed Sunny's cheek with his hand. "This is the last Christmas we'll ever have to spend in a place like this. I give you my solemn word."

His wife stared back at him. "Just go get her. Please, Ford."

As Joe Wayne ran out the door ahead of him, eager to claim the promised boxes, Marvella came bounding up the stairs, one hand on Homer's collar. Homer was wagging his tail happily, as if to explain to Ford that he had abandoned the boxes in favor of a higher duty—protecting his daughter. Ford patted his head. "It's okay, boy. I didn't mean to leave you down there so long."

The double bed looked like a banquet table when Ford and Joe Wayne finally returned to the room. Marvella had intertwined the paper chains she had made in school around the various dishes of food. A lopsided silver star shaped out of tin foil hung from the only lighting fixture in the room, a bare bulb directly above the bed.

"I'll never take chairs for granted again," said Sunny, pulling the one straight-backed chair the room possessed to the foot of the bed. "You sit here, Ford. This will be the head of the table."

"No, you take it," he insisted, carefully removing his new jacket, then stretching out on his side against the head of the bed. He propped a pillow under his elbow, taking care not to upset any of the dishes. "After that climb I'm ready for a rest."

As was their custom whenever they gathered for a meal, they each took a turn talking to God. "Thank you for letting us be together again," Marvella began. "Especially Homer."

Ford laughed and opened his eyes to look at Sunny. But her hands covered her face, and she was shaking with silent sobs. Joe Wayne said an impatient prayer, then there was silence. "Come on, Mama," he urged, "it's your turn. We all have to say something before we can eat."

"I can't," said Sunny, rising suddenly and hurrying toward the bathroom. "Go ahead, all of you, start without me. I'm feeling kinda funny."

The children looked expectantly at Ford, waiting for his permission. "Thank you, God, for this day," he said quickly. "And all the blessings it has brought." He nodded at the children to begin, then moved to the bathroom.

"Come on, honey, it's Christmas Eve," he whispered. He tried to open the door but it was locked. "Try not to think about what we've been through or what lies ahead. God took care of us today and we've got to be thankful for that." But the only reply was the sound of dry heaves coming from the bathroom. "Are you all right?" he called anxiously.

Finally the toilet flushed and the lock turned. He opened the door. Sunny was bending over the basin washing her face. He stood behind her, encircling her waist with his arms.

"I haven't seen that much food spread out in front of me since we left Iowa." She laughed weakly. "Nothing that happens to us surprises me anymore—being stranded on the top floor of a building so dirty and dangerous you don't dare let your children leave the room, planning to serve your last can of beans for Christmas dinner, knowing you're never going to find an apartment you can afford because they simply don't exist. But I'm not prepared for something like this that just comes out of nowhere. Something so wonderful. All those feelings I thought were dead start coming to life again—and I don't know how to deal with them."

Ford turned her around to face him and cupped her face in his hands. "You've been on your own too long. I'm not leaving here tonight. I've got plans for that bed," he whispered, "as soon as we finish eating what's on top of it." He took Sunny by the hand and led her back to her chair.

"Are you okay, Mama?" Joe Wayne asked anxiously as he dipped his spoon into the candied yams.

"She's just hungry," said Ford. "But who isn't?"

"I want some turkey," said Marvella, brandishing her fork.

Ford took off his tie and rolled up his shirtsleeves. "I'm stripping for action. Did any of you ever see a man take apart a turkey with his bare hands?" He pulled off a wing and handed it to Sunny. "Here, angel, I bet you could use an extra wing."

"You don't look like you belong here with the rest of us, Ford, all dressed up like that," she said, her eyes full of questions.

"It's the three of you who don't belong here," Ford replied, using the knife and fork from his place setting in a clumsy attempt to carve the turkey. "After dinner we're going to get you outfitted so I can take you anywhere. Where do you want to go first?"

"Disneyland," cried Marvella without a moment's hesitation.

49

"You said that was why we were moving to Los Angeles but we never got to go."

"We'll get there, sweetheart. And somewhere in those boxes we'll find you something pretty to wear when we do."

Sunny continued to eye him as they filled and refilled their plates. "Where have you been all day?" she asked finally. "Church people might have cooked this dinner, but they sure wouldn't have given you all those nice clothes. You look like a man who's never had to worry about money."

"I'm wearing another man's Christmas," said Ford. "I don't know what he did to make his wife so mad, but she took all his presents from under the tree and gave them to me."

"And what did you have to do to get them?" Sunny was looking at Ford with an expression he had never seen before.

"Nothing you wouldn't have done in my place."

"How did you meet her?"

"My car broke down in front of her house—just as her husband was heading out the driveway. She called the AA for me."

"Alcoholics Anonymous?" Sunny asked in alarm. "Oh, Ford, you haven't started drinking?"

"No, the Auto Club."

"The AAA. Thank God!"

"And while we waited for them to come, she gave me some soup and let me take a bath."

"So the two of you were alone in the house?"

"Not alone." He paused to see the effect this would have on Sunny, then added with a grin, "Homer was there the whole time."

"When are you seeing her again?" Sunny was not smiling.

"Seeing her again? I don't even know her last name."

"But you know where to find her."

"I know her address," he admitted, "and I'd sure like to be able to do something to thank her. I saw a lot of things that needed tending around the house. I got the feeling that husband of hers hadn't paid any attention to it in a long time—or to anything in it. How a man could own such a beautiful house and turn his back on it is a mystery to me."

"And the woman in it? Was she beautiful too?"

"Had been, I'd say. Could be again. But it looked to me like she was suffering from neglect same as the house."

Sunny got up from her chair and sat down on the bed beside Ford. She took his hand and held it against her cheek. "I'm grateful to her, God knows—but I'm glad she sent you on your way today."

Suddenly for Ford there was no one in the room but the woman next to him. He took her in his arms and held her close. He could feel her heart beating against his chest. He pressed his mouth to hers, breathing life back into their marriage, but the connection was severed by Joe Wayne shouting, "Come on, you two. No making out till we see what's inside those boxes."

Reluctantly Ford and Sunny pulled apart but he continued to hold her hand as they leaned back against the pillows.

"We'll open the boxes as soon as the two of you put away what's left of dinner," he said.

"Why do we have to do all the work?" Joe Wayne grumbled, taking the roasting pan with the remains of the turkey to the corner of the room that served as a kitchen.

"No one in this family does everything, but we all have to do what we can," Ford said. "Marvella, you wash off the plates and silverware in the bathroom sink and put them back in the basket so they'll be nice and clean—in case we decide to have a midnight snack."

"A midnight snack! I really must be dreaming," Sunny said with a laugh. "Pinch my arm, Ford. I want to be awake for every minute of this."

While the children cleared the dishes from the bed, Ford pinched her arm, then began to tickle her. Laughing helplessly, she lifted his hand to her mouth and bit his finger.

"I can't leave the two of you alone for a minute, can I?" Marvella chided them as she returned from the bathroom with the plates and silverware neatly washed and dried.

"If you've got all that energy to burn, you can put it to work helping me," shouted Joe Wayne as he crammed the turkey into the small and now very overcrowded refrigerator.

"You two sound like me talking," sighed Sunny. "I used to listen to my mother and swear I would never, never let that tone creep into my voice—no matter how many children I had or how hard life got. Oh, Ford, I don't want to end up like her. Working so hard every day and nothing to show for it. I've got to get a job!"

"As soon as we find a place to live, honey. That's the first step."

"No one's going to hire me, looking the way I do."

"You look beautiful," Ford said, removing the rubber band that held her hair in a ponytail and letting the soft blond curls fall down around her face. He began to sing softly, "You are my sunshine. . . ."

"When you sing to me, it makes everything all right," she whispered. "When we were first married, you used to play your guitar and sing me to sleep."

He nodded, remembering.

"I wish you'd brought your guitar with you today," she said wistfully. "I love to listen to you play."

"I had my hands full," said Ford brusquely, reaching in his pocket to make sure the pawn ticket was still there. He stood up and clapped his hands. "This is no time to be talking about the past. Joe Wayne, why don't you play Santa Claus and pass out the things inside those boxes?"

Joe Wayne ran to the biggest box and began to paw through the contents. "Nothing but clothes for girls," he said in disgust.

"Clothes for girls? Let me see." Marvella hurried over to the box.

"Take the things out slowly, Marvella, one at a time, so we can all have a chance to see," said Ford, hoping that somewhere in one of the boxes would be a piece of clothing that would make Sunny believe in herself again.

Marvella held up a bulky pullover worn thin at the elbows. "Try it on, Sunny," Ford urged.

She slipped it over her head and smiled gamely. "It won't get me a job but it'll keep me warm. That's something."

"Can I have this, please?" cried Marvella, clutching a strapless pink chiffon party dress.

"It's a little old for you sweetheart," said Sunny, laughing, "and a little big."

"Please let me just try it on," begged Marvella. "And look, Mama, here are some high-heeled shoes to go with it."

"Go on then." Sunny smiled as Marvella ran into the bathroom with the clothes.

Ford moved to the box, found a pair of sweatpants and a shirt. "Hey, Joe Wayne, there's something here for you after all. And these sneakers look about your size. And what about this down vest and jacket—just the kind you like, with lots of pockets. You won't know yourself in these new clothes."

"They're not new," said Joe Wayne, taking the clothes without enthusiasm. "Somebody we don't even know was throwing them away."

"Were you there?"

A sullen no was Joe Wayne's only response.

"First of all, I do know the person who gave them to us. As much as you can know anyone in a couple of hours. But someone who's willing to share with a stranger is someone I consider a friend for life. And I hate to think how it would hurt her to see the way you're behaving."

Just then Marvella came tottering out of the bathroom in the high-heeled shoes, wearing the strapless pink dress. "This is the way I look in my dreams," she announced happily, her face wreathed in smiles.

Ford kissed her. "Honey, you look like a rose that's just about to burst into bloom. You remind me of your mother the first time I took her out dancing." He began to hum a waltz and held out his arms to his daughter. "May I have the pleasure of this dance?"

"Just be careful you don't break your neck trying to dance in those high heels," warned Sunny.

"Don't listen to her," Ford whispered to his daughter. "She's just jealous because I've lost my heart to another woman."

"Who?" asked Marvella, never taking her eyes off her feet as Ford tried to steer her in a dance.

"Why you, honey—who else?" Ford replied, lifting her into his arms and twirling her around the room.

"Stop, Daddy," she cried. "My shoes are falling off—and so's my dress."

Still sulking, Joe Wayne turned the box upside down. Hidden among the clothes was a gift-wrapped package. "Look, it's for me," he shouted, his voice hoarse with excitement, showing them the card with his name handwritten on it.

"Open it," cried Marvella.

"Wait," said Sunny. "If we're careful, we can save the paper." She took a knife from the picnic basket and slit the tape, then folded the paper neatly while Joe Wayne opened the box to reveal a portable tape deck with a set of earphones.

"Wow!" shouted Joe Wayne. "What a great present! And look what came with it," he added excitedly, taking half a dozen cassettes out of the box.

"How could she have had something like that all wrapped and waiting?" Sunny asked as Ford showed Joe Wayne how to insert a cassette.

"She must have bought it for someone else," Ford said as the majestic strains of a Bach cantata filled the room.

"What kind of music is that?" Joe Wayne asked in disgust. "It feels like we're in church."

"Maybe we are." Ford smiled.

"Look what else I found!" Marvella suddenly pulled a leather shoulder bag from the box.

"That looks like something your mother could use," said Ford firmly, taking the bag from Marvella and handing it to Sunny.

"Look inside," urged Marvella. "See if there's a card."

"It's not meant for me," said Sunny. "It's probably just something she got tired of carrying. Except it hardly even looks used." Almost hesitantly she unzipped the bag and put her hand inside. Her eyes widened. "It's full of things," she whispered.

"Let's see, Mama," cried Marvella. "Turn it upside down on the bed."

Sunny shook the contents of the purse onto the bed. "Everything a woman could want," she said slowly as she opened the makeup kit, the manicure set, the miniature sewing box, and a new datebook for the coming year with a gold pen attached. She saved till last the leather billfold, not daring to believe she would find anything inside. When she finally opened it, a card with her name fell out of the change purse. Slowly she pulled from the leather folds ten ten-dollar bills. "I can't believe someone could be so kind," she said, the tears flowing without embarrassment from her eyes. "The world has been so cruel to us for so long."

"Most people are kind when given the chance," said Ford. "They just don't know how to reach the rest of us. If my car hadn't broken down in front of her house, she wouldn't have known about us."

"Or cared," added Sunny.

"She wouldn't have had any reason to care," said Ford. "Most people don't go out of their way looking for trouble. They have enough at home. One kind of trouble or another. We may not have a house—or even a table . . ."

"Or chairs," chimed in Marvella.

"God knows we could use a few chairs," Ford agreed. "But here in this room we have a family—a husband, a wife, a son, and a daughter. Any one of us would give his own life to keep harm from coming to the other three. How many people living in fancy houses this Christmas Eve can say that?"

"We've got more than each other," said Joe Wayne impatiently. "We've got two more boxes to open."

Ford laughed. "Go ahead then. See if there are any more surprises."

As Joe Wayne tore open another box, Sunny slowly began to repack her purse. She opened a zipper compartment she had not noticed before, reached inside, and pulled out a slip of paper covered with writing on one side.

"What's that?" Ford asked. "Did she write you a letter?"

"Not exactly," Sunny replied with a smile, then began to read: "Eggs, milk, orange juice, cheese, crackers, champagne—" She stopped abruptly. "Imagine living like that. Just being able to write down anything you felt like eating—or drinking—never having to figure up how much it was going to cost, what you could do without."

Ford took the list from her and began to study it. "Do you realize what this means?"

"That she can spare a few old clothes and even some cash," said Sunny, her voice suddenly hard. "Anyone who writes down champagne on her grocery list can afford to be charitable."

"This was her shopping list for today," Ford said. "See, it says Christmas Eve right here at the top."

"So?"

"So she gave you her own purse," said Ford. "She'd probably bought herself the datebook to start the new year. And everything else must've belonged to her—the billfold, the powder, the lipstick. Not quite the coat off her back, but I'd say for a woman it comes pretty close."

Sunny opened the compact and, moving in slow motion, began to make up her face. Her blue eyes sparkled as she applied mascara and eyeliner. When she was finished, she turned to Ford. "Well, how do I look?"

"I hardly know you."

"I hardly know myself." She looked down at her worn jeans. "If only the rest of me went with the face."

"Maybe it will before we're through," said Ford, opening the last box. There on top was a taupe-colored linen suit with matching pumps. Underneath was a silk paisley blouse and skirt in deep shades of red and green. "It looks like it's just your size, honey," Ford said hopefully as Sunny held the suit next to her.

"Then it must be just her size," replied Sunny, imagining how the suit must have looked on its original owner.

"Once maybe," Ford said. "But not anymore."

Suppressing a grin, Sunny put the blouse inside the jacket to see the effect. "Maybe I can wear these together."

"I think that's what was intended." Ford pointed to the jacket lining—the same paisley fabric as the skirt and blouse.

"Look at all the different outfits I can make." Sunny laughed as she held up the clothes in different combinations.

"Now you have to dress up too, Mama," cried Marvella. "Just like me. You'll be the queen and I'll be the princess."

"Go on," Ford urged her. "Now that you've got the clothes to match your new face."

Sunny smiled shyly and took her new clothes into the bathroom while Marvella continued to search the box. "What are you doing, sweetheart?" Ford asked. "Why don't you take off that fancy dress and try on some of these everyday clothes? I know they're not exactly your size but some of the sweaters should be okay and here's a skirt with an elastic band. Your mama can take up the hem if it's too long."

But Marvella just shook her head stubbornly. "I don't want to try on everyday clothes. It's Christmas Eve. I want to stay dressed like a princess." She continued pawing through the contents of the box, throwing clothes on the floor. "I knew it!" she shouted, holding aloft a furry teddy bear with a bow around his neck and a tag that said "Marvella." "I just knew there had to be something with my name on it."

"I envy you your faith, child." Ford smiled.

"Hurry up, Mama," shouted Marvella, pounding on the bathroom door. "I want to show you my present."

"What present?" asked Sunny, stepping tentatively into the room like an actress trying on her costume for the first time, wondering if it was right for her character.

"Mama, you look beautiful," said Joe Wayne appreciatively.

"Well, if you say so, it must be true," said Sunny with a laugh, kissing her son on the back of his neck before he could protest and brushing his thick brown hair out of his eyes. "You never notice what people are wearing."

"That's because there's never anything to notice," he said.

"What do you think, Ford?" Sunny asked shyly.

He moved in a circle around her, admiring her from every angle. "You look too good for this place. In fact, we all do. What we need is a night on the town."

"A night on the town—oh, boy!" shouted Joe Wayne. "Where will we go?"

"Out for a walk—to see the Christmas decorations and the

store windows all lighted up. Maybe find a mirror so your mother can see how pretty she looks. Then she'll have a picture to hold in her head."

"I'm not walking down all those stairs just to see how I look," said Sunny firmly.

"Well, I don't have any choice," said Ford. "I've got to take Homer for a walk—after all the turkey he's eaten."

"I'm coming with you," said Joe Wayne. "We'll have a night on the town—just the fellows—okay, Dad?"

"You're not leaving me," Marvella burst in. "I can go down the stairs if I take off my high heels and put on my sneakers. But I'm bringing my high heels with me—so I can see how I look in a mirror."

Sunny laughed. "All right, I give up. I'm not staying here alone."

"That's more like it." Ford gave her a hug. "Come on, Homer," he called, opening the door into the hallway. "We're going for a walk—to rejoin the human race."

SIX

Marvella gripped Ford's hand as they walked out the front door of the rundown hotel, ignoring the surprised stare of the clerk at the front desk.

"Remember the way we used to drive into town to see the Christmas decorations at home every year?" Ford reached for Sunny with his free hand but she walked briskly ahead with Joe Wayne, who was having a hard time restraining Homer.

"If I start remembering last year, I'll never get through this year," she said, putting an end to any further reminiscence.

They walked on in silence and when the lighted windows of The Broadway came into view, Marvella ran ahead with Joe Wayne to gaze at the moving figures of Santa Claus and his elves. Ford watched as Sunny caught sight of her own full-length reflection in the glass. "I told you you were beautiful," he whispered. "Maybe now you'll believe me."

"It's like a dream," Sunny said. "If only I didn't have to wake up before I go to sleep."

"That doesn't make sense," Ford laughed.

"Nothing that's happened today makes sense." Sunny took his hand. "Oh, Ford, I don't want to go back to that place. Not tonight. Not ever."

"Let's keep walking," said Ford.

As they approached the lighted facade of one of the luxury hotels that were changing the face of downtown Los Angeles, Ford stopped abruptly. "Let's go inside."

Sunny looked at him suspiciously. "What for?"

Ford shrugged. "Just sit in the lobby for a while. Pretend we're staying there."

"What about Homer?" Joe Wayne asked. "We can't take him inside a hotel."

"Tie him to that meter over there." Ford gestured toward a deserted side street where a row of parking meters stood guard over the empty spaces. "There's not going to be any demand for parking places in downtown Los Angeles on Christmas Eve night. He'll be fine."

Ford led the way into the lobby. As he approached the escalator that led up to the reception area, Sunny hesitated. "What if we get caught?"

"It's not a crime for us to be here," he said gently. "You don't have to pay to sit in a hotel lobby."

At the upper level they were greeted by a chorus of voices singing "It Came Upon a Midnight Clear." Her spirits buoyed by the music, Sunny smiled at Ford.

"We learned that song in school," Marvella shouted proudly, and suddenly added her voice to the carolers' as she stepped off the escalator.

"Hush, Marvella," said Sunny nervously, but the head caroler motioned them to come closer. As the carol ended, he quickly handed them song sheets.

"You're just in time for 'Oh, Come, All Ye Faithful,' " he said happily. "We were afraid we weren't going to have any audience at all. We were supposed to be here at six just as the stores were closing but our bus broke down. Now come on, everybody, join in—raise your voices," he urged, then sounded a note on his pitch pipe.

Sunny looked at Ford for guidance as the carolers launched into the familiar strains. He smiled reassuringly, then added his deep baritone. Shyly Sunny and the children followed his example. With each chorus their confidence swelled along with their volume and when the carol ended, several clerks standing behind the reception desk broke into spontaneous applause.

"What a great voice," the head caroler said to Ford, clapping him on the back. "Are you and your family here for the holidays?"

Ford nodded.

"Where you from?"

"Iowa."

"Guess you asked Santa to bring you a little sun for Christmas."

Ford smiled. "Among other things."

As the carolers packed up their sheet music, their leader blew on his pitch pipe to get their attention. "Five minutes, folks. Then I want to see you on that bus. And no stopping till we get home—so take advantage of the facilities. As far as we're concerned, there are no bathrooms between here and San Bernardino."

Marvella tugged at Ford's coat. "Daddy, can I go with them?"

Ford laughed. "On the bus?"

"No. To the bathroom."

Ford nodded at Sunny. "Sure, honey, as long as your mama goes with you."

The caroler smiled after them. "Nice family," he said to Ford. "Wish you could come with us. We could use that voice of yours in our church choir. And we really could have used you tonight. We've been to all the downtown hotels. We figured people who found themselves away from home over the holidays might be sympathetic to our cause. But we figured wrong." He held out a can in which a few coins rattled plaintively. "We're collecting for the homeless. Can you spare any change?"

Stalling while he looked around for an escape, Ford asked,

"Why do you drive to downtown Los Angeles? Don't you have any homeless in San Bernardino?"

"Sure we do. That's who we're collecting for. But we don't have any fancy hotels. However, judging from the size of this take, I'm voting next year to stay home and hit Howard Johnson."

"Look, I'm sorry, I left my billfold upstairs," Ford said awkwardly. "I'll go back up and get it. Come on, Joe Wayne, we'll take the elevator."

"But, Daddy," Joe Wayne started to protest. Ford grabbed his hand and headed for the elevator before he could finish.

"Are we really going to stay here?" Joe Wayne asked hopefully as they stepped off the glass-enclosed elevator on the tenth floor.

"Not tonight, but someday maybe," Ford replied. "Let's just look around, see if it suits us."

Marvella was crying when Ford and Joe Wayne returned to the lobby. When she saw Ford, she ran to him and flung herself into his arms. "Daddy, we didn't know where you were."

"What were you doing?" Sunny demanded.

"Just checking on a room," he said.

"Ford, have you lost your mind? We can't stay here."

"No, but there's nothing to keep us from looking—and hoping."

She sighed. "Yeah, I know. It took everything in me to leave that bathroom. I washed my face and my hands, then my arms up to my elbows. What I'd give for a clean tile bathroom with enough hot water to shampoo my hair without worrying about it turning cold before I rinse."

"I know how you feel," Ford agreed. "That bath today may have been the best present I got."

As they walked reluctantly back to the only room to which they had a key, Sunny begged Ford to describe the house where he had spent the afternoon. "Take me through it room by room. Make it seem so real I can pretend we're living there instead of where we're going."

So as they walked down the dark street past winos lying

unconscious on hot-air grates and women trying to shelter children underneath shopping carts, Ford described a brick house with a flower-lined flagstone path leading down to a curving street. "Even the mailbox was set into a brick column," he said, "and on top there was a planter with all kinds of flowers trailing down from it. Imagine having a mailbox in full bloom."

"That's what I dreamed California would be like—for all of us," Sunny said wistfully.

They continued walking while his words etched the details of the house into a shared memory. Sunny listened as he described the gaslamps garlanded with holly that lit the way to the front door. Then he took her inside, past the ceiling-high Christmas tree in the bay window, through the living room with its down-cushioned furniture and French doors opening onto the terrace. Then into the wood-paneled country kitchen with a brick fireplace flanked by outsized armchairs and copper skillets hanging from the beams.

As they climbed the stairs to the top floor of their temporary shelter, Joe Wayne and Marvella ran ahead with Homer. "I'm going to close my eyes and pretend I'm walking up the path to her front door," said Sunny. "You're going to lead me to the bed and I'm not going to open my eyes till morning."

Ford laughed and took her elbow. But there was no way to close their nostrils to the stench from the hallway. "Describe the flowers, the way they smelled," Sunny begged him. "And what about the front door? Was there a pine wreath for Christmas? There is nothing better than the scent of evergreen. I could live in a forest."

Suddenly there was a scream from the top floor. Sunny's eyes flew open and her fingers dug into Ford's arm. "Oh, God," she said. "That's Marvella."

Ford was already racing up the stairs, with Sunny close behind. Joe Wayne burst out of the room to meet them while Homer ran in frantic circles from one member of the family to another.

"They took my Walkman, Dad," Joe Wayne shouted, trying manfully to hold back the tears. "And everything we left in the room." He pounded on his father's chest. "I wanted to take it with me. You . . . you," he stuttered, choking on the words, hitting his father in the ribs with his tightly clenched fists, "you said to leave it here. You said it would be all right. You said we could lock the door and everything would be safe inside. But nowhere is safe for us. Nowhere!" And he started down the stairs.

"Joe Wayne, you come back here," Ford called in a firm voice. Then with a sigh he forced himself to follow Sunny into the room.

Marvella was sobbing quietly in a corner. "I want my bear," she cried. "He was going to sleep with me tonight."

Ford walked over to her and stroked her hair. "Homer is going to sleep beside you tonight. He'll take better care of you than a toy bear. And you still look like a princess. Nobody can take that away from you."

Sunny slammed the door of the small refrigerator. "They even took the leftover turkey," she said dully.

"They were hungry," said Ford.

"They couldn't eat my Walkman," Joe Wayne muttered, standing defiantly in the doorway.

"Come inside, Joe Wayne, and shut the door," Ford ordered.

"What good will that do? The lock's busted." But finally, at a stern look from Ford, Joe Wayne did as he was told.

"Now listen to me," said Ford. "We're leaving this place in the morning and we're never coming back."

"Damn it, Ford," exclaimed Sunny, "don't make promises you can't keep."

"I swear on my life," said Ford, raising his hand in a solemn pledge. "I'm taking all of you with me tomorrow."

"Where are we going, Daddy?" Marvella asked, her voice hungry with hope.

"You'll find out when we get there," said Ford, astonished by his own faith. "But for tonight we're just going to pretend we're camping in the woods somewhere. Think of how little we used to take with us."

"Yeah, but we used to have a house," Joe Wayne protested. "We could leave things there and they'd be safe."

"We'll have a home again. I promise," Ford said. "But tonight we're on the road and traveling light. I don't know about the rest of you but I'm getting tired. I think it's time to pitch our tents."

"I don't want to sleep outside," Marvella protested tearfully. "I'm scared."

"Not outside," Ford said cheerfully, pulling the mattress off the bed and onto the floor. "We're pitching our tents right in this room."

"What are you doing, Ford?" Sunny asked, her voice seesawing between exasperation and anticipation. "I don't want to sleep on the floor."

"This isn't your tent," said Ford, pushing the mattress underneath the window. Then, while the children watched with growing excitement, he took a sheet from the bed and, climbing on the only chair in the room, opened the window from the top and closed it again on the hem of the sheet. Then he set the chair at the foot of the mattress and draped the sheet over it to make a tent.

"Oh, boy, I'm going to bed right now." Joe Wayne crawled inside with Marvella close behind him.

"Good idea," said Ford, reaching for Sunny and pulling her close. "I'm making a sleeping bag for your mother and me on the box springs." He threw a blanket on the bed and motioned to Sunny to crawl under it with him. She pointed at her new clothes and hurried into the bathroom.

"Daddy, can we sing ourselves to sleep the way we used to do when we were really camping in the woods?" Marvella called out sleepily from inside the tent.

"Just keep your eyes closed," Ford cautioned, turning out the only light in the room and moving to the bathroom door where he could hear the water running. "That way there won't be anything to keep you from believing you're not where you want to be."

Ford closed his own eyes for a moment as he began to sing softly, "On the first day of Christmas, my true love gave to me, a partridge in a pear tree." From their improvised tent the children added their voices to his.

At the sound of the bathroom door opening Ford turned to see Sunny standing naked before him. She held out a hand to him. "I have nothing else to give you," she whispered. "Merry Christmas."

"Keep singing," Ford mouthed a silent command before claiming the gift that had just been presented to him.

Sunny's soprano joined his baritone as she caressed his face, her fingers tracing the contours of his cheeks, trying to erase the lines of suffering engraved around his eyes by the hardships of the year just ending.

Still singing, Ford moved his hands slowly from her shoulders down the length of her arms, as if taking her measure. Then he encircled her waist with his hands, realizing for the first time how very thin she had become. Dressed tonight in her new clothes, she had looked young and slim. But her naked body betrayed all the days she had gone to bed hungry. He could feel her ribs outlined beneath his fingers. Closing his eyes to keep her from seeing the tears, he pressed his head to her chest and gently cupped her breasts in his trembling hands. Their soft fullness was the only part of her that seemed undiminished by the deprivation she had suffered and for which he felt responsible.

Suddenly he realized her voice was the only one still singing. The children had sung themselves to sleep. He motioned Sunny to continue with another chorus and he joined her in a low voice. He walked quietly over to the makeshift tent and looked inside. Joe Wayne and Marvella, still in her pink party dress, had fallen asleep, each with an arm around Homer, who lay between them. At Ford's approach the dog looked up and began wagging his tail. But Ford shook his head sternly and put the sheet back in place.

Then he quickly removed his clothes and slipped under the blanket where Sunny lay waiting. Her arms cradled him as he stretched out next to her. The full length of her body against his quickened every cell into life.

"Welcome home," she murmured.

SEVEN

On Christmas morning Kate awoke alone in the king-size bed, her head still fuzzy from all the champagne she'd drunk the night before. There had been so many toasts—to Ruth and Henry on deciding to sell their house, to Nina on her first year of law school, to Cliff on his film.

Pressing her fingers to her throbbing temples, Kate seemed to recall that someone had even proposed a toast to her. She closed her eyes and tried to think. Adam. Yes, of course, it must have been Adam. Late in the evening, after the others had been congratulated on their various accomplishments, Adam had opened another bottle of champagne and said, "But we're forgetting the most important person here—the one who's provided us with a home for the holidays." And so they had all lifted their glasses to Kate. Even Cliff. "They also serve who only stand and wait," Adam had said as he refilled Kate's glass and then his own. But he was looking at Nina as he said it, and Kate realized he was not drinking to her this time but to himself.

Kate sat up in bed, stretching her arms behind her on either side like flying buttresses to steady her. She felt so dizzy. She had forgotten the effect champagne had on her. The only other time she had drunk so much of it—and that was before she knew how light-headed it made her feel—had been on her wedding night. Then she had been terrified of living with a man. Now she was terrified of living without one.

She stood tentatively. From her bedroom window she could see Adam's car parked in the driveway. Knowing that he was still in the house made her smile.

She was glad Adam and Nina had found each other so early in life. When they continued to remain faithful to each other through four years of college, despite the months and miles that separated them, Cliff had begun to share Kate's gratitude that their daughter had survived the risks to which a generation that prided itself on its sexual freedom had suddenly become prey. Promiscuity now carried a price far more severe than moral censure. Even Cliff had come to appreciate the irony that his daughter, in becoming seriously involved with a boy before she was eighteen, had been proven by time and changing circumstances to have been playing it safe.

Kate knew she was being foolish and old-fashioned, but she wished with all her heart that Nina would greet her this Christmas morning with the announcement that she was getting married instead of going back to law school. If Nina were acquiring a husband then Kate wouldn't mind so much losing one.

There was much pleasure, Kate had found, from being at one remove from a romantically active relationship. She could share the obvious joy Nina and Adam took in each other without experiencing the pain of separation and the stress of a still undefined commitment.

Standing alone at the bedroom window where she had so often waited for Cliff to come home from a late night in the editing room, Kate bit back angry tears. Whatever her failures as a wife, she had succeeded in steering her daughter through the treacherous shoals of a California childhood. Sometimes it seemed to her like a miracle that Nina had reached adulthood without succumbing to the easy and easily available excitement of drugs and alcohol—a miracle for which Kate took no credit but which had provided her with immense comfort at the time and even more now, looking back.

If anyone deserved credit for keeping Nina safe from all the temptations to which her generation was prey, Kate thought, it was Adam. She had liked him immediately the first time Nina had brought him home from high school with her to study for a test.

The only child of divorced parents, he spent more time in his car than he did in either home. He had his own room in both houses, but he kept all the things he cared about locked in the trunk of his car. When he stayed with his father, he felt guilty about leaving his mother alone. When he was with his mother, he worried about his father. Only at Nina's house, halfway between his mother in Sherman Oaks and his father in Pacific Palisades, could he relax and feel comfortable.

Thinking back to that first conversation with Adam—how touched she had been on learning of his conflicting loyalties—Kate remembered the man whose station wagon had broken down outside her front door the day before. Like Adam, that man kept everything he cared about stored in the back of his car.

Ford. His name was Ford. She could see him clearly now. She smiled, remembering how handsome he had looked in Cliff's Christmas presents. Then she thought of the presents she had tagged for his wife and children. What were their names? She couldn't remember now. Damn that champagne! Last night she had wanted to forget everything. Now she struggled to bring the family into focus. The man she would never, could never forget. He was the first man she had ever met who seemed to have no defenses. His face was so open, so trusting, so grateful for any kindness. What kind of a Christmas was he having today? She tried to imagine him with his family, envisioning their joy as they opened the presents she had sent them.

Sunny. That was the wife. And the children— She scanned her memory, searching for their names, unfamiliar names, not like the names of anyone she knew. What was it the man—Ford

—had said? "Once you can call a thing by name, you start to care what happens to it." Suddenly she could hear Ford, in that strong, rich voice of his, telling her the name of his son.

Joe Wayne. The boy was named Joe Wayne. And the girl? A strange and wonderful name. Miranda? Was that it? No, she knew a Miranda. This was a name she'd never heard before. Marvella. That was it. Marvella. What a marvelous name! But how sadly wrong for the life the child was living. Kate's heart ached for the children of the world, born into lives they had done nothing to deserve, helpless inheritors of their parents' mistakes or misfortunes.

Kate could not stop the tears. But she was not crying for the children of the world. She was thinking how much she hated sleeping alone. Suddenly she crossed to the door. The hell with Cliff. She had devoted the better part of her life to trying to make him happy. If another woman had succeeded where she had failed, so be it. There was someone else, too long ignored, whom she had a much better chance of pleasing. Herself.

She went downstairs to the kitchen. From a storage shelf high above the washing machine, she took down a wicker breakfast tray. Cliff had surprised her with it one Mother's Day when Nina was still a baby. He had brought her breakfast in bed that year for the first and last time in her life. Kate had used this tray whenever anyone was sick in bed but this fall, after Nina had left for law school and Cliff for location, she stored it out of sight.

Now she dusted it off and set it with her favorite china. She measured coffee beans into the electric grinder, then brewed a carafe of the extra strong coffee that only she liked. She heated a saucepan of milk and poured it into a pitcher so she could have café au lait along with the croissants Nina had brought home last night.

Kate opened the front door to retrieve the morning paper. She stood there for a moment, breathing in the soft morning fragrance of the garden. She shivered slightly in the cool air, then slammed the front door more loudly than she intended, tucked the folded newspaper into the side basket of the tray, and started toward the stairs.

Cliff suddenly emerged from his study and took the tray from her hands. "You sure don't need an alarm clock around this house the way you slam that front door getting the paper."

Kate stared at him in amazement as he set the tray down on his desk. "What do you think you're doing?" she demanded as he pulled a croissant apart and began to butter it.

"I know I shouldn't be using butter," he muttered. "My cholesterol count has probably skyrocketed this past month. But I'm too upset to take care of myself." He filled the cup with black coffee and took a sip. "Are you trying to poison me?" he yelped. "This coffee is undrinkable."

Calmly Kate took the cup from him and added steaming milk to the black coffee. "I decided to make café au lait," she said, keeping the cup for herself.

"Why would you do that when you know I have to start the day with black coffee?" he demanded.

"You don't ever have to start another day as far as I'm concerned," Kate said coolly, picking up the breakfast tray and heading out the door. "Or finish one either for that matter," she added. And kicked the study door closed behind her.

She climbed the stairs to the bedroom. Setting the tray down on the huge bed, she stared at the half-eaten croissant. The mood was broken. She was too angry to eat.

Cliff followed her into the bedroom. "Look, Kate, I know we have to talk. But may I please finish my breakfast first?"

Kate crossed to the window. "It's not your breakfast, it's mine. I wonder when you would've noticed. If ever!"

"I'm not going to stand here arguing. I don't have the strength. Not after all the champagne I drank last night. I'll go downstairs and fix myself something."

"Oh, go ahead and eat what's there," Kate said wearily. "I'm not hungry." However, she continued sipping the café au lait. "But if you want coffee, you'll have to make it yourself."

Cliff sat awkwardly on the side of the bed. "No, it's okay. I don't really want to be awake."

He looked so miserable and so out of place Kate had to laugh. "The whole point of breakfast in bed is to stretch out and be comfortable," she said finally, "not to sit there like some frightened schoolboy. Anyone would think you'd never been inside this bedroom before." And with that she kicked off her slippers and stretched out languidly on her side of the bed, the breakfast tray standing like a border guard between them.

Cliff turned to face her but kept his feet on the floor, as if the scene they were about to play would have to be approved by the Hays Office. "I should've just lied to you," he said finally. "At least until we got through Christmas. But I couldn't take you to bed with another woman inside my head."

"Why not?" asked Kate, reaching for the half-eaten croissant. "You've done it before."

"What are you talking about?" Cliff turned away abruptly, jostling the breakfast tray and causing Kate to spill her coffee. It quickly soaked through her nightgown, burning her chest. She screamed.

"Oh, Christ, I'm sorry." Cliff rushed to her. "Get that off—away from your skin." He pulled the nightgown over her head, then led her into the bathroom. "Cold water. That's the thing for burns. Get under the shower." He turned on the shower full force and pushed Kate under the spray.

"What are you trying to do?" she shouted. "Kill me? Turn that thing off before I get pneumonia."

"How badly were you burned?" Cliff asked anxiously, wrapping her in a terrycloth robe and patting her dry.

Kate looked down at her chest. "Right now all I feel is cold. But I don't think it's even red, is it?"

Cliff steered Kate until she stood directly under the light. Then he parted her robe, pressing his fingertips gently down her chest.

"Does that hurt?" he asked.

Kate shook her head, not trusting herself to speak. Her breath came faster as he continued to probe the injured area. After a long silence, she reached for his free hand and placed it against her breast.

Responding eagerly to her cue, Cliff pressed her to him. "Oh, Kate," he murmured, "you're still—"

"No," she cried out. "Please. Don't say a word." And with that she put her hand behind his head and pulled it down until she could seal his lips with her own.

Kate had a pot of black coffee waiting when Cliff came downstairs in his terrycloth robe, his hair still wet from the shower. "Merry Christmas," she said, greeting him with a kiss.

He looked at her in some confusion before saying slowly, "You have to know, Kate, that what happened just now is not going to change anything. I'm still going back to Toronto tonight without you."

"I know," she replied. "But that was your Christmas present to me. You said yesterday you hadn't had time to shop. The best possible present is something you can't, or won't, do for yourself —so thank you. And since I have nothing for you, you can consider this morning my present to you as well."

"You have nothing for me?" Cliff asked, as hurt as a child. "What about all those presents I saw under the tree when I came home?"

"I gave them away," Kate said matter-of-factly, "when you said you had nothing for me. You've spent enough time feeling guilty about me this Christmas, Cliff. So from now on, let's just call it even—and concentrate on Nina."

Her calm demeanor caught him off guard. He had steeled himself for tears and accusations—but not for this. "What did you mean just now," he said finally, "when you said I'd done it before?"

"Come on, Cliff," Kate replied. "Do you really think coming home and telling me about it makes this time different from all the other locations?"

"But you've always come to visit me on location," Cliff protested.

"I assumed that added to the thrill," Kate said quietly, "pretending that you were coaching some actress or working late into the night on script changes. Then crawling into bed on top of me, daring me to doubt you, fooling yourself into thinking you were buying my silence with sex."

"If you knew, then why didn't you say anything?" Cliff was genuinely puzzled. Kate could not remember the last time he had looked at her so intently, trying to decipher her motives.

"I didn't know—till now. I only suspected. I didn't want to know. I wanted a home. And a family. I wanted to give Nina the things I never had—starting with a father. But she's left home now. Gone for good if you don't count flying visits—and I don't. So why pretend any longer? I might as well face the fact that along with my future, I've lost a past I never had."

Kate suddenly had the feeling that if she stayed in the house another second, it would come tumbling down on top of her. She pushed open the kitchen door and headed for the safety of the towering live oak whose forked trunk still sheltered the tree house Cliff had built for Nina the summer she was six, when she finally convinced him that she was old enough to climb trees.

In the beginning Kate would climb right behind her and stay there till she was ready to come down. Lying braced against the branches, watching with endless fascination the shifting patterns of light filtered through the leafy canopy, Kate would feel herself completely immersed in the present moment, with nothing to push her back into the past or forward into the future.

Now, with her heart pounding, she climbed up the tree trunk and wedged herself into position, then closed her eyes, waiting to be enfolded once again in that well-remembered sensation of calm. But Cliff was calling to her from below. "Come down, Kate. It's been years since anyone climbed up there. The boards have probably rotted by now. It's not safe."

"I can't live in this house without you, Cliff," she said, her arms reaching behind her to encircle the branch that supported her back.

The whole of her marriage had been spent in this house. The day Cliff signed his first studio contract he asked Kate to marry him and together they found the house that would provide a setting for their life together. Cliff used all his savings for the down payment and the monthly mortgage check took more of his salary than any business manager would have permitted. But

Cliff always managed his own money, and he considered the house an investment in his future.

In spite of the hours Kate had spent taking care of it, she always felt the house belonged to Cliff much more than it did to her. His earnings paid for it and maintained and improved it. He was the one who decided when a new roof was needed or when they could afford to remodel. He would draw rough sketches, then go over the plans with the architect and hold daily consultations with the contractor while the work was in progress. Each year the house came a little closer to being the best possible building it could be, but Cliff was never satisfied and no sooner was one project completed than he would begin thinking about the next.

Yet all the while Cliff was bringing the house closer to his private vision of what a home should be, Kate could feel herself falling further and further short of his image of the perfect wife. Age, of course, was against her—but it only felt like the enemy when she was around Cliff. Alone, away from a mirror, she took pleasure in the richness of experience that was the legacy of the passing years. Though she considered herself reasonably attractive, she had never counted her looks as an asset, especially in a city where so many women made a career out of being beautiful. Many of her friends organized their days around activities designed to enhance their physical attractiveness—exercise classes, facials, manicures, massages, hair styling and streaking and setting—but Kate felt time invested in her outward appearance tended to be a losing proposition and could be better spent on other people.

In the beginning "other people" meant Cliff. From the day he married her and brought her home to this house that so far exceeded her childhood dreams, her sole purpose in life had been to be where he wanted her to be. Until Nina came into their lives and demanded her care. Once Nina started school, Kate suggested to Cliff that she might get a job, but he took it as a reflection on the decline in his own career and asked how she could be so insensitive to what he was going through. What did she want that he had failed to provide? Nothing, she was quick to assure him. Then how could she justify taking a job away from someone who might really need it?

She couldn't—and didn't.

With Nina in school, Kate began to see beyond the needs of her own family. A friend invited her to a luncheon to raise money for a shelter for abused children. The luncheon bored her but she was haunted by the pictures on the brochures. The next day she got into her car and drove to the shelter. The overworked woman running the office hardly knew how to reply when Kate asked what she could do to help—besides writing a check. "I don't know where to begin," she said. "Why don't you just spend some time with us and see for yourself."

And so, after dropping Nina at school, Kate would drive to the shelter and try to discover what needed to be done. She never felt as if she was accomplishing anything very concrete, but she did listen to the children and ask questions and remember their names, and each time she came she felt as if she was getting a little deeper into their lives.

But the shelter was only a temporary solution; the children would either be returned to their own families or assigned to foster parents, and Kate would never see them again. She could not seem to learn to strike the necessary balance between caring for someone yet accepting the fact that he or she will soon move beyond your reach. And though she continued to go to the shelter, she had to learn to steel herself against thinking of the children she met there as sons and daughters who owed her an account of their lives.

What she really wanted, of course, was to bring them home, all of them, to fill every corner of the house with bunk beds and air mattresses and sleeping bags—a house wall to wall with children. Even now the thought made her smile. Looking up at the sturdy branches of the live oak, she imagined a child entwined around every branch. What a harvest that would have been!

The sound of Nina's voice pulled Kate back to reality. She was standing in the doorway calling to them. "Good morning.

Merry Christmas. What are you two doing out there? Come on inside. I want to open my stocking."

Cliff stretched out his arms to Kate. "Come down. Please. Nina doesn't suspect anything. Don't buckle now. I'm not asking for my sake. I'm asking for hers. Let's have one last Christmas together—as a family."

Kate looked down at him from the safety of the tree house. "I'll come down on one condition," she said. "Tomorrow I'm putting this house on the market. I don't want to live here without you. You have to promise not to stand in my way."

"How could you even think of selling this house?" Cliff asked, outraged. "Do you realize what it's worth?"

"That's why I want to sell it," Kate said calmly. "I want something tangible to show for all the years I've put into this marriage. It's not as if I've been earning a salary."

"I bet this house has made more money than my career," Cliff said with a sour laugh. "Just sitting here—increasing in value every day. They say this is no town to grow old in—but that applies to people, not houses. This house is the best investment we've made, Kate. I hate to think of you getting rid of it. God, I feel guilty enough about all this—it gave me some small comfort to think at least you could continue to live in a safe, comfortable home. I'm prepared to give you full title to it. I want you to know that. It's the least I can do."

"Good," said Kate briskly, climbing down from the treehouse, avoiding Cliff's outstretched arms. "Then it's up to me to decide what to do with it. I've lost a husband but I've gained a house. Some people would say I've come out ahead."

"But where will you go?" Cliff asked anxiously as they walked toward their daughter, who stood waiting at the door. "Do you have any idea how much another house is going to cost? You're likely to end up spending more—and getting less in return."

"I don't want to buy another house," said Kate, surprised at her own conviction. "It's an illusion to think anyone owns anything—ever!"

"But you have to stay somewhere," Cliff insisted.

"Have you forgotten what season this is?" asked Kate. "We're celebrating the birth of someone whose parents didn't even know where they were going to spend the night."

EIGHT

"I can't do it," said Sunny, clutching Ford's elbow as he started to open the car door. "I can't go in there."

"Well, we can't stay here any longer," Ford said. "We've been sitting in this parked car for ten minutes. Do you have any idea how suspicious we look? It's a wonder we haven't been taken somewhere for questioning. People who live in houses like this have private patrols that come around night and day."

"Have we done something wrong, Dad?" Joe Wayne asked anxiously. "Aren't we allowed to drive down any street we want?"

"You bet," said Ford decisively. "And to stop anywhere we want too. Besides, we're here for a reason. Now, everybody out."

"What about Homer?" asked Marvella as she climbed out of the car.

"Homer can come too. He'll be as welcome as the rest of us," Ford said with a glance at Sunny, who continued to sit motionless in the front seat of the car.

"And how welcome is that, Ford?" she asked quietly.

The children ran up the flagstone path, holding Homer tightly by his leash. They stopped outside the bay window to gaze at the lighted Christmas tree.

"I'm ringing that doorbell, Sunny," Ford said. "If you don't want to come with me, you can sit in the car, but I'm not waiting for you any longer."

And he strode up the front walk. Marvella came running to meet him.

"Daddy, there's an angel on top of that tree," she whispered.

"We always used to put an angel at the top of our tree. Don't you remember, honey?" he asked gently, squeezing her hand and allowing her to lead him to the bay window to look at the tree.

"No, I don't mean a decoration. I mean a real angel. I saw her face on the top branch. Only somebody with wings could've flown up so high."

Ford looked down at his daughter and smiled. "I don't know about the wings, honey, but you're right about an angel living in that house." Then his eyes focused on the direction she was pointing.

"See, Daddy, there she is—but why is she crying?"

"She doesn't see us," said Ford quietly. "Come on, move out of the way before she does." He walked to the door and rang the bell quickly before he could forget what he had just seen.

He was propelled forward by the sound of the lock turning in the front door. But a chain appeared abruptly across his line of vision, like a slap across the face. The door, secured against further entry, opened only a few inches. "Yes?" called a disembodied voice. "May I help you?"

Ford felt his confidence ebbing away.

"What is it?" she called, her voice becoming more anxious. Was it his imagination or was the door beginning to close?

Ford stammered, spluttering out words like chips of wood to wedge the door open until he and his family were safely on the other side. "You may not remember me," he began. Fool, he thought. You were here yesterday. Tell her your name. No, he checked himself. The name won't mean anything. Remind her how it happened. "My car broke down outside your house yester-day," he continued hesitantly. The door moved toward him. Oh, God, it's over, he thought.

Suddenly the chain was released and the door flew open. "Ford!" Kate cried, opening her arms as if to embrace him, then, embarrassed, extending her hand.

He took it gratefully. "Merry Christmas," he said awkwardly. "I mean it was for us—thanks to you."

Her eyes filled with tears. "Thank you," she said, "for letting me feel I've made one person happy."

"More than one," he assured her. "I've brought the whole family to say thank you." He was about to introduce the children when Kate took Marvella in her arms, smiling to see her in the pink evening dress and high-heeled shoes. Ribbons Kate recognized from the Christmas presents she had wrapped were braided into her hair.

"This must be Marvella," she said. "You're as beautiful as your name."

"She started feeling pretty from the time she put on that dress yesterday." Ford smiled at his daughter. "She hasn't taken it off."

"If I had, it would've been stolen," said Marvella.

"Like my Walkman," added Joe Wayne.

"Stolen?" Kate's face clouded.

Ford flinched. "Let's not talk about that now, Joe Wayne. You haven't even said thank you."

Joe Wayne remained stubbornly silent. Kate would have known he was Ford's son without having to be told—something about the way he stood, shifting his weight from side to side. He had the same unruly brown hair, the same trusting eyes. She crossed to him and put an arm around his shoulder. "I don't blame you for being mad, Joe Wayne. Why don't you come inside and tell me all about it?"

"Can Mama come too?" Marvella asked with an anxious look toward the car.

"Well, of course," Kate replied warmly. "Where is she?"

"Waiting in the car," Ford explained. "She wasn't sure we'd be welcome."

Kate's eyes signaled her understanding. She pushed the front door open wide. "Go on inside—all of you. Make yourselves at home. Homer too." She nodded at the children, who continued to stand hesitantly in front of the open door, not trusting their good fortune.

"It's okay," said Ford. "Go ahead. Just mind your manners."

As the children hurried into the house, Kate turned to Ford. "I wasn't sure I'd ever see you again. I've been thinking about you, wondering what happened. It was nice of you to come back."

"Nice?" Ford could not contain an incredulous laugh. The enormity of his need was beyond the scope of polite conversation. He was a fool to think she'd be able to sense why he had come. "You don't understand anything, do you?"

Kate looked hurt and confused. "I'm sorry. Did I say something wrong?"

"No, I'm sorry," said Ford. "I'm the one who's in the wrong. Sunny was right. We shouldn't have come." He stepped inside the front door, calling for Joe Wayne and Marvella.

Kate started after him, then, changing her mind, turned abruptly and walked to the car where Sunny continued to sit staring straight ahead. Kate was surprised to see how young she was—at least ten years younger than Ford, not that much older than Kate's own daughter. She was wearing the suit Kate had bought for herself as an incentive to lose weight—but had never worn. Kate opened the door on the driver's side and slid behind the wheel. "Do you know how much I envy you?" she said softly.

Sunny's head spun around in surprise. "You walk out of that beautiful house and expect me to believe I have anything you could want?"

"You have a husband who loves you."

Sunny shrugged. "It doesn't keep me warm."

Kate gripped the steering wheel as if she were driving to some unknown destination. "My house is centrally heated but I've been shivering all afternoon—ever since my husband flew back to Canada. I built a fire as soon as he walked out the door, but it doesn't seem to help. Why don't you come sit in front of it for a while? It's a shame to waste it."

"I don't think I'd ever be lonely if I could build a fire every night when it got dark," Sunny said softly.

"Please come in the house with me," Kate urged, sensing that Sunny was beginning to relax. "I'm taking down the decorations from the Christmas tree. I could use some company." She opened the car door.

"Taking them down?" Sunny protested. "So soon? We never take down the decorations till after New Year's. I mean we never did. When we had a tree." She paused, then added under her breath, "When we had a house."

As they walked to the front door, Kate said to Sunny, "That suit looks great on you."

Sunny stopped, embarrassed. "I should have said thank you. I should have said it first thing."

Kate laughed. "I didn't give you a chance. I was too busy feeling sorry for myself. As if you didn't have troubles enough of your own."

"Not as many today as yesterday." Sunny smiled for the first time—and Kate saw how pretty she must have been once, before fear and worry had creased her face. "At least now I've got something I can wear to look for work. If you look desperate, nobody wants to have anything to do with you."

Kate nodded in sympathy. "My husband says that the only way to get a job in Hollywood is not to need it. And the more you don't want it, the more they want you to have it. I guess it's true everywhere—not just in show business."

Suddenly the front door flew open and Marvella ran into her mother's arms. She was sobbing so loudly she could hardly speak.

"What's wrong with you?" Sunny asked. "Did you hurt yourself?"

Marvella shook her head.

"Come inside," said Kate.

Ford was standing in the front hallway, one arm around a

sullen Joe Wayne. Homer, straining at his leash, was barking loudly.

"Dad says we have to go back," Joe Wayne said, his teeth clenched with disappointment.

"But you've just come," said Kate. "It would be very rude to turn right around and leave." She turned to Ford with a pleading look. "Besides, I thought we could have a tea party beside the Christmas tree—before I take down the decorations."

Ford relaxed visibly when he saw Sunny step through the door with a tentative smile. "So that's why the ladder was out," he said. "You were taking it all down. Marvella thought you were an angel when she saw your face above the star."

"No angel," said Kate. "Just a lady who doesn't want to be alone on Christmas Day."

What happened next seemed inevitable to Kate when she looked back on it later that night. First she put away the ladder and told the children she would leave the decorations in place as long as there was anyone around to enjoy them. Then she asked Sunny to come into the kitchen with her and help her make the sandwiches for tea.

But when Sunny opened the refrigerator door, she just stood in front of the shelves, transfixed by the abundance within easy reach. Finally Kate crossed to her, quietly took what she needed, and closed the refrigerator.

While she waited for the kettle to boil, Kate trimmed the crusts from the bread. Sweeping them into the sink, she was just about to turn on the disposal when Sunny suddenly reached into the sink and began scooping up the crusts. "What are you doing?" Kate cried. "Do you want to lose a finger?"

"How can you throw away good food?" Sunny asked. Then she flushed with embarrassment and turned away. "I'm sorry."

"No, I'm sorry." Kate shook her head. "I feel so stupid and wasteful. I should have thought—"

But before she could finish, Sunny started for the door. "We shouldn't have come. It's your house—and your food. You can do whatever you want with it."

Kate moved to her. "If you go, I'll feel worse than I already do."

With a shrug Sunny turned back into the kitchen. Kate opened a drawer, removed a plastic bag, and began to stuff the crusts into it. "I never saw my mother throw away a piece of bread, no matter how stale it was. She'd make stuffing or bread pudding or—"

"I used to have a recipe for bread pudding," Sunny said. She closed her eyes, then slowly began to recite in a singsong voice, "Three eggs, three cups milk, a half cup sugar, a fourth cup raisins . . ."

"Why don't we make some now?" Kate interrupted. "It can be cooking while we make the sandwiches. I haven't had bread pudding since I was a child."

"Could I do it?" Sunny asked eagerly.

"Don't you want me to help?"

Sunny shook her head. What she wanted more than anything was just to be left alone in that kitchen, its cupboards stocked with supplies, its counters lined with shining appliances. "Would you trust me in here alone?" she blurted out.

"Of course," Kate said and started to touch her hand, but Sunny turned away. "I'll take Ford and the children outside and show them around the garden. If you decide you could use some help, just give us a call."

Sunny took a jar of peanut butter from the shelf. "Would peanut butter and jelly sandwiches be okay?"

"My favorite," said Kate, thinking of the cucumber she'd been about to slice.

Joe Wayne and Marvella were standing at the French doors that opened onto the terrace when Kate entered the living room.

"Sunny wanted to be left alone in there," she said, looking at Ford for approval.

"I learned a long time ago that when Sunny says she wants to be left alone, it's better not to argue," he said with a smile.

Kate could not help feeling, as she often did around men to

whom she was not married, that there was nothing easier than pleasing another person. All you had to do was look and listen.

"Come on outside," she said. "I'll show you around the garden. I'm sorry the heat's not on in the pool. It's almost warm enough for a swim."

"You have your own swimming pool?" Joe Wayne asked, disbelieving. "You don't have to share it with anybody?"

"See. What did I tell you?" Marvella was dancing with excitement. "Daddy said when we got to California we'd see a swimming pool in every backyard."

"Not in every backyard," Ford corrected her, "but in a lot."

"We haven't seen one," said Joe Wayne.

"That's because we haven't been in any backyards," Ford replied.

"Nothing you told us about California turned out to be true." Joe Wayne's voice was hard and accusing.

"It takes time, son." Ford's voice was gentle but Kate could see the hurt in his eyes.

"You said we'd be able to pick oranges off the trees for breakfast." Marvella began remembering the other promises.

"Come with me," said Kate, taking her by the hand. They walked past the pool to a citrus grove, where grapefruit, oranges, and lemons weighted the branches. "Help yourselves," said Kate. "There is so much more here than I can use. I hate seeing it go to waste. I used to try making marmalade, but I'd end up with jars and jars that nobody wanted. So now I just let the fruit fall and rot—and try not to think about it."

While the children ran among the trees, filling their arms with fruit, Ford walked around the garden, stopping every so often to examine the soil in the flower beds. "You could grow enough behind your house to feed a family."

"That was my husband's plan when we moved into this house," Kate remembered. "He wanted us to be self-supporting so he could turn down any script that had nothing to say."

She thought back to that first summer. She and Cliff would spend every afternoon working in the garden. When a belated wedding check arrived from an uncle Cliff had not seen since childhood, he spent it on citrus trees—even though their living room was still without a couch. "I'd rather spend my money on something with roots," he said—and Kate smiled and worked happily alongside him while he laid out a vegetable garden.

Neither of them was too sure of what they were doing. Kate put in a whole bed of tulip bulbs upside down and Cliff planted the green bean seeds so far underground they never did sprout, but they watched the zucchini swell into shape as proudly as if they'd given birth to them and when the first ones were ready to eat, Cliff insisted on cooking them himself—the only time Kate could ever remember his showing any interest in what happened in the kitchen.

"Zucchini," Kate murmured. "We had good luck with zucchini." Then she forced herself back into the present and tried to pay attention to what Ford was saying.

He was talking enthusiastically about the climate—how the planting season in California continued right through the calendar. Not like Iowa, where at Christmas you could tell the ground good-bye till spring.

Kate looked at Ford more closely. Talking about the land, he seemed to acquire a dignity and sense of purpose that stood in vivid contrast to the desperate mood in which she had first encountered him. She suddenly felt ashamed, thinking of her refusal to acknowledge the humanity behind the outstretched hands and pleading voices she'd learned to ignore around the shops in her own neighborhood.

The first time a man had approached her car as she was loading the trunk with sacks of groceries and said he was hungry, she had emptied her coin purse into his outstretched hand and fled back to the safety of her house, forgetting the other errands she had planned to do that day. For weeks after that, she never left the house without several dollar bills in her pocket, so she could buy her way in and out of the grocery store without guilt— and without having to open her purse.

Then she read an article in the *Los Angeles Times* about how panhandling in affluent neighborhoods had become a big-time business and she felt like a sucker, taking the easy way out by giving loose change to the first needy-looking person who crossed her path. From then on, she wrote an end-of-the-year check to the Los Angeles Mission and steeled her heart against the men who prowled the parking lot of the shopping center.

But she couldn't imagine this man panhandling—even to feed his children. Marvella was hugging his neck as he knelt beside the rose bushes, scooping up the earth and letting it fall through his fingers.

All through her childhood Kate would watch other girls with their fathers, trying to fill in the blanks of a relationship she would never know. Usually she was on her guard against succumbing to any easy illusions about family life. She would watch the father carefully for signs of impatience or ill temper, which were seldom long in coming, and she would usually come away feeling that the child was asking for more than the father was prepared to give. Better never to know your father, she concluded, than to be disappointed daily by his lack of response.

But watching as Ford picked up a flower that had fallen to the ground and presented it to his daughter, Kate felt her eyes fill with tears for what she had missed. You couldn't learn to live with a man for the first time as an adult. First you had to be a daughter. Then a friend, a lover, and finally a wife.

Suddenly Sunny opened the kitchen door and called for them to come inside. She had removed her suit jacket and rolled up the sleeves of her blouse. She was wearing one of Kate's aprons to protect her skirt. Her cheeks were flushed from the heat of the oven and little blond tendrils of hair, fugitives from her ponytail, curled softly around her face. Shyly she led them into the dining room, where she had set the table with the Christmas china Kate unpacked every year. The children's eyes grew wide with delight as they saw the centerpiece Kate had constructed around a miniature sled overflowing with candy.

"Something smells wonderful," Kate said, giving Sunny a reassuring smile.

"It's the bread pudding," Sunny said. "It's in the oven—but I thought we might as well get started on the sandwiches."

"Good idea. I'm starving," Kate replied, motioning Ford to sit down. He was standing awkwardly in the doorway while the children clambered into their seats. "I haven't eaten all day," she continued, passing the platter of peanut butter sandwiches dripping with jelly.

"Neither have we," said Marvella, stacking her plate with sandwiches.

"Don't take more than you can eat," Ford said sternly, returning all the sandwiches but one to the platter.

"I didn't," Marvella replied, her lips trembling.

"If we eat all these sandwiches, we can make more," Kate assured her. "I have another loaf of bread in the freezer."

At a signal from Ford the children bowed their heads. "Why don't you say the blessing today, Marvella?" he suggested.

"Okay," she said, "but first everybody close your eyes."

As Kate bowed her head, she saw Marvella easing the platter of sandwiches closer to her plate.

NINE

The children were roasting marshmallows in front of the fire when Kate noticed that Sunny had fallen asleep in her chair. Motioning for Ford to follow her, she moved to the hallway and started up the stairs without a word. He looked around hesitantly before climbing slowly after her.

"I want to show you something," she said, opening the bathroom door and switching on the light.

"You think I'm ready for another bath?" He grinned as she turned on the faucets.

The image of the way he had looked the day before, a towel wrapped loosely around his hips, his dark brown hair still wet, flashed in front of Kate's eyes. She sat down quickly on the edge of the tub.

"What's wrong?" asked Ford, putting his hand on her shoulder to steady her.

"They leak," said Kate, pointing to the faucets. Twin trickles of water were making parallel paths down the tiles into the tub.

"I noticed that yesterday," said Ford, reaching across Kate to turn off the water.

Kate stood abruptly and walked over to the mirror. Her cheeks were flushed. Her eye was caught by a jagged crack across the bottom of the mirror. How long had it been there? She couldn't remember. She couldn't even remember how it had happened. All she knew was that she could no longer walk through the house without seeing something wrong in every room—a rotting plank in the parquet floor (hidden by an area rug to every eye but Kate's), smoke stains on the kitchen wallpaper (from the time she had set the electric oven on broil instead of bake and returned to find the pan of brownies in flames), drawers that no longer shut, temperamental appliances that seemed to operate on whim instead of electricity. She had even noticed when Cliff closed the heavy, fortresslike front door behind him today that the wood had begun to split—just a tiny seam but enough to admit daylight. And when Kate put her hand to it, she could feel the cold air invading the front hall. The house was coming apart, just like the marriage.

She should have taken better care of it, called a repairman at the first sign that something was wrong. When the plumbing or the heating broke down—something major, something that disrupted their lives—she went into action and the wrong was righted immediately. But these minor flaws were easy to overlook. Each one, taken alone, was insignificant. But now there were so many things wrong with the house—everywhere she looked.

"Are they beyond repair?" she heard herself asking as Ford examined the faucets.

"Nothing is beyond repair," he said, "but I think you're going to need some new fixtures."

"Do you really think that would do it?" asked Kate. "I was afraid we'd have to break through the tiles and go into the pipes."

"Do you have a wrench?"

"I'll be right back," said Kate. And she ran down the stairs to the kitchen. At the sound of the dishwasher entering the rinse cycle she stopped and smiled. She hadn't used a machine to wash the dishes since Nina had left home. With only two people there were not that many dishes. Then Cliff left for location and there were hardly any dishes at all.

She glanced into the living room. Sunny was still sleeping in her chair, but the children were nowhere in sight. Then she noticed that the French doors opening onto the terrace were ajar. She was crossing to close to them when she heard the sound of frantic barking.

Her heart pounding, she ran into the garden. Homer was racing around the swimming pool, barking an alarm. As Kate reached the edge, she saw Joe Wayne struggling to keep his head above water as he pulled a choking and spluttering Marvella to the side.

"Oh, my God!" Kate exclaimed, kneeling to help them out of the pool. "Are you all right?" She took off her cardigan and wrapped it around Marvella. "We'd better get you inside where it's warm."

As she hurried the children through the kitchen door and into the house, Ford came running to meet them. "I heard Homer," he said, kneeling to comfort his daughter. "What happened?"

"I fell in," sobbed Marvella, her teeth chattering with cold.

"You jumped in," said Joe Wayne. "And I had to jump in to save you."

"This is no time to argue," said Ford. "Now, both of you, take off those wet clothes before you die of pneumonia."

"I don't want to die," Marvella began to scream hysterically.

"Of course you're not going to die, sweetheart," Kate said, putting her arm around Marvella as she guided her up the stairs. "That's just an expression. We'll get you into a hot bath and find some dry clothes and you'll be fine." Kate looked back at Ford. "You take Joe Wayne into that bathroom and I'll take Marvella into mine."

"I'll take Marvella," a voice said coldly from the bottom of the stairs. The shy, frightened woman Kate had had to talk into entering her house now walked up the stairs as if she owned them and took her daughter by the hand. "Come with me, honey." Opening the door to the bathroom, she pushed Marvella inside, then turned back to Ford. "I told you we shouldn't have come."

Kate suddenly felt like an outsider in her own home. "I'll go find some dry clothes for the children," she said hurriedly.

She was standing on a stepladder in Nina's bedroom, taking a storage box down from a high cupboard, when Ford entered. He rushed to Kate and took the box from her. "That's too heavy for you. Why didn't you ask me to help you?"

Kate shrugged. "I'm not used to asking anyone for help around the house." Then she laughed. "There's usually no one to ask."

Ford held out his hand to help her down from the ladder. "Are the children all right?" she asked anxiously.

Ford nodded. "I gave Joe Wayne that robe to wear—the one I didn't see yesterday hanging on the door."

Was he laughing at her? Kate wasn't sure. "And Marvella?"

"I left her alone with her mother. She was more scared than anything else."

"Who? Marvella or Sunny?"

"Both, I guess." Ford seemed hesitant, uncertain. "I'm sorry for the way Sunny sounded just now. You've been so good to us and all we've done is cause you trouble."

Kate began to sort through the box of clothes she had taken down from the cupboard. "I need your help here—in this house," she said slowly. "Why do you think I showed you those faucets in the bathroom? There are a hundred things like that around here —things I don't know how to fix. I don't even know who to call to fix them for me." She crossed to her daughter's bed and sat down, defeated. "I hate being alone here," she said, picking up the stuffed dog Adam had given Nina the night of their high school graduation and stroking it as if it were alive.

"I owe you so much already," Ford said. "Show me anything you want done and I'll do it."

"The problem is I can't pay you," said Kate. "I don't have any money—I mean not any money of my own. All I have is this house. My husband pays the bills." She paused. "That's embarrassing to admit in this day and age. I guess I'm going to have to get a job, but I don't even know where to begin."

Ford laughed bitterly. "You begin with an address—which you've got—so you're a long way ahead of me. You can't get a job in this town without one but you can't get one till you've got a job." He started for the door. "Did you ever find a wrench? I'll get to work on those faucets."

"Oh, dear, I must have left it by the pool. But don't worry about that now. Let's get the children dressed—and then we can talk about how we can help each other."

She picked out a dress from the box of clothes Nina had long since outgrown but Kate had stubbornly refused to give away. "Take this to Marvella," she said. "I remember my daughter wearing it the day she started the first grade. It should be about Marvella's size. I'll keep looking through these things, see what else I can find."

When Ford left the room, Kate pulled out a pair of footed flannel pajamas and held them to her face. She closed her eyes and hugged the pajamas to her chest. She could almost feel Nina sitting in her lap.

"Why are we keeping all these old clothes?" Nina had asked last summer before she left for law school. She had been cleaning her room ruthlessly from floor to ceiling and storing all her senti-mental keepsakes. "I could use this space. Besides, these clothes could be doing someone some good."

"They're doing me some good right where they are," Kate had protested, thinking of how often she got down the clothes and looked through them—from the handknit baby sweaters to the ruffly party dresses to the trendy T-shirts dating from the time Nina had demanded a voice in choosing her clothes. She could see Nina in each outfit, and she was flooded with memories of the places they had been together, the happy times they had shared. But the happy times were over and Nina was right—the clothes could no longer do Kate any good at all. She picked out several more outfits and headed to the bathroom.

"No," Marvella was screaming as Kate knocked at the door. "I'm not getting out."

An embarrassed Sunny opened the door to admit Kate. "Usually I can't get her into the tub for a bath. Now I can't get her out."

Marvella had let all the water out of the tub and was sliding from side to side.

"Let her play," said Kate. "I found some more clothes for you, Marvella," she added, handing the outfits to Sunny.

"Come on, Marvella," said Sunny, holding out a towel. "Get out of the tub and get dressed. We've got to go."

"Where are we going?" asked Marvella fearfully.

"Back where we came from," said Sunny. "Back where we belong."

"We don't belong there." Marvella began to cry. "It's dirty and horrible and there's never enough hot water to take a bath. Plus it stinks." And she stopped crying long enough to hold her nose.

"How would you like to stay here?" Kate asked tentatively, looking at Sunny.

"Oh, yes, please," said Marvella. "Can we roast more marshmallows?"

"No," said Sunny fiercely. "No one's going to separate us from our children."

"Of course not." Kate touched Sunny's shoulder to reassure her but felt her stiffen at the touch. "I meant all of you—the whole family—spend the night."

"Just one night?" Marvella's voice sank with disappointment.

"I'm all alone here," said Kate. "There's plenty of room. You can stay as long as you like."

By now Marvella had dried herself off and was getting dressed as fast as she could. "Where will I sleep?" she asked, almost tripping over a towel in her excitement.

"You can have my daughter's room," said Kate. "She's all grown now. Would you like me to show you?" She held out her hand to Marvella, who began pulling her out the door. "But first we have to make sure it's all right with your mother."

Sunny nodded and tried to smile. "I don't know why you're doing this, but thank you."

Kate left Marvella in Nina's room trying on clothes and went in search of Ford. She was haunted by the look of fierce, defeated pride in Sunny's eyes. From the moment Ford's car had broken down outside her front door, Kate had followed her instincts. But how far would they take her? She was frightened to think how fast she had become involved in the fate of this family. Once they stayed the night, their lives would be inextricably interwoven with hers. There would be no turning back. She took a deep breath and put a hand on the banister to steady her as she walked down the stairs. She had to find Ford—in his presence everything would seem clear and simple and right.

She realized with a start that there was a light on in Cliff's study—as if to remind her of his existence. What would happen if he came home unexpectedly and found every room occupied by people he had never even met? The thought amused her. Kate looked into the study. Stretched out on the couch, wearing Cliff's robe, was Joe Wayne. The television set was on and he was changing channels every few seconds with the remote control. Kate smiled and walked quietly away without letting Joe Wayne know she had seen him.

Kate remembered how pleased Cliff had been the day he brought home that set—a Christmas gift from the studio. Cliff preferred to watch television alone—for him it was work not play, he had explained to Kate—and he had bought her a set for the bedroom. But she was uncomfortable watching a show with only a laugh track for company and seldom turned it on.

Cliff, however, retired to his study every night after dinner and stretched out on the couch to "do his homework" (as he put it to Kate). But more often than not, she would come downstairs late at night to find him asleep, remote control in hand, the television set still sending its flickering images into the darkness like a lighthouse beacon warning ships at sea that they were approaching shallow water.

Looking back now, Kate wondered if the introduction of that

remote control television into the house marked the beginning of the end of her marriage. If a man can control a complicated piece of machinery by lifting one finger, he can grow to resent exerting any more effort to communicate with his wife.

But perhaps Cliff was equally resentful of all the miracle workers plugged into her kitchen counter, Kate thought as she turned on the light—the microwave, the food processor, the pasta machine, the bread maker. One flick of the switch and you felt like Superwoman. It did tend to ruin you for the work required in human relationships.

The sound of clothes tumbling in the dryer echoed her thoughts—until she remembered that she hadn't washed today. She turned on the light in the utility room and opened the door of the dryer. The clothes Joe Wayne and Marvella had been wearing when they came to her front door collapsed into a pathetic little heap.

Ford must have taken his children's wet clothes and put them in the dryer. The fact that he just did it—without asking her —seemed oddly touching to Kate. He already felt at home here. Something in her relaxed. Whatever the consequences of her action in inviting this family into her home, she had no regrets. At least not yet. She had to find Ford, tell him that everything was going to be all right. But where had he gone? She looked out the front window. The car was still parked by the mailbox, as if to say, "Now that I've finally got an address, I'm not budging."

A noise from the upstairs bathroom led her to him. He had found the wrench and was tightening the faucets.

"You're not going to need new fixtures after all," he said proudly, turning on the water full force to demonstrate. "One of the fittings had just come loose."

"Do you know how much it would have cost me to have a plumber come to that same conclusion?" she asked with a smile.

"I can put in a new mirror for you," Ford said. "Then your bathroom will be good as new."

"It's your bathroom now," said Kate. "I'm giving you and Sunny the master bedroom."

Ford stared at her. "I don't understand."

Kate spoke slowly, choosing her words with great care. "It's simple. You need a house. I need someone to take care of this one." And to take care of me, she said without words, her eyes pleading with him not to let his pride prevent him from accepting what she was offering. "I can't pay you, but I can share what I have with you—this house and all the food you can eat."

"Why would you do that?" asked Ford. "You don't even know us."

"The people I know don't need my help," said Kate. "I haven't made a difference to someone else in a long time. It would give me a reason to get up every morning if I thought I were making a difference to you."

"The difference between life and death," said Ford. He sat down heavily on the edge of the tub and covered his face with his hands.

Kate longed to take him in her arms, to reassure him that the worst was behind him, that whatever the future held, it would be better than what he had just lived through. His shoulders were shaking now. He was like a soldier who could not experience the full horror of battle until he was safely home.

"It's going to be all right," Kate said softly, putting her hand on his shoulder. "I can't give you much, but I can give you an address."

Ford took her hand and pressed it to his lips, not daring to look at her. Finally he released it and rose to his feet. "The address we can accept," he said with a smile, "but not your bedroom. We have sleeping bags in the car. We can spread them on the floor in the living room and in the morning we can roll them up and you won't even know we're here."

"But I want to know you're here," said Kate. "I want to walk into every room in this house and feel it being used. I've felt so guilty living here alone—all this space for just one person. It makes no sense. The life I live here makes no sense. I need you to make it make sense—perhaps even more than you need me. Now, come on, let me show you your room."

"What about Sunny?" Ford asked anxiously as Kate turned on the lights in the master bedroom.

"She's already agreed to all this—if that's what you're worried about," Kate reassured him, taking clean sheets from the cupboard and stripping the bed.

"You asked her first—before you asked me?" Ford seemed surprised.

"Actually, I asked Marvella." Kate laughed. "Sunny just happened to be in the same room."

"Where is she now? I think I'd better talk to her."

"I left her in the bathroom," said Kate.

When she was alone, Kate took a suitcase from the back of the closet. She had packed it the week before so she would be ready to leave for Canada with Cliff. She had not been able to face unpacking it when he left without her. Was it only a few hours ago?

She put the suitcase on the bed and opened it. Slowly she removed the heavy woolen clothes. What a waste, she thought as she hung the down coat and cable-knit sweaters in the closet. I'm not likely to need any of these things unless *I* end up sleeping on the street.

When the suitcase was empty, she closed it decisively as if closing a chapter of her life and started toward the hall to store it out of sight, if not out of mind. But she stopped at the door and began looking around the room as if she were seeing it for the last time. Suddenly she flung open the suitcase and began filling it again with books and photographs from her bedside table, papers from her desk, clothes from her closet, and the bag of toilet articles she had packed for the trip. Then she took one last look around the room and started down the stairs with the suitcase.

Marvella, wearing an ill-matched outfit she had put together from Nina's old clothes, came running after her. "Where are you going?" she cried. "You can't leave us in this house by ourselves!"

Kate set down the suitcase and took Marvella in her arms. "I'm moving," she said, "but only to another room. That is, if we can talk Joe Wayne into giving up the study."

"It's your house," said Marvella. "We have to do what you tell us. Don't we?" she added tentatively. "My daddy said we did when we came here."

"If we're all going to live here together, we have to try to make each other happy," said Kate. "Now let's go find Joe Wayne. I have a surprise for him."

Kate opened the door off the kitchen that led to what had been designed as a maid's room but never put to that use. It was plainly furnished—a bed, a desk, a bureau. "Okay, Joe Wayne," she said, "how would you like your very own room?"

"It's a long way from everybody else," he said, looking long-ingly back toward the study. "I was almost asleep on that couch. It felt real nice. I'd rather have a TV than a bed."

Kate walked over to the kitchen counter and unplugged the small television set next to the stove. "Would this do?" she asked, setting it down on a table at the foot of the bed and plugging it into the wall.

"You mean I can have my own set and I'll be the only one who decides what to watch on it?" Joe Wayne's eyes widened with delight.

Marvella came running into the room. "See, Joe Wayne, I told you we were going to like it here."

Joe Wayne lay down on the bed and lifted his foot toward the television.

"What are you doing?" cried Marvella.

"Just testing." he grinned as he turned on the set with his big toe. "I don't even need a remote control."

In the bathroom Ford was growing impatient with his wife. "First you won't get out of the car, now you won't get out of the bathtub."

Sunny lay back and closed her eyes. "Do you know how long it's been since I took all the time I wanted in the bath—without somebody banging on the door wanting a turn. Besides, I don't know when I'll get to take another one."

"You can take another one tonight and then another one tomorrow morning," Ford said in an exasperated voice. "We're staying. This is where we're going to live. She told you. I told you. Now believe it."

"It just doesn't make sense," said Sunny stubbornly.

"She wants to help us."

"She wants a man in her house. She wants one bad enough she's willing to take in his family to get him."

"Your sister took us in for six months before we came to California. You didn't see anything wrong with that."

"That's blood. Blood is different," said Sunny, wrapping a towel around her wet hair.

"Here. Put on this robe." Ford took a thick white terry-cloth robe from the bathroom door and held it open for Sunny.

"Is it hers?"

"It's her bathroom, so I guess it has to be. But she's giving us her bedroom, so she's hardly going to mind if you wear her robe."

"Her bedroom?" Sunny looked at Ford with disbelief. "She's moving out of her room? Why would she do that?"

"Well . . ." Ford hesitated, searching for an answer he hadn't been able to find himself. "There are two of us and only one of her. Maybe it's as simple as that."

"She's given us so much. I just don't know what she wants from us," said Sunny, putting on the robe and tying the cord around her waist.

"I'm not sure she does either," Ford had to admit.

"And that's what worries me," Sunny said, following Ford reluctantly into the bedroom.

TEN

Ford was dreaming that he was back on the family farm. He never thought of it as his, even after his father died and he had to work it alone. He felt he was holding it in trust for his son just as his father had done for him and his grandfather for his father. "Banks can fail," Ford had grown up hearing his father say, "but the land will never let you down."

Ford could feel the breeze fanning his face as he rode his tractor through the fields, fields he owned as far as the eye could see in every direction. "A man doesn't have to have money in the bank to feel rich in this country," his father had said as he bought more equipment and took out more loans to make improvements. "There'll always be a market for what we've got to sell. No matter how bad times get, people still have to eat."

Ford stirred uneasily in his sleep. A cloud hovered at the back of his unconscious but he refused to allow it to enter his line of vision. The sun was high in the sky. He shaded his eyes with his hand and squinted into the distance, then his face relaxed into a smile. Sunny was just leaving the farmhouse with a wicker basket on her arm.

Ford drove his tractor to the edge of the field and parked it beneath a grove of oak trees. He climbed down and walked through the trees to an old mill pond ringed with willows.

Sunny was approaching, wearing a peasant blouse and a full skirt that could not conceal her swelling contours. He put his hand against her stomach. "How do you feel, honey?" he asked.

"Fat," she replied.

"I like making things grow," he whispered, pulling her blouse off her shoulders. "I couldn't keep my hands off you before we were married."

"Which is why we had to get married," she reminded him.

"But I'm even more attracted to the mother of my child than I was to my sweetheart," he said softly, holding her close to his chest.

Turning restlessly in his sleep, Ford reached for Sunny, but there was no one beside him. Confused, he opened his eyes and wondered if he was still dreaming. An arched canopy of spring flowers rose above him, the pattern echoed in the drapes that framed two French windows opening onto a balcony. Ford got out of bed and walked to the windows.

The sound of splashing coming from the swimming pool alarmed him and he stepped onto the balcony. Then, suddenly realizing he was naked, he lunged for the bed and grabbed the terrycloth robe lying across it. He walked to the far end of the balcony but could barely see the swimming pool through the leafy branches of the trees. He had no sense of the seasons here in California. In the calendar of his mind December evoked a scene of bare black branches in stark relief against white fields. But here it was the day after Christmas and the surrounding land-scape seemed to be in full bloom.

"Is everybody all right out there?" he called as the splashing sounds continued, punctuated with bursts of laughter. Homer came running to greet him, then, frustrated at finding his master beyond his reach, began barking up at the balcony.

"It's okay, Homer, I'm coming down," Ford said. "I didn't hear you barking before so I guess everybody is managing to stay afloat today."

Just then a dripping Joe Wayne came into view. "Come on in, Dad," he shouted. "The water's great."

"I thought the two of you had learned your lesson yesterday," Ford said sternly. "You almost caught pneumonia."

"Kate turned the heater on last night so we could swim this morning. She said for you to look in her husband's closet and find a suit."

"Where is she?" asked Ford.

"In the pool with Marvella—teaching her to float like a dead man."

Ford laughed. "Well, you hurry up and get back in there with them. I hope the water is warmer than the air out here or you're all going to be dead men."

"It's great, Dad," Joe Wayne assured him. "Like a giant bathtub—only you don't have to wash behind the ears."

"Sounds like my kind of place," said Ford.

He went back into the room and stared at the empty bed. How long had he been sleeping there alone? Where had Sunny gone so early in the morning? Then he looked at the clock in disbelief. Ten o'clock? It couldn't be.

Ford had never slept that late in his life—though as a boy on the farm, lying in bed for five more minutes after his father had shaken him awake at 4:00 A.M. to help with the milking, he would dream of the day he could sleep till noon. He never wasted time dreaming of money or fame. The farm provided him with everything he needed and he liked working hard—if only the work could have waited for him to wake up on his own. He would almost fall back to sleep every morning milking, his cheek pressed against the warm flank of the cow, lulled by the steady rhythm of his hands as they squeezed and pulled and the syncopated beat made by the milk hitting the sides of the pail.

Of course this past year, after they lost the farm, there were no chores to rouse him from bed before sunrise. He could have slept all day for all the difference it made—but fear got him out of bed earlier than the farm. Once they shut the door on their home for the last time, Ford stopped sleeping through the night. He seldom got more than three or four hours' sleep at a stretch.

But last night . . . he looked at the clock again. It had been nine o'clock at night when he looked at it last—just before Sunny fell asleep in his arms. Once he had coaxed her into the bedroom, she had climbed into the king-sized, canopy-covered bed and refused to leave it. "From the time I was a little girl I wanted to sleep in a bed with a canopy," she said. "It always seemed so safe somehow. I used to cut pictures out of magazines and paste them in a scrapbook. One whole scrapbook was bedrooms, nothing but bedrooms, and every bed had a canopy. Every Christmas I would write 'canopy bed' at the top of my list for Santa Claus, but I never got one. I remember one day my mama sat me down real serious and said she had a surprise for me. I was so excited I almost fainted. I knew what she was going to say. I was finally going to get a canopy bed. But all I got was a baby sister." Sinking back into the pillows, she looked up happily at the fabric arching above her like a flower-strewn sky. "Even if we have to leave this house tomorrow, I will have finally gotten my wish."

"Honey, please stop being scared." Ford lay down beside her, slipping his hand beneath the robe she had borrowed from the bathroom. "We're going to be able to stay here till we get our lives back on track. I told you last night I was going to take care of you."

"Oh, Ford." Sunny was trembling now, eager for him to finish what he had started. The pleasure she took in him, pleasure she was never embarrassed to show, was what had drawn him to her in the first place. So different from his mother, who denied his father her bed every time he did anything that displeased her.

Ford could still remember the time his father had come into the barn unexpectedly and found him masturbating in the hayloft. Flushed with guilt, Ford had closed his eyes and wished he could disappear from the face of the earth.

"It's okay, son," his father said gently, sitting down beside him, putting a companionable arm around his shoulders. "I know your mother doesn't approve, but she drives me to it at least once a week."

"Once I'm married," said Ford, "I'll never do it again."

"Maybe not," said his father. "But fortunately for all men who want to stay faithful to their wives, it's something you never forget how to do. And I'll tell you, son, there are times when the woman in your head can be a lot more accommodating than the woman in your bed."

"Dad, can I have the car tonight?" Ford asked, anxious to end the conversation.

"She's still pretty young—and you're getting in pretty deep," his father warned him as he handed him the keys.

"All I know is when I'm with her, I'm where I want to be," Ford replied.

And it was true. Ford had never met a girl like Sunny. Most of the girls he had dated had come from farms like his—and couldn't wait to move away to the city. Sunny lived in town—in a crowded apartment on top of the mom-and-pop grocery store her parents ran. The first time Ford took her out to the farm, she ran from tree to tree like a child let out of school for summer vacation, intoxicated by the endless space. "Imagine looking out your window and seeing nothing but fields and trees and knowing they all belonged to you," she said. "If I could live in a place like this, I'd never ask for another thing."

She even liked the idea of sharing the farmhouse with his parents, just as his parents had done with his grandparents when they were first married. "They can help us take care of the kids," she said. "I want to have a lot."

"We'll need a lot to help with the chores." Ford grinned.

And so they were married the day after Sunny graduated from high school. Joe Wayne was born five months later.

Their plans for a big family disappeared as the farm drove them further and further into debt, but when a baby daughter arrived four years after their son, her overjoyed father named her Marvella. Sunny, however, saw little cause for rejoicing in the arrival of another mouth to feed. Their financial situation became desperate as government policies made a mockery of the improvements Ford's father had borrowed heavily to finance. As if admitting defeat, his mother was hospitalized for cancer and died within the year, leaving her survivors a few antiques and a stack of unpaid bills.

Her husband shrank from the confident, vigorous man his son had idolized into a stumbling, frightened shell of his former self. When he died of a heart attack a year after his wife, Ford was almost relieved to be able to remember him as he once had been instead of having to confront the daily reality of what he had become.

Ford and his family worked longer and longer hours, desperate to make the farm pay, but finally they could no longer meet even the interest payments on the money they owed. The day his farm was sold at auction, Ford went to his father's grave and cursed him for the blind optimism that had led them so far into debt. Then he fell to his knees and thanked God for sparing his father the sight of the land he had so loved passing into the hands of strangers.

Sunny took Joe Wayne and Marvella back to the apartment on top of the grocery store, where her sister now lived with her husband and four children. Sunny had wanted no part of the store once she married Ford and moved to the farm. The apartment was even more crowded now than it had been when Sunny was growing up. At least then she had had a bed of her own and a room she shared with her sister. Now she and her family slept on bedrolls in the living room.

Ford waited until everyone but Sunny was asleep at night before he would set foot in the apartment, and he left in the morning before anyone was awake. He couldn't bear to see the pity with which Sunny's younger sister treated her. Each day he would drive in a different direction looking for work, but it seemed to him that every house in the state sheltered homeless relatives who had lost their land or their jobs.

After six months of living like a fugitive, forced to depend on the ever more reluctant charity of his in-laws to feed and house his family, Ford decided, as a final, desperate gamble, to drive his family and their few possessions west to California where at least they could count on the weather to be kind.

The promise of work, which had lured them west like an ever-receding mirage in the distance, disappeared at the end of the road. Factories closing up and down the state flooded the job market with skilled workers who were also lifelong residents with an inside track to whatever employment was available. A farmhand from out of state didn't have a chance.

Ford looked at the canopied bed and sighed. Every day for the past year he had expected Sunny to say she had had enough, she was taking the kids and leaving him for good. But she had clung to him, whatever the cost. And while at times he resented her dependence, it was finally the centripetal force that kept him centered. Without her and the children looking to him each day for some miraculous solution to their increasingly desperate circumstances, he could no longer have summoned the strength to continue looking for jobs that didn't seem to exist.

It was not until he brought her to this house, where his own faith in the future had been somewhat shakily restored, that Ford had felt Sunny's blind trust in him begin to weaken. It was the first time he had seen her so reluctant to follow him wherever he had chosen to lead.

And even last night in bed, the urgency with which she had welcomed him had demanded a response so total it summoned any possible emotion he might have been holding in reserve—as if she were taking his full measure as a man before deciding to what degree he fell short.

Looking back on the whispered shards of sentences that seemed to escape her lips almost against her will in the brief intermission between the act of love and the onset of sleep, Ford felt an ominous sense of foreboding.

"Promise me you'll keep a close eye on the children here. You're so trusting. You don't see what's coming." He had thought she was talking about the swimming pool, warning him about the danger, but listening to her words replaying in his mind, he heard something else in her tone—a distancing of herself from their new circumstances, as if she were somehow trying to free herself from the sticky net of family.

Frantic, he began to search the bedroom for some sign that she had disappeared only from the room, not from the house, not from his life. But the clothes she had been wearing the night before, which she had left folded on the chair beside the bed, were gone—including the handbag Kate had given her, which contained enough cash, it suddenly occurred to Ford, to buy a bus ticket back to Iowa.

He ran into the hallway and opened every door—closets, bathrooms, and the bedroom Kate had given to his daughter. The foot of her bed was piled with stuffed animals. Kate must have taken them out of storage, he thought, to make Marvella feel at home. He smoothed the sheets and straightened the down comforter. Comforter—what a wonderful word, he thought—it described exactly what it did. The warm, safe feeling that greeted him the first time he set foot inside this house pervaded every room. His children felt it, he could see from how quickly they had made themselves at home here. Why couldn't Sunny? Why wasn't she here to share their happiness?

He hurried down the stairs. Surely somewhere she had left a clue. There was evidence connecting every other room to the person who had last occupied it. Pillows and blankets were still piled on the couch in the study where Kate had slept. She doesn't even have a bed in here, Ford realized, wondering again why she had given them her bedroom.

Joe Wayne's clothes were scattered on the floor in the room off the kitchen. I'm going to have to talk to him about taking care of his things, Ford thought, picking up the clothes and spreading them on the bed—but then he remembered how long it had been since any of them had owned anything in which they could take pride. This new life was going to take practice.

The fragrant aroma of freshly brewed coffee drew Ford into the kitchen. There was a pitcher of orange juice on the breakfast table and a basket of warm muffins. Maybe Sunny had just gotten up early and come downstairs to make breakfast. Ford began to relax. She was probably outside in the garden, keeping an eye on the children.

He stepped outside. The wet grass felt soft and welcoming under his bare feet. A woman who appeared to be naked emerged from the water and walked toward him. Kate!

He barely recognized her with her hair pulled back and so much bare flesh showing between the lines of what he realized now was a very brief peach-colored bikini. Her figure was far from perfect. In fact, there was more of her than he would have guessed from seeing her fully clothed. Yesterday, in her well-tailored slacks and elegant wool sweater, she had looked to him like a glamorous actress or at least like someone who was accustomed to dressing for an audience. No detail of her appearance had been neglected. Her ash-blond hair had been carefully cut to frame her face, and artfully applied makeup had created the illusion she was as young as he was. Looking at her now, in the bright light of morning, her face scrubbed clean, he saw she was at least five years older. But her openness in showing herself exactly as she was seemed oddly endearing.

"Good morning," she said. "I'm glad you were able to sleep so late." The warmth of her smile transformed her unadorned appearance and made her seem more beautiful to Ford than she had the day before.

"In a bed like that who would ever want to wake up?" He smiled back, trying to keep his eyes on her face and off the generous curves of her body, offered so openly for his inspection.

Marvella came running over to him. "Daddy, come see me swim," she said excitedly, untying his bathrobe.

"Not yet, sweetheart." Ford suddenly remembered he was not wearing anything under the robe.

"Have you had breakfast?" Kate asked. "I made muffins."

"Oh. I thought maybe Sunny—" He stopped abruptly.

"We haven't eaten yet," Kate explained. "We decided to go for a swim first. Would you like to have breakfast with us? Or maybe you'd rather wait for Sunny."

Ford just stared at her. "She's not here," he said finally. "She's not anywhere in the house."

"Well, she can't have gone far," said Kate. "Your car is still parked in front. Maybe she just went for a walk."

"Why would she do that? Leave the rest of us here and go out by herself?"

Kate was more puzzled than she wanted to admit. "I didn't hear anyone leave the house and I was up early making the muffins."

Ford put his hand on her cheek and turned her face so she could not avoid his eyes. "You were up early because you had a hard time sleeping on that couch, admit it."

Kate shook her head and turned away. "No. I would have ended up on that couch last night even if there had been no one else in the house. That room belongs to my husband. It's his study —where he goes to work, where he goes to be alone."

She talks about him as if he's still in the house, Ford thought.

"I can't tell you how many times he's fallen asleep on that couch," Kate continued. "I thought maybe if I lay down there, I could feel his presence, fool myself into believing he was sleeping beside me."

What kind of a man could leave a woman like this, Ford wondered. She bared her heart to him as trustingly as she bared everything else. "I'd better get on some clothes," he said, hoping Kate would do the same.

Alone in the bedroom, Ford took off the robe and flung it across the bed. He thought of Kate lying there alone night after night while her husband fell asleep on the couch downstairs. Ford hated waste of any kind and for a man to turn his back on a woman, leave her so unused, make her feel so unwanted, was waste.

He reached for his trousers, and a piece of paper fluttered to the floor. He picked it up and read, in Sunny's childlike hand: "Dear Ford, I don't want to have to depend on anybody ever again. I'm going out to look for a job. I won't be back till I get one. Love, Sunny."

ELEVEN

"You left him alone in the house?" Ruth stared at Kate in disbelief.

"I invited him to come with us, but he was painting the bathroom."

"You've lost your mind, Kate. It's as simple as that." Ruth stood up and shook the crumbs from her lap. Two sparrows immediately swooped down from the roof to scavenge under the table. "I haven't been to the Farmers Market in years," Ruth said, shooing them away. "I'd forgotten how open it is." She picked up her purse and looked around.

"Are you leaving?" Kate asked in surprise. "Don't you have anything else to say to me?"

"I have a lot more to say," Ruth assured her. "But I need a cup of coffee. I think I saw a stand over this way. Would you like some?"

Kate nodded. "Please. But I think I'd better stay here—in case the children come back."

Ruth shook her head. "I hope you know what you're doing."

"I don't," Kate said. "All I know is I'm happier today than I've been in a long time. And I've been able to make four other people happy too. So how could I be doing anything wrong?" Suddenly she waved and shouted, "Over here."

Joe Wayne was wandering through the tables, trying not to let Marvella see that he was lost. Marvella came running over to Kate, holding a dripping ice-cream cone. "I finally decided," she announced, "but Joe Wayne still can't make up his mind."

"You haven't lost your money, have you, Joe Wayne?" Kate asked. He unclenched his fist to show her the two dollar bills wadded inside.

As Ruth approached with the coffee, Kate hurriedly opened her purse and handed them each a five-dollar bill. "Why don't you buy something to take home to your mother and your daddy? Some candy or nuts. Whatever you think they'd like. Take as long as you want to decide. I'll be sitting right here. We won't leave till you're ready."

As the children moved off in the direction of the candy stall, Kate took a sip of coffee and braced herself for Ruth's next attack.

"Did you ever know Hillary and Tom Mackintosh?" Ruth asked.

Kate was thrown off guard. "I remember being introduced to them, but I never really knew them. Why?"

"They moved out here from New York when he sold a play to the movies for a lot of money. They bought a big house and hired an Asian couple to take care of it—Korean, I think. They seemed like very sweet people and Hillary and Tom trusted them completely, thought nothing of leaving them alone in the house when they were out of town. Then one night they came back early from a trip and found over twenty people living in the house—relatives in every room."

"So what happened?" asked Kate. "Did they fire the couple?"

"Well, they tried," said Ruth, "but they were outnumbered. All those Asians just descended on them in a horde and forced them into a closet. They were locked in there for three days before Tom's agent got worried because there was never an answer when he called. The one thing the Mongol horde forgot to do before they fled with all the silver was switch on the answering machine."

Kate couldn't help laughing but then she had to ask, "So what does all this have to do with me?"

"The point is," Ruth explained patiently, "Tom and Hillary were paying those people and they still turned on them. What chance are you going to have with total strangers?"

"You take a risk any time you let another person into your life," said Kate. "An employee, a friend, a husband . . . You have to trust your instincts and, I tell you, Ruth, there is something about this man that is so decent, so honest, so good."

"What about his wife?"

Kate hesitated. "I haven't gotten to know her yet. She was gone this morning when I got up."

"Gone? Where?"

"She left a note saying she was not coming back without a job."

"Well, that's admirable, I must say." Ruth was appeased by this information. "I like her better than I do him."

"He wants to get a job but he sees how much I need his help around the house. We've let it go during these last few years when Cliff was out of work so much." She paused, thinking of the eagerness with which Ford began working on the bathroom this morning, washing the walls, sanding the rough spots, replastering around the windows. Cliff had never taken much interest in maintaining the house. He only got excited about spending money on something that would make a dramatic difference—a new room, a swimming pool, a sauna. Spending money to keep things the same bored him. "I just wish I could afford to pay him," she murmured.

"If you're feeding and housing him and his family, I'd say you were paying him more than he has a right to expect," Ruth replied. "And how are you going to explain all this to Cliff? All these people living in his house?"

"Cliff is in Canada." Kate spoke in a monotone. "He'll be on

location for the next few months. I don't have to explain anything to him."

"I thought you were going to be joining him there." Ruth
gave Kate a puzzled look.

Kate shook her head. "No, I'm staying here."

"Too cold for you?" Ruth laughed.

Kate stared into the distance as if she hadn't heard.

"Is something wrong?" Ruth prodded gently.

Kate turned back to her. "I've decided to sell the house.
That's why I want to get it into shape."

"Welcome to the club." Ruth opened her purse and began
fishing in it for a card. "You must use my realtor. He's marvelous
and you wouldn't believe the price he thinks we can get for our
house. Ten times what we paid! That was twenty years ago admit-
tedly but still, when I think how scared we were signing the
mortgage . . . We'd always lived in rented apartments. Owning
a house—well, the responsibility was just overwhelming."

"Was—and is," agreed Kate. "When I married, all I wanted
was a house of my own. Now I never want to own another one."

Ruth looked at her curiously. "What will you do? Where will
you go?"

"I haven't thought about it."

"You've always been impulsive," Ruth said, "but somehow I
can't see Cliff living anywhere but his own house."

Kate's face froze. Finally she forced the words from her
throat. "Cliff is in love with someone else. He's not coming home.
At least not to me." She tried to smile—a funny, crooked smile—
but the tears were running down her cheeks.

"Oh, Kate." Ruth reached across the table and touched her
hand. "When did this happen?"

"It happened to *him* in Canada. It happened to *me* Christmas
Eve. That's when he told me."

"Does Nina know?"

Kate shook her head. "No. He made me promise not to tell
her. He didn't want to ruin her holiday."

"What about *your* holiday?"

"I knew from the minute he set foot inside the door that he

hadn't really come home. At least when he finally told me I could stop wondering what was wrong." She took a deep breath, trying to control the feelings that were flooding her, making it impossible to think. "Oh, Ruth, I can't live in that house without him."

Ruth nodded sympathetically. "Now I understand about the man and his family. It was certainly good timing on their part."

"His car broke down outside my front door," Kate stated quietly. "It was hardly a calculated move. But I need them—all of them—and they need me."

"Actually, I need your help too." Ruth smiled at the irony. "That's why I called you to meet me for lunch." She went on to explain that once their house sold, she and Henry would be without an address—for the first time in their lives. "We don't need a home, but we've got to have an address—a home base—with someone we can contact to forward mail and take care of business."

"You wanted me to be your home base?" Kate was touched.

"I know it would be asking a lot," Ruth replied, "but you're one of the few people we could trust to open our mail and decide what to do—if something had to be decided. However, if you're selling your house, we'll have to think of someone else."

"I wish I could help you, but I don't know what I'm going to be doing. I can't think beyond tomorrow." Kate found herself envying Ruth the future that stretched out ahead of her. "I always imagined, once Nina was grown, that Cliff and I would finally have time to do all the things we talked about when we were young. I never minded getting old, because I thought each birthday was bringing me closer to my dreams. We were planning a trip to Mexico when he suddenly got the call from Canada."

"You mean Cliff wasn't the first director on the film?" Ruth asked in surprise.

"He didn't want me to go around publicizing the fact that he was a replacement," Kate explained. "He was hired two weeks into filming. They needed someone who knew how to move a camera and wouldn't argue with the actors. Cliff was so thrilled to get another crack at directing a feature—and I was thrilled for him. With us the work has always come first. But Cliff promised we'd go to Mexico in the spring—for our silver wedding anniversary." Her voice suddenly broke and she could not stop the tears. "Oh, Ruth, I don't want to grow old alone!"

They sat in silence until Ruth finally said in a low voice, "We all grow old alone—even when there's another person sleeping in the same bed."

"It's not the same."

"Of course it's not the same. Loneliness takes a different shape inside every house. But don't think just because your dream hasn't come true that mine has." She turned away abruptly, as if regretting what she had just said.

"What do you mean?" Kate asked. "Aren't you and Henry happy?"

"As happy as a brother and sister could be," Ruth said in a whisper. She looked around to make sure the children were nowhere in sight and no one she recognized was in the vicinity of their table. "Henry hasn't slept with me in over a year."

Kate was stunned. "But the two of you have always been so close. What happened?"

"Nothing. That's the trouble. If something traumatic had happened—an accident, a death in the family—then I could understand and wait for time to heal whatever private hurts he was hiding. But he acts as if nothing has changed—he's as devoted to me as he ever was."

"Have you tried talking to him about it?"

"He says he's just depressed—and talking about it just depresses him even more."

"Has he seen a doctor?"

"He had his yearly physical last week. The doctor said he saw no reason why Henry couldn't live to be a hundred—which has always been his goal—but Henry said that was the most depressing news yet. Lately all he talks about is death." Ruth paused, staring into her empty coffee cup. Kate could not think of anything to say. "I blame cable television," Ruth continued finally. "Ever since we had that twenty-four-hour news channel installed, he turns it on first thing every morning and turns it off last thing every night. And in between, he's a walking catalogue of disasters. Much as I'm going to miss my garden, selling our house may be our last chance at happiness. I just hope once we start traveling, Henry will remember how"—she hesitated, searching for the right word—"how rich life can be."

Kate shook her head in disbelief. "You're my best friend—and I didn't suspect what you were going through. I feel as though everyone I know has turned into a stranger, starting with my husband."

Ruth stood to leave. "As long as I didn't tell anyone, I could pretend it wasn't true. Besides, I thought you and Cliff were happy—I didn't want to inflict our unhappiness on you."

Kate grimaced. "Well, now you have no reason to keep anything from me."

Ruth laughed and bent down to kiss her cheek. "That's more of a comfort than you can possibly imagine."

Suddenly Marvella came rushing over to Kate, her eyes shining with excitement. Joe Wayne followed more slowly, carrying a big box.

"I love this place," Marvella said. "Can we come back here tomorrow?"

"Maybe not tomorrow," said Kate, laughing, "but soon, I promise. Did you buy a nice surprise for your parents?"

"A giant pie," Marvella announced proudly, showing the box to Kate.

"It looks delicious," said Kate, peeking inside. "What kind is it?"

"Lemon meringue," Joe Wayne replied. "It's my dad's favorite. My mom used to make it every Sunday when we lived on the farm. But she hasn't made it in a long, long time. She's probably forgotten how."

Marvella punched him in the stomach. "Don't say that. She hasn't forgotten how to do anything she ever did."

"We'll have to test her on it." Kate smiled. "Put her in the kitchen with some eggs and sugar and lemon and see if she comes out with a lemon meringue pie."

"No, don't make her take a test—please." Marvella was suddenly whimpering with fear. "She might not remember and then you'll be mad at her."

Kate pulled the frightened child onto her lap. "I was joking, Marvella. Your mother doesn't have to prove anything to me. As far as I'm concerned, she never has to make another lemon meringue pie for the rest of her life. Whenever we want one, we'll just come back here and buy one. How about that?" Marvella smiled happily. "How about you, Joe Wayne?" Kate asked. "What did you buy?"

Joe Wayne stared at her defiantly. "I helped Marvella pay for the pie," he said. "It cost ten dollars."

"Ten dollars for a pie!" Ruth was horrified. "This place has really turned into a tourist trap."

"It's all right, Ruth." Kate quieted her quickly. "Cliff is still paying my living expenses—despite having ruined my life."

Ruth gave her a hug then reached in her purse for her car keys. "Let's do this again soon. Meanwhile, call me anytime you want to talk. And do give my realtor a ring. At least let him come give you an appraisal. To quote Henry, it's a seller's market—this is the time to cash in your chips."

"Thanks for the advice," said Kate. "And for making me feel less alone."

"Can we go home now?" begged Marvella as Kate waved good-bye to Ruth. "I want to see if I still remember how to float like a dead man."

"I can't wait to see your daddy's face when he cuts into this pie," Kate said when they reached her car.

"My mama likes it too," Marvella said quickly.

"I'm sure she does," said Kate as she handed the box carefully to Joe Wayne, who had claimed the backseat. As he held out his arms to take it, she saw he was still clutching in his fist his five-dollar bill.

TWELVE

Ford was painting the bathroom window when he noticed the police car circling the block. He put down his paintbrush, then stepped back quickly from the window so he wouldn't be seen.

The police parked behind his car. They walked over to inspect his license plate. One of them reached down to flick a piece of mud off the plate so he could read the numbers.

Ford felt beads of sweat breaking out on his forehead. He started to wipe them off with his hand and realized he had streaked green paint across his cheek. He looked into the mirror. The man he had been this morning had disintegrated into a desperate character on the verge of pleading guilty to any crime with which the authorities decided to charge him.

Now the police were walking around the car, noting the dents, the cracked windshield, the broken springs, the hood held in place by a piece of wire.

Ford was breathing heavily. That wreck of a car was his only refuge if all else failed. He couldn't risk losing it. But what was wrong? Why were the police so suspicious? He had a perfect right to park on a public street. Didn't he?

Oh, God, they were coming to the front door.

He wiped his hands on a rag and started slowly down the stairs. The doorbell rang insistently.

Ford opened the front door and tried to look as if he belonged where he was standing. "Yes?" he said, his voice cracking from the effort to stay calm. "Is there a problem?" He saw that both policemen were younger than he was but instead of reassuring him, that fact made him even less secure. His generation had been left behind, overrun by kids who had grown up being given everything before they were even sure of what they wanted. What did they know about being cold or hungry or having nowhere to go?

"How long has that eyesore from Iowa been parked out front?" the short, stocky officer asked.

"Since yesterday." Ford eyed him, taking his measure.

"We had a complaint from one of your neighbors," the taller officer explained. "We've been finding abandoned cars all over the city. You didn't happen to see who left it, did you?"

Ford cleared his throat and tried to smile. "It's my car," he said in what he hoped was a casual tone—but to his ear his voice sounded shrill and unconvincing.

"Your car?" The short policeman looked skeptical. "You live here?"

"I'm . . ." Ford hesitated, praying for the right words to come. "I'm visiting."

"Who does live here?" the policeman persisted, taking out his pad. "I'd like to talk to the owner."

"He's out of town," Ford blurted out. Everything about his behavior was making him look guilty and yet he had committed no crime, done nothing even to stretch the law.

"What's his name?" The short, stocky officer was growing more suspicious by the minute.

"He's in Canada, making a movie," Ford offered as a diversionary tactic while he strained his memory for the name of the man in whose bed he was now sleeping.

"A movie—huh?" The officer smiled, suddenly tolerant of the erratic behavior he had just been witnessing. He looked at Ford curiously, seeing for the first time his well-built frame and finely chiseled features. "Are you in the business too?"

Ford shook his head. "I came here looking for work—but so far I haven't had much luck."

The taller officer nodded sympathetically. "You gotta give it time. I'd say you could give a lot of those guys I see on the big screen a run for their money." He extended his hand. "Sorry to have bothered you, but we have to check out these calls. Good luck. Maybe next time we see you, *you'll* be in uniform—playing a cop. Feel free to call on us any time for technical advice." He laughed and gave a friendly wave as they got into their car and drove away.

Ford stepped cautiously out the front door and looked around. Which neighbor had called to complain? The houses on the street seemed empty, deserted—no sign of life behind the windows—like facades on a movie set. This town was unreal. What was he doing here?

He started down the flagstone path to the street. A noise made him turn around. The front door had just blown shut behind him. He reached in his pockets in an involuntary gesture but realized as he did so that it was futile. Kate had not thought to give him a house key, and it had not occurred to Ford to ask for one. The last thing he wanted was to leave.

He walked back to the garage. The green Jaguar which had almost crashed into him on Christmas Eve was parked on one side. The other side, which housed Kate's tan Buick, was empty.

Ford walked to his car, put the key into the ignition, and prayed for it to start. For once it rumbled immediately to life. He turned into the driveway and headed for the empty garage.

Kate felt a flutter of panic when she turned into the street and saw that Ford's car was no longer parked in front of her house. Where could he have gone? Her mind sifted through the possibilities, but none of them made sense.

Then she pulled into the driveway and saw that the garage door was down. She didn't remember closing the garage when she left for the Farmers Market. She reached into the glove compartment for the remote control and handed it to Marvella. "Here's your chance to be a magician. Just point this at the garage and push the button."

Marvella did as she was told. "There's my daddy's car," she cried in surprise. "I really am a magician. How did I do that?"

"Put the door back down, Marvella," Kate said brusquely, annoyed to find her space in the garage occupied. It was one thing to share with people who were less fortunate but quite another when they started helping themselves to what belonged to you. She was going to have to have a talk with Ford. Ruth's words of warning replayed in her head.

She crossed to the back door and unlocked it. The children ran ahead of her into the house. "Daddy," Marvella called, "come see what we brought you." Homer nearly knocked them to the ground with the exuberance of his greeting, but Ford was nowhere to be seen.

"He's not here," Joe Wayne announced as Kate climbed the stairs. The light was still on in the bathroom and a paint can stood open on the window ledge. "Something's happened to him," Joe Wayne said fearfully. "He never quits in the middle of a job."

"They've left us," Marvella suddenly cried.

"No, honey," Kate was quick to assure her. "Parents don't just go off and leave their children behind. I'm sure he just remembered something he needed and decided to walk to the store."

But Marvella would not be comforted. "It happened to a girl in her class," Joe Wayne explained. Kate listened as the children kept interrupting each other. The girl had attended ten different schools over the past two years while her father drove from state to state looking for work. His wife had walked out on him when he lost his job, leaving him to take care of their only child alone.

The day before Thanksgiving as he put her on the bus for school, he gave her a sealed letter addressed to the teacher. Marvella was seated at her desk in the classroom when the little girl handed the letter to the teacher. She read it without saying a word but at the end of the day when the other children got back on the bus carrying the holiday favors they had made for their families, the teacher took the little girl aside and spoke gently to her, holding her close to quiet her sobs. Marvella watched from the window of the bus as the teacher led the crying child back into the school building.

Marvella never saw her again, but the next Monday she overheard the teacher telling someone, "He said she was so happy in this school he couldn't bear to take her away. He hoped maybe I could keep her home with me until he got enough money together to look after her right." The teacher shook her head. "I would've given anything to keep her, but I've got kids of my own. Anyway, I had to notify the authorities that she'd been abandoned and then it was out of my hands." She turned to enter her classroom. "I don't think I'm strong enough for this job."

Her eyes pleading, Marvella asked Kate, "Do you think her daddy came back for her when he found out the teacher couldn't take her home?"

Kate nodded with a conviction she didn't feel. "I'm sure he did. I bet he got a job playing Santa Claus in a big store where they paid him in presents instead of money and . . ." Kate was improvising desperately now, but the look in Marvella's eyes kept her going. "And I bet he came back for her on Christmas Eve still dressed in his Santa Claus suit, with his pack full of toys, just for her." Marvella had stopped crying and was beginning to smile.

"There he is now!" Joe Wayne had been looking out the window. Suddenly he jumped up and dashed down the stairs to the front door just as the doorbell began to ring. Marvella ran after him and Kate followed close behind.

Ford entered carrying a brown paper bag. "I've got a surprise for you," he said, smiling at Kate.

"A surprise for us?" Joe Wayne and Marvella chorused.

"Don't you think the two of you have had enough surprises lately?" he asked. "This one's for Kate. But what's inside this bag is only the last part of the surprise. First you have to come out back with me."

As he led them outside past the swimming pool, he told Kate about the police checking on his car. "How dare they?" she said indignantly, thankful she had kept her irritation on finding his car in the garage to herself.

"Well," said Ford, "what do you think?" He pointed proudly to the piece of land behind the row of palm trees that bordered the swimming pool. The ground had been spaded and cleared of weeds and neatly raked into long rows.

"Is this the surprise?" Joe Wayne asked, his voice heavy with disappointment.

"What is it?" Marvella was equally let down. "It just looks like dirt to me."

"That's all it is now," said Ford, "but wait till summer." He held open the brown paper bag to Kate. "Reach inside."

Kate's fingers closed around a small paper packet. "Seeds," she said, strangely touched. There was something so brave about the gesture—as if a packet of seeds could change the future. She smiled at Ford.

"Seeds today," Ford said, turning the bag upside down so that all the packets tumbled to the ground, "but by summer you'll have carrots, onions, potatoes . . ."

"Zucchini?" asked Kate hopefully.

"You bet," replied Ford, placing a packet at the end of each row. "When you get hungry, all you'll have to do is step outside your back door and pick yourself a meal."

"When can we plant?" asked Joe Wayne, getting caught up in Ford's enthusiasm.

"We can get started with the root vegetables right away."

Kate closed her eyes. She felt dizzy, as if she were about to faint. Summer! By summer the house would be sold and she would be living . . . where? She wanted to scream, "Don't do this to me. Don't depend on me. Don't count on staying here. We're in this day by day."

"You're not angry with me, are you, Kate?" Ford's voice cut into her thoughts. "I know I should've asked you before I started digging up the ground but the thing is, I got locked out of the house, so I came around back to try the kitchen door and it was locked too. Then I saw all those tools lined up in the shed and I thought of this land just lying here useless, so I said to myself why not just get to work and surprise her. Once I got the ground cleared, I decided to walk down to the hardware store and see what kind of seeds they had for sale. Next thing I knew, I was emptying my pockets to pay for them."

"You shouldn't have spent your money." How could she tell him she was putting this house on the market?

"I wanted to do something for you that you wouldn't be able to do for yourself," he said. Something in her expression filled him with panic and he added hurriedly, "The only hard part about a garden is getting it started. I mean, once it's planted, you can take care of it by yourself. You won't need me. I hope you don't think that's why I did it—so you'd have to keep me around for the harvest."

"You must be tired," Kate said softly, her defenses disarmed. "Come inside and have some lunch."

"Then you can have dessert," Marvella said, taking his hand and pulling him toward the house. "Guess what we brought you?"

"I don't know," Ford replied. "But whatever it is, I'll love it."

"No, you have to guess," Marvella insisted. "It's your favorite dessert."

"Chocolate ice cream," Ford guessed, but at the look of disappointment on Marvella's face he quickly amended his answer. "No, I'm forgetting, that's your favorite."

Marvella beamed. "I know. That's what I had at the Farmers Market. But guess what we brought you."

Kate moved behind Marvella and mouthed the words "lemon meringue pie."

Ford bent down to Marvella. "You didn't by any chance bring me a"—he paused for dramatic effect—"a lemon meringue pie."

"I knew it was your favorite," said Marvella, opening the box and showing it to him proudly.

"I never saw such a big one," said Ford.

"Everything in California is bigger," Joe Wayne assured him. "You should've seen the strawberries."

"What would you like for lunch?" Kate asked him, opening the refrigerator and looking inside. "We have ham, cheese, all kinds of things for a salad—"

Ford walked over to her, pulled her away from the refrigerator, and shut the door. "You've done too much for us already. We're staying in your house, we're eating your food because right now we don't have any choice. Not that we're not grateful. We'll be beholden to you for the rest of our lives. But don't offer to do anything for me that I can do for myself."

"Are you telling me Sunny didn't fix your meals when you were living on the farm?"

"That was different. She was getting something in return. I took care of her and she took care of me."

"Well, look at what you're doing for me," said Kate. "Painting the bathroom, planting a garden—and you've only been here one day."

"Fixing meals is something we can do for ourselves—and for you when you're hungry. So don't ever worry again about what we're going to eat."

"Can we go swimming again, Kate?" Joe Wayne asked impatiently.

"Not just yet," Ford answered for her. "As soon as I have something to eat, I could use some help finishing up in the bathroom. But first, why don't you take Homer out back for a run. He's been locked in this house all the time I was locked out of it."

"Then why don't you bring him in and we'll give him a bath?" Kate suggested. "He's the only one of us who hasn't had one."

"Bathe Homer?" Joe Wayne and Marvella found the idea very funny. "Do you think he'll like that?"

"He used to love to go swimming in the pond when we lived

on the farm," Ford reminded them. "I imagine he could use a bath if we're going to keep him in the house with us," he added, glancing at Kate. The grateful look she gave him was proof he had read her mind.

THIRTEEN

The front door was locked when Sunny returned home in the late afternoon, carrying a sack of groceries, and there was no sign of Ford's car. She rang the doorbell but there was no answer. She tried to imagine how he would have reacted to her note. How angry had it made him?

She had had no idea where she was going this morning when she left Ford asleep and walked quietly down the stairs. The children were already playing in the pool with Kate. Sunny heard the sounds of their laughter when she stepped into the garden. She turned around and went back into the house. Her children had no need of her here. She couldn't even swim.

She closed the front door behind her and started walking. Farther down the street she noticed a delivery truck parked in front of an imposing house. A husky young man who looked like a high-school halfback was carrying a box of groceries to the front door. When he returned to the truck, Sunny was sitting in the front seat.

"Where did you come from?" he asked.

"That doesn't matter," she replied. "What matters is where I'm going."

He looked at her curiously. The linen suit she was wearing didn't belong with those hard-edged features, those worn hands.

"I grew up working in a grocery store," she said. "Will you take me back to yours? I need a job."

He liked the way she just came right out and said what she wanted. She didn't play games, like the girls he dated.

"I've got some more deliveries to make before I go back," he said, "but you can keep me company if you want. Just don't say anything to my boss. I'm not supposed to give anybody a ride."

"You're not just giving me a ride," Sunny reassured him with a smile. "You're taking me to work."

It was two hours later before he stopped his truck a block from the store and let Sunny out. "Good luck," he said. "And if you're introduced to me, don't look like you know me."

Sunny found the store manager in his office. He looked puzzled when she told him what she wanted. "Why did you come here?" he asked. "I haven't put an ad in the paper. You didn't see any 'help wanted' sign on the window, did you?"

"I like your service," said Sunny. "Not many stores can be bothered to make deliveries anymore. But some people need help getting food into the house. My folks made deliveries every day, even though it meant they didn't eat themselves before nine or ten at night."

The manager's face brightened. "We've got a new owner here. He wants to cut out home delivery, says it's not cost efficient. I suppose he's right. We're not a fancy place like Jurgensen's, after all, or some big chain. We're just a little neighborhood store. But we've been here twenty years. People depend on us. Some of our best customers are too old to drive. What would they do if we stopped delivering?"

"I used to take all the telephone orders," said Sunny. "And then I'd fill them. I'd try to pick out the biggest head of lettuce, the most perfect tomatoes. I felt like people trusted me to make their choices for them. I didn't want them to be disappointed when they unpacked their groceries."

"I like the way you think," the manager admitted. "But I've got to account for every penny I spend here. I just can't justify putting somebody else on the payroll."

Sunny stood there silently. As long as she kept standing by his desk, she had a chance. Once she left the store, she was lost. She hadn't gotten anywhere looking for work until today. She had to think of something. Then she noticed a basket of food by the back door.

"Do you want me to put those things away for you?" she asked. "I might as well make myself useful as long as I'm here."

"I just took that stuff off the shelves," he explained. "Once we pass the 'sell by' dates, we have to get rid of it. There's an organization that comes by to collect it and distribute it to the hungry but they don't always show up."

"What if I took my pay out of that basket every day?" Sunny asked. "Just what my family could use—nothing more."

The manager looked at her in disbelief. "You'd be willing to work here all day just to feed your family at night?"

There were tears in Sunny's eyes. "More than willing."

She spent the rest of the day learning her way around the store—pricing items, restocking shelves, taking telephone orders, checking out customers. She felt such a sense of physical comfort from the plenty that surrounded her she forgot she hadn't eaten all day herself. The manager passed her as she was standing on a ladder taking down a sign advertising the day's specials. She closed her eyes for a moment and put a hand to her head.

"You look tired," he said.

"I am," Sunny admitted, "but it feels good to work this hard."

"You haven't taken a break since you started. I didn't even see you eat lunch."

"There's a lot to learn, but I think I'll know what I'm doing tomorrow."

"Why don't you go on home now?" he suggested. "We'll be closing soon. You've done enough for one day."

Sunny looked at him closely to make sure he meant it, but he was smiling kindly. "Do you have a car?"

"My husband needs the car to look for work," she said. "I don't mind walking."

"Do you have far to go?"

"I don't think so." Sunny was not really sure where she was. The delivery truck had made so many stops this morning she had lost her way. Well, she'd just have to ask directions and start walking.

"Look, the truck is about to leave with the afternoon deliveries. I'll tell him to give you a lift." He started for the back door. "But don't forget to take your day's pay." He nodded toward the basket of food.

Sunny held open a grocery bag and began to fill it. She had always hated planning meals. Now her choices were limited to what was in front of her.

"Congratulations," said the driver as she climbed into the front seat beside him. "I guess you got what you came for."

Sunny smiled happily. "Do you remember where you found me?"

"Sure."

"Good." She sighed with relief. "Because I couldn't have told you how to get back there."

"We have several customers on this street," he said as he turned onto a block of houses that Sunny recognized. "I go by here twice a day. Do you want a lift tomorrow morning?"

She wanted to say yes, but she was frightened. "I don't want to do anything to upset the manager," she said. "I can't lose this job."

The young man smiled protectively. "He told me tonight to look after you. I'm just following orders."

Sunny gave him a hard stare. "I've got a husband to look after me. But I can use a lift to work. You can let me out right on this corner—and this is where I'll be waiting in the morning. 'Bye —and thanks."

As she jumped down off the truck, holding her bag of groceries, the driver tried to figure out which house she had come from.

These were expensive properties. He couldn't imagine one of them housing a woman willing to work all day just to feed her family.

Finally Sunny accepted the fact that no one was going to open the front door. Hesitantly, she picked up the sack of groceries and moved around the driveway to the back.

The sound of laughing and shouting followed by loud splashes drew her toward the swimming pool. Was Kate having a party? Sunny peeked timidly through the azalea bushes. A double-decker water fight was in progress—Joe Wayne astride his father's shoulders and Marvella atop Kate, clutching her hair as if it were a horse's mane.

Sunny put her hand to her cheek to wipe away angry tears. They looked like some magazine ad for the all-American family. "A boy for you, a girl for me"—wasn't that how the song went? And no place for Sunny in the picture.

She put away the groceries and set five places around the kitchen table. Then she looked down at the clothes Kate had given her. She'd better take them off before she started cooking dinner. She had to take care of them. She was determined not to ask Kate for another thing.

She was undressing in the bedroom when Ford, a towel wrapped around his waist, came bounding up the stairs. He enveloped her in a bear hug.

"Oh, honey. Thank God you're home. I've been so worried about you."

"Yeah, I could see," she said, pulling away from him with a shiver. "You're getting me wet."

"Why don't you come in for a swim?" he suggested. "And tell us where you've been all day."

"Nothing to tell," she said flatly. "I got a job and I'm getting paid in groceries." She pulled on an old pair of jeans and a T-shirt. "And now I'm going downstairs to cook dinner."

"Hold on a minute, honey. You don't have to start cooking dinner right away," Ford said awkwardly. He could see a storm coming but he didn't know how to stop it. "Kate took the kids to the Farmers Market for lunch and I just had a big sandwich a couple of hours ago. Nobody's very hungry."

"Well, I'm starving," Sunny said fiercely. "I haven't eaten all day."

"Just fix something for yourself then," Ford said gently. "I'll come down and keep you company while you eat—as soon as I get on some clothes." He peeled off his wet suit, rolled it up in the towel, and crossed to the closet.

Something about the confidence with which he crossed the room troubled Sunny. She hadn't seen him so unashamedly naked in the full light of day in a long time—not since that first summer on the farm. She closed her eyes and gave a low moan. Why did he have to be so handsome?

Ford turned and came toward her. "What's wrong, honey?" He put his arms around her and steered her toward the bed. "You're all worn out. Why don't you just lie here for a while and rest?"

Sunny suddenly began beating her hands on his chest. "Stay away from me, damn you. Don't come near this bed. That's what got us in this mess in the first place."

Ford backed away, embarrassed. Defensively, he reached for the robe lying across the foot of the bed. "I've never seen you behave like this. You've been so brave this past year. And now, just when things are beginning to work out, you go all to pieces."

Sunny's voice was hard as steel. "I took one step out of the pit today, Ford—and I'm never, never falling back in." There was a long pause while she eyed him coldly. "Now, what have you done about getting us out of here?"

"What do you mean? Why would we want to leave here?"

"Then you didn't look for a job today?" Her voice was hard and unforgiving.

"My work is right here in this house," he said, speaking with an authority that sounded hollow to his ear. "For as long as we're staying here and as long as there's anything that needs to be done. I owe her that. You just said you were getting paid with groceries. Well, I'm working for a roof over our heads."

"You can work around the house at night—and on the weekends," said Sunny, unrelenting. "Like other men."

"What about Joe Wayne and Marvella?" Ford was getting angry now. "Did you even give a thought to them when you walked out that door this morning?"

"She'll look after them," Sunny said sullenly. "What else does she have to do? She was swimming with them when I left this morning and now they're all in there again."

"She likes children," Ford said slowly. "Her daughter's grown and gone off to school and she's lonely here in this big house all by herself. But that doesn't mean we're going to take advantage of her. As long as the kids are on vacation, I'm not leaving them in this house without one of us to keep an eye on them." He reached for Sunny's hand. "Now come on downstairs and let's get you something to eat. You get real out of sorts when you're hungry."

Sunny had the refrigerator door open and was showing Ford her day's wages when Joe Wayne and Marvella came running into the kitchen.

"Mommy," Marvella cried, throwing herself into Sunny's arms. "Come watch me swim."

"We didn't know where you were," Joe Wayne said, searching Sunny's face for signs of trouble.

She gave him a reassuring smile. "That's because I didn't know where I was going when I left this morning."

Marvella looked at her curiously. "Where did you go?"

"I'm working in a grocery store—just like I did when I was a little girl helping my mama and papa. And every night I'm going to bring home something different for our dinner."

"What did you bring us tonight?" Marvella was getting caught up in Sunny's enthusiasm.

"How about tacos?" Sunny suggested. "I've got meat and tortillas and lettuce and—"

"Tonight we're going out for dinner," Joe Wayne interrupted. "Isn't that right, Kate?" He turned to Kate, who was standing hesitantly at the kitchen door.

"Why look, your mother has already set the table," she said with surprise. "And did I hear talk of tacos? There is nothing I like better."

"But what about the restaurant on the ocean?" Joe Wayne was almost shouting in his determination to hold her to her promise. "Where the waves come right up to the window."

"It will still be there tomorrow," Kate replied.

"You've already been out once today," Ford reminded the children. "I think we'd better stay home tonight." He could feel the happiness spreading through him at the prospect of being safely locked inside this house, surrounded by his wife and children, as darkness fell. He smiled tenderly at Sunny, but she was deep in her own thoughts and did not glance in his direction. "Besides," he continued, focusing his attention on the other woman in the room, whose eyes seemed to follow his every movement, "we can't keep letting you take us places, Kate. We owe you too much already."

"I haven't taken *you* anywhere yet," Kate reminded him. "Or Sunny," she added quickly. Then turning to Joe Wayne and Marvella, she said, "Why don't we save the place on the ocean till Sunday when your mother hasn't had to work all day?"

"What did you do today, Ford?" Sunny asked abruptly.

"We painted the bathroom," Ford replied with false bravado. "Right, kids?" He looked to Joe Wayne and Marvella for support.

"And don't forget about the vegetable garden," Marvella reminded him. "We're going to grow carrots and onions and . . ." She paused, looking to Ford to continue the list but he suddenly moved to the door. "You kids better get out of those wet suits before you catch cold."

"You tell her what we're going to grow, Daddy," Marvella said as she ran out of the room.

"We'll talk about it at dinner," Ford said, avoiding Sunny's eyes. "You stay where you are, honey," he added in a placating tone. "I'll look after the children."

"You don't have to look after me," Joe Wayne said. "I've got my own room now. I can take care of myself."

"Glad to hear it," said Ford. "I'll go up and see how Marvella is getting along."

Sunny waited for Kate to follow him. She felt uncomfortable treating the kitchen as if it were her own but she was growing faint with hunger. However, Kate fixed herself a glass of instant iced tea and settled companionably into a chair opposite her.

"Did you ask him to plant a vegetable garden?" Sunny blurted out.

Her intensity caught Kate off guard. "Well, no, not exactly." She hesitated, not wanting to say anything in the confrontation she sensed was building. "I mean we talked yesterday about how there was room for one—about how much good land is going to waste out here when we could be growing things to help feed hungry people."

"So it was his idea—actually planting a vegetable garden?" Sunny's voice cut into her conviction.

"He got locked out of the house," Kate explained. "There was no one here and nothing else for him to do." Hating how defensive she was suddenly feeling, she got up from the table. "That reminds me. I have some extra house keys around here somewhere." She began rummaging through a drawer. "I want you and Ford each to have one—so you can come and go as you like."

"Don't you ever watch the news?" Sunny asked as she took a package of ground meat from the refrigerator.

"What?" Kate never seemed to be prepared for what Sunny was going to say next.

"It's not like Iowa here. We were scared when we lost the farm—scared of not having a job or a place to live, but we weren't scared of other people. But in this city no one is safe. People are attacked right inside their own homes—in nice neighborhoods." She took a skillet from the cupboard and began browning the meat, chopping it forcefully with the spatula.

"You sound like my friend Ruth," Kate said. "She blames the Cable News Network for what's happened to her marriage." She shuffled some papers around, trying to see into the corners of the cluttered drawer.

Sunny waited expectantly for the story. Finally she had to

ask, trying not to sound too curious, "What did happen to it? Her marriage, I mean."

Kate looked up from the drawer. "Her husband doesn't make love to her anymore."

Sunny started to laugh but then she saw that Kate was serious. "She blames the news for that?"

Kate shrugged. "All these years I thought she had a perfect marriage. But she probably thought the same about me."

Sunny concentrated on what she was cooking. If Kate was waiting for her to pour out the secrets of her marriage, she'd have to wait a long time.

"Here they are!" Kate handed a key to Sunny. "You keep it before I put it down someplace and forget where."

"How can you do this?" Sunny persisted. "Give a total stranger a key to your house?"

"But you're not a stranger. Not anymore," Kate said, taking a head of lettuce and two tomatoes from the refrigerator. "I'll chop the lettuce and tomatoes. We've made a new rule around here—no one prepares meals for anyone else. Everybody pitches in."

"Ford's not going to like that rule." Sunny couldn't help smiling.

"You're wrong," Kate said. "He's the one who thought it up." She slipped the other key in the pocket of her robe. "I'll give him this and tell him to get down here and lend us a hand."

As Kate left the room, Sunny reached for an onion and began chopping it furiously. Now she had an excuse for tears.

FOURTEEN

"Good night," Kate called and closed the door of the study, surprised by the feeling of relief that came over her.

After they had finished dinner and washed the dishes, Ford
built a fire in the living room. Kate stacked the stereo with her
favorite Simon and Garfunkel albums. Her musical taste had
never moved out of the sixties, and even her daughter, far from
trying to convert her mother to more current music, still went
around the house singing the songs which she had first heard as
lullabies. Kate claimed an armchair by the fire, kicked off her
shoes, and stretched out her bare feet on the ottoman.

But Ford and Sunny sat stiffly on the couch with a child on
either side—like relatives paying a duty visit. Since they had arrived the day before, everything had gone with surprising ease,
Kate reflected. True, all of them had been careful with each other,
afraid of offending or of overstepping the invisible boundaries
that divide those who need help from those who provide it. And

of course until this evening they had been united in some common activity—preparing food, buying paint, even staging a water fight. Kate smiled at the memory, then another difference occurred to her—Sunny had been away all day.

To Kate the room seemed strained with the tension of unspoken thoughts. Thank heaven for the music to color the silent canvas of the evening that stretched ahead of them. "I remember that song," Ford said suddenly as Simon and Garfunkel cradled them with their voices in "Bridge Over Troubled Water." He reached for Sunny's hand. "It was playing on the car radio the night we—" He stopped abruptly, his words braked by the memory. "The night we met," he continued softly.

A smile played on Sunny's lips but she continued to stare straight ahead. Kate closed her eyes and tried to lose herself in the music. Odd to feel so out of place in your own home, she thought.

Nothing else was said—and Kate suspected she was the only one in the room who needed words to anchor her into the moment. Funny how some people were able to be so comfortable together without talking. Ford and Sunny had barely shifted position on the sofa, but it seemed to belong to them now. He put his arm around her and drew her close. She leaned her head against his shoulder and closed her eyes. Ford kept his eyes focused on the fire as if hypnotized by the flames. Marvella had fallen asleep with her head in her mother's lap. Joe Wayne slid to the floor and lay next to Homer, who was already asleep in front of the fire.

When was the last time Cliff and Kate had sat in silence in front of a fire? Kate couldn't remember. In fact, Cliff only bothered to build a fire on the nights when company was expected. "It's so much trouble," he would complain. "It would be different if you could do it once and count on it staying done. But you have to keep tending it all night—or it'll die on you."

Like a marriage, Kate thought. But all she said to Cliff was, "No wonder you never wanted to direct in the theater." He didn't deny it. One of the things he loved most about working in film was having his vision preserved. Once the work was done, it stayed done.

And so a few years into the marriage Kate had bought a huge copper cauldron, filled it with flowers and greenery from her garden, and set it in the cold, black emptiness of the fireplace. She replenished it year round with blossoms and branches, and the colors spilling out of the burnished copper bowl warmed her heart even on winter nights when her feet got cold.

Not until the Christmas holidays, on the night she decorated the tree, would she ceremoniously remove the cauldron from the fireplace and build the first fire of the season while carols played on the stereo. On New Year's, when the tree came down, the fireplace would once again be filled with flowers.

But this year was going to be different, Kate vowed silently. Cliff was not coming home again—and the fireplace was going to be put to the use for which it was intended as long as the nights were cold enough to warrant it. And as far as she was concerned, the Christmas decorations could stay up until the tree disintegrated into dust. The colored lights and silver tinsel kept the darkness at bay—and with it a despair in which she could drown.

Kate stood suddenly. For the past twenty-four hours—since Cliff had left the house and Ford and Sunny had moved into her bedroom—she had immersed herself in the present tense. Last night, when she had closed the door of Cliff's study, she had thrown a sheet over the couch, curled up under a blanket, and fallen asleep almost immediately. But tonight she was lonely. Whatever was left of Cliff in this house would be found in his study.

"I'm falling asleep," she said in a whisper to Ford and Sunny. "Do you mind turning off the lights before you go to bed?"

Joe Wayne scrambled to his feet. "Can I watch television in my own room?"

Kate started to say yes, of course—then checked herself. She was not the parent here, as easy as it would have been to assume the role.

Ford looked at his watch. "Just for an hour. Then lights out. We've got a lot of work to do around here tomorrow. I need your help."

Joe Wayne kissed his parents good night, then gave Kate a shy wave as he headed toward the kitchen, Homer trotting behind.

Tomorrow. Kate's mood brightened at the thought. This house was clamoring for attention, and every task she undertook to improve it opened her eyes to a new one. The newly painted bathroom demanded new curtains. She would take the children to the Beverly Center tomorrow. They would love the escalators and all the shops. And she'd turn them loose on the top floor for lunch. Maybe she could even talk Ford into coming with them.

"Good night," she called from the hallway—and closed the study door behind her. It suddenly felt so good to be alone—not to be responsible for anyone besides herself. The suitcase she had brought down from the bedroom was standing untouched beside Cliff's desk. Packing it the night before had been a gesture—even though Cliff had left her behind, she had to feel she was going somewhere. Tonight she had to face the fact that this room was her destination, at least for now. But perhaps here, where he had spent so many solitary hours, she could find the key to what had gone wrong between them.

Kate opened her suitcase and spread the contents on the leather couch. She felt almost like an intruder as she moved the assorted jackets still hanging in his closet to make room for the clothes she had brought from the bedroom. She stored the empty suitcase on a high shelf and closed the closet door.

She felt an illicit sense of satisfaction at the thought of taking over his study. This was her house as much as Cliff's—and yet one room in it had been virtually off-limits to her all the years of their marriage. There was no room in the house where Kate could close the door and count on being left alone. Even in the bathroom when she was lying in the tub, Cliff thought nothing of coming in to ask a question. If she locked the door, he'd just bang on it and shout his question to her.

In the early days of their marriage it would never have occurred to Kate to lock a door. And Cliff never entered the room when she was bathing without pausing for an appreciative assessment. It was only in recent years, when he'd burst in and start talking as if she were seated at a desk, that Kate began to resent his interruptions. But she had never really wished for a room of her own in this house. Now, however, she began to be excited about laying claim to this space—partly, she had to admit, as a way of displacing Cliff but also as a means of discovering who she was without him.

She settled into the swivel chair at his desk—and felt like an army captain taking over a command. His desk was twice the size of the graceful burl one in the bedroom where she sat to write letters and pay bills. And the machinery at her command! She would have to learn to work the computer and the video cassette recorder and the telephone answering machine. If she was going to have to live in this house without Cliff, she could at least take advantage of everything he had bought to make his life easier.

She started going through the desk drawers systematically, looking for instructions. You could get to know a person better by looking through his desk than you could over a candlelight dinner, Kate thought. On the surface Cliff was organized and efficient. Writing supplies were laid out in neat stacks. Household bills were filed. Unanswered correspondence awaited his return. Despite what he had told her, this did not look like the desk of a man who was not coming home.

Cliff had consigned the debris of his personal life to a deep bottom drawer. There was no order here. Things were piled at random—newspaper clippings, photographs, invitations to events long since past, even a box of condoms.

Kate picked up the box and turned it over in her hand. It looked fairly new. She was hardly surprised—she had always known there were other women on location—but she was hurt. She had dared to hope that at least while Cliff was at home he had belonged to her and she had never stopped wanting to have a child of her own, though she had long since given up hope of it ever happening. Angrily she threw the box across the room. "Bastard!" she cursed him in a whisper. "You've taken away my future. Couldn't you have left me my past?"

Fighting tears, she dug deeper into the drawer. Her fingers suddenly struck metal. Scattering papers in all directions, she pulled a long metal box from the bottom of the drawer. She held it on her lap warily for several minutes before trying the lock. No use. Cliff must carry the key with him. She sat frozen while her thoughts raced. Maybe it was better not to know what was inside.

Kate started to put the box back inside the drawer—but she couldn't bring herself to relinquish it yet, not without making some attempt to discover what secrets it held. A sense memory led her fingers to an inlaid wooden box on top of the desk. It was filled with keys of all shapes and sizes. A few were identified with tags—extra car keys, house keys, luggage keys—but most of them had long since survived whatever purpose they originally served. Cliff was adamant about saving keys—even when whatever they unlocked was no longer anywhere to be found.

Kate overturned the box on the desk and spread the keys in front of her. Starting with the smallest, she tried one after another in the lock. With each frustrated attempt, she grew angrier at Cliff. What kind of a man saves keys that don't unlock anything? What does a man keep in a box only he can unlock? As if in answer, the key she was trying suddenly turned in the lock. Kate had so completely accepted the fact that she would never see what was inside that it took her a moment to summon the courage to look.

The box was filled with official-looking papers. With trembling hands Kate unfolded the first one and began to read. Suddenly she was laughing with relief. Their marriage license! Flattering to realize Cliff considered it a document of sufficient value to keep under lock and key but infuriating to think he stored it with his private papers, hidden out of her sight in a box to which she didn't even have a key. He acted as if he were the only one who might ever require legal proof of their marriage. Kate found herself wondering if you had to turn in your marriage license when you got a divorce, or did someone just stamp it null and void?

Her mind was still on her marriage as she unfolded the next set of papers. All legal documents concerned with Nina's adoption. No secrets here—Cliff and Kate had both signed them.

They had tried so hard for a baby of their own. In fact, once Cliff had installed a wife in his new house, he couldn't wait to have a child. Kate was probably the only one of her friends who had never used birth control. But to no avail.

Without telling Kate, Cliff went to a doctor to be checked. Once he had been assured that there was nothing wrong with him, he insisted that Kate go in for a checkup. Blocked tubes was the verdict and adoption the recommended course of action.

At first Cliff would not even discuss the possibility—he wanted his baby, not another man's—but watching Kate cry herself to sleep and feeling powerless to console her had finally convinced him that their marriage was never going to be complete without a child.

Once they started making inquiries, however, they discovered that trying to adopt a baby could lead to as much heartache and disappointment as trying to have one. Access to the pill and legalized abortion had made unwanted babies an increasingly rare occurrence and in an age when unmarried movie stars were keeping their babies (and often even refusing to name the fathers, let alone live with them), society lost its power to force lesser mortals into giving up their out-of-wedlock offspring for adoption.

After two years of putting their names on endless waiting lists, placing ads, writing letters, pursuing leads that led to nothing, Cliff and Kate finally got a call from their lawyer. He had been in contact with a young girl, eight months pregnant, whose boyfriend refused to marry her. She had decided to give up her baby for adoption and go to college.

Cliff and Kate happily agreed to pay her tuition and expenses, and within a month the cradle in the nursery they had decorated with such care was filled. They gave their son Kate's maiden name—Saxon—and by the time he was six months old he recognized it and responded with a smile when they spoke to him. Cliff and Kate felt their long wait, the false leads, the heartache, had been more than repaid by the joy they took in their son, and on the way to the lawyer's office to sign the final adoption papers they began to talk about the possibility of giving Saxon a baby sister.

But when the lawyer took them into his office, he said the young mother had changed her mind. She was getting married after all and she wanted her baby back.

Kate began to scream, "She can't do this to us. She can't do it to Saxon. He won't understand." Cliff dropped into a chair and put his hands in front of his face. He just sat there, refusing to talk, while Kate cried and cursed and pleaded. The lawyer put his arm around her and said he had been on the phone with the girl all morning. Nothing he said could persuade her to change her mind and the law was powerless to do anything about it. A waiting period before the final papers were signed was part of every adoption agreement, but he had never, in all his years of practice, known the natural mother to take advantage of it to reclaim her child.

Kate and Cliff mourned their son as if he had died. Kate left everything in place in the nursery—tiny knit suits folded in drawers, toys on the shelf—but she shut the door and never looked inside the room. She put away the framed baby pictures and hid the photograph album out of sight. The high chair and playpen and pram were dismantled and stored in the garage.

But despite all her efforts not a day passed without some reminder—a tiny sock caught in the clothes hamper, a sentence in a letter from an out-of-town friend who hadn't heard the news, a sale notice from the neighborhood baby shop—and then the pain would seize her heart again as mercilessly as it had the first time, and she would pull the curtains in her bedroom and pour her grief into the pillow.

Cliff stopped coming home for dinner. Kate seldom felt like cooking and on the rare occasions when she did, she couldn't bear to face Cliff across the table. She would leave what she had prepared in the refrigerator or on the stove and pretend to be asleep when he finally came to bed. It was a relief to both of them when he got a job directing a picture being filmed on location in upstate New York.

The day he left, Kate put on stockings and high heels and

drove to the lawyer's office. She told him she had to see Saxon—and demanded to know the name and address of the natural mother. She wouldn't do anything foolish, she promised. She just had to know he was safe—and loved.

As gently as he could, the lawyer explained that this information was confidential. As painful as it was for Kate, the natural mother wanted no further contact with her. The baby was never to know where he had spent the first six months of his life.

"Can you at least tell me what they've named him?" Kate begged, but the lawyer shook his head. He urged her to stop tormenting herself, to accept what could not be changed and to concentrate on the future. But she couldn't stop crying. "If he'd died, at least we could have had a funeral," she sobbed. "But he was taken from us so abruptly. And we don't know what's happened to him."

"He's with his natural parents." The lawyer patted her hand.

"Some consolation that is." Kate would not be comforted. "Every day there's another story in the paper about what natural parents have done to their children. No one could love Saxon as much as I did. As much as I still do."

"Maybe not." The lawyer opened his desk drawer and removed a photograph. "But look at this picture of Ralph on his first birthday and maybe you'll feel better."

"Ralph?" Kate reached for the picture. A little boy whose face was achingly familiar stared back at her. He was walking toward the camera, arms outstretched. In a corner of the photograph a pair of unidentified hands held a cake with one candle.

"I knew he'd be walking by his first birthday." Kate smiled through her tears. She stood to leave, continuing to hold tightly to the photograph. "Please, may I keep this?" The look in her eyes dared the lawyer to say no.

He nodded. "He may not remember you, but no one can ever take away from him what you gave him."

Driving home, Kate was surprised by the sudden happiness she felt. She had a son. He was alive and well, even though he had a new name and another set of parents. It was a mistake to have such a narrow idea of family, she thought. Family means anyone you hold in your thoughts. You pray for their happiness and fear for their pain, but there is not much you can do about either. You have to accept that your parents will probably die before you, and your children will leave home to live their own lives long before you're ready to see them go. In the end you're alone just as you were in the beginning, and the sooner you learn to love people in absentia the better off you'll be.

Cliff was astonished at the change in Kate when he arrived home three months later. She seemed younger and happier than she had on their honeymoon. Over a lovingly prepared dinner his first night home, she told him she wanted to adopt another child. To her surprise he offered no objection. In fact, he said, he had been just about to bring up the subject with her. The only way they were going to put their grief to rest was to bring another baby into the house. Cliff put his arms around Kate and told her he would take care of everything. And this time he was going to make sure nothing went wrong, even if it meant interviewing the prospective mother himself.

"Just don't tell me anything until there is an actual baby we can bring home," Kate begged him. "I can't take any more disappointment."

And so she knew nothing until six months later when Cliff told her he was going out of town—with the lawyer. He said to get the nursery ready and make sure she had plenty of diapers on hand. He was bringing home a baby daughter.

Kate threw her arms around his neck. "I've been praying for a girl," she said, "but I was afraid to say anything. How were you able to find a baby? Where are you going to get it? Can't I come with you?"

Cliff touched his fingers to her lips. "You said you didn't want to know anything," he reminded her. "Now leave everything to me. You've got enough to do here."

The house was filled with flowers when Cliff returned with the baby. Kate had brought everything blooming in the garden into the house. "What are we going to name her?" Cliff asked as he placed the baby in Kate's arms.

"No name from either side of the family," she said. "We're

not making that mistake again. This baby is a gift. She's not descended from either one of us, and it's wrong to pretend she is."

Finally they decided on "Nina"—Spanish for young girl. They put the baby in bed between them and reached across her to touch each other, as if they were conceiving in spirit what they had been unable to do in fact.

Thinking back now to that night, Kate felt her whole body responding to the memory. It was as if in bringing her a child, Cliff had given her himself more completely than he ever had before or since. He might never come home again, but she could take comfort in the knowledge he had belonged to her once. And Nina had been allowed to grow up in the atmosphere of love her presence had created. The fact that it hadn't lasted didn't mean it hadn't happened.

Kate refolded the adoption papers and returned them to the metal box. She had seen enough. If the legal proofs of their marriage and the adoption of their child were important enough to Cliff to keep them under lock and key, then perhaps she had not lost him completely.

As she started to close the box, her eye was caught by a snapshot. She pulled it out and examined it more closely. A dark-haired young woman holding a baby. She turned it over. On the back was written in Cliff's bold handwriting, "Nina, two days old, with her mother." Kate stared at it. She had never seen a picture of Nina's mother. It had not occurred to her that Cliff might have one.

Kate felt dizzy with a sense of displacement. Nina had never shown any interest in learning the identity of her natural parents or finding out anything about them. Yet Kate couldn't help feeling suddenly jealous, wondering what Nina would think of her real mother.

Reaching deeper into the box, she found more photographs —one of Cliff with two-day-old Nina and another one of Cliff with Nina and her mother. Kate stared at the photo in disbelief. Cliff had his arm around the woman, and he was smiling at her, not the baby.

Kate ripped through the papers at the bottom of the box.

Buried among real estate deeds and car insurance papers was a birth certificate for a baby girl born on the day they celebrated as Nina's birthday. The parents were listed as Cliff Hart and Wenda Stone.

Wenda Stone. Kate felt her heart stop beating. So the woman who had refused to marry Cliff when he was a struggling actor had borne him a child when he returned as a successful director. She had not just come back into his life on this trip.

Kate examined the birth certificate more closely. The birth was registered in Toronto. Of course! Cliff had been filming in upstate New York, not that far from Canada, when he came home with the idea of adopting another child—his child. She took a deep breath. How many times had he seen Wenda Stone in the years since Nina was born?

Kate's eye suddenly fell on the telephone number Cliff had written on his desk pad—where he could be reached in an emergency. She had no idea when she started dialing what she was going to say, but her thoughts crystallized when she heard the voice on the other end.

"Could I speak to Wenda Stone?" She struggled to sound as calm and self-assured as the woman who had answered on the first ring.

"Speaking," the voice replied.

Kate hesitated. Her right hand, in which she cradled the receiver, was trembling so hard she had to use her left hand to steady it.

"Hello. Hello. Is anyone there? Can you hear me?" The voice had lost some of its assurance and was straining to make contact.

Slowly, using both hands, Kate put the receiver back on the hook, severing the connection.

FIFTEEN

It was absurd to feel so nervous, Kate thought as she entered the darkened restaurant. After all, they had spent hours under the same roof, shared countless meals in the past. But she had never before asked to be alone with him, demanded his total attention.

Dinner had been his idea. All she had said last night on the phone, staring at the picture of Nina with her real parents, was that she needed to talk to him, face-to-face. Could they meet somewhere for a drink? He had seemed to sense, without her having to explain, that she did not want him coming to the house. She needed an impersonal setting, a place with no associations for either of them, for what she had to say.

"Hello, Kate." Adam stood to greet her as she joined him at the table. "You look different tonight." His voice made it clear that he was not just doing her a favor by meeting her for dinner; he was happy to be seen in her company.

"This is a new dress." She tried to sound casual. "I can never resist the after-Christmas sales."

He shook his head. "It's not the dress. Maybe it's me. I'm usually with Nina when I'm around you. I never really stopped to look at you before." He turned away quickly. A waiter appeared to take their drink orders and handed them each a menu. Adam opened his and pretended to study it until the waiter was out of sight. "Sometimes I wish there were more of you in Nina," he said in a low voice, his eyes firmly fixed on the menu.

Kate smiled, her eyes brimming with tears. "When I asked you to meet me, I wasn't sure what I wanted to say to you, how much I could tell you. But maybe what I really wanted was to hear what you just said to me." Then she quickly put her hands in front of her face.

"What's wrong, Kate?" Adam reached across the table to touch her elbow. "Do you want to go?" She shook her head and opened her menu as the waiter approached with their drinks.

When they were alone again, Kate smiled bravely at Adam and lifted her glass. "To a new year! And a new beginning—for both of us."

He looked at her curiously as he raised his glass to touch hers. "To a new year," he said, repeating only the first part of her toast.

"I know I'm a few days ahead of the calendar," she said softly, "but I'm wiping the slate clean—starting today." And suddenly the words were tumbling out of her.

Adam listened as she told him, in often incoherent detail, of how she had been doubly betrayed. Cliff had left her on Christmas Day to return to his first love—in Canada—with whom, it seemed, he had been having an affair off and on all the years of their marriage. And Nina was the product of that affair.

"Are you telling me Nina is Cliff's daughter but not yours?"

Kate nodded. It felt better somehow to have said it. For the past twenty-four hours she had carried her discovery inside her, invisible to outside eyes, like one of those poor souls she had seen on television who smuggle bags of cocaine past customs by swallowing them, risking death if a bag bursts inside them. What were they called? "Mules." That was it. And that was just how

Kate had felt—like some poor mule, her poisonous cargo pressing against her intestines—until now when it was finally, safely, out of her system.

"What a shock for you!" Adam gave a low whistle. "Does Nina know?"

Kate shook her head, not trusting herself to speak. She reached for her wineglass, but her hand was trembling so violently she set it down again.

Adam covered her hand with his. "It's not going to change the way she feels about you. Nina's not like that."

Kate stared past him, unaware of his hand on hers, his eyes searching her face. "When you adopt a child, you take nothing for granted. You feel right from the beginning that you're on trial —you have to prove you're worthy of being a parent. And that feeling never goes away." She paused, then continued in a whisper. "I've been so afraid of failing Nina. . . ."

"Well, you can stop worrying. You've been a wonderful mother. And you've raised a wonderful daughter." Adam smiled warmly at Kate and withdrew his hand. He opened his menu but Kate continued to sit in silence, her hand gripping the stem of her wineglass.

"Not wonderful enough," she said finally.

"What?" Adam was still studying his menu.

"Now that I know whose child she is," Kate began slowly, "I'm seeing her clearly for the first time. Seeing how much alike she and Cliff really are. They both put what they want ahead of everything and everybody."

Adam shifted uncomfortably in his chair. "Don't take the way you're feeling about Cliff out on Nina. She's the same person she was before you found out who her natural parents were. And I still love her. Nothing is going to change that."

"If you didn't love her, I wouldn't be here. I love her too, but I don't like the kind of person she's becoming." Kate sighed. "Maybe it's my fault. I never said no to her. Probably because I knew that if I did, she'd just go to Cliff and he'd take her side. He admires people who know what they want, and he used to say it was important to teach a child—especially a daughter—not to be afraid to ask. I should've realized," she continued, her voice breaking, "that he was trying to teach Nina to be the kind of woman he would never stop loving."

The waiter approached to take their order, but Adam shook his head and waved him away. Kate kept talking, oblivious to everything but her own pain. "You are everything a mother could want for her daughter, Adam—but you deserve better than Nina. Or at least a better Nina. I have the courage to say that now only because I have finally accepted the fact that I deserve better than Cliff."

"Look, I'm sorry as hell for what Cliff has put you through this Christmas." Adam's voice was kind, but his eyes had grown cold. "However, it has nothing to do with me. Or with Nina." He pushed his chair back from the table as if he were about to leave.

"Please don't go, Adam." Kate could see how upset he was, but she was determined to curb for once her reflex to apologize. Even though it meant putting their friendship at risk, she had to finish what she had started. "You and I are alike in so many ways. And seeing something of myself in you makes me stronger, makes me want to fight for both of us. At least tonight I have finally done something I wanted to do—without worrying about what you would think of me for doing it." Then she had to laugh at herself. "That's not true. I did worry. I worried all afternoon about what I'd be doing to our friendship by unloading all this on you. I picked up the phone three different times to cancel. But I love you, Adam, and when you love a person, you owe them your honesty. I've watched you with Nina since you met in high school and I've envied her—oh, God, how I've envied her—the kind of unquestioning love you give her. But you've got to make her fight harder for it—and for you. So she'll appreciate what she's got." She stopped abruptly. She'd let the momentum of her emotions carry her words, not stopping for breath until she had spilled out all her feelings. She rose from the table. "I'll go now. Thank you for listening."

Adam signaled the waiter.

"Are you ready to order, sir?"

Adam shook his head. "Not yet. First we'd like a bottle of champagne." He smiled at Kate. "We're welcoming a new year tonight."

SIXTEEN

Ford heard the doorbell ringing as he climbed down from the attic, but when he opened the front door there was no one in sight. However, the white Mercedes parked in the driveway proved there was a visitor somewhere on the premises.

Ford reached in his pocket to make sure he had a house key before pulling the front door shut behind him. He moved along the driveway to the back of the house. A tall, well-dressed woman was showing a younger man around the garden. As they moved toward the swimming pool, Ford approached them hesitantly. "Excuse me, did you ring the doorbell just now?"

"We'd decided no one was home," the woman said, giving him an appraising look.

"I was in the attic, fixing some wiring," Ford explained.

"Are you an electrician too?" The woman seemed surprised.

Ford stared at her. An electrician too? What did that mean? How much did she know about him? "I can do almost anything that needs doing around a house," he said slowly.

"May we see the house?" The man seemed impatient to get on with whatever he had come to do.

Ford didn't know what was expected of him. "I'm the only one here right now," he began.

Suddenly the woman extended her hand. "Forgive me. I haven't even introduced myself. My name is Ruth Gibbons. I'm Kate's closest friend." Seeing the blank look on Ford's face, she put her hand down and continued hurriedly. "At least I thought I was. Has she never mentioned me to you?"

Ford shook his head. "She's not here. Do you want to come inside and wait for her?"

The young man looked at his watch. "As long as we're here, do you think we could look through the house? I have to get back to the office."

Ruth smiled, trying to put Ford at ease. "This is my realtor, Laird Cooper." Ford transferred the piece of wire he was holding to his left hand, and the two men shook hands awkwardly. "I told Kate to call him," Ruth continued, "when we had lunch last week at the Farmers Market."

Ford's face brightened at the mention of the Farmers Market. "My kids are still talking about that place."

"I met your son and daughter. They're beautiful children," said Ruth. "Unusual names . . ." She paused, trying to remember.

"Joe Wayne and Marvella."

The realtor was getting restless. "I'll just go on ahead, if you don't mind—take a quick look around." He loped toward the house.

"I'm sorry for barging in on you like this," Ruth said as they walked toward the house. She searched Ford's face for a clue to what he was feeling. His expression revealed nothing, but there was something substantial and reassuring about his physical presence. "I guess you're finding a lot to do around here."

He nodded. "You can't just turn your back on a house. When little things start going wrong, you should tend to them right away. This house has been left on its own too long."

"I'm afraid I've made the same mistake with my house,"

Ruth said. They were in the kitchen now. Ford moved toward the hallway, clearly anxious to get back to work. "How about a coffee break?" Ruth motioned toward the full pot on the coffee maker.

Ford nodded hesitantly. Ruth filled two mugs and set them on the kitchen table. She took a seat and, smiling at Ford, willed him into the chair across from her. "I can always count on Kate for a cup of coffee. No matter what time of day I drop by, there's a freshly made pot. As far as I know, it's her only vice." She laughed.

There was an awkward silence as Ford shifted in his chair. "I wish I'd had the foresight to get my house in shape before I put it on the market," she continued. "There are so many things wrong with it. I get tense every time a prospective buyer comes through, hoping he won't turn on the shower or look under the carpet. Oh, well, what's that saying? Buyer, beware!" She knew she was talking too much, but she couldn't help herself. All a man had to do was sit in silence and a woman would tell him everything she'd ever thought or felt. She lowered her voice confidentially. "I haven't even told Laird everything and he's my realtor."

At that moment Laird entered the kitchen on the run. "Great house," he said enthusiastically. Handing his card to Ford, he added, "Tell Mrs. Hart we could get two million—easy. That's if she wants to sell tomorrow. If she's willing to wait, we can go higher. I'd sure like to be the one to handle this property. We've got folks standing in line to buy in Los Angeles. There just aren't enough houses to go around." And he was out the door.

"I've noticed," said Ford, putting the card in his pocket while one thought played and replayed inside his head. Kate was selling this house. Now everything made sense. No wonder she seemed so happy to have him around. For the first time since Christmas Eve he began to see that maybe the giving was not all going in one direction. There even seemed to be a note of envy in her best friend's voice.

"Every penny you spend on improving a house before it goes on the market comes back to you doubled—at least—or so I've been told," Ruth said. "Kate's going about this exactly right. It's not like her, really."

"Why not?" Ford started calculating what it would have cost to hire a professional—or, more likely, several professionals—to do the work he'd been doing around the house for the past week. Even by Iowa prices, he'd more than repaid her for room and board for his family. By Los Angeles prices, he'd be showing a profit.

"Well, Kate's usually so impulsive," Ruth explained, pouring another cup of coffee for herself and for Ford. "She tends to get carried away—doesn't stop to think things through. But getting you to work here around the clock—that seems very enterprising. You can't imagine how impossible it is in this city to find somebody who can do more than one thing." She sat back down, ignoring the fact that Ford was looking restlessly toward the door. "I had a plumbing problem last year," she continued. "The plumber had to knock through the wall of the shower to get to the pipes. He fixed the plumbing but he left this huge hole in the wall. Then he had the nerve to hand me a bill. I just laughed in his face. 'I'm not paying you a cent until you put things back the way they were,' I told him. He just shrugged. 'I'm a plumber,' he said. 'I don't do that.' I was furious. 'You undid it, didn't you?' He looked at me like I was some kind of halfwit. 'Lady, you wanted your pipes fixed, didn't you? Well, I fixed them. That's all I'm paid to do.' I told him to come with me. I guess he thought I was going to write him a check because he started to smirk like he'd made his point. Instead I opened the front door and told him to get out. 'And don't bother me with a bill,' I said, 'until you finish what you started.' "

"Did he?" asked Ford with a barely suppressed grin. "Finish, I mean?" He was beginning to think maybe there was a future for him in Los Angeles after all.

"At the end of the month he mailed me a bill," Ruth replied. "I wrote across it in big red letters Job Not Completed and mailed it back. This went on for three months and then I got a summons to small claims court. I was going to fight it—I even checked out a book from the library on how to be your own lawyer—but my husband said he didn't give a damn about the principle of the thing, he just wanted to be able to take a shower again. So I paid the plumber and called a plasterer. He gave me an estimate for filling in the hole but said I'd have to call somebody else to do the tiling—that wasn't what he did. I looked in the Yellow Pages under 'Tile' and called three separate numbers. They all came and looked at the hole in the wall that the plumber had left and said to call them again when the hole was filled in. That wasn't what they did. I was ready to give up and forget about ever taking a shower again when I decided to ask my poolman for advice. He's always been pretty good at patching things. He scratched his head and said he thought he could figure out what needed to be done. He'd work at night after he finished his pool cleaning rounds. I was so grateful I offered to fix him dinner. Six weeks, thirty dinners, and sixteen hundred dollars later, the shower looked more or less like it did before the plumbing broke. I swore the next time something went wrong in the house, I'd leave it for the next owner to fix. My husband and I have had it with home owning. If we can just unload the one we've got, we'll never saddle ourselves with another piece of property. We decided early in our marriage we didn't want the responsibility of raising children. We didn't realize owning a home would be even worse."

"I sure hate being at the mercy of other people," Ford agreed sympathetically. "When you live on a farm, you've got to learn to take care of yourself—and your property. You can't pay people to come driving out to the middle of nowhere every time something breaks down on you."

"I don't suppose you'd have any free time to do some work around my house?" Ruth asked casually. "I don't know what the going rate is for what you do—since I've never found anybody who can do what you do—but I'll happily pay you fifteen dollars an hour."

Ford got up from the table and walked slowly toward the door. "I don't like leaving a job half done," he said, threading the piece of wire he was holding through his fingers. "It's going to take me the rest of the day to finish this wiring. But I could be at your house in the morning—as soon as I take my kids to school."

"I'm so grateful to you." Ruth extended her hand. This time Ford took it. "By the way," she added as she opened the front door. "My husband works at home—he's a writer—so I'm used to cooking lunch."

"You would have made a good farmer's wife." Ford smiled.

"I could never be one of those wives who kisses her husband good-bye in the morning and doesn't see him again till night. I like knowing what he's doing all day."

"Watch out or he'll put you to work alongside him. It doesn't matter what kind of work you do, you can always use another pair of hands," Ford said.

"Or feet, in my case," Ruth replied. "Henry stays home and writes. I do the errands. He hates leaving the house—except to travel."

"I know just how he feels," said Ford. "But sometimes you don't have a choice. See you tomorrow."

As he closed the front door he took the realtor's card from his pocket and tore it into small pieces.

SEVENTEEN

Sunny was adding up the change in her cash register. Two days ago one of the checkers had called in sick, and the manager had asked her to take over the stand. She had felt a sense of pride ringing up each item and sacking the groceries neatly. Even as a little girl she had been fascinated by all the products for sale in the store. On a rainy day at home when she couldn't play outside, she would amuse herself by taking groceries from the kitchen shelves and arranging them on orange crates in her bedroom. Her mother would have to pretend to shop to get all the items back into the kitchen.

Sunny could tell a lot about a person from the groceries in their basket—whether they were buying for themselves or for a family, whether they had plenty of money or had to watch every penny. The majority of customers in that neighborhood never checked prices. Ringing up their totals, Sunny would think how much more she could have bought with the same amount of money. But when she took telephone orders, she pretended she was spending her own money and prided herself on getting the best value for everything.

The sense of plenty that surrounded her in the store was beginning to erase the bitter memories of the past months. Even when she went all day without eating, the shelves of food that met her eye in every direction kept her from feeling hungry. And though she never knew till the end of the day what she'd be taking home for dinner that night, she was secure in the knowledge that no one in her family would be going to bed hungry. That was salary enough, at least for now, Sunny thought as she wrote down her totals for the day and locked her cash register.

She picked up her purse to leave—and saw the manager smiling at her. He reminded her of her geometry teacher in high school. Not just his gray hair and rimless glasses. But the feeling he was rooting for her—wanting her to succeed but knowing he could only go so far to help her. Geometry had been such a struggle for her in the beginning. But once she got the hang of it, it became her favorite subject. She loved using her ruler and compass—reducing everything to clean lines and recognizable shapes. For a few months in high school, when she was at the head of her geometry class, the world had seemed within her grasp. But never again. Sunny sighed.

"You've been a godsend these past couple of days," the manager said in a friendly voice. "I don't know how we would have managed without you."

"I like being here," Sunny replied, wondering what food she would find in the surplus basket to take home tonight.

"Everybody seems to get sick once the holidays are over," he lamented. "We're always shorthanded in January and February. I'd like to know I can count on you to come in every day."

"Oh, you can," Sunny assured him. "I like waking up in the morning and having somewhere to go, a place where I can work at something I know how to do."

"This is all I can afford to pay you right now," the manager said, handing her a sealed envelope, "but if you stick around, I'll try to do better by you."

Sunny tore open the envelope and looked at the check. "If we were still living in Iowa, I could support my family on this," she said, quickly opening her purse and putting the check inside.

"Unfortunately, this isn't Iowa"—the manager smiled—"but you're a good, dependable worker, and you seem to have a real feeling for this business. There's a place for you here if you want one."

"Oh, I do!" Sunny answered quickly. She had worked hard all her life, but this was the first time she'd ever had a paycheck to show for it. Her parents would occasionally reward her with candy or odd change, but the store paid for their food and shelter and everybody in the family was expected to put in a certain number of hours each week. Once she married Ford and moved to the farm, she found herself working even harder—but their bank account just kept getting lower. Even though the account was in both their names, Ford signed all the checks—he had inherited the account from his father, along with the farm.

"Is there a bank around here?" Sunny asked impulsively.

"Sure. A block away. A big one. You could go there on your lunch hour. Not that I've ever seen you take a lunch hour—or even a coffee break." There was concern behind his smile. "If I'm going to be able to count on you, you've got to promise me you'll start taking better care of yourself."

"Don't worry," Sunny reassured him. "I'm strong. I have to be. I won't let you down." She saw the delivery truck at the back door and started toward it. "I don't know how to thank you for this," she said, patting her purse.

"You've more than earned it," the manager assured her. "But until I can afford to pay you what you're really worth, keep taking out the difference in groceries."

Sunny's face broke into a smile. "I didn't feel right about asking, but if I had to start spending my paycheck on groceries, I probably wouldn't have anything left to put in the bank." Filling a brown paper bag with items from the surplus basket, she confided shyly, "I've never had my own bank account before."

"It's high time you did," the manager said. "I've been watching the way you fill telephone orders. If you spend your own money as carefully as you spend our customers', your bank account is going to grow faster than your children."

A warning honk from the truck sent Sunny running to the back door. "I don't want to keep my ride waiting," she said with a quick wave. "Thanks again. See you in the morning."

As Sunny hurried around the truck to the passenger side, a hand reached for the sack of groceries.

"Ford!" she exclaimed. "You scared me. What are you doing here?"

"Anything wrong with a man meeting his wife after work?" He put his free arm around her shoulders and kissed her.

Sunny pulled away, embarrassed. "Not here, Ford." She waved to the driver. "It's okay. I've got a ride." He nodded and started the engine.

Ford put the groceries in the back of his battered car, then climbed in behind the wheel.

"He could've taken me. It's right on his way." Sunny was fighting tears of anger and embarrassment as she got in the car. "Why are you wasting gas?"

Ford stared straight ahead as he turned the key in the ignition, praying silently that the car wouldn't make a fool of him here. But the engine started smoothly. "The car hasn't left the garage in a week," he said, "and I haven't left the house. I had to make sure both of us were in working order before tomorrow."

"What happens tomorrow?" Sunny detected a note of excitement that was new to her ear.

"I'm taking the kids to register at their new school."

"I know. I wish I could go with you," Sunny said. "I'm so scared for them."

"You don't have to be scared about this school," Ford said. "We're in a nice neighborhood now."

"That's why I'm scared," Sunny said. "They're not going to fit in. I can't stand to think of the other kids making fun of them just because they talk different or dress different."

"I think Kate was worried about that too," Ford admitted. "That's why she took them shopping this afternoon—to buy them some new clothes."

"Without even asking me? I'm their mother. I'm the one who should pick out their clothes."

"As long as she's paying, she can pick out anything she pleases. And since she's making Joe Wayne and Marvella happy, it seems to me we oughta be happy too."

Sunny sat silently, watching the traffic through her window. "See that drugstore," she said abruptly. "Pull in there."

Ford swerved to make the turn. "What do you need?" he asked. "You're not sick, are you?"

Sunny shook her head with a smile. "I got paid today."

"I know," Ford replied. "I put the groceries in the back." Sunny opened her purse and handed the check to Ford. He looked at it in astonishment. "What's this for?"

"One week's work."

"You mean you're going to get this much every week?"

Sunny nodded. "Plus groceries. For now. I may get a raise later."

Ford pulled into a parking space in front of the drugstore and turned off the engine. "So what are you going to do now? You're not going to try to cash it in there, are you?"

Sunny stepped resolutely out of the car. "I've still got the money Kate gave me for Christmas. This check is not going to be cashed. I'm taking it to the bank tomorrow and opening an account."

Ford hurried to catch up with her. "I may have something to put in it myself," he announced. "Starting tomorrow, I'm going to be doing some work for a friend of Kate's. She said she'd pay me fifteen dollars an hour."

Sunny turned to look at him. "So that's why you wanted to make sure the car was running right." She reached for his hand. "Oh, Ford, things are going to get better for us now, I can feel it. If Kate will just let us stay with her until we save enough money for a place of our own."

The realtor's words echoed inside Ford's head: "Two million —easy. That's if she wants to sell tomorrow. If she's willing to wait, we can go higher." He muttered to Sunny, "We just gotta be grateful for every day we have a roof over our heads and enough to eat. But we can't count on anything, honey—except each other."

Sunny's face hardened. "I'm not counting on her." She patted her purse. "This is the only thing I'm counting on. And if you want a bank account, *you* open one. With the money *you* make. I'm never going to depend on you the way I did when we were living on the farm. I went down with you once. I won't do it again." And she marched into the drugstore.

Ford turned and walked slowly back to his car. He had been feeling so good when he left the house to meet Sunny. He thought they might even drive out to the ocean and watch the waves crashing against the rocks in the moonlight.

When they had first reached Los Angeles last summer, they had kept right on driving to the Pacific Ocean. None of them had ever seen a body of water larger than a lake, and the immensity of the endless vista provided an awesome conclusion to their journey, along with the promise of an unimagined future.

Ford was suddenly drowning in memories. A sob escaped his lips. He had to get to the ocean, to try to recapture that sense of hope. This time he was going to hang on to it. He started the car engine and pulled out of the parking space. Suddenly Sunny was running across the parking lot, shouting at him. He screeched to a halt and she climbed in the car in a fury. "Are you crazy?" she screamed. "Why were you driving off without me?"

"I just thought I might die if I didn't get back to the ocean."

"To the ocean?" Sunny looked at him as if he'd lost his mind. "You go where you want, but I've gotta get home to the kids." She motioned to the two shopping bags at her feet. "I bought them some things. For tomorrow." She put her hand on Ford's shoulder hesitantly. "I didn't mean everything I said just now."

He shrugged but kept his eyes fixed firmly on the road. "You didn't say anything that wasn't true. I did take you down with me. I can't blame you for wanting to be on your own."

"I'm not leaving you, Ford." Sunny's voice was clear and steady. "I just want my own bank account. Can you understand that?"

"Sure, honey." He managed a smile. "You put your money in

the bank and I'll pay cash for whatever we need. We won't touch your paycheck. We'll just watch that bank account get bigger and bigger every week. Until we have enough for a place of our own." He reached out his arm and pulled Sunny close to him.

She leaned her head back against his shoulder with a long, contented sigh. "Sometimes I dream I'm standing in an empty apartment. Nothing but space around me. Brand-new carpet from wall to wall, everything freshly painted, and sunlight streaming through the windows. I start imagining how I'd furnish it if I didn't have to think about money. I'd have a couch with lots of soft cushions that makes into a double bed and a dining table with eight chairs in case we want to have company and a desk where I can sit and write checks on my new account and a fire-place—we have to have a fireplace—and bookshelves on either side filled with books and plants everywhere you look and a stereo player . . ." She paused for breath, then added in a final burst of enthusiasm, "And a nice easy chair for you in front of the fire. How does that sound?"

"I'm glad to know I made it into this dream." Ford grinned. "I thought maybe you were planning on living there alone." He stopped the car in front of a darkened house. "Sometimes I just ache for you," he murmured, gathering her into his arms. "That's why I had to come get you tonight. I just hate having you out of my reach all day."

"We're acting like teenagers." Sunny giggled. "Necking in a parked car."

"Who needs an ocean?" Ford asked when the car was once again moving down the street. "When I'm holding you, I feel like everything is still possible."

Sunny squeezed his hand. "We're gonna make it, I know we are."

"I can't make it much longer without something to eat." Ford laughed as they turned into the driveway. "How about you?"

"I'm starving," Sunny admitted.

The spicy smell of pizza with sausage and green peppers greeted them as they entered the kitchen. Kate was sitting at the kitchen table with Joe Wayne and Marvella, a cardboard box open in front of them.

"Mommy! Daddy!" Marvella ran to hug them, her face glowing with excitement. "We went shopping and now we're having pizza and—where were you?"

"I had to get some gas for the car," Ford explained, "so I decided to surprise your mama at work and drive her home."

"Gas?" Joe Wayne looked alarmed. "We're not leaving here, are we?"

"No, son," Ford reassured him. "Not unless Kate's ready to get rid of us." He watched her closely to see if her face would reveal more than her words.

"You have a home here with me as long as you want one," she answered simply, looking him right in the eye. "You're my family now." She seemed to be fighting back tears. But quickly turning her attention to the table, she gestured toward the pizza. "Sorry we didn't wait for you," she apologized, "but shopping makes you so hungry."

"I'm famished myself," said Ford, taking a slice.

"Have you been shopping too?" Marvella asked.

Sunny started for the door. "Oh, Ford, we forgot to bring the bags in from the car."

"I'll go get them in just a minute. You sit down and have something to eat," he said, his mouth full of pizza. "This is so good." He could see Sunny getting tense. It happened every time she and Kate were together in the kitchen. She resented it if Kate suggested cooking something for them or taking them out to dinner or bringing something in. And yet she felt Kate was being condescending if she shared the food Sunny brought home from the store to fix for her family.

"I'll go get them myself. I'm not hungry," Sunny said—and she was out the door. Ford felt as if he were losing his mind. Was this the same woman he had held in his arms only moments earlier?

"Joe Wayne, go help your mother," he said wearily.

"What did you bring home tonight?" Joe Wayne asked as he took the bag of groceries from Sunny and started unpacking it.

"See for yourself," she replied, holding tightly to the two shopping bags from the drugstore.

"Eggs, milk, canned biscuits, bacon—looks more like breakfast to me," he said.

"And that's what you need before you start school tomorrow morning—a good hot breakfast." She put an arm protectively around her son. "I'm going to set my alarm so I'll be awake in plenty of time to cook breakfast for you and Marvella before I go to work. And while you're eating, I'll make sandwiches for your lunch. See that bologna? I brought it home especially for you because I know how much you like it."

"I don't," volunteered Marvella. "I like peanut butter and jelly."

"I like peanut butter and banana," Joe Wayne announced.

"That's fine. I brought home a big bunch of bananas." Sunny was trying her best to please. Her face was lined with fatigue and Ford knew she was hungry though she seemed determined to deny it, but she was putting her heart into the role she was playing now and he knew better than to get in her way. He picked up another piece of pizza and bit into it. "I'll use the bologna to make sandwiches for your dad," Sunny said, staring at Ford.

"He's not going to school," Marvella giggled.

"No, but he's going to work," Sunny said quietly.

Ford saw the questioning look in Kate's eyes but decided to ignore it. Suddenly Marvella ran over to him and put her arms around his neck. "Please take me to work with you, Daddy," she begged, beginning to cry. "I don't want to go to school."

"Of course you do, sweetheart," he said soothingly. "You like learning to read and you're the champion speller in your class."

"In my old class," she corrected him. "I don't want to be in a new class—with people who don't know my name."

"We're living in a different house now," he reminded her. "You'll be going to a school right here in the neighborhood. And tomorrow I'm going to drive you up to the front door myself." The image of the realtor clouded his thoughts. How long could they count on living in this neighborhood? How long did it take to sell a house in California? What if someone made an offer tomorrow? They'd be back on the street by Easter, if not sooner—and his children would have to change schools again.

"Will you stay with me at school all day, Daddy?" Marvella begged.

"I can't, baby. I've got work to do," he said, hugging her to him.

"Then I'll go with you and help you work," she replied.

"Do you know how many children there are in this country who don't even have the chance to go to school?" Ford said quietly. "Their parents are always on the move, looking for work, living in trailers or tents or sometimes just in packing crates on the sidewalk because they can't afford anything permanent. If it weren't for Kate, we'd be right there with them. Any of those kids would be glad to trade places with you tomorrow for the chance to wake up in a warm bed and spend the day in a school-room learning something to keep them from ending up as scared and hungry as their mothers and fathers."

Marvella looked from Ford to Sunny and suddenly began to cry.

"Stop, Ford. You're scaring her," Sunny said. She held out her arms to Marvella, who ran to her and crawled in her lap.

Kate tried to erase her presence from the scene by putting the leftover pizza in the refrigerator and stacking the plates in the dishwasher.

"I brought you something tonight," Sunny said soothingly, handing a shopping bag to Marvella and the other one to Joe Wayne. "Something to get you off to a good start tomorrow."

Joe Wayne tore into his sack. "A notebook?" His disappointment was clear but Sunny didn't seem to notice.

"And packages of blank paper and brand-new pencils that have never even been sharpened and ballpoint pens and paper clips and rubber bands . . ." Sunny was pulling packages out of Marvella's sack and displaying them on the kitchen table. "I even bought a box of gold stars to put on every paper you bring home with a good grade."

"Hey, my notebook has Superman's picture on the cover." Joe Wayne brightened considerably at this discovery. "It's a bird, it's a plane, it's Superman!" he shouted, climbing on a chair and standing with his arms outstretched.

"He grew up watching those cartoons on television," Ford explained to Kate. "He jumped from the hayloft when he was four, thinking he could fly. Broke his arm. Lucky he didn't break his neck."

"I can fly," Joe Wayne insisted. "I just can't do it when anybody's looking."

"Remember that tomorrow." Sunny smiled as she reached over and swung Joe Wayne down from the chair. "You're just like Clark Kent. You've got secret powers."

"I'm flying," shouted Joe Wayne as he ran out of the room, waving his arms up and down.

Marvella was carefully opening her notebook and fitting the lined paper inside.

"Do you like yours, Marvella?" Sunny asked softly.

In reply, Marvella began to kiss the picture of Snoopy on the cover of her notebook.

"Who's that getting all my kisses?" Ford joked. The tension that had choked the atmosphere in the kitchen earlier had dissolved into a gently protective bond, as if all three adults were conspiring to weave a web that would keep danger away from these two young lives entrusted to their care.

"I love you, Snoopy," exclaimed Marvella, hugging the notebook to her.

"You can't take Homer to school, but you can take your dog Snoopy," Sunny said with a smile.

"And if anybody tries to hurt me, he'll bite them, won't you, Snoopy?" Marvella said.

Kate handed Sunny a mug of coffee. "You look like you could use something hot," she said. Then she filled two more mugs and brought them to the table.

"Thanks," said Sunny.

The warm feeling flooding Ford's chest had nothing to do with the coffee. Thank God for the children, he thought.

Marvella suddenly jumped up from the table. "Come upstairs, Mama, and see the new clothes Kate bought me."

Ford sighed inwardly. If only it were possible to freeze everybody in place when they finally forgot themselves long enough to be happy. "Let your mama finish her coffee," he said—but it was too late. The moment had passed.

Sunny stood abruptly, leaving her half-filled mug on the table. "That's okay," she said. "I don't really like drinking coffee at night. It keeps me awake and I have to be up early in the morning."

As soon as Sunny had left the room, Kate took the half-filled mug to the sink and, with her back to Ford, stood rinsing it over and over again. He continued to drink his coffee in silence. Finally she put the mug into the dishwasher and crossed back to the table. "I don't know how to make her feel at home here," she said softly.

"Maybe she just doesn't want to get used to something she knows is not going to last," he said, staring down at the mug, both his hands wrapped around it, remembering the times when a cup of coffee was the only thing he had to keep him warm. "She wants a place of her own."

"I can understand that," said Kate. "But until you find something, you're welcome to stay here."

"Until we find something—or until you find a buyer?"

Kate looked at Ford sharply. "A buyer? What are you talking about? What makes you think I want to sell this house?"

Ford stood up. "Look, you don't owe us any explanation. It's your house. You can do anything you want with it. I just need to know how long we've got."

Kate put her hand on his arm. "What happened here today? Did someone say something to you?"

"Your friend Ruth stopped by with her realtor."

"I see." Kate poured herself another cup of coffee.

"He left you his card but I—I lost it," Ford muttered, still refusing to look at her.

"It's true, I was thinking about selling the house," Kate admitted. "I told my husband I didn't want to live in it alone. But then you came."

"I thought I was doing all this work for you—so you'd feel

good about living here. I didn't know what I was doing was just part of what you were selling. Now your friend Ruth wants me to do the same kind of thing for her. She's going to pay me fifteen dollars an hour. Don't worry, I'll work here nights and weekends to pay for our room and board. But I can't just keep breaking even. I've got to find a way to get ahead—to put something aside."

Ford headed for the hallway. Suddenly he was so tired. He just wanted to sleep. Kate started after him but the ringing of the phone summoned her back to the kitchen. Ford stopped on the stairs to listen. "Two o'clock tomorrow?" he heard her say. "Well, I guess I could be here. The thing is, I haven't really made up my mind to sell." Ford waited, wondering what was being said on the other end of the line. Finally Kate spoke again. "That much? I don't believe it. That's twenty times what we paid. What? Oh, well, let's see, that was almost twenty-five years ago. Still, I can't believe we've made that kind of money without doing anything to earn it except owning a house." There was a long pause before she spoke again. "No, I don't suppose there's anything wrong with letting them look. All right. Tomorrow at two then." Ford hurried up the stairs and closed the bedroom door.

Sunny was stretched out in the middle of the big bed with Marvella on one side of her and Joe Wayne on the other. She was holding her purse in front of her. "Close your eyes," she ordered, "and don't open them till I say so." She took the envelope from her purse and held the paycheck out in front of her. Her happiness reached out to Ford and drew him to the bed. He stood watching her—wishing he could have been the cause. "Now!" Sunny announced in a voice so triumphant it sounded as if she were about to break into song.

The children opened their eyes and stared at the check. "That's your name," said Joe Wayne, looking at Sunny with new respect.

"What is it?" asked Marvella.

"My first paycheck," Sunny said, stroking the piece of paper as if it were a living thing. "I'm going to get one every week."

"What are you going to do with it?" asked Joe Wayne.

"Tomorrow I'm going to the bank and I'm going to open an account. I'll have checks with my own name on them," Sunny said proudly. "But I'm not going to spend a penny if I can help it."

"Are you gonna be rich, Mama?" Marvella asked hopefully.

Sunny hugged her. "No, sweetheart, we're probably never going to be rich but maybe someday soon, if we work real hard and save our money, we'll at least be able to pay the rent on a place of our own."

Joe Wayne reached deep into the pocket of his jeans and pulled out a crumpled five-dollar bill. "Here," he said, handing it to Sunny. "Give this to the bank too."

Ford crossed to Joe Wayne. "Where did you get that, son?"

"It's mine," Joe Wayne replied defensively. "Kate gave it to me."

"Why would she give you money?" Sunny asked.

"Why didn't she give me any?" Marvella was about to cry. "I want to give Mama some money to put in the bank."

"She gave you five dollars just like she did me," Joe Wayne reminded her.

"Not today she didn't."

"Last week—at the Farmers Market," Joe Wayne said in a low voice.

Ford put his hand on Joe Wayne's shoulder. "Were you supposed to buy something with that money?"

"Something to take home to you," Joe Wayne answered defiantly. "And I gave you the money. I didn't buy anything for myself."

"And I bought you a lemon meringue pie," Marvella reminded him. "Joe Wayne told Kate we bought it together but we didn't. I spent all my money to pay for it. It's your favorite, isn't it, Daddy?"

"It was the best one I ever ate," Ford assured her. "The best *bought* one I ever ate. Nobody makes better lemon meringue pie than your mama."

"You still remember how to make one, don't you, Mama?" Marvella asked anxiously.

"Sure, honey, you never forget something like that."

"See, I told you." Marvella turned to her brother. "Joe Wayne said he bet you'd forgotten how."

"I'll make one tonight and prove it to you." Sunny was suddenly in such a good mood. Like the sun coming out from behind a cloud, her good humor warmed the whole family.

"But first I want to show you my new clothes." Marvella began pulling at Sunny's hand.

"Let your mother go on down to the kitchen and get started," Ford intervened, afraid mention of the clothes Kate had bought her children would darken Sunny's bright spirits. "She hasn't even had anything to eat herself. Why don't you two change into your new clothes and give us a fashion show? But first, Joe Wayne, you've got to give that five-dollar bill back to Kate."

Joe Wayne looked as if he'd been hit across the face. He grabbed the bill from Sunny and stuffed it back in his jeans. Then he ran past Ford, shouting, "It's mine. I won't give it back. I shouldn't have showed it to you."

Sunny followed Ford as he started down the stairs after Joe Wayne. "Go easy on him, Ford," she pleaded. "He was just trying to help. It's not like he stole the money. She gave it to him."

"I may not have anything else to give my children," Ford said, "but I can teach them the difference between right and wrong. That's about the only thing my father gave me that I've still got—but I'll go to my grave believing it has some value in this world." He cupped her chin in his hand, forcing her to look him in the eye. "At least when it comes to the children I've never let you down. Have I?"

Sunny nodded. "You're a good father, Ford. I'll never say otherwise."

He smiled. "Then trust me. And call me when that lemon meringue pie is ready."

Joe Wayne was watching television in his room with a chair pushed under the doorknob when Ford knocked. "I want to talk to you, Joe Wayne. I'll be in the living room."

Without waiting for a reply, he strode across the hallway. He paced for a moment, then started back to Joe Wayne's room just as Sunny and Marvella were coming down the stairs.

"Mama's going to teach me to make a lemon meringue pie," Marvella announced, "so if she ever does forget how, I can help her remember."

Ford gave her a kiss, then turned back toward the living room. "I'll get a fire started."

Ford was just putting a match to his carefully laid pile of logs and kindling when Joe Wayne entered hesitantly. Ford pretended not to hear him and busied himself fanning the flames. Finally Joe Wayne slumped on a corner of the sofa. Ford continued to kneel in front of the fire until Joe Wayne spoke.

"You're gonna have to tell me what I did wrong," he said stubbornly.

Ford stood slowly. "No, I'm not. I'm going to let you work that out for yourself." And with that he stretched out in the easy chair by the fire, put his feet on the footstool, and closed his eyes.

"Kate said to spend the money on you and I gave it to you, didn't I?"

Ford nodded but did not speak.

The weight of his father's presence pressed down on Joe Wayne, forcing the words out of his mouth. "I know she said to buy something to bring home to you, but we need a lot of things worse than we needed another pie. Maybe I should've given you the money right away—but what difference does that make?"

"None. Absolutely none," Ford agreed without opening his eyes.

There was a long pause. Joe Wayne got up and started out of the room. At the door he turned to look back at Ford, who was still sitting with his eyes closed. Joe Wayne took a deep breath and shifted from one foot to the other. "I guess it was wrong to tell her that the pie cost ten dollars."

Ford opened his eyes and turned toward his son. "You guess?"

Joe Wayne lowered his head and spoke into his collar. "I know."

Ford stood up. "Then I guess you know what to say to Kate."

And he marched to the study door and knocked softly. He could hear voices inside. He hesitated for a moment, then glanced at Joe Wayne, who looked as if he were about to bolt out the front door. Ford knocked again sharply.

Kate opened the door. "I'm sorry. I was playing one of Cliff's old movies. I didn't hear you at first."

"I'm sorry to bother you," Ford began, "but Joe Wayne has something to say to you."

Kate took one look at Joe Wayne and gathered him into her arms. "Joe Wayne, is something wrong?"

He nodded furiously and burst into tears.

"Come inside and tell me what happened," she said, pulling him down on the couch beside her while Ford stood awkwardly in the doorway. She pressed a button on a box beside the couch and turned off the television. "He's more talented than I realized —my husband," she said to no one in particular. "I'll have to show you some of his movies."

"Will you show me how to play movies on that machine?" Joe Wayne brightened at the prospect.

"The VCR? Sure," Kate promised. "I've only learned to work it myself these past few months while Cliff's been away. But you know something? It's not as hard as he always made me think it was. I've been so in awe of all his equipment. Now I've even recorded a new message for his answering machine."

"Can I hear it?" Joe Wayne asked eagerly.

"Joe Wayne!" Ford's voice held a warning note.

Joe Wayne reached quickly into his jeans pocket and handed the five-dollar bill to Kate. "This is yours. I'm sorry." And he started for the door but Ford was blocking his exit.

"I don't understand." Kate looked in confusion from Ford to Joe Wayne. "You don't owe me any money."

"It's your money." The words came tumbling out of Joe Wayne. "You said to buy something to bring home from the Farmers Market—only I didn't. I told you the pie cost ten dollars but it only cost five. I kept my money. I'm sorry." And he started to cry again.

This time Ford put his arm around his shoulders and hugged

him close. "It's okay, son. You've said what you had to say." He smiled at Kate.

Kate knelt down beside Joe Wayne and folded his fingers around the five-dollar bill. "It's still your money, Joe Wayne, not mine. But I bet you can think of something to buy with it that will last a lot longer than a lemon meringue pie."

EIGHTEEN

Sunny was walking down the street, a sack of groceries in each hand, when she saw the "For Sale" sign in front of the house. What was happening? She had never heard Kate say anything about selling her house. There was nothing Sunny wanted more than a place of her own but it was going to take time to find one they could afford to rent—and to save the money for a deposit. Despite her brave words to Ford the day before, she was still counting on Kate—more than she'd dared admit.

She hurried into the house. Silence greeted her. She ran up the stairs to the bedroom and was reassured to see her clothes on a chair, just as she had left them that morning. She crossed to the windows and stepped out on the balcony. The weather had been unusually warm, even for southern California, and the evening air still held the sun.

The panic that had seized her throat gradually subsided. She closed her eyes and took a deep breath. Surely Kate wouldn't just turn them out onto the streets again. Once you intervene in someone's life, you can't just abandon them. You have to stay with them, see them through, until they're on their feet again. Don't you?

The sound of laughter coming from the swimming pool told her where she could find her children. Kate was with them. Sunny could hear her voice. She was besieged by the now familiar feeling of jealousy that lay in wait for her every night when she came home from work exhausted and saw another woman enjoying her children.

But it made her happy to see them having fun again. Hard times had robbed them of the childhoods she and Ford had taken for granted. But too often now she felt as if she were watching them through the wrong end of a telescope. Their good fortune had distanced her from them, putting them beyond her reach. She was only allowed to watch now—she could no longer touch. Or at least that was the way she felt. Only Ford seemed to be able to move freely in and out of all their lives. She had to find him and ask him what the "For Sale" sign meant.

She heard Homer barking in the garden and Ford calling to him. She hurried down the stairs and out to the back, where she found Ford building a trellis.

"What are you doing?" she asked. "It looks like you're getting ready for a wedding."

"Green beans have to climb on something," he said. "Everybody puts up poles. I thought I'd do something different."

"You just put in the seeds last week. They haven't even sprouted yet. Do you know how long it's going to be before they start to climb?" Sunny was rigid with anger.

"We'll be ready for them when they do." Ford smiled.

"We won't even be here." Sunny was shouting now. "Did you see that sign in front of the house?"

Ford shrugged. "It's her house. She can do what she wants with it."

"And what are you going to have to show for all this work?"

"Seeds don't stop growing just because the land changes owners."

"People who live in houses like this don't care about growing vegetables, Ford. When they're hungry, they go to the grocery store. Why aren't you spending your time working on something we can keep, something we can take with us when we have to leave here?"

Ford continued to hammer at the trellis, avoiding her eyes. "I had seventy-five dollars in my pocket when I finished work today. I got in my car feeling like a man for the first time since we lost the farm. I sang all the way to school to pick up the kids. I parked right in front so they couldn't miss me. Marvella came running out as soon as the bell rang, her arms overflowing with papers. She couldn't wait to start showing me things." His voice suddenly softened. "Her teacher made every child in that class write her a letter of welcome."

Sunny's eyes filled with tears. "Thank God! She was so scared this morning. I was afraid that big breakfast I made her eat wouldn't stay down."

Ford grimaced. "It didn't. She threw up out the window on the way to school."

Sunny moaned in sympathy. "I bet she wanted to turn around and come right back home."

"No, she was real brave. She said if she didn't go today, she'd dread it all the more tomorrow. She just wanted to get it over with."

"How about Joe Wayne? How did he do?"

Ford dropped to his knees without saying a word and began to go over the ground, pulling out any trace of weed.

Sunny knelt beside him. "What happened, Ford?"

Ford was focusing on the ground, scooping up the dirt and letting it sift through his fingers. "He was real quiet on the way to school. I took them both inside and got them registered and walked them to their classrooms. If I could've figured out a way to be invisible, I would've stayed to look after them but finally I had to leave them on their own."

Sunny clutched his arm. "I just saw him in the swimming pool. He seemed okay."

"Yeah—now that he's home." Ford stood and leaned heavily

on his hoe. "I thought he was never gonna come out of that building this afternoon. We were the only car still waiting. I was getting ready to go look for him when he comes around the corner on the run, throws himself into the backseat, and tells me to step on the gas. I try to make light of it, ask him if he's in trouble with the law. He breaks into tears, tells me from now on he's walking to school." Ford's voice cracked.

"Why would he say that? What happened?" Sunny's voice was threaded with helpless concern. She had always taken her children to school the first day, met their teachers, made sure everything was going to be okay.

"It started with the notebook." Ford's voice cut into her thoughts.

"The notebook?"

"That Superman notebook you gave him last night. Some of the boys in his class made fun of it—they said Superman was a joke and asked Joe Wayne if he came from another planet."

"I guess we do," Sunny muttered.

"Then after school they saw him heading toward my car. They started teasing him, asking him if the car was in disguise like he was. He hid in the bathroom until everybody had gone so no one would see him getting into it. How do you think that makes me feel—knowing my own son is ashamed of me?"

Sunny shook her head. "It was my fault. I bought him the notebook."

But Ford wasn't listening. "All I could think about driving home was how proud I'd always been of my father. I used to point him out to people and let them know I was his son. And here I am with a son who doesn't want to claim me." He paused, then blurted out, "I know what I did next is not going to make sense to you, Sunny, but I just had to do it."

"Do what?" she asked in alarm.

"I drove straight downtown to that pawnshop where I hocked my father's guitar. Thank God it was still there."

"How much did it cost you to buy it back?" Sunny's voice had turned to ice.

"A day's pay."

"Seventy-five dollars? You spent seventy-five dollars on a gui-tar?"

"Not *a* guitar. The guitar my father used to play when I was a boy. Just holding it reminds me of him. It's the only thing he left me that I can still reach out and touch. When I play it, I hear him singing to me. Even now. You gotta understand how I feel." His eyes were pleading as he turned to Sunny.

"How *you* feel? Do you ever stop to think how *I* feel? You are living in the past, Ford, and I am bone-weary of being the only one in this family willing to fight for our future." She turned toward the house. "I'm going to get something to eat now and then I'm going upstairs to bed. I'm worn out. Try not to wake me or, better yet, sleep somewhere else."

NINETEEN

It was close to midnight. Kate stood outside the garage door, listening to the notes of a song she half remembered from her childhood. Ford must have been sitting in his car all night. Thank God he's safe, she thought to herself. She'd come out to the garage to see if his car was gone. She hadn't seen him since he brought the children home from school. In fact, she hadn't actually seen him then. She had been in the pool when she heard his car pull into the garage. Joe Wayne and Marvella had wasted no time before changing into their suits and jumping in with her.

Kate had waited for Ford to join them. All the awkward, invisible boundaries that seemed to separate them when they were in the house together dissolved in the water. The four of them felt like a family, playing games and making jokes. Thank heaven Sunny doesn't swim, Kate had thought more than once since Ford and his family had moved into her house.

But Ford never came anywhere near the pool and the children seemed strangely subdued. Especially Joe Wayne. Kate tried to ask them about their first day of school and Marvella had begun chattering away, when Joe Wayne suddenly burst out that it was enough he had to go to school all day, he didn't want to talk about it all night.

Kate was looking in the refrigerator, trying to decide what to do about dinner, when Marvella wandered into the kitchen and announced she was going to make her own and so was Joe Wayne as soon as her mama got through talking to him. When Kate asked where her daddy was, she shook her head and said she didn't know.

Marvella was just getting a box of cereal down from the shelf when Joe Wayne came in. He looked as if he'd been crying. Kate wanted to put her arms around him and tell him whatever had gone wrong today they would make right tomorrow, but instead she offered to make pancakes. Joe Wayne replied defiantly that they could take care of themselves. Besides, their mother had made them promise not to bother Kate. What bother, she wanted to cry out. You're the children I never had. I could spend the rest of my life making pancakes for you and count myself blessed. But she sat quietly at the table saying nothing while they ate their cereal and carefully washed and dried their dishes. Then she told them good night and said she thought she'd take a bath and go to bed early.

She made her bed on the couch in the study and slipped a cassette of Cliff's most recent film into the VCR. She felt in a funny way she was getting to know him better through his work than she had sitting across the table from him or even sleeping in the same bed. Every night for the past week she had played one of his movies. Interwoven with the images flickering on the screen were scenes from their marriage. She would remember how she felt about the script when he first showed it to her, what had been happening in their lives while he was filming it, the critical and box-office response to the finished product. No matter how much you believed in something while you were working on it, the public verdict was what stayed with you.

But tonight Kate could not keep her mind on what she was

seeing. She left the study door open so she could hear Ford going up or down the stairs. He wasn't with Sunny and he wasn't with the children. Where could he be? Had he gone somewhere? Something was tearing this family apart and she couldn't figure out what it was.

Finally she turned off her light and tried to fall asleep but to no avail. At midnight, with the hall light still burning, she put on her robe and went outside.

But she was stopped at the garage door by the sound of a guitar, and then Ford's voice came floating toward her, "I gave my love a cherry that has no stone . . ." Kate closed her eyes and pressed her head against the door, imagining what it would be like to have that voice singing in her ear.

Then the singing stopped. The silence frightened her. Hesitantly she opened the side door. It was so dark inside the garage all she could be sure of seeing were the solid forms of the two cars, huddled like sleeping animals. She reached for the door of Ford's car and opened it. He did nothing to make it easier for her, just sat in the front seat strumming his guitar and staring straight ahead.

"I was worried about you," she said softly. "Have you been sitting out here all night?"

He nodded. "In the old days I would've gone for a long drive to try to get my head straight. But I can't afford the gas."

Kate shivered in the night air. "Do you mind if I sit with you for a while? It's sort of chilly just standing here."

Ford shrugged and started to slide behind the wheel. Kate quickly put her hand on his shoulder to stop him. "No, don't move. I'd rather stretch out in the backseat and listen to you play." As she climbed into the backseat, she asked hesitantly, "Would you sing that song you were singing just now one more time—for me?"

"Do you know it?" Ford asked.

"I'm not sure of the words but I remember hearing it a long time ago."

"Then will you sing with me?"

"I'll be your backseat back-up singer," Kate said—and was rewarded by a deep-throated chuckle from the front seat.

Kate was not wearing a watch and it was always three-thirty by the clock in the car, so time lost all meaning as song followed song. Ford sat facing ahead, bending over his guitar as if it were a long-lost love. The deep reverberating sounds coming from his throat seemed to be carrying on a dialogue with the chords of his guitar.

Kate had never been musical herself. Her mother had hated taking piano lessons as a child and refused to inflict them on her daughter. Kate had never felt she was missing anything—until tonight. The sound of someone singing set right all the discordant elements in the universe—at least until the song ended.

"Did you and Sunny have a fight?" The question had been circling inside her head all night like a plane waiting for permission to land, and now suddenly there it was on the ground. "You don't have to answer that," she added quickly. "It's none of my business."

"That's not exactly true," Ford replied in a low voice. "As long as we're living under your roof, you're in the middle of it, whether you want to be or not." And still facing ahead, playing chords on his guitar, he said slowly, "I spent the money I made working for your friend to get this guitar out of hock. Sunny went a little crazy when she came home and saw the 'For Sale' sign. She thinks we should be saving all our money so we can move into a place of our own."

"Look, I'm not trying to do anything behind your back." Somehow, from the distance of the backseat, Kate felt safe saying things she would never have had the courage to confess face to face. "The truth is, I don't know myself what I'm doing from day to day. I seem to be at the mercy of whoever knocks at my front door. And when that realtor got through talking to me today, it just seemed to make sense to put the house on the market. I was going to tell you and Sunny at dinner tonight so we could start making some plans, but she went straight to bed and I had no idea where you were."

"Inside this car is the only place where I know who I am."

The guitar was mute now but even in the silence Kate had to strain to hear what Ford was saying.

"Sunny is using all her strength to stay above water. She's afraid if I touch her, I'll take her down with me, and maybe she's right. So I'm not going to risk it. This car has been my only real home since we lost the farm. I've slept here more nights than I've slept anywhere else. When I'm alone here, I feel like I can handle whatever happens. But as soon as I open the door, things start going wrong. I can't even drive my kids to school without causing trouble for them." He put his head down on the steering wheel. His shoulders began to shake with sobs. Kate watched helplessly from the backseat. He was so alone in his despair she was afraid to touch him and remind him there was someone else in the car.

Finally the sobs subsided. "That's been locked inside me all night. Thanks for opening the floodgates before I drowned." And then the story came spilling out of him. "When I pulled into the garage this afternoon, I vowed I'd come back tonight—when everybody was asleep—and turn on the engine."

"Oh, Ford! How could you even think of such a thing?"

"I made up my mind my family would be better off without me."

"No woman is better off without a husband—if he loves her."

"She is if she's stopped loving him," Ford replied in a voice drained of emotion.

"I felt like a fool coming out here tonight—getting in the middle of your marriage," Kate confessed. "But thank God I did if thoughts like that were going through your head."

"I never even turned on the ignition," Ford admitted. "When I got behind the wheel, there was my daddy's guitar lying beside me on the front seat reminding me of how much I loved him when I was a boy, of how much more I love him now that I'm a man." He paused, putting his hand gently on the guitar, drawing strength from the feel of the wood beneath his fingers. "I stopped being afraid of death after he died. It's not an ending at all, you know. It just frees someone to be with you all the time." He cradled the guitar in his arms, strumming chords as he talked. "I've got to live long enough to make my son proud of me again —so he'll want to keep me with him the rest of his life, the way I keep my father with me." He began to sing softly, as if he were alone.

Kate sighed and stretched out on the backseat. Suddenly she felt so tired. There were worse places to sleep than the backseat of a car, she thought. It was a time capsule, self-enclosed, separate from the responsibilities that have a way of attaching themselves like creeping vines to any structure rising from a solid foundation. But just as she was closing her eyes, Ford began to sing a lullaby. "Hush, little baby, don't say a word. Papa's gonna buy you a mockingbird. And if that mockingbird don't sing, Papa's gonna buy you a diamond ring."

"Please stop," Kate cried. Then, while Ford sat silently in the front seat, she explained, "I used to sing that to my daughter when she was a baby—except I changed 'Papa' to 'Mama.' If she wasn't asleep by the last verse, I'd keep making up verses until her eyelids started to close."

"Then I'll do the same for you," Ford said—but Kate shook her head.

"I can't stand hearing it now—now that I've lost her."

"Lost her? How? By letting her grow up and go away to school?"

"She'll never come home. Not to me. Not when she finds out her father is in love with another woman."

"But you're still her mother. That hasn't changed."

Kate shook her head. "She's Cliff's daughter, not mine."

Ford laughed. "I know what you mean. Joe Wayne is Sunny's child. Marvella is much more like me."

"You don't understand. Nina is adopted." And she told him how Cliff had brought Nina home to her.

"He must have loved you a lot," Ford said.

"That's what I thought," Kate said. "I thought it then and I kept right on thinking it for twenty-two years. Nothing else he did or didn't do seemed very important compared to Nina. But then I found out she didn't just think like him and talk like him —she really was his daughter." And she finished the story.

"Are you sure about that?" Ford's voice was scored with concern. By sharing her pain, Kate had taken him into her life more fully than she had on the day she invited him into her house. And now, even though they were sitting in the garage in the dark, going nowhere, they seemed to be traveling together. She was leading him into her past.

Kate went back to the beginning. Her life seemed more interesting when she was telling Ford about it than it had while she was living it. Never knowing her father had left a hole nothing could fill. Her mother had never recovered from his loss. Kate used to look at pictures of her mother as a young girl and try to see what her father had seen. Nothing about the woman Kate knew growing up would lead a man to fall in love with her. She couldn't help wondering if their love would have survived if he'd stayed alive to nurture it—or would time have inevitably worn the girl he married into the grim-faced woman who shepherded Kate so joylessly through the first two decades of her life.

That was what had drawn Kate to Cliff—his ability to have fun at whatever he was doing. Kate had grown up with a mother who looked on every day as an obstacle course that had to be run between getting out of bed in the morning and going back to it in the evening. Her work at the post office brought her no pleasure beyond a regular paycheck which she spent with resigned reluctance on rent and utilities and groceries. What little was left went into a savings account for rainy days. For Christmas Kate could expect new underwear and pajamas and two crisp ten-dollar bills, supposedly hers to spend as she pleased except that her mother could invariably be counted on to ask what she had bought and how much it had cost.

Her mother had always made going to work seem like such a chore, so Kate was surprised to discover, when she graduated from high school, how much she looked forward each day to her job at the Universal commissary. She never knew who she was going to see or what was going to happen. And the thrill of earning money never wore thin.

"I guess that must be what Sunny is feeling," Ford said, more to himself than to Kate.

Kate was so immersed in her own past it took her a moment to realize Ford had brought someone else with him on this trip— his wife. But then Kate was hardly traveling unaccompanied. Cliff was right there beside her.

Suddenly she laughed out loud, remembering the day they had met. He had been having lunch in the commissary with a very attractive girl who was wearing clothes that called attention to her figure. Obviously an actress, Kate thought, envying her self-assurance. Kate made a point of dressing not to be noticed. Cliff approached the cash register where Kate was stationed and handed her his bill, along with a credit card. Kate ran it through her machine but just as Cliff was about to sign the receipt she glanced at the card again. "Sorry," she said, quickly pulling the receipt from under his hand and tearing it in two. "Your card's expired."

"I'm sure there's a new one in the mail," he said in a low voice, glancing at the girl, who was now pacing restlessly outside the door. "It's just that I moved recently and my mail hasn't caught up with me."

Kate smiled, trying to keep things as light as possible. "I don't doubt it, but until it does, I guess you'll have to pay cash."

Cliff pulled out his billfold and showed it to Kate. Empty except for a one-dollar bill. "You've got to help me out," he whispered. "She just got me this job in casting. Her uncle's an agent, I think. I called to thank her and said I'd take her to lunch in the commissary some time and she asked what I was doing today. But I don't get paid till the end of the week."

"Why don't you ask her to lend you the money?" Kate suggested, ignoring the people lining up behind Cliff.

"I can't. She'd think I was a real loser. Next thing I know, I'd be out of a job."

"Well, you've got to ask somebody," Kate whispered. "I'd do it if I were in her place."

"Would you do it if you weren't?" The sheer nerve of the

question so stunned Kate she said yes before she had time to think about it.

"I'll pay you back at the end of the week," Cliff promised as Kate reached into her pocket for the money.

"How are you going to eat till then?" she asked anxiously.

He shrugged. "Something will turn up. It always does."

"Something?" she asked. "Or someone?" As the bell on the cash register rang, she laid two bills inside the drawer and scooped up some coins. "Your change," she said. "You might as well owe me for an even amount." She quickly wrote some numbers on his receipt and handed it to him. "My phone number," she said, "in case you get hungry before you get paid. I'm a very good cook. But I'd better warn you—I live with my mother."

Over a week went by. Kate had given up hope of seeing either Cliff or her money again when her phone rang late one night. "Has your mother gone to bed?" a voice asked.

Kate almost hung up but something about the voice sounded familiar. "Who is this?"

"You said to call if I got hungry before I got paid. I'd made up my mind not to take advantage of you twice but I just finished my last jar of peanut butter."

"It's been over a week. Have you spent your paycheck already?"

"Turns out I'm in management. We only get paid every other week. Last week was an 'other.' "

Kate laughed. "I'm not going grocery shopping at this hour. You'll have to make do with whatever I can find on the shelves."

"Then I wasn't the first hungry man you let into your life." Ford's voice brought Kate abruptly back to the present. But she wasn't ready to leave Cliff—Cliff as he was when she first knew him. Not yet.

"I like someone who's not afraid of improvising," Cliff said later over a huge bowl of linguini with clam sauce. Then he told her what he really wanted was to be a director—to create something that would last.

"Unlike linguini with clam sauce," Kate said, watching with

a smile as he turned the serving bowl upside down over his plate to get the last bit of sauce.

She was so filled with happiness that night. Whether it would last or not seemed beside the point. Cliff was the first person Kate had ever met who had ambitions far beyond what he was doing at the moment. He was driven by a desire to achieve something of permanence. In Kate's experience people only went to work to make money to pay the bills. But for Cliff work was the end, not the means.

He took advantage of the free tickets available to anyone in casting at all the smaller theaters around town, and he could count on Kate to keep him company without resenting the attention he paid to the actresses onstage. He even began to rely on her judgment. She responded to people instinctively. If she liked someone, it was a pretty good bet the audience would too.

Cliff felt comfortable with Kate. He could share his future plans with her, but she never made him feel that their relationship was in any way conditional on his achieving his ambitions. She liked him just the way he was. But he didn't have the courage to ask her to marry him until the day he signed his first studio contract.

By that time he was directing regularly for television and they were married during spring hiatus. Kate quit her job at the commissary. Cliff told her he needed a silent partner—someone to read scripts, make phone calls, write letters, pay bills. She was never happier than she was during those early years of marriage when Cliff's only office was the study where she now slept. But along with his first feature film came an office at the studio with his own secretary. And suddenly Kate felt as if she were out of a job.

Unlike her own mother, Kate had looked forward to living each day. She had been as generous as she dared with money she never really felt belonged to her. She had made their home into a place to which a man could look forward to returning and a child would never want to leave. So how had she ended up living here alone?

198

"You see why I have to sell this house," she suddenly blurted out to Ford. "I feel like a failure here."

"Will you buy another one?" he asked. "There's always a lot to do with a new house. I could help you get it into shape."

"I never want to own anything again," Kate said. "It gives you a false sense of permanence—encourages you to start taking things for granted."

"That's how I felt when I lost the farm," Ford said. "But I can't make Sunny understand. She dreams of putting down roots. I'll tell you something I could never tell her. If it weren't for worrying about the kids, I wouldn't mind living in a car—just traveling wherever the spirit took me, working long enough to buy a meal, then moving on."

"I know what you mean," Kate replied. "When I used to visit Cliff on location, I'd sit in his trailer and I'd imagine the two of us living in it—driving all over the country, stopping in the mountains one night and the desert the next. I thought once Nina was grown, Cliff would stop worrying so much about his career and we could finally start having fun again, the way we did when we first met."

Ford picked up his guitar and began to play. "Would you sing with me?" he asked.

"If I know the words."

"If you don't, I'll teach you." He stretched out along the length of the front seat, his back braced against the door, his long legs extended in front of him, cradling his guitar in his arms. He looked straight ahead into the blackness and sang of rolling hills and clear skies. They were still parked in the garage but Kate could swear they were heading toward the open highway.

Some of the songs were new to Kate but Ford went over the words line by line and if she got lost, he stopped and started over, his strong voice carrying her hesitant soprano along if she faltered. Kate was facing him, leaning against the opposite side of the backseat, but he was looking past her to some distant, half-imagined destination, allowing her to focus on his features without embarrassment. He had not touched her and yet he was inside her and through her and around her. She stopped singing so there would be nothing between his voice and her ear.

Ford was almost whispering the words of the lullaby she had stopped him from singing earlier, laying the melody gently over her like a quilt.

The memory of singing it to Nina when she was a baby now seemed like a souvenir of a trip she would never take again, but sweeter in the remembering than it had been at the time. She remembered Nina as an earnest three-year-old asking her what a memory was. She couldn't grasp Kate's explanation. "But how do you make a memory?" she asked.

"You don't always know when you're doing it," Kate had said, pulling her onto her lap and hugging her close, "but you're making a memory for me right now."

After that day Kate would make a point of calling Nina's attention to anything they did that had the makings of a memory —a pony ride in the park, a day at the ocean, her first kitten.

Cliff had always had his camera ready to record the big events in their life as a family—birthdays, Christmas, trips, school plays, graduation. He was the director so Kate never had any interest in owning a camera. Photographs provided a public record, but once she began to create a game out of making memories for Nina, Kate felt she was teaching her something much more important than how to take a picture—how to stamp a moment in time so it would stay with you and sustain you later.

The lullaby that Ford was singing flooded Kate with images and sensations. She could feel a sweet-smelling baby softening into sleep against her shoulder, making contented little animal noises, and suddenly there was Cliff smiling down at both of them. He loved coming into the room just as Nina was falling asleep. He would sit patiently beside Kate, stroking her hand while she sang to Nina, never taking his eyes off the two of them. Kate would feel so embraced by his attention that as soon as she put Nina into her crib to sleep she would melt into his arms. But she felt more loved while he was watching her rock the baby than she did during the lovemaking that followed.

A sharp pain suddenly pierced her heart and she cried out. It was his own child Cliff used to look at with such love. Cliff was the father but Kate was only the caretaker, not the mother. A hand began to shake her gently and a voice asked what was wrong. Kate opened her eyes. Ford was leaning over the front seat, looking down at her. "I must have been dreaming," she murmured sleepily. "Please don't stop singing," she remembered saying just before she closed her eyes again.

TWENTY

Kate awoke to find herself alone in the car. Her back ached from the half-sitting position in which she had slept and her mouth felt stale and musty. She hadn't emerged from sleep feeling so un-rested and grubby since her childhood summers when she and her mother would travel by train to visit her grandmother, sitting up two nights in a row because they couldn't afford Pullman berths.

How could anybody actually live in a car, she wondered, stepping from the darkened garage into the morning sun. She held her wrist to her eyes, then realized she had left her watch in the study when she undressed the night before. She had no idea from looking at the sun what time it was. It seemed early. If only she could get into the house without running into Sunny. Though she had no reason to feel guilty, she could hardly deny that she had spent the night with Ford in his car.

She moved hesitantly to the kitchen door and opened it. The

smell of coffee greeted her but there was no one in sight. She knew she should have headed straight for the study and closed the door behind her but she couldn't resist filling a mug. A slight movement caught her eye. Sunny was standing at the door to Joe Wayne's room, staring at Kate.

"I went out to the garage to look for something," Kate began lamely, pulling her bathrobe closer around her.

"Did you find him?" Sunny's tone was abrupt and unforgiving.

"What are you talking about?" Kate was determined not to say more than was absolutely necessary.

"Ford never came to bed last night. I woke up early this morning worried about him. I thought maybe he was sleeping in his car so I went out to the garage to check. The only one sleeping there was you."

Trying not to let Sunny turn her into an adversary, Kate said slowly, "I knew something was wrong when he didn't come in the house yesterday after he brought the kids home from school. I couldn't sleep for wondering what had happened. When I went out to the garage to see if his car was gone, he was just sitting in it, playing his guitar. I got in the backseat and fell asleep listening to him sing. That's all that happened. Really. You've got to believe me."

Sunny sighed. "I've been in that car with Ford. You don't have to explain anything to me."

Kate crossed to Sunny, put a hand on each shoulder, and looked her right in the eye. "He didn't touch me. I swear."

Sunny turned away and clutched a kitchen chair as if her feet could no longer be counted on to support the weight of her body. "I wish to God I'd never let him touch me," she said, her voice choked with sobs.

Kate sat down beside her. "What's wrong?"

"I'm pregnant," Sunny said dully.

Kate's eyes filled with tears, imagining the joy of saying those words. But Sunny was spitting anger and pain. "It must have happened at Thanksgiving." She seemed to be talking more to herself than to Kate. "We were both so tired and I guess I

wasn't expecting—" She turned away, embarrassed, then continued in a low voice, "I swore, when things started going bad after
Joe Wayne was born, that I wouldn't have another one till I was
sure we could take care of it."

"What about Marvella?" Kate asked. "I thought she got her
name because you had to wait so long for her."

"Ford named her," Sunny replied in a flat voice. "I was the
one that made the vow, not him. He thought she was a miracle. I
knew she was an accident." She sighed. "Ford believes in miracles. And maybe he's right. God knows the way you opened your
door to us was nothing we had any right to expect. I guess that's
why I don't trust it. Why I wasn't really surprised to see that 'For
Sale' sign staring me in the face last night." Her voice was devoid
of emotion, but her frail shoulders were shaking with sobs.

Kate moved to her and put her arms around her. "Just because I'm selling my house doesn't mean I'm abandoning you. I
don't know what I'm going to be doing myself, but we'll work
something out, I promise. You've got to stop worrying so much—
especially now, with another baby on the way."

But Sunny would not be comforted. "You can't take all of us
on your back. You don't even have a job. You've got to be able to
take care of yourself before you start making promises to other
people. You made the same mistake I did—and now we're both
paying the price."

"What price? What do you mean?" Kate never knew what
Sunny was going to say next. All she could be sure of was that it
would upset her.

"You married someone you thought would take care of you
for the rest of your life, didn't you?"

"Well, I guess that was part of it," Kate had to admit, "but
that didn't mean I didn't love him."

"I didn't say I didn't love Ford. I still do. But I can't risk
letting him back in my bed again." She turned to Kate in despair.
"We can't afford the two kids we've got now. What are we going
to do with another one?"

"Have you told Ford?"

Sunny shook her head. "I wasn't sure myself until this morning, but only one thing makes me that sick." She looked at her watch. "I've got to go to work, but if Ford doesn't show up, I don't know how the kids are going to get to school."

"You go on," said Kate. "I'll drive them. I need to take the Jaguar out anyway. It's just sat in the garage since Cliff left."

Just at that moment Joe Wayne burst out of his bedroom. "The Jaguar!" he shouted with glee. "Oh, boy!"

"I'll be dressed by the time you finish your breakfast," Kate assured him. "Where's Marvella?"

"She's getting dressed," said Sunny. "She had breakfast early —with me." She stood hesitantly at the door. "Well, I guess I'd better go now, or I'll miss my ride."

Kate wished there were something she could say to make Sunny feel a little better about her future. Her whole body was stiff with anxiety. "Try not to worry," Kate said softly, putting her hand on Sunny's arm. "Things are going to work out, you'll see." But Sunny just clenched her lips tightly and left without another word.

Kate dressed quickly. As she opened the study door, she heard shouting coming from the kitchen.

"You're my son and you're going to ride in my car." Kate had never heard Ford so angry. "I will not have a son who is ashamed of his own father."

Joe Wayne came running to Kate as she entered the kitchen. "Tell him, Kate. You said you were going to drive us to school in the Jaguar."

Kate smiled at Ford. "Somebody has got to take the Jaguar out today or the battery will go dead." She took the keys from her purse and handed them to him. "Would you mind? You'd be doing me a big favor."

Ford gave her a hard look. "You want me to drive your husband's car?"

Kate nodded.

"Hooray!" shouted Joe Wayne—and he raced out the door toward the garage.

Ford moved close to Kate. "What would he say if he knew?"

"He's not using it. Why shouldn't you?"

Ford put his hand lightly against the small of her back. "Will you come with me? Make sure I can handle it? I'm not used to such a fancy piece of equipment."

"The more expensive a car, the easier it is to drive. I imagine you'll do better at the wheel of Cliff's car than he would at yours," Kate said with a smile.

"I doubt if he could even get mine started," Ford agreed.

"If I go with you, you'll have to bring me back home," Kate reminded him.

"I know."

"What about Ruth? What time is she expecting you?"

"I told her my hours would have to be my own. I said you came first."

The children did all the talking on the way to school. Joe Wayne ordered his father to stop right in front of the building so everybody could see him getting out of a Jaguar. Marvella waved good-bye and ran into the building. But Joe Wayne stopped beside the driver's door, leaned in the window, and kissed his father. "You can bring your car to get me," he said. "And I won't wait till everybody's left to get in it this time. I promise."

"Way to go, Superman," Ford said, putting a hand around his son's neck and pulling him close for a hug.

Joe Wayne flinched at the reference, then bravely turned his notebook over so the picture showed and marched into school.

"He hasn't kissed me in public since he was six." Ford was grinning happily as he pulled into the traffic.

Sitting beside him, watching the ease with which he maneuvered the car through the early morning traffic, Kate felt as awkward as a teenager on her first date. Ford and his family had been living with her for two weeks now but she had never been alone with him, without the children, until last night. However, in the darkened garage their eyes never met, their hands never touched. They had poured out their separate hurts like strangers who meet on a train, knowing they will probably never see each other again. She looked at Ford and wondered how much of what he had said in the dark he would remember in the daylight.

"Where did you go after I fell asleep last night?" Kate asked shyly.

"There was so much going on inside my head. I had to walk around for a while." Ford kept his eyes on the road. "I didn't dare go back inside the house and risk waking Sunny. She doesn't want any part of me anyway." He paused for a moment as if expecting Kate to protest, but she remained silent. "Then I started wondering about those rooms on top of the garage."

"The original owners built them as servants' quarters but Cliff and I have never had any servants, so we just used the space for storage. I always wanted to redo the rooms into a guest apartment but Cliff hated the idea of people staying overnight."

"Probably because he knew they'd never want to leave." Ford turned to look at Kate. "I spent last night there."

"How did you get in?"

"I looked through that drawer in the kitchen where you keep the extra keys till I found the one I needed."

"I haven't been out there in ages," Kate said. "It must be a mess."

"Anybody who's ever slept in a shelter would think it was a dream come true—a kitchen, a bathroom, a living room, a bedroom—who couldn't be happy with all that?"

Kate turned away from Ford and stared out the window. Tears were running down her cheeks.

He put his hand to her face, tracing the tears. "Did I say something wrong?"

Kate shook her head. "No. I'm just so ashamed to think of those rooms going to waste when there are so many people in this city, in this country, without a roof over their heads. Everyone I know has empty rooms in their house, empty guest cottages, empty garage apartments, not to mention empty summer houses on the ocean or empty weekend cabins in the mountains. I'm ashamed of all of us. How dare we be so selfish?"

"I wasn't trying to make you feel sorry for me," Ford said gently. "I just thought if I cleaned the apartment up, got it into shape, you might be able to sell your house for even more than two million dollars."

Kate looked at him sharply. "How do you know what I'm asking?"

"That fellow the other day said he thought you could get two million easy—more if you were willing to wait. I thought he was kidding but then I looked at some real estate ads. He's right on the money." He gave a low whistle. "When I think how many acres two million dollars would buy in Iowa!"

"When I think how many families you could house and feed for that kind of money!" Kate exclaimed, surprised at her own passion. "It's obscene to think of one family spending that much just on themselves."

Ford was strangely quiet as he pulled the Jaguar into the garage. He walked over to his old car and stood beside it. "I shouldn't have given in to him," he muttered.

"You didn't give in to him," Kate said gently. "It was my idea —driving the Jag."

"I don't like him thinking a car is the measure of a man. I should've stood my ground."

"There's nothing wrong with him seeing that his father knows how to handle all kinds of cars," Kate reassured him. "What you showed him today was that you're the same man no matter what kind of car you're driving. That's a lesson a lot of his classmates may never have the chance to learn."

TWENTY-ONE

"What are we celebrating?" Ford asked, looking curiously at Kate as she brought a glazed ham into the dining room and put it on the table. All Kate had said to any of them was that she was cooking dinner tonight. But when Ford returned from work and saw the table set in the dining room, a centerpiece of fresh flowers and candles waiting to be lit, he went upstairs to shower and change into the clothes Kate had given him for Christmas.

"What's going on?" Sunny had asked suspiciously when she arrived home from the store and found him in the bedroom.

"Kate's gone to a lot of trouble for dinner," he said, avoiding all the other questions waiting to be answered between them. "If she's going to treat us like company, then I guess we ought to act like it."

"I knew this was coming the minute I saw that 'For Sale' sign," Sunny said. "If you think I'm putting on my good suit just to be told we're back on the street, you can guess again."

"Do as you please," said Ford, "but you're not being fair to her."

"Granted you know her better than I do," Sunny said, sitting down on the bed and taking off her shoes.

"What does that mean?"

"I've never spent the night with her."

"She fell asleep in the backseat of my car. Period. End of story."

"Skip it," Sunny said as she flopped back against the pillows and wiggled her toes in the air. "I never knew standing still could be so hard on your feet. I'm not putting on shoes again today for anybody."

At that moment Marvella knocked at the bedroom door. She wore a long dress and fresh flowers were braided into her hair.

"Honey, I'd like to take your picture and send it back to Iowa," Ford exclaimed, giving Marvella a hug.

"And write on the back 'see you soon,'" Sunny muttered.

Marvella crossed to the bed and laid a Mexican caftan and a pair of sandals in front of Sunny. "Kate thought you might like to wear these. So you could take off the clothes you wore to work and be comfortable."

Ford avoided looking at Sunny and took Marvella's hand. "Let's go downstairs and see if we can help with dinner."

"I already helped make a coconut cake for dessert," Marvella announced proudly.

Watching Kate put the food on the table, refusing help from any of them, Ford felt his stomach contract with tension. "What are we celebrating?" he asked again, searching her face for some clue to his future.

"I'm selling this house," Kate announced, passing the basket of rolls to Sunny. Sunny clutched the basket against her chest as if it were a baby. Ford felt the muscles in his throat tighten. He couldn't have made a sound even if he'd known what to say.

"How soon?" Sunny's voice betrayed her fear.

"They want to move in as soon as we get all the papers signed. They've been transferred here from the East, so they're living in a hotel. They didn't even try to bargain—they offered exactly what I was asking."

"We have to leave this house?" Joe Wayne looked from one adult to the other, trying to figure out what was happening.

"I know how much you want a place of your own," Kate said to Sunny. "That's what we're celebrating. I only made one condition for the sale. I said I had a family living here who helped take care of the house. They had to be allowed to live in the apartment over the garage for as long as they liked, rent free, in return for looking after the house and garden."

"What apartment over the garage?" Sunny asked.

"The servants' quarters," Ford said in a low voice.

"It needs some work," Kate continued, "but this way you can pick out the paint and the wallpaper and fix it up just the way you want."

Sunny's face brightened. "Why would you do this for us? You could've lost the sale."

Kate smiled. "They loved the idea of having people around to take care of the house for them—and at no cost. Who wouldn't? I explained you both had other jobs so you'd have to work out your hours, but they said that wouldn't be a problem."

"Why can't we keep living here with you, Kate?" Marvella was about to cry.

Kate patted her hand. "Because I can't afford to keep living in this house without my husband. He paid all the bills."

"You could get a job—like Mama did," Marvella said.

"Even if we all had jobs, we wouldn't make enough money to live in this house. But if I sell it, I'll have more money than I could've made if I'd worked all the years I was married. It doesn't seem fair, but it's a fact."

"But you have to live somewhere, don't you, Kate?" Joe Wayne was trying manfully to come to terms with this puzzling new development.

She nodded. "I'd like to live a lot of different places." Ford was very quiet. Kate could not tell what he was thinking. She quickly began passing the serving platters. "Anyone for seconds?"

Only Sunny took a second helping.

"I don't feel like eating," said Joe Wayne.

"You'll change your mind when you see the coconut cake," Kate promised him. "Why don't you and Marvella help me clear the table, and Ford can take Sunny out and show her the apartment."

"When did you see it, Ford?" Sunny could not hide her surprise.

In reply he grabbed her elbow roughly and steered her out the back door. "Where do you think I slept last night when you told me to stay out of your bed?" he asked as soon as they were out of hearing of the others.

"Any man who would spend the first money he's earned in months on a guitar doesn't need a bed or a house. Or a wife," she added. "Kate said you slept in your car. I had no reason not to believe her."

"What else did she tell you?" he asked, unlocking the door to the garage apartment and climbing the stairs ahead of Sunny.

"She said she came out to check on you and fell asleep in your car. When she woke up this morning, you were gone. She said you didn't touch her."

"Would you have cared if I had?"

But Sunny wasn't listening. A big room with windows overlooking the garden extended in front of her. She began opening doors, looking in closets, going back and forth from the living room to the bedroom. "Do you know how much it costs to rent an apartment like this?" She could not suppress her excitement.

"Several hundred dollars a month for sure," Ford said.

"In Iowa maybe. In Los Angeles you'd be lucky to find an apartment this big, in a nice neighborhood, for a thousand dollars a month. You don't know how hard I looked when we were living at the shelter—the bus rides I took—trying to find a place we could afford. And nothing I saw was anywhere near as nice as this. With you working and me working and us not having to pay rent, maybe we're finally going to be able to dig ourselves out of this hole." She walked to the window and stared back at the big house, past the swimming pool and the citrus orchard and the floodlit garden. "It's funny. I never really felt safe living in her house, having to depend on her for everything, but here we can earn our keep. I'll do the housework at night and on the weekends, and you can take care of the garden and we'll get the kids to help us—" She stopped abruptly. "That's why I can't have another one. You've got to understand."

Ford pushed a chair against a wall and sat down heavily. What was she saying? "A baby?" he whispered, reaching for Sunny. He wanted to hold her in his lap, the way he used to do when they were first married. But she moved across the room and stood with her back against the wall as if protecting herself from a surprise attack. "Why didn't you tell me?"

She shrugged. "I didn't know for sure till today. There's a clinic near where I work. Anybody can walk in and they treat you for free, no questions asked. I can go back there to get rid of it."

Her voice was hard and determined. This was no one Ford knew speaking. "No," he cried out in pain. "It's my baby too— and I want it."

Sunny just shook her head. "We can't take care of the ones we've got. I shouldn't have told you—just gone ahead and done what I had to do—but I didn't want you to hear it from her."

"Her?"

"Kate. I was upset this morning. It all just came spilling out before I had a chance to get my head clear. But now that she knows, you have to know too."

"Too? I'm the father, God damn it!"

"Ford, if we're gonna get ourselves back on our feet, everything has got to change. Nothing can stay the way it was—starting with you and me. I don't want to split up the family—the kids need a father and a mother. It's going to take the two of us together—working as hard as we know how—to make sure Joe Wayne and Marvella grow up right. If I have any strength left over after that, I'm going to use it on myself. I'm not asking anything more from you, and you better not expect anything more from me. I always thought getting married would make life easier. It doesn't—it makes it harder than I ever imagined it could be."

Ford put his head in his hands. Sunny crossed to him and touched his shoulder. "I'm not mad anymore. I was last night, I admit. I guess I was still feeling like you owed me some kind of accounting. You don't. I'm going back in the house now and go to bed. You can come with me if you want—as long as all we do in that bed is sleep. This will be the first night since long before we left the farm that I've been able to fall asleep without being afraid of tomorrow."

Sunny was almost dancing after she saw the garage apartment. She stunned Kate by throwing her arms around her as she was loading the dishwasher and thanking her for everything she had done for them. Then she insisted on washing the rest of the dishes herself, talking nonstop about the curtains she planned to make, the herb garden she wanted to plant in the kitchen window. She called the children into the kitchen while she ate the coconut cake Kate had cut for her and began to describe the apartment. Kate found herself getting caught up in Sunny's enthusiasm. "We'll buy the paint this weekend," Kate promised. "If we all pitch in, we can have it done in a day."

"Can I help paint?" Marvella asked. "I want to use a roller."

"You and Joe Wayne are going to have to help do a lot of things," Sunny said.

"Where will we sleep?" Joe Wayne didn't like change.

Sunny looked at Kate for support. "We could put two daybeds in the living room," Kate suggested.

"Daybeds? I don't want to go to bed in the day," Joe Wayne protested.

"Daybeds are made up to look like couches in the day and you sleep on them at night," Kate explained.

"I like sleeping in my own room—with a television," Joe Wayne said.

"You can take that little set with you, Joe Wayne—wherever you go," Kate assured him. "In fact, you can use any furniture in the house for the apartment. I'm not taking anything with me. All the furnishings are included in the price of the house, but no one has made any inventories. Besides, as long as the furniture is somewhere on the property, I haven't violated the agreement."

"I want to see where we're going to live," Marvella begged.

"It's time for bed," Sunny said, turning on the dishwasher, but then she looked at Kate and softened. "But your dad is still out there, so why don't you and Joe Wayne go give him a good-night kiss." As they headed for the door, she added, "You might take him a piece of this coconut cake—I never tasted anything so good." She put a large slice on a plate.

"I'll carry it," said Marvella. Then she turned to Kate, "Can I tell him I made it all by myself?"

Kate bent down to kiss her. "You tell him whatever you like and I'll stand by you." She stood in the doorway watching the children cross the garden, then turned back to Sunny. "The same goes for you."

Sunny poured herself a glass of milk and sat down at the kitchen table. "Too late. I already told him the truth, the whole truth."

Kate filled a mug with coffee. "You told him you were having a baby?"

Sunny put both hands around the glass of milk and held it so tightly Kate was afraid it would break. "No. I told him I wasn't going to have it." Ignoring the look of pain that clouded Kate's face, she continued, "It's only because of you we've been able to take care of the ones we've got. What would we do with a baby? How could I work?"

I'll have it for you, Kate wanted to scream, but she bit her lip and remained silent. "What did Ford say?" she asked finally.

"He wants it. But it's not his decision. Not this time." She picked up an *Architectural Digest* lying on the table. "Did this just come today?" Kate nodded. Sunny began leafing through it. "You've got a stack of these by your bed. I look at one every night before I fall asleep. I build this house in my mind and I furnish it from the pictures. But tonight when I close my eyes I'm going to be moving into that apartment over the garage."

And where am I going to be? The silent question reverberated in Kate's mind. She seemed to have answers for everyone but herself.

"I've never had a place of my own before," Sunny confided. "I lived with my parents until I married, then I moved to the farm with Ford's family. I've never chosen so much as the color of a wall." She paused, slowly turning the pages of the magazine. "Soft yellow," she said suddenly. "We'll paint the bedroom a soft yellow. Then it will seem like the sun is always shining."

Kate crossed to the kitchen door and looked out. "You don't have to decide right away about the baby," she said, turning back to Sunny.

"What?" Sunny was engrossed in the magazine.

"Once you're settled in the apartment, you may feel differently. I know how hard it is to keep a family together," she said, her voice cracking with her own pain. "Especially when times are bad. I want to help you."

To Kate's surprise, Sunny took her hand and held it against her cheek. "You've done something for me today no one has ever done for me before. Not my parents, not my husband. You've made me feel like I can make it on my own. I don't ever want to need anybody again the way I've needed Ford. If I have this baby, we'll be right back to where we were before—and I'm not going to let that happen. I don't know where I'm going—all I know is it's going to be different than where I've been. If the four of us stick together, I know we can make it. But we can't add another soul. Not now, when things are finally beginning to work out for us." She stood up, then suddenly put her arms around Kate and kissed her. "Thanks, Kate. For everything. Sleep well. See you in the morning."

But Kate did not sleep well. In fact, she did not even try. She put Cliff's most recent film on the VCR but the flickering images could not compete with the movie unreeling inside her head. Cliff and the life they had shared seemed no more real than the story unfolding on the screen in front of her. She felt as if she were in the process of detaching herself from her own past and free-falling through the present toward an indeterminate future. For the first time in her life she was absolutely and terrifyingly alone. She could depend on no one but herself, and now that she had provided for Ford and his family, no one was depending on her. The proceeds from the sale of her house, no matter how she chose to invest them, would keep her from ever being cold or hungry, and now at last she could afford to follow her imagination to any number of possible destinations.

But instead of filling her with elation, the prospect of so much freedom seemed underscored with a sense of loss. She had to admit that in the past two weeks her life had become inextricably interwoven with the combined fate of Ford and his family, each of whom she had grown to love in a different way. She was having a hard time imagining a future that did not include them.

But she had no choice. Since last night, when she fell asleep in his car, things were different between her and Ford. There was the kind of tension that charges the air when a man and woman sense their attraction to each other. And the more they refuse to acknowledge it, the more it colors every exchange between them.

It was clear to Kate that Ford had ceased to feel like a man around his wife, and the more Sunny struggled to become self-sufficient, the shakier his sense of self-esteem grew. With Kate, whom he had never failed, he became the man he had once been, the man who came of age knowing he could have any woman he chose.

But the attraction was mutual. In Ford's presence Kate could forget that her husband had left her for another woman. Without saying a word, Ford let her know that her very presence in a room could change the way a man felt about himself, give him a reason to keep going.

I can't let this happen, Kate said to herself sternly. Every marriage goes through rough times but, deprived of easy alternatives, a man and woman who loved each other in the beginning can usually rediscover their feelings in the end. Ford and Sunny will work things out once they move into the apartment. She had to get out of their lives, leave them alone together.

She'd never traveled. Now that Nina no longer needed a home, this was her chance. Once she'd seen everything she wanted to see, she'd rent an apartment somewhere—maybe in

Boston, near Nina. Even though Kate could no longer claim her as a daughter as confidently as she always had, she hoped they could find a way to be friends.

Yes, that's what I'll do, she thought, walking to the kitchen for a glass of milk. She had to stop drinking coffee at night. It had never kept her awake before, but now she was tense and restless. Maybe she was just getting old. She grimaced at the thought. Five more years and she'd be fifty. If she didn't start traveling now, she'd have to see the world from a wheelchair. How much longer could she count on her health? She'd always taken it for granted. Besides, she wouldn't want to be traveling once the grandchildren started coming. Why was Nina so determined to go to law school? Why couldn't she just marry Adam and settle down? She had hated being an only child and always said she planned to have lots of children. She shouldn't be wasting time. Kate sighed. Growing old wasn't so bad if you could look forward to grandchildren. But what if Nina never married? She was determined to let nothing get in the way of her career. She had no intention of turning out like her mother.

The thought of a future without a home, without a husband, and maybe even without grandchildren flooded Kate with waves of despair. Looking through the kitchen window, she saw the light in the garage apartment still burning. Like the moon pulling the tide, it drew her out of her house, out of her past.

The night air was soft and fragrant. Kate knelt down by the vegetable garden Ford had planted and touched her fingers to the earth to see if any of the seeds had sprouted. Whatever else happened, at least now he would be able to reap his harvest.

She sensed a presence behind her and looked around to see Ford. He was wearing an old pair of jeans cut off at the knees and his chest was bare. Kate was afraid to speak. Her need was so blatant, there was no way to hide it. It was useless to pretend she had left the house for any reason other than the one they both knew.

Kate hid her face in her hands, ashamed her honorable intentions had been so short-lived. Ford began to stroke her hair, raking it with his fingers and watching as it fell back into place.

His hands made delicate furrows the length of her back. Kate abandoned herself to the sensations that were taking possession of her, releasing her from guilt. But then she pulled away from him. "No, Ford, we can't be doing this."

"Don't leave me, Kate," he begged. "You've turned my life around. You can't walk out on me now."

"Once I'm out of your life, you and Sunny will be able to work things out."

He turned away and stood for a long time with his back to her. "That's what that dinner tonight was all about, wasn't it? You were telling me good-bye."

"I was trying," she replied softly. "I didn't take your family into my home so I could break it apart."

He rested his forehead against the live oak tree where Kate had taken refuge on Christmas morning. "You can't break something apart from the outside unless it's already started dying on the inside. Sunny doesn't want me in her bed. She told me that last night and again tonight. I'm not going back to that bedroom again. When I'm with her, I feel like I'm no use to anybody—I'm no good as a husband, no good as a father."

"Don't say that."

"If it weren't true, she wouldn't be afraid to have another one."

"Oh, God, I wish I were the one having the baby," Kate said with a strangled cry. "I wanted so much to have a child by a man who loved me, really loved me—a man who would never, ever leave me." Her body racked with great choking sobs, she sank to the ground and hid her head in her lap. Her pain made Ford forget his own. He gathered her into his arms, gently kissing the top of her head and murmuring soft, comforting words.

"If only we could stay like this forever," Kate said finally, "not hurting anyone."

"Just make me one promise," Ford said.

"I'm not sure I can."

"Don't leave me." He hesitated, then amended his plea. "Don't leave us."

"I'm not going to come between you and your family. That's

why I'm selling the house—so I can help you, all of you, without getting mixed up in your lives. You and Sunny need to be by yourselves for a while."

"Why do people always think being by themselves will help a man and a woman get along better? There's nothing harder than being alone together. When a building gets shaky, you reinforce it, you don't start stripping it. The only way Sunny and I have any hope of putting the pieces back together again is with your help. Now come upstairs and see what I've done to the apartment."

At the top of the stairs Kate exclaimed, "But what have you been doing here?" A large area of the scarred linoleum that covered the floor had been removed, exposing a parquet wood surface underneath. "Who would cover such a beautiful wooden floor with linoleum?"

"Maybe they thought it was too good for the servants," Ford said. He knelt down and pulled back a strip of linoleum to reveal a thick layer of tarlike substance covering the wood floor.

"How did you get rid of that stuff?"

"Turpentine. I had a can in the back of my car. I've been working all night just to clean that square."

"It's going to take a lot of work to get this place ready," Kate said.

"You can't know what it means that my family is finally going to have a place they can count on staying. I wish there were some way I could repay you."

"Look at the work you're putting into this place," Kate said. "You're transforming it." She walked around the room. "How would you like to go into business with me?"

"Doing what?"

"I've never had any money of my own, but when I sell this house I'm going to have so much it scares me. I've been awake all night trying to decide what I'm going to do with it."

Ford smiled. "And?"

"The answer just came to me. The two million dollars I'm going to make didn't come from anything I've done. This house made that money for me, so the best thing I can do with it is put it right back into another one."

"You're going to buy another house?"

"Not a house like this one. An old, neglected house in a rundown neighborhood. I'll buy it and you can fix it up, then we can sell it and split the profits."

Ford spoke quietly. "There is no work I'd rather do than take an old house and remind it of what it was when it was first built —of everything it started out to be."

Kate's eyes filled with tears as she realized he was talking about himself.

TWENTY-TWO

Kate had stopped in the driveway to wipe the paint from her hands when she saw the taxi passing the house. A taxi on a residential street in Los Angeles looked as alien as a rickshaw. She wondered briefly who was going where, but her mind was much too occupied by the activity taking place in her own backyard to speculate for long.

They were spending Saturday painting the apartment. Kate had bought enough rollers and brushes so everybody in the family could pitch in. Sunny took charge of the kitchen, Ford kept an eye on the children while they painted the living room, and Kate worked alone in the bedroom, taking a bittersweet pleasure in making the room clean and ready for Ford and Sunny to share.

It was good to be doing something that projected her thoughts into the future. She had been spending the evenings going through her personal possessions, all the things she was not selling with the house, deciding what she could give away and what she was willing to pay to put in storage. She had no idea where she was going to go, but the idea of living in temporary quarters—a place that held no memories and made no claims on her future—was oddly liberating.

Each day the stack of things she could not live without—which in the beginning filled half a dozen footlockers—grew smaller. She was like a plane abandoning ballast so it could keep climbing. Finally she was down to three suitcases in the study closet, filled with clothes, scrapbooks, her few pieces of jewelry, and a small painting she and Cliff had bought in Carmel on their first trip together. She knew she was being premature—the house couldn't even go into escrow until Cliff had signed the papers—but somehow it seemed important to be prepared, like a refugee from a war zone, for imminent departure.

Meanwhile, during the past week she had begun to look for a house to buy—one that she and Ford together could make new. She relished the prospect of using the profits from the house where her marriage with Cliff had come apart to keep Ford and his family together and in the process to provide not only a living but a reason for living—for herself as well as for Ford.

The idea of reclaiming space that was not being used or used to its full potential excited Kate. She had never thought of herself as particularly creative. Cliff was the artist—the one who had provided a home for them and made a reputation for himself by using his imagination. But being creative, Kate realized now, didn't necessarily involve a product—a painting, a play, a film. It could just mean thinking of a new way of doing something, a different way of living one's life.

From the day Ford had first appeared in front of her house, Kate had experienced the exhilaration of making choices she had never made before—choices she had never heard of anyone else making, for that matter. There were no patterns, no preconceived rules, for the way she was living now. Trying to make the best possible use of what she had been given seemed to her as great a challenge as writing a book or making a movie. For the first time in her life, she felt as much an artist as Cliff. It was a heady feeling.

Kate was startled by a noise, as if someone had overheard her thoughts. She crossed the entrance hall just as a key turned in the lock. Kate's heart stopped. It had to be Cliff. Who else had a key to the house? Instead of signing the papers and expressing them back to her as she had asked, he was bringing them himself. She hurried to the door just as Nina, carrying an overnight bag, stepped into the house.

"Nina, what are you doing here?"

"Just the question I flew across the country to ask you."

Kate checked the impulse to kiss her daughter. "I'm a mess," she said quickly, glancing down at her paint-stained clothes. "Why don't you come to the kitchen? I'm making sandwiches for lunch."

"Are you having a party?" Nina asked in surprise. She had never known her mother not to drop everything when she appeared.

"No, just the family," Kate said, fighting the panic that always seemed to overwhelm her when Nina started asking questions. She knew she wasn't making sense. Why did her daughter always put her on the defensive? Her daughter . . . No. Nina was Cliff's daughter, connected to Kate only by a childhood.

"What family?" Nina's voice tugged at the tangled skein of her thoughts. It was inevitable that this relentlessly logical child she had raised would grow up to be a lawyer, Kate thought. Once Nina sensed that parental authority could be challenged by cold logic, Kate had given up trying to win an argument with her.

"I felt guilty living in this big house all by myself, so I'm sharing it with a family who didn't have anywhere else to go." The rightness of what she was doing reinforced Kate's confidence. The panic began to ebb. Her words seemed to resonate with moral certainty.

"When did you acquire this concern for the homeless?" There was a defensive note in Nina's voice that was new to Kate.

"The first time I saw a picture of a family living in their car. Before that, I thought people who slept on the street were there because they didn't want to work—you know, drunks, bums— people who'd walked out on their families, turned their back on society. I didn't have much sympathy for them. But a whole family forced to live in a broken-down car, a husband and wife willing to take any job but still not able to make enough money to pay the rent, innocent children dragged from school to school while their parents looked for work, no safe place to sleep at night—well, it changed the way I felt completely." Kate was busy spreading sandwiches as she talked. She handed Nina a knife and nodded to her to continue while she arranged fruit and cookies on a platter.

Nina stared at her, then finally took off her suit jacket, rolled up the sleeves of her silk blouse, and went to work. "So you went out and found that family in the picture and brought them here?"

Kate shook her head. "No, I'm just like everybody else. I thought how shocking, then threw away the paper, went off to the grocery store, and filled my cart. So much for my concern for the homeless. But that picture stayed in my head—then on Christmas Eve I saw this man. His car had broken down in front of our house." And she told Nina the whole story.

"So that's what you did with the turkey." Nina smiled. "But how can you sell the house? Where will they go?"

"They'll live in the garage apartment. I made it a condition of the sale. That's why we're working so hard this weekend to get it painted so they can move in." She stopped abruptly and stared at Nina. "How did you know I was selling the house?"

"Don't you think I have a right to know? I live here too."

"Not that I've noticed. One night at Christmas doesn't really count."

"Are you angry about that? Why didn't you say something?"

"I'm angry about a lot of things. I hardly know where to start."

Nina reached to touch her arm but Kate pulled away and began rolling lemons on the cutting board, then halving them with a knife and squeezing them by hand into a glass pitcher. "You have a right to be angry," Nina said softly. "Daddy flew to Boston last week after you sent him the papers for the house. He told me everything."

"I doubt it."

"He thinks you're selling the house to punish him."

Ignoring the accusation, Kate turned eagerly to Nina. "Did he sign the papers? Did you bring them with you?"

Nina shook her head. "He wants to talk to you first."

Kate was determined not to cry. She squeezed the lemons fiercely. "I don't want to hear anything else. Damn it, he said on Christmas morning he was giving me full title to the house. He said it was the least he could do. I didn't ask—he offered. But I'm holding him to it. I don't want alimony—I can support myself. I don't want a percentage of any of his pictures—but this house is all I have to show for twenty-five years of marriage. He may have broken every other promise he ever made me, but I'm going to see that he keeps this one." She stopped finally, out of breath, and stared at Nina. "Do you think I'm being unfair?"

"No," Nina said. "Speaking as a lawyer, I would have to say you're being more than fair. But I'm still your daughter too, you know." She picked up a lemon and held it against her face, breathing in its sharp fragrance. "You know what I miss most about California—being able to walk out the back door and pick a lemon off my own tree." Moving to the window, she looked into the garden. "This is such a wonderful house. Our whole life as a family is here—written on these walls. How can you even think about selling?"

"It's not a house that makes a family. It's people who love each other and want to live together." Kate could not stop the tears from coming.

Nina took her in her arms. "Daddy will always care about you. He knows you're safe and comfortable here. That's why he wants you to keep the house."

Kate pulled away angrily. "He doesn't give a damn about me. He just wants to think that if things don't work out where he is, he can always come home. Well, he can't. He destroyed his home at Christmas. I have nothing to show for the marriage, but at least I can turn a profit on the house."

Nina shrugged. "We'll talk about it some more later. Right now I'm going to my room to unpack and change clothes. I think

I'll lie down for a while. I've been up since before dawn—Boston time."

She started toward the front hall. Kate hurried after her. "Why don't you just stretch out on the couch in the study? No one will disturb you there."

Nina picked up her suitcase and started up the stairs. "Why wouldn't I go to my own room?"

"Because Marvella is using it now."

"Marvella? Who's Marvella?"

"Ford and Sunny's daughter—she's six."

"You gave her my room?"

"Don't act so outraged. You weren't using it. Besides, I gave Ford and Sunny mine. I've moved into the study, but you can have it while you're here. I'll sleep on the couch in the living room. How long are you planning to stay?"

"I have to be back tomorrow. I was planning to stay overnight, but I think I'll take the red eye instead," she said, the sharp edges of her voice cutting any further communication between them.

Kate refused to be put on the defensive. "Do you really expect me to keep your room empty on the off-chance you'll come flying home for an overnight stay?"

"It's your house. You've made that clear enough to everybody. Fill the rooms to your heart's content. I'm going to call Adam and tell him he can take me to dinner." And she disappeared into the study, slamming the door behind her.

Kate decided to serve lunch by the pool. There was so much talk about the apartment and what they were going to do next, no one seemed to notice that Kate said almost nothing.

Afterward Joe Wayne and Marvella went for a swim while Sunny stretched out on a lounge chair in the shade. Kate kept looking anxiously back toward the house, waiting for Nina to make an appearance, but there was no sign of her. Finally she began loading a tray with the lunch dishes.

"Let me carry that for you," Ford insisted. Sunny started to get up from her chair, but Kate motioned to her to stay where she was, adding that someone needed to keep an eye on the children. Sunny sank back gratefully against the pillows.

"Is something wrong?" Ford asked when they were alone in the kitchen. Kate took the tray and started loading the dishwasher.

"It's my daughter," she said. "She's always getting on me for not standing up for myself, but as soon as I do, she walks out in a huff."

Ford looked confused. "Your daughter? Is she here?"

Kate nodded.

He smiled. "Then you haven't lost her after all?"

"I'm not so sure about that. She's here to try to talk me out of selling the house."

"Are you having second thoughts?" Ford looked troubled.

"Absolutely not. I'm more determined than ever to go ahead with it."

"It's not just because of us, is it?" Ford was searching her face anxiously. "I mean your own family has got to come first."

Kate reached for his hand. "You're part of my family now—you and Sunny and Joe Wayne and Marvella and—" She broke off, thinking of the baby Sunny was so determined not to have. Suddenly she heard a noise and, releasing his hand, turned to see Nina entering the kitchen.

"Ford, I'd like you to meet my daughter Nina."

He turned and awkwardly extended his hand. "Pleased to meet you."

Nina gave him an appraising look. "I hope you're enjoying your stay," she said in a flat tone, devoid of nuance.

"Your mother saved my life," he replied, his eyes enveloping Kate.

"Did you reach Adam?" Kate asked, anxious to change the subject.

"I'd better get back to work." Ford seemed grateful for an excuse to leave.

Avoiding Kate's eyes, Nina made a pretense of looking through her purse. "I've called a taxi to take me to the airport. I was able to get a reservation on the five o'clock flight."

"But you just got here," Kate protested. "Can't you at least stay for dinner?"

"I've said what I came to say. I promised Daddy I'd try to get you to change your mind. But you're not the same person you were at Christmas."

"Thank you," said Kate. She took a tentative step in Nina's direction. "Can you honestly say you're sorry? I'm not."

Nina tilted her head. She reminded Kate of Cliff when he was trying to frame a shot, looking for just the right camera angle. How could she have failed to see the resemblance all these years? They had the same dispassionate eye, always at a safe distance from whatever drama was taking place. What was Nina saying now? She used to feel she could count on Kate. But no longer.

"You're just like your father." The words came hissing out of Kate. "Thinking you can shelve people when you don't need them, then find them right where you left them when you return."

To her surprise Nina began to cry. "You sound like Adam," she said. "He told me at Christmas he wanted more than I seemed able to give. He said the next time I came home he might not be here waiting."

Kate interrupted. "At Christmas? He told you that at Christmas?"

Nina looked at her curiously. "What does it matter *when* he told me? The point is, it wasn't an idle threat. When I called his house just now, his mother said he was away for the weekend. She wouldn't say where he'd gone—or with whom. That woman has never liked me."

"Every mother wants her child to be loved unconditionally," Kate said. "That's what I've always loved about Adam—how much he loves you, so much more than you love him. Who can blame his mother for wanting you to feel the same way?" She laughed. "Too bad Cliff's mother died before we could meet. She would've been crazy about me."

Nina was pacing the room, apparently oblivious to what Kate was saying. But suddenly she wheeled around to confront her. "How dare you say Adam loves me more than I love him! How can you possibly know what I'm feeling inside?"

"I can't. I can only judge you by your actions—just like you judge me. It hurt me for Adam to see the way you were taking him for granted. So I told him how I felt."

"You told him how *you* felt? What business was it of yours?"

For once Nina was not putting her on the defensive. The words came easily to Kate. "I found myself identifying with him. I thought maybe I could help him avoid making the same mistake I did."

"And what mistake was that?" Nina picked up a dish towel and began twisting it without realizing what she was doing.

"Forgiving too much. Asking too little."

"I can't believe this. You've never interfered in my life."

"You've been telling me for years I should speak out when something bothers me. You're right. I've felt a lot better since I started taking your advice."

"When did this conversation with Adam take place?"

"Last week. Over dinner."

"You took him to dinner and told him to dump me?"

"No. He took me. He even ordered champagne—so we could toast a new year."

Nina threw the dish towel angrily to the floor. "No wonder you're selling this house. You've made it impossible for anyone to live with you."

Kate stared at her. "Why has it taken me so long to see how alike you and Cliff are? You both just expect me to sit back and take whatever you're dishing out. Well, no more! You can tell him that every day he waits to sign those papers is going to cost him. I wasn't even that anxious to get a divorce, but I'm calling my lawyer in the morning."

Nina's voice softened. "Why can't you just admit how angry you are at him and stop taking it out on me? He and I are not the same person. And I hate him for the way he hurt you. I mean, to tell you on Christmas Eve that he was in love with another woman . . ." Her voice trailed off helplessly.

"To *tell* me? It wasn't the telling that hurt, it was the doing!"

Kate felt as if she were seeing Nina clearly for the first time. "So what's his name?" she asked suddenly.

"Who?" Nina looked at her watch. All she wanted was to get back to the safety of her studio apartment—a continent away from this unexpected inquisition.

"The boy in Boston."

"You mean Roger?" The words were out of her mouth before Nina realized she'd been trapped.

Kate's eyes were drilling into her. "It wasn't work keeping you in Boston over Christmas, was it? But you didn't want to hurt Adam by telling him there was someone else."

"I'm not sure I'm in love with him." Nina walked to the window to avoid facing Kate. "I mean any more than I'm in love with Adam."

"You don't want to choose, do you?" There was a fury building inside Kate. "You want to keep all your options open—no matter what the cost to anyone else. The rest of the world can keep their lives on hold to suit your convenience. You are exactly like your father. No wonder he sent you to plead his case. Well, it's no use. I'm going ahead with this sale. I need the money to make a life for myself. And as for Adam, I hope he's having a wonderful weekend somewhere, with a beautiful girl in his bed, someone who will love him as much as he loves her."

Nina suddenly lunged forward and struck Kate across the mouth. "Why are you doing this to me? I didn't leave you, your husband did."

"You're his daughter," Kate cried, shaking Nina by the shoulders, "and I hate how much of him I see in you."

"Why do you keep saying that? I'm no more his daughter than I am yours. I don't belong to anyone. I'm adopted—did you forget?"

"Only by me. It turns out I'm the one who doesn't belong to anyone." Kate sank into a chair.

"Only by you? What do you mean?"

"I mean I'm the only one who did any adopting."

"But I thought—"

"So did I. Until a week ago. I found the papers locked in his desk. That's what comes of sleeping in his study." Kate hid her face in her hands, all passion spent.

Nina moved to the kitchen door and stood with her hand on the knob, locking and unlocking the door as if it led to a past she was afraid to face. Finally, with her back to Kate, she asked in a low voice, "If he's my father, my only father, then who's my mother?"

"He's with her now." Kate's voice was cracking with pain. "She was his first love, long ago, before he left Canada."

"He told me that much. Why didn't he tell me the rest?" Nina moved to Kate and stood behind her, her hands on her shoulders.

"He doesn't know I know. I guess he was trying to leave me something," Kate said, staring straight ahead, afraid to respond to Nina's touch and reveal how much she still needed her. "So now you know," she continued finally. "I have to accept the fact that whatever we had here—the three of us—is over now. Why should I keep this house when I no longer have a family?"

A loud honking outside the house provided the only answer to her question.

Nina started toward the door. "There's my taxi."

Kate sat in silence—already alone in her mind. Nina suddenly ran back to her. "Come with me."

"What?" Kate turned to her in surprise, not sure she had heard her correctly.

"Back to Boston. Your suitcases are already packed. I saw them in the study." Then Nina reached for her hand and began to pull her toward the door.

"Why? Why would you want me?"

"I felt for a terrible moment just now that I'd lost you from my life. It was like falling into some kind of black hole. I'm not going to let that happen. I don't care who gave birth to me. You're my mother and I need you." She paused, fast-forwarding childhood memories through her mind. Suddenly she laughed softly. "Remember when I was six and I decided to give a party all by myself. I wouldn't let you write out invitations or call the other mothers or anything. I told my six best friends at school to come to my house at noon on Saturday."

Kate smiled at the memory. "You wouldn't even let me help you make the sandwiches—you were so determined to do everything yourself."

"By eleven thirty I was sitting by the front door in my best dress waiting for everybody to come. At twelve thirty I was still sitting there—all by myself. Finally my least favorite friend showed up."

"Only because I went next door and took her by the hand."

"I never knew that," Nina said.

"Of course not. I snuck out the back door."

"What was her excuse?"

"She'd forgotten."

Nina sighed. "I never knew what happened to the others. They'd probably forgotten too—or at least forgotten to tell their mothers."

"I always felt it was my fault," Kate said. "I should've protected you, called behind your back. At that age nobody takes an invitation seriously unless it comes from a mother. But you were so brave. You came upstairs to the bedroom and invited me to come to the party and there we sat, the three of us, eating honey and raisin sandwiches—"

"My own invention."

"And drinking chocolate milk."

"Then you saved the day," Nina remembered. "You said, 'Aren't we lucky that there are just the three of us, because I couldn't have taken everybody to Disneyland.' "

The taxi honked again. "I'm going to tell him to wait while you get ready," Nina said. And she was out the door.

Kate was in the study, looking through the clothes in the closet, when Nina dashed into the room. "Hurry and change. I'm so happy you're coming with me!"

Kate turned to face her, closing the closet door behind her. "I actually got as far as choosing what I'd wear on the plane . . ."

"You're going to love Boston. There are so many places I want to show you."

"And I can't wait to see them. You don't know how much it means to me that you asked me. But I can't come with you today. I'm needed here. Once I'm on my own, though, I may just surprise you and show up some time without being asked. I plan to live the second half of my life a lot differently than I've lived the first half."

Nina's eyes were filled with concern. "But what will you do when you sell the house? Where will you go?"

"There was a time, not that many weeks ago, in fact, when that question would have terrified me. But now I like not knowing."

"When you decide, will you let me know?" Nina asked, giving her a hug. "A daughter deserves a forwarding address, don't you think?"

Kate held her close. "I love you, darling. And I love you for caring what happens to me."

"I'm going to tell Daddy to sign the papers and send them back to you by overnight express," Nina said as she picked up her suitcase. "He owes you a house. At the very least."

Kate walked with her to the front door. As she opened it, Nina suddenly leaned over and kissed her on the cheek. "I love you, Mother," she said softly. "And there's as much of you in me as there is of him. I've just been afraid to show it."

TWENTY-THREE

On an impulse Kate unplugged the Cuisinart from her kitchen counter and, wrapping the cord around the base, walked across the garden and up the stairs to the garage apartment. This is ridiculous, she thought to herself. Most people live their whole lives without a Cuisinart. It took me years to stop being afraid of it and start depending on it. But something in Kate rebelled against admitting any inherent differences between her and Sunny. They were alike in every way that mattered. Giving her the Cuisinart seemed to be a way of showing how she felt.

"Here," she said, presenting it to Sunny, who was busy arranging cooking utensils in the kitchen shelves. "A housewarming present. There's a cookbook that goes with it. I'll find it for you."

"But everything in this apartment is a present from you," Sunny protested. "You shouldn't give us anything else. Besides, you don't have another one." Kate was pleased to see that Sunny found nothing inappropriate about the gift.

"I don't see that much cooking in my future." Kate smiled. "At least not the kind of cooking I used to do—when we gave dinner parties."

"I never gave a dinner party," Sunny said. "I'd be scared to death cooking for anybody but family."

"I was too—always," Kate confessed. "I used to have nightmares that my living room was filled with people who had come for dinner and I had nothing to serve them."

"I have nightmares about not being able to feed people too," said Sunny, "but I thought it came from not having enough money to buy groceries." Surveying the well-stocked kitchen, she smiled with satisfaction. "I can't wait to start cooking dinner in here. I should've gone with Ford and the kids to get the groceries. They'll never remember everything."

"Why don't we surprise them and see if we can get the bed assembled while they're gone," Kate suggested. "We'll show Ford that women are not so helpless."

Sunny followed Kate into the bedroom. All the separate parts of the canopy bed were lying spread out on the floor. Kate and Sunny stared helplessly at the curved and polished pieces of wood that resembled abandoned ribs. Kate began to laugh. "Now I know how Noah felt! I'd have a better chance of building an ark than putting this bed back together."

Sunny knelt on the floor, trying to figure out how the various pieces fit. "I bet you're sorry you let us move it out here."

Kate shook her head. "No, I'm not sorry about anything. I'm not even sorry I'm sleeping alone. I don't want to go back to the way everything was before. I feel like such a failure in that bedroom"—she paused, then added in a low voice—"in that bed. As long as I'm on the couch in the study, I feel like a guest in my own house. Nothing is expected of me." She suddenly pointed to the headboard. "Look, here are all the pieces for the frame—and all four posters. We can put that much together, I know. Then Ford can help us with the canopy."

Kate and Sunny struggled wordlessly with the heavy pieces of wood until they had assembled the frame and fitted in the slats. They tugged the mattress into place atop the box springs, then Kate stepped back to admire their efforts with a sigh of satisfaction. "At least now you have somewhere to sleep tonight. That canopy is just for looks."

"But it makes me feel so safe," Sunny confided. "It's like having an extra roof over my head." She picked up a curved wooden rib and held it like a bow. It was as tall as she was.

"Wait a minute," Kate said with excitement. "Now I see how to do it." And she and Sunny lifted and fitted the pieces of wood until the canopy had been miraculously re-created, complete with floral covering.

"I never had matching anything in my life." Sunny had climbed on a chair to hang the curtains on the rod Ford had nailed in place the night before. Their bright floral pattern matched the canopy and the bedspread.

"That's why it didn't make sense to leave the curtains in the bedroom when the bed was here," Kate said spreading a fitted sheet over the mattress.

"You haven't just given us your bed, you've given us your whole room," Sunny said, looking at the burl desk and the cane-back bentwood rocking chair.

"I want you and Ford to be happy," Kate said in a low voice as she continued to make the bed, fluffing the comforter until it settled lightly as a cloud over the smooth white sheets.

"He hasn't been in that bed since he brought home that guitar and I told him about the baby," Sunny said, continuing to hang the curtains. Her back was to Kate and her voice was muffled by the heavy folds of material, but Kate could hear every word. "He's been working out here till late every night. He took one of those old sleeping bags out of the back of the car. I found it just now in a closet. I guess he spread it on the floor up here. I thought maybe he'd been sleeping in the car."

"So did I," Kate whispered, not daring to confess that she fell asleep with the study door open, listening for Ford to come in the house. But for the past week, once dinner was over and he'd told his children good night, he'd go to the garage apartment to work and, except for a glimpse of him as he backed his car out the driveway to take the children to school, Kate would not see him again till dinnertime.

"I don't want to lose him," Sunny said, climbing down from the chair and sitting on the edge of the bed. She picked up a pillow and, holding one end tucked under her chin, shimmied it into a pillowcase. Then she began thumping it into shape as she talked. "But I don't want to go back any more than you do. I can't depend on him to look after me, but if I have this baby, I won't have any choice. I won't be able to take care of myself."

"What about me?" Kate asked, hugging a pillow to her chest to keep her hands from trembling. "Would you trust me to take care of the baby?"

"You? Take my baby?" Sunny began to cradle her pillow protectively in her arms.

"Well, not take it exactly. That is, unless you wanted to be completely free of any responsibility for it."

"There's only one way I can be completely free of it—and that's not to have it," Sunny said flatly.

"But what if I was willing to do all the work? And pay all the expenses?" The words were tumbling out of Kate as a plan began to take shape in her mind. She hurried to say everything she was thinking before Sunny could abort the idea.

"And what would I have to do?"

"Nothing. Just not stop what's already happened."

"Then whose baby would it be?"

"It would belong to you and Ford—and to me."

Sunny looked at Kate as if she were a child with no concept of reality. "How could a baby belong to three people?"

"Just because it takes two people to conceive a baby is no guarantee there will be two people around to take care of it. A lot of babies have to settle for only one. What I'm suggesting is three times better than that." Kate sat down on the bed beside Sunny. "Why is it so hard for you to trust me?"

Sunny looked away. "Because I don't understand what you want." There was a long pause before she blurted out, "It's Ford, isn't it? You're in love with him. You want his baby."

"I could be in love with him," Kate admitted. "In another

time. In another place. He's a fine man. But I can't separate Ford from his family. Not even in my own mind. I love all of you." Kate walked to the window and looked across the garden to her house. She seemed to be speaking to another part of herself. "So many things can pull a man and a woman apart, but a baby can put everything back together again, at least for a while . . ." Her voice trailed off as she followed her memories into the past.

The summer Nina was five, Kate had made up her mind to divorce Cliff. He was out of work and irrational about money. Without even consulting her, he had canceled their plans for a vacation in Laguna at the beach. And yet when Kate asked to see the checkbook, he refused to show it to her, saying as long as he was the one who earned the money, he was the one who would decide what they could and could not afford. He slammed out the front door and she packed her suitcase.

When Nina saw her packing, she thought they were going to the beach after all. In great excitement she ran into her bedroom and filled a shopping bag with her favorite toys.

Cliff returned home just as Kate was loading her suitcase into the taxi. "Daddy," Nina cried, throwing herself into his arms. "We almost had to go on our vacation by ourselves, but now you can come with us."

"Where do you think you're going?" he asked a tight-lipped Kate.

"To the ocean. To see the waves," Nina answered for her. Then she tugged at his sleeve. "Daddy, does the ocean have arms?"

"No, sweetheart," he said, "the ocean is nothing but water. Boats sail in it and people swim in it."

"Then how can it wave?" she asked earnestly.

Even Kate had to laugh. Cliff reached for her quickly, before her mood could change. "I guess we'll just have to show you," he said to Nina. Then he took the suitcase from the taxi and tipped the driver five dollars, saying there had been a change in plans.

"I never thought you'd go on a vacation without me," he said to Kate as they drove through the winding curves of Laguna Canyon down to the Pacific. "Thank God something made me turn around in time. I would never have forgiven myself if I hadn't been with you to see Nina waving at the ocean and waiting for it to wave back."

Kate just smiled and allowed him to apologize that night in bed, where he could always find the right words. She vowed never to tell him that far from going on vacation, she and Nina had been headed home to her mother, who had retired to San Diego.

"For how long?" Sunny demanded harshly, jolting Kate back into the present.

"What do you mean?"

"A baby can put everything back together again for how long? I'll tell you—until it starts crying to be fed." Her eyes clouded with pain. "There was a woman across the hall from us at the shelter with a brand-new baby—a boy. I never heard a baby cry like that. And sometimes late at night, I'd hear her cry along with it. I'm not going to let that happen to me."

"I wouldn't let it happen to you, I promise," Kate said. "Just think about it, please. I can't have any children of my own, and at my age and without a husband I wouldn't be allowed to adopt one."

"So which do you really want? My husband or my baby?"

"I don't want anything for myself. I'm just trying to help you keep what you've already got."

The sound of Ford's car pulling into the garage put an end to the discussion.

"I'm sorry. I was wrong to get in the middle of this," Kate said quickly to Sunny. "It's between you and Ford. But finally, you're the only one who has the right to decide. I won't say anything else about it—but I'm here to help if you need me."

"Need you for what?" Ford came bounding up the stairs, followed by Joe Wayne and Marvella, each carrying a large box of pizza.

"Dad let us each pick out a pizza," Joe Wayne announced proudly.

"Because we couldn't decide," Marvella explained.

"I said thick crust and she kept saying thin." Joe Wayne

glared at Marvella. "If I'd said thin, she would've said thick. She just wants to be different."

"You kids sure are getting choosy." Sunny shook her head in dismay. "Two weeks ago I didn't know there was but one kind of pizza. And now we've got two big boxes. How much did that cost, Ford? I thought you were just going to buy groceries. I was all set to cook supper."

"We were too hungry to wait, weren't we, Dad?" Joe Wayne had learned to jump on the first sparks of an argument between his parents.

"Besides, you've been working since dawn scrubbing shelves and washing windows and getting this place ready for us to live in," Ford said gently. "You shouldn't have to cook dinner on top of all that. You've got to look after yourself, honey," he said with a pleading look that Kate wished she hadn't seen.

"I am looking after myself," Sunny said. "I'm not going to take on any more than I can handle."

"That's good," Ford said gently. "You're looking awful tired."

"I'm going to bed right after I have a piece of pizza," Sunny said.

"Here, Mama," said Joe Wayne, shoving his box in front of her. "You like thick crust, don't you?"

Marvella's lip trembled. "I want Mama to have a piece of my pizza."

Sunny opened the drop-leaf table by the window and took five plates from the kitchen cabinet. "I was planning to have one of each. What about you, Kate?"

"Me too," she said, smiling at Sunny. "If you're sure there's enough to go around."

"More than enough," Ford assured her. "We were counting on you to eat with us."

"Yeah, that's the only reason we got to order two," Marvella said.

"So if it weren't for Kate, we wouldn't have a choice," Sunny said as a funny little smile played on her lips. The tension seemed to have drained from her body, leaving her relaxed and calm.

Ford saw the look she exchanged with Kate. He didn't know

what it meant. "I'll get the bed set up so you can go to sleep as soon as you finish eating," he said, brushing the back of Sunny's neck with his fingertips. "You need your rest."

Sunny picked up her plate in one hand and his plate in the other and followed him into the bedroom.

"Who did all this?" he exclaimed, staring in surprise at the canopy-covered bed and the newly hung curtains.

"Kate and I figured it out together."

"Well, I guess the two of you can manage just fine on your own." Smiling, he took his plate and started back into the other room.

Sunny put her hand on his arm to stop him. "You must be as tired as I am, Ford," she said softly, pushing the door closed with her foot.

"I guess we won't know till we're both lying down," he said with a playful twinkle in his eye. "But what about the kids?" He looked toward the other room.

"Kate will look after them," Sunny said. "She was telling me again today how much she loves children."

TWENTY-FOUR

Kate deliberately chose to sleep late the next morning. She dreaded waking up in the house alone. The sound of Ford's car backing out of the driveway to take the children to school made its way into her dream, but in her mind's eye she saw the whole family piled into the old car, their suitcases strapped to the top. "Where are you going?" she cried out, running to the window.

"Back to Iowa," Ford called, waving cheerfully.

"Please don't go," she sobbed. "Don't leave me here alone." The only response was Homer barking good-bye as the sound of the car engine disappeared into the distance. Kate clutched her pillow in despair. However, the barking continued, finally rousing her from her sleep.

Half awake, she stumbled into the kitchen, stopping at the thermostat to turn up the central heating. The temperature must have dropped twenty degrees overnight. Homer was running around in circles in the backyard, barking loudly. Kate opened the kitchen door and called to him. He came bounding into the house, almost knocking her to the floor in his eagerness for human companionship. Kate knelt down and put her arms around him. He licked her face gratefully. "You don't like being left alone here any more than I do, do you, boy?" she crooned, rubbing behind his ears.

It was the first morning since Ford and Sunny had arrived that Kate had the kitchen to herself. Usually Sunny was the first one up. Kate would find the coffee made and the children eating breakfast while Sunny packed their lunches for school. She missed their talk. A house without children was an empty shell. If only Sunny would decide to have that baby and let Kate share in its upbringing. You didn't have to give birth to a child to make it part of your life. She thought of Nina and smiled. She felt closer to her now than she had in years. They had survived being mother and daughter to become friends—and blood ties had nothing to do with it.

The doorbell interrupted her thoughts. She pulled her robe around her and peered cautiously through the living room window. "Ruth!" she exclaimed, throwing open the front door. "I'm so happy to see you. Come in the kitchen. I was just making coffee."

Surprised at her reception, Ruth followed Kate. "I was beginning to wonder if I was ever going to see you again. Every time I call, you're on the run and you're never free to have dinner."

"We've been working night and day—all of us—getting the apartment ready."

"Then you're not angry at me?" Ruth stood hesitantly in the doorway.

Turning on the coffee maker, Kate looked at Ruth in astonishment. "Angry at you? Why?"

"For taking Ford away from you?"

Kate laughed. "You haven't taken him away from me. You've given him a job. I'm as grateful to you as he is. I can't afford to pay him. All I can provide is a place to live."

"But what about the work he's doing for you?"

"It's mostly done. Now that the apartment is fixed, he'll be able to work evenings finishing up around here."

"So when do you move?"

"As soon as Cliff signs the papers."

"Have you decided what you're going to do?"

"I've been looking at some houses in Inglewood."

"Inglewood?" Ruth looked at Kate as if she'd lost her mind. "I don't think I've ever been to Inglewood except on my way to the airport."

Kate smiled. "I've been all over the city this past week. At first I was just restless with Joe Wayne and Marvella at school, Sunny working at the grocery store, and Ford at your house. For the first time in my life, no one was depending on me for anything. My family was gone, my house was being sold, I was free to start my life over—except I didn't know where to begin. So one day I just started driving. I've lived in Los Angeles all my life but it was a shock to realize what a small area I know my way around in." She looked at Ruth. "Have you ever been to Boyle Heights?"

Ruth shook her head. "I'd have to look at a city map to know where it is."

"We lead such insulated lives. You would be shocked to see the way people are living all over this city. Whole families living in garages. And they're lucky compared to the ones camping in cardboard boxes on the street or sleeping in drainpipes in the park. What's happening to this country?"

Ruth shook her head. "I don't know. All I know is we're not going to stay around to watch." Then she told Kate why she had come. She and Henry had just been offered the use of an apartment in Paris. Would Kate be willing to live in their house until it sold?

Kate threw her arms around Ruth. She had been surprised this past week at how calmly she had been facing her uncertain future, refusing to worry about where she would live once the new owners took possession of her house. Now her faith in providence or God—or possibly just in herself—had been justified.

Kate had to laugh when Ruth began to thank her for the favor. "You've just answered the biggest question in my life," Kate said.

"You're not the only one starting a new life," Ruth confided to Kate. "Thank God Henry doesn't know French. Even if the apartment has a television, he won't be able to understand it. If I can just get his mind off the news, maybe I can get him back into my bed. It's not the sex I miss so much," she confessed, "it's the closeness. I can't bear the way he keeps his distance. To him even a kiss is a promise he's afraid of not being able to keep."

Listening to Ruth describe the apartment awaiting them in Paris—the top floor of an old townhouse on the Ile St. Louis with windows opening onto a balcony that overlooked the Seine—Kate felt her throat tighten with unspoken regret. She and Cliff used to talk about the places they would live once Nina was grown and the school calendar no longer dictated where they would spend their days. A new location with every assignment was what Cliff liked best about his profession, but Kate, her loyalties divided between husband and child, had never been able to share his enthusiasm. Now, when she was finally free to travel with him, he had left home without her. She had never even been to Paris. She could hardly bear to listen to Ruth rattle on about the life she imagined awaiting her—long walks along avenues canopied by chestnut trees, punctuated by impromptu meals at small cafés or improvised picnics in sun-dappled parks evoking impressionist paintings.

"Will you mind being alone in the house?" Ruth was asking, looking anxiously at Kate.

"I'd much rather be alone in your house than mine," Kate replied, surprising herself with the force of her response. "Not that I'm ever alone in my house. Every time I close a door, I'm assaulted by memories of what might have been. I'm not sure what I would've done if Ford and his family hadn't come along."

"You'll have Ford to keep you company during the day at my house. There is so much work still to be done," Ruth said, adding with a laugh, "Why don't we take better care of our houses while we're living in them? Do you know I haven't used my bottom oven in over a year—since a pizza box caught on fire inside it and burned out the wiring. I thought the whole oven would have to be replaced and it just didn't seem worth it. Yesterday I finally called someone out to fix it. He replaced one small connection, charged me thirty-five dollars, and now the oven is as good as new. I felt like such a fool for letting it go so long. Why do we only begin to pay attention to our surroundings when we decide to sell them to someone else? What does it say about us—about the value we place on ourselves—that a house is more important as a property, an investment that has to be protected, than it is as the place where we live our lives? Even though I'm excited about where we're going, I'm almost sad to be leaving my house now. It's the first time since we bought it that I can walk through every room without being besieged by these nagging feelings of things that need to be done. It's like a wife who's neglected herself until it's too late. She doesn't get around to losing weight and dyeing her hair until her husband has fallen in love with another woman." Ruth caught herself suddenly. "Oh, God, Kate, I'm sorry. I didn't mean that."

Kate turned on her angrily. "Why apologize—unless you were thinking of me when you said it? I don't blame myself because I'm alone. I don't think I deserve to be punished for having spent more time in the past twenty-five years thinking of Cliff and his needs than of my own. If that comes under the heading of neglecting myself, I plead guilty, but I refuse to believe that gave Cliff the right to betray me. I took being married as seriously as anybody takes a paying job and I thought I was earning the right to a secure old age, shared with the man I love."

Her anger spent as suddenly as it had erupted, Kate crossed to Ruth and took her hand. "Forgive me, Ruth. I'm the one who should be apologizing to you. All this anger. It has nothing to do with you. I should be saying these things to Cliff. But he's safely out of reach. You just happen to be in the line of fire."

Ruth squeezed her hand. "At least you're not ashamed of your anger, not afraid to put it into words. I can't even acknowledge mine. I ought to be grateful I still have a husband who loves me and wants to live under the same roof, but at night . . ." She couldn't finish.

Kate picked up her purse. "At least we're not just standing still and taking it. We're both doing something to shake up our lives. Now let's go back to your house and you can show me everything I need to know. As many times as I've been there, you don't really know a house until you've lived inside it."

"Just like a marriage," Ruth agreed.

Ford was repapering the guest bedroom when Ruth unlocked the front door and handed Kate the key.

He listened as Ruth told him the plan. And now that Kate had agreed to be there to show prospective clients around, there was no urgency about selling. Just the opposite, in fact, since Kate had nowhere to go.

"I can't stay here alone, Ruth," Kate suddenly blurted out. "I just can't."

Ford stepped down from his ladder and started toward her. "If you're frightened, Kate, I can—"

"No, I'm not frightened," she stopped him midsentence. "But think of the waste. All these empty rooms." She walked to the wall and gently stroked the flowered paper Ford had just hung. "Look at this beautiful guest room. Who wouldn't love spending the night in a room like this?"

Ruth sighed. "I always meant to paper this room. But Henry never really wanted guests. Now, just as I'm leaving, I have the guest room I always wanted." She walked to the window and looked out. "I would've liked guests too."

"I can only stay here on one condition, Ruth," Kate announced in a firm voice. Ford looked at her curiously. Ruth continued to stare out the window, not hearing. "If I'm going to live in this house, even for a few weeks, I have to be free to fill the rooms with the people I choose."

"Well, of course." Ruth turned to her with a relieved smile. "I wouldn't ask you to live in my house without expecting you to treat it like your own. Invite anyone you please to visit you." Her eyes glittered with curiosity as they searched Kate's face for clues. "Are you expecting anyone in particular?"

"No," Kate answered steadily, then walked slowly to the ladder where Ford was standing, watching her in silence. "Ford is going to have to help me find them."

"Find who?" His eyes narrowed in confusion.

"People who have nowhere else to go. People for whom even one night in a clean, safe house with running water and food in the refrigerator would be a miracle—and maybe give them the strength to go on living."

Ruth looked at Kate in horror. "You want to turn my house into a shelter for the homeless?"

Ford quietly measured a length of wallpaper and turned his attention to his work, trying to remove himself from the crossfire of conversation.

Kate pushed aside the new chintz curtains piled on the loveseat covered in matching fabric and sat down. "No, I'm only one person. I'm not going to attempt the impossible. But I've been thinking a lot this past week about what I'm going to do with the rest of my life. Not just *where* I'm going to live but *how* I'm going to live. From now on, I'm going to share whatever I have with at least one other person."

She turned to Ruth. "That's why I've been looking at houses in Inglewood and Boyle Heights and East Los Angeles. I don't have any money of my own but when I sell my house I can buy another one, one that's been neglected and needs work, and while Ford and I are fixing it up, I can fill the rooms with people who will be grateful just to have a roof over their heads. Once we've gotten the house into shape, we'll sell it and buy another one with the profits and do the same thing with it. And on and on. I don't ever plan to have a permanent address again. Or to live alone in a house with empty rooms."

Ruth shook her head. "Your heart's in the right place, Kate. It always has been. You're the most generous and loving person I know. But you've lost your head. This idea is just plain crazy. You can't start taking in complete strangers—people who've been living on the street. Think of the dirt, the disease. And what about the alcoholics, the drug addicts, the mentally retarded? How would you know what you were getting into? Most of those people are homeless for a reason—and they need professional help to turn their lives around. All the good will in the world is not going to change that. And I'm not just worried about my house—though my realtor would faint the first time he took a client through and found vagrants camped in every corner—I'm concerned about you, your safety."

"How can you talk like that in front of Ford?" Kate confronted Ruth angrily.

"Ford's different."

"No, I'm not." From the stepladder, Ford's voice descended on them like a judgment.

"The only difference is that he's just one man." Kate looked at him with an affection that overflowed into feelings much deeper. A passion she had never experienced seemed to be gathering force from someplace deep inside her. "You're seeing him as a person and not part of some faceless mob. That's all I want to do, Ruth. Find one other person I can help and then another person and then one more. I'm not going to open my door to the whole world. And of course I'm not going to ask complete strangers to share my life. I know how dangerous that would be. If Ford's car had broken down outside my house on any day but the day my husband told me he was leaving me, I would never have asked him inside. Even then I knew I was breaking all the rules of safe conduct, but I didn't care. On Christmas Eve I was ready to die. My life meant nothing to me. But now I'm excited about being alive. And I'm not about to endanger my future—it's become much too precious to me.

"I know this idea sounds crazy and impulsive, and I can't tell you I've been thinking about it for a long time because I haven't. I seem to be living my life moment to moment, but it's amazing what miracles happen when you concentrate all your energy and attention on the immediate present. You see things with a clarity that takes you right out of your own body, makes you feel as if you're viewing everything from a perspective that is absolutely objective. You look at your own life and it's like a thread, separate and distinct, a color all its own, but when you look again, it's part of this huge, intricate, fantastic pattern."

The look Ford gave her was like an electrical charge. In that instant they were welded by a sense of shared purpose that was stronger and more life-enhancing than the most thrilling sexual encounter. Suddenly he was descending the ladder and walking toward her. She held out her hand to him. "Will you help me find someone?"

Ruth's voice came crashing down like an ax, severing the connection between them. "I'm sorry, Kate. Not here. Not now. I guess I'm just not as old a soul as you are. I envy your way of looking at things, I really do, but I'm afraid I haven't gotten nearly as far as you have down the path of enlightenment. This house is all Henry and I have in the way of security. I have to protect our future and I'm sorry that means putting a damper on your plans for the present."

Ford slowly put away his tools and left the room without looking back.

Kate heard the sound of his car starting as she returned the house key to Ruth. "You know where to find me if you change your mind. But now you know my price. And it's clearly more than you're willing to pay."

TWENTY-FIVE

Kate had no idea where she was headed when she left Ruth's house. But behind the wheel of her car, with the doors locked and the engine running, she felt calm and in control, not just of a complicated piece of machinery, but of her life.

Unlike Cliff, unlike most of the drivers who crowded the California freeways, Kate had never thought of a car as more than a convenient way of getting from one place to another. The idea of a piece of equipment shaping your self-image seemed to her ridiculous and rather pathetic. But lately, every time she left the house, she had found herself seated behind the wheel of Cliff's Jaguar, as if unconsciously laying claim to the sense of power and purpose with which it had always provided him. And she, who had never owned anything but an automatic, had even begun to enjoy shifting gears, making the decisions that in the past she had been quite content to leave to the machine.

Driving without a destination still felt strange to Kate. Until this week she could never remember getting in her car without knowing exactly where she intended to go. But lately the very act of driving had become an end in itself, and the streets Kate followed seemed to be taking her not just to parts of the city she never knew existed but far beyond the boundaries of her own experience into depths of despair she would have been incapable of imagining.

In the past week, telling herself she was looking for houses, Kate had headed toward the outer perimeters of the vast, sprawling metropolis she no longer felt she had the right to call her hometown. That cozy epithet was forever at odds with the disparate collection of neighborhoods through which she had traveled, feeling as alien as a foreigner. But despite the mileage recorded on her instrument panel, she had still not come close to the dark, disintegrating inner heart of the city, where lives came to a dead end.

Ford had told her about the shelter where Sunny had been forced to stay with the children while he circled the city in his car on a futile search for work. He could hardly bear to look back on those months, and Kate didn't really want to hear him describe the desperate lives, the constant fears, the inescapable filth. She had closed her eyes and ears to the horror from which they had emerged and made a silent vow that no matter where her life took her, she would make sure they never had to go back. She had intervened in the fate of one family, and at first that seemed like enough.

Kate was not a crusader, out to change the world. She had always preferred the view from her living room window, safe in the comfort of her own home. But once she had opened her door to Ford, there was no way to close it again and bolt it against the terrors of the outside. She could no longer even sit quietly at home.

Now, fleeing the safe suburban neighborhood where Ruth lived, Kate found herself driving toward downtown and felt as if she were calling her own bluff. She had been almost as surprised as Ruth by her condition for house-sitting. However, she realized now, the idea must have begun taking shape in the back of her consciousness during the past week, as she saw one rundown house after another and tried to imagine how she and Ford could transform them and in the process provide temporary shelter for people who had nowhere else to go.

The idea was too good, made too much sense, to abandon at the first sign of resistance. If Ruth could not stomach the idea of poverty-battered strangers living within her impeccably redecorated walls, then Kate would find somewhere else to house-sit while she looked for a property to buy and renovate. Marriage to a director had given her a lifetime connection to a creative community that was in a constant state of flux by any number of standards, not least of which was real estate. Her friends were always coming and going, on location with films, on the road with plays. Travel was so much a part of the lives of the actors and directors and writers she knew that even when their work didn't require them to leave home, they still traveled for pleasure.

At any given time within her circle of friends there were at least half a dozen houses standing empty while their owners were living in hotels or sublet accommodations or second homes in New York or England or the south of France. Second homes. Until now the idea had seemed extravagant but exciting to Kate —using space to cheat time, leading a double life within the unyielding framework of a single lifetime. But as her car moved past the imposing lines of the Music Center, where even the most conservative residents of Orange County felt safe, toward the inner city, she began to burn with a slow, steady anger. The street sign read "No. Hope." "No." stood for "North" but the abbreviation was more accurate. Her conscience questioned how a phrase like "second home" could fit so comfortably into common usage. It seemed like a contradiction in terms in a world where innocent children had to sleep in cardboard crates.

I'm becoming a woman obsessed, Kate thought to herself as she drove down a street of imposing office buildings. All I see are buildings that are empty as often as they're occupied. Isn't there some way to open them at night when they're deserted, to share all this expensive space with the other residents of downtown Los Angeles—the unacknowledged refugees of this affluent society?

She shivered. But it was more than the bitterly cold weather that was causing her hands to tremble. A man was moving down the sidewalk ahead of her, clutching a ragged quilt around his shoulders. It trailed behind him like a tattered train, giving him the look of some dispossessed emperor driven mad by betrayal and misfortune.

Kate gripped the steering wheel and turned the corner. She couldn't believe what she was seeing just outside her car window, close enough to touch. Drug dealing right out in the open. Dirty, desperate faces staring at her without shame, daring her to avert her eyes.

Suddenly she was engulfed by waves of panic. She must have been crazy to drive the Jaguar down to this part of town. She could feel the hostility pressing against the car like a high desert wind, threatening to topple it.

At a stoplight a gang of young boys—they couldn't have been more than ten years old—pressed their faces against the car window and held out their hands for money. Refusing to look at them, she stared straight ahead. One of them angrily kicked the tires of her car. Urged on by the cheers of his companions, he suddenly scrambled onto the hood and stood on it, facing her defiantly. Praying for the light to change, she sat behind the wheel and watched in frozen horror as he slowly unzipped his ragged jeans and sprayed her windshield with urine.

All the anger Kate had been feeling in the abstract for the victims of poverty and injustice was suddenly directed toward them. "Get down from there, you little bastard," she screamed as the signal glared green. The car lunged forward, throwing the boy into the gutter.

Somehow the car found its way back to the freeway and then across Coldwater Canyon into the comforting foothills of the Santa Monica Mountains. Kate had no memory of having driven there. She could not stop her hand from trembling as she reached for the remote control to lower the automatic garage door. Leaning her head against the steering wheel, Kate began to sob. What a fraud she was—only caring about people from a safe distance.

At least Ruth was honest about her feelings. Kate's high-minded plans crumbled at the first exposure to reality.

Finally regaining her composure, Kate climbed out of the car and hurried into the house. It was early afternoon but all she wanted to do was sleep—to hide from her waking self who had turned out to be someone she didn't much like.

She collapsed onto the couch in the study, pulling the handknit afghan that lay folded at one end over her shoulders. Her bones ached with the exhaustion of despair. The problems that loomed beyond her front door in streets stretching across the continent were beyond her power to combat. Someone else would have to figure out what to do about the homeless. She was only one woman, alone and without income, abandoned by her husband, no longer needed by her daughter. Just learning how to take care of herself after all these years of depending on someone else to pay the bills and make the decisions would be an accomplishment.

Hostile faces peopled her dreams. Wherever she went, she was followed by unshaven men in dirt-stained clothing, gaunt women holding babies to the breast with one hand and begging with the other, and bare-bottomed children defecating in the gutters. And she was no longer inside her car—no protective shell of steel and glass to insulate her from the abusive sound of their anger and the suffocating stench of their poverty. Shouting at them to leave her in peace, she ran along the alien streets, searching desperately for a place to hide. Hands tore at her skirt, and every time she turned a corner, there were more faces coming toward her.

Finally she found her house, but her heart was still pounding and the sound was echoed by insistent knocking at the windows and doors. She saw that the crowds of people had followed her home and were laying siege to her house, trying to get inside, She ran to the door and with trembling hands somehow managed to put the chain in place, averting her eyes from the accusing stares. She turned back to the other side of the room and saw nothing but hands reaching through the windows.

Then the lock on the door was forced. Only the chain kept

the crowds from flooding into the room. Kate leaned against the door, bracing it with her shoulder, but disembodied hands reached through the space above and below the chain, clutching at her. "There are too many of you," she cried helplessly. "I don't know what to do."

A hand was shaking her awake. "Kate," said a voice hoarse with concern. "You've got to come with me."

Jolted awake by the familiar tone, Kate opened her eyes and saw Ford looking at her. "What time is it?" she asked.

"After four. Thank God you're here."

Kate started to stand. The dream was still vividly imprinted on her mind. Not until she looked through her living room window and saw the peaceful street outside would she believe her house was no longer under siege by an angry, homeless mob.

Then she saw the way Ford was looking at her. "What's wrong?" she asked. As he struggled to find the words, she started toward the back door. "Where are the children?" she shouted, her voice frantic with fear as she ran through the garden to the swimming pool. Its surface lay tranquil and undisturbed in the fading light of a January afternoon.

"It's not the children," Ford said as he caught up with her. "It's not Joe Wayne and Marvella." He stopped abruptly. Kate could hear the catch in his throat. "They're upstairs in the apartment watching television on that little set you gave Joe Wayne."

"Sunny wouldn't like them watching television in the afternoon," Kate murmured. "Not until they've done their homework. I'll bring them down to the house, keep them with me till she gets through work."

She started toward the apartment but Ford put out a hand to stop her. "Sunny's up there with them."

"Oh, I see."

"She's locked in the bathroom. She won't talk to me. I'm scared she's fainted again." The words spewed out of Ford in short, anxious gasps.

"Again? How long has she been in there? What's she doing home so early?"

"The manager called from the store. Lucky I was here working. When I left Ruth's house, I came back here and went to work on that front door lock, the one that keeps jamming."

"What did he say?" Ford looked disoriented at her question. Kate could see he was in a state of shock. She took his hand and held it in both of hers. "The manager—what did he say when he called?"

"He said she was gone a long time at lunch and when she came back, she looked pale and like she'd just been sick at her stomach—more than once. He tried to get her to lie down, but she said work was the only thing that would take her mind off things. She was standing at the cash register checking out a customer when her knees buckled. She just missed hitting her head on the edge of the counter as she fell. As it was, she could've had a concussion. That's why he called me to come get her. He thought she needed somebody with her."

"Why didn't you tell me?"

"Your car wasn't in the garage when I brought her back. I didn't know where you were."

Kate pressed her hands to her throbbing temples. "I don't know where I was either." She tried to shake the images out of her mind as she followed Ford to the garage apartment. "Shouldn't you have taken her to the hospital?" Kate whispered. "I mean, after a fall like that and especially since she's—"

Ford cut her off quickly. "She said she was fine—just weak. All she wanted was to come back here and lie in bed and look up at that canopy."

"I wish there were someplace where I could feel as safe as Sunny feels in that bed," Kate said with a sigh.

"She was asleep when I left to pick up the kids at school," Ford said. "But when we got back, she was locked in the bathroom and every time I knocked, she screamed at me to go away. I was afraid to keep knocking—because of the kids."

Suddenly Joe Wayne and Marvella came running down the stairs to meet them. Marvella was whimpering softly. "What's the matter, honey?" Ford lifted her into his arms.

"It's Mama," she sobbed. "I can hear her crying but she won't open the door."

"I asked her what was wrong"—Joe Wayne was trying not to show how frightened he was—"but all she said was she'd been sick all over the bathroom and she couldn't come out till she cleaned it up." He wrinkled his nose in disgust. "I don't like seeing someone be sick. It makes me feel funny inside."

Kate put an arm around him. "Why don't you and Marvella take Homer outside and play with him. He misses you when you're at school all day."

"But put on a warm jacket," Ford warned as Marvella wriggled out of his arms. "It turned cold last night. When winter finally makes up its mind to come to California, it doesn't let you forget it's here."

As soon as the children were out the door, Kate turned to Ford. "Maybe you should talk to her first. I'll go straighten up the bed. Let's try to get her back into it."

While Ford spoke softly to Sunny through the closed door, Kate went into the bedroom. As she turned back the covers of the bed she and Sunny had put together with such pride the night before, she saw that the sheets were stained with blood. She rushed into the other room. The door to the bathroom was open and Sunny was huddled on the floor, her hands around her knees. Ford was kneeling beside her. "Stop blaming yourself, honey. You couldn't help getting sick."

Kate stood in the doorway staring at Sunny, then said in a low voice, "You did it, didn't you?"

A moan was Sunny's only response. Ford put his arms around her and lifted her to her feet. The moan grew louder, turning into a mournful wail. Ford looked in confusion from Sunny to Kate, but neither was looking at him. "You need to get in a warm bed with the covers around you," he said gently. "Don't try to talk now." But as he started toward the bedroom with his arm around her, Sunny broke free and ran to the couch. She lay with her face to the wall, trembling violently.

Kate brought the comforter from the bedroom and laid it over her while Ford looked on helplessly. "Can I get you something to drink?" he finally asked. Sunny closed her eyes as if she had not heard.

"I'll make some tea," Kate offered.

When she returned, Ford had pulled up a chair and was sitting beside the couch, stroking Sunny's hair and reassuring her as if she were a frightened animal who understood nothing beyond the touch of a hand and the sound of a voice. "You don't have to tell me anything," he kept saying. "Nothing is gonna change how much I love you."

Watching him comfort her, Kate felt her eyes fill with tears. She poured a cup of tea and handed it to Sunny. It seemed to give her the strength to confront whatever she had been hiding from. "I lost it," she said finally.

"What?" Ford was struggling to understand.

"The baby."

"Is that where you went at lunch? To get rid of it? How can you say you lost it when you did it on purpose?" He walked to the window. The sound of his two children laughing and shouting at each other as they raced around the flowering fruit trees with Homer in barking pursuit comforted him, and he watched them in silence until Sunny spoke again.

"I did go to the clinic. It's true." She turned to Kate. "It was what you said to me last night that settled things in my own mind."

Ford spun around, his eyes searching Kate's face. "What *you* said? What does this have to do with you?"

Kate was trying not to cry. "I don't understand. I said I'd take the baby, help raise it . . ."

"Take our baby?" Ford was clenching his fists with helpless rage.

"Not to keep. I just wanted to take some of the burden off Sunny. It's hard to have a baby if you're trying to hold down a job. I thought if she could count on me to help, she wouldn't be so afraid to have it. I knew how much you wanted it."

Ford sank, defeated, into a chair. "I'm not a fool. The last thing we need is another mouth to feed. But what kind of a man am I to give my wife so little faith in the future?" He hid his face in his hands.

Sunny slowly eased her legs over the side of the couch and

put her bare feet on the floor. She walked to the chair where Ford was sitting and, childlike, sat in his lap, clasping her hands behind his neck and resting her head against his chest. "Don't take it so hard," she murmured. "This doesn't have anything to do with the kind of man you are."

"I'll just check on Joe Wayne and Marvella." Kate started for the stairs. "In fact, why don't I take them in the house with me and fix them some dinner. You two need some time alone."

"No," Sunny cried, rising from the chair and moving to Kate, "I haven't finished." Kate guided her back to couch and sat down beside her. "I went to the clinic on my lunch hour, just like I said," Sunny continued. "All last night, after we talked, I kept thinking about that woman across the hall from us at the shelter. The one whose baby kept crying."

"Teresa." Ford's voice was low and intense. "Her husband walked out on her before the baby was born." He gave Sunny a pointed stare, then muttered, "Bastard."

"There are hundreds and hundreds of women like her, with babies they can't feed." Sunny was staring intently at Kate. "If you want to help raise a baby, find one that's already been born. Help a woman who doesn't have a husband. I have Ford." She smiled at him—a tender, forgiving smile—but then suddenly her eyes were brimming with tears. "I was going to do it for you, Ford. That's what you've got to understand. You have all you can handle right now—worrying about Joe Wayne and Marvella and me. I was afraid another baby might break you—and I knew for sure it would break us apart. I didn't sleep all night trying to think things through and this morning my mind was made up. But when I got to the clinic there were all these people marching around it carrying Bibles and pictures of dead babies and singing hymns like they were some kind of army from God. When I tried to get past them to go inside, they screamed at me and called me a murderer. I was so scared." Sunny was sobbing hysterically now. "They pushed and shoved me and told me I'd burn in hell for my sins . . ."

Kate took Sunny in her arms to comfort her. "How dare they try to frighten you like that? Why don't they do something about all the hungry, homeless babies who've already been born instead of trying to bully women into having babies they can't feed? They're the criminals, not you."

"But they act like God is on their side," Sunny cried. "They made me feel so ashamed."

"I've never been as angry as I am right now," Kate said in a steel-edged whisper. "I mean I've always believed in the principle of a woman deciding her own fate, but not being able to have children of my own, I thought having a baby was the most wonderful thing in the world. It was just hard for me to imagine being pregnant and not wanting to have it. That's why I came to you last night and asked if I could share yours. But it was wrong of me to ask. Nobody—not me, not those crazy people marching around the clinic, not even Ford, as much as he loves you—has the right to make you have a baby you don't want. It's your decision. Yours alone."

"I couldn't do it," Sunny said. "I was too scared. I ran all the way back to the store. But I killed it just the same. As I was running, I fell. Then I felt sicker and sicker." She hid her face in Kate's lap, but her shoulders were shaking.

"It was an accident," Kate said, patting her back to calm her. "The fall probably started the hemorrhaging. But even if it hadn't been an accident, even if you'd stayed at the clinic, you wouldn't have done anything wrong."

"I was in bed asleep, but I kept seeing those people shouting at me, their eyes just burning with hate. And then I felt it happening—all that blood." Sunny was sobbing again. "Oh, my poor little baby," she cried.

"Stop it, honey." Ford put his arms around her. "You can't think like that."

"I know I don't have the right to grieve for it when I was all set to get rid of it—but I can't help it. Nothing about this was my choice. I didn't want to have it but I didn't want to lose it either. Not the way I did. I just feel so empty inside."

"You've lost a lot of blood," Kate said. "I'm going to call my doctor and have her come take a look at you."

"Thank you, Kate." Ford helped Sunny to her feet. "Come on, honey, let's get you back into bed."

"I'll fix it for you." Kate hurried into the bedroom, stripped the stained linen from the bed, and quickly remade it with clean, smooth sheets. "Now try to rest," she said as she helped Sunny into it. "You've been through a lot today but you've given me a reason to get up tomorrow. If Ford will go with me, we'll go down to that shelter and find Teresa and her baby." She patted Sunny's hand. "You didn't take a baby's life today—you saved one."

TWENTY-SIX

Kate was awakened the next morning by a call from the realtor. His clients were getting anxious. They needed a place to live and even though Kate had agreed to a short escrow, the clock could not start ticking until her husband signed the papers. Was he going to be a problem?

As she listened in helpless anger to the disembodied voice coming over the wire, her fingers tightened around the pencil she kept by the grocery list in progress. "No," she wrote over and over again under the words "milk" and "eggs." Cliff could not do this to her—she would not let it happen.

Kate assured the realtor that her husband was eager to get rid of the house. She had no doubt the signed papers were already on their way back to her but she would call him tonight to be sure. She was pressing the pencil against the pad so hard it splintered just as Ford entered the kitchen.

Kate told him what had happened but swore nothing about

their immediate future was going to change. They were driving downtown today to try to find Teresa and her baby.

With Ford at the wheel of his old station wagon and Kate seated safely in the passenger seat beside him, the downtown streets did not seem quite as alien and threatening as they had the day before. She reached for his hand as they turned a corner and pulled to a stop in front of a once-elegant hotel now rotting with neglect. "Is this the shelter?" Kate asked as two derelicts pressed their faces to the car window.

"Move on, brothers." Ford opened the door for Kate, waving the men aside. "Can't you tell from this old heap I'm driving that we're no better off than you are?"

"You've got four wheels and an engine. You can get out of here," one of the men muttered. "That makes you a lot better off than we are."

Ford suddenly reached into his pocket and pulled out a handful of change. "If I can get out of here, so can you," he said hoarsely, dividing the coins between the two men. "Don't give up hope."

Watching the men thank Ford, Kate saw the suffering behind the hostile masks that had been haunting her thoughts, waking and sleeping. She started to open her purse but Ford put a protective arm around her and hurried her into the building.

Inside what was once a lobby but now more like the entrance to a prison, Kate was assaulted by the smells of garbage mixed with vomit and urine. She felt like gagging, then forced herself to take a deep, calming breath. "How can people stand it here?" she blurted out, then was immediately ashamed of speaking her thoughts aloud. "I'm sorry. I didn't mean that."

"Of course you did," Ford said. "Everybody who comes in here feels that way. Even the ones who have to live here." He guided Kate to the elevator and pressed the button. "We're in luck today," he said as the doors creaked open.

"In luck?" Kate looked around her.

"Do you know how many times I've had to climb the stairs to the top floor where Sunny and the kids were living? And how many more times they had to climb them?" His voice was cracking. "When I think of Sunny riding buses all day, walking block after block, trying to find a place we could afford to live and a job to help pay for it—then coming back here to this hellhole and having to climb all those stairs . . . God, no wonder I wake up every morning and expect to find her gone."

Kate patted his hand. "She's lucky to have you to look after her, Ford—to care what happens to her. And she knows it now."

"All she said to me this morning was that she was praying we weren't too late."

"So am I," Kate whispered as the elevator groaned its way to the top floor. "Imagine having to keep a newborn baby in a place like this."

The muscles in Ford's jaw tightened. "In this place I can't see beyond where I've been. The day Sunny moved in here with the kids I hit bottom. But the worst of it was how relieved I felt that I couldn't stay here. Much as I wanted to be with my family, I couldn't wait to get out of this place. Alone in my car I could feel like a man. Inside these stinking walls I had to face what a failure I was—as a husband and a father. I still have to face it," he said in a low voice as the elevator doors opened and they stepped into a dank and mildewed hallway.

The crying of a baby led them to a battered door striped with dirt stains and peeling paint. Kate knocked timidly and Ford called out, "Teresa, it's me—Ford. Remember Sunny across the hall and Joe Wayne and Marvella."

The door opened hesitantly and a slender young woman with long, dark hair and deep brown eyes stared out at them. She was holding a tiny baby, who was pawing at her half-buttoned blouse.

The woman's face brightened when she saw Ford. Kate reached instinctively for the baby. "What a beautiful baby! A little boy, isn't it?" Kate looked into the wrinkled face, whose features were almost hidden by an unruly cap of thick black hair. Handing the baby reluctantly to Kate, the woman looked to Ford for reassurance. "It's all right, Teresa," he said gently. "We've come to help you."

Between Teresa's broken English and Kate's half-remembered high school Spanish, a tentative bridge was built but there was no way to convey the full extent of what Kate wanted to do for her. Finally, desperate to understand, Teresa knocked at the door across the hall. From the apartment where Sunny and her children had lived emerged a sturdy young woman with an open, freckled face and reddish-gold hair plaited in a long braid down her back. A pair of boisterous boy twins, talkative toddlers, came clambering after her.

Something about her struck Kate as familiar—but she could not think of any context in which they might have met. Introductions were exchanged and neither recognized the other by name. Teresa launched into a rapid-fire account in Spanish, pointing with emotional gestures to Kate, who was cradling the baby in her arms and crooning to it. The girl, whose name was Sharon, listened sympathetically, asking an occasional question in what sounded to Kate like fluent Spanish. Finally, when Teresa had run out of words, Sharon patted her hand reassuringly and turned to Kate. "She's afraid you want to take her baby."

Kate quickly handed the baby back to Teresa and put an arm around her shoulders. "Not without you," she said. "I want to give both of you a home." Then with Sharon translating, she explained what she wanted to do.

Understanding at last what she was being offered, Teresa fell to her knees and crossed herself. "She says God must have sent you in answer to her prayers," Sharon explained. "She came into the country illegally and she's terrified the authorities are going to take her baby away from her. He's all she has in the world but she can't feed him. She hasn't had anything to eat herself in three days and her milk has dried up. The baby cries all the time because he's hungry."

"Why didn't I think of that?" Kate whispered to Ford. "We could have brought something with us."

"She'll feel better once she's out of this place," Ford said. "We can stop at McDonald's on the way home and buy her a hamburger and a milkshake."

At the word "McDonald's" the twins threw themselves at

Ford. "Hamburger," one cried, straddling his leg. "Milkshake," shouted the other, swinging on his arm.

Embarrassed, Sharon grabbed them. "Come on, boys, time to go." At this they broke into loud yelps of protest. Ford turned to Kate. "What do you think? Can we make room in the car for three more?"

"Look, you don't have to feel sorry for me," Sharon began. "I can take care of my kids. I get food stamps. We can manage. Besides, we're leaving this place today. My husband may have walked out on me, but his mother still writes. She said she misses the boys. Well, we'll see how much she misses them when we land on her front door."

"Can we give you a lift?" Kate asked.

"She lives in Florida."

"How are you getting there?"

"By bus."

"Do you want us to take you to the depot?"

"I don't understand why you want to bother about me. You came for Teresa, didn't you?"

"I just keep feeling I know you from somewhere," Kate said, "and you don't look like the kind of person I'd expect to find at a place like this."

Sharon laughed bitterly. "The first thing you learn at a place like this is not to be surprised by who you find here." Then, as she stuffed her few possessions into shopping bags, she explained that she had been deserted by an out-of-work husband soon after the twins were born. She had worked at three different jobs to make ends meet, leaving the boys in the care of her mother. Then her mother died unexpectedly and Sharon suffered a heart attack. The illness wiped out her savings, and the bank reclaimed her house. The doctor warned her if she went back to work, she risked a second, probably fatal heart attack. She could no longer give her sons a home, she said, but she was going to make sure they had a mother. She was all they had, and they were the only thing that kept her going.

"How do you happen to speak such good Spanish?" Kate

asked as Sharon and the twins climbed in the backseat of the station wagon next to Teresa and the baby.

"My husband worked in Mexico once," Sharon replied in a tone that made it clear she was not prepared to furnish details. "We lived there several months. We lived a lot of places before the twins were born. Sometimes he took a job just so we could go somewhere we'd never been. He never worried about having enough work in those days. But once he had a family to feed and he really needed a job, he never seemed to get one."

"Having a family changes everything for a man," Ford muttered. His hands clenched the steering wheel as he pulled to the curb in front of the bus depot. The twins were half asleep in the backseat and protested loudly when Sharon roused them. "I'll carry them inside." Ford hoisted the two small boys into his arms.

Teresa began to cry when she realized Sharon and the boys were leaving. Sharon reassured her that everything was going to be all right.

Kate pulled a twenty-dollar bill from her purse and handed it to Sharon. "I wish I could do more for you," she said.

"It's not your problem," Sharon said, "but thanks anyway." Then she stuck the money into her blue jeans. At the door of the depot she turned back to them with a funny little wave. *"Hasta la vista."*

Getting Teresa and the baby settled in Nina's bedroom helped Kate forget how angry she was at Cliff for not signing the papers and allowing her to get on with her life. Though she was still depending on the sale of the house to finance her future plans, she was excited about the immediate prospect of filling all the empty houses she could find—starting with her own.

Teresa lay down in Nina's bed for a nap, the baby nestled beside her. A deep feeling of content descended on Kate as she closed the bedroom door behind her. She was not sure Teresa understood that they would soon be moving, but for the moment she seemed happy to accept whatever Kate was able to offer. In the meantime Kate was going to have to brush up her high school Spanish or communication could prove to be a problem. If only Sharon were around to translate.

Kate kept turning over the image of that proud, defiant face in her mind. She remembered a younger Sharon. They had spent time together in the past—but when, where?

Kate moved into the now-empty master bedroom. Stripped of its curtains and furniture and canopied bed, it felt like a no-man's land. Over the weekend, while Ford was moving all the furniture his family could use into the garage apartment, Kate had finished packing the remaining personal possessions into cartons ready for storage. There was nothing left in the room to link it with her life.

She moved slowly down the stairs and into the study—the one room in the house unchanged by the prospective move. Kate had made no effort to collect Cliff's things—once he signed the papers, she would have to confront him about what to do with all the artifacts of his career. The dark, walnut-stained shelves were crammed with framed photographs, awards, leatherbound scripts. Even in his absence Cliff asserted his presence in this house more strongly than she did. Little wonder it was so easy for her to accept the prospect of spending the rest of her life in other people's houses, Kate thought. It was what she had been doing all along.

A photograph taken on location in Mexico ten years earlier caught her eye. Cliff had been directing a Western near Guadalajara. In the photograph Cliff was sprawled in his director's chair, flanked by actors leaning over him and laughing. Kate remembered taking the picture when she and Nina went down to join him over spring vacation. Nina was twelve then and had a hard time keeping up with her classes if she missed even a day of school. So although Cliff begged Kate to stay with him when the vacation ended, she reluctantly took Nina back to Los Angeles.

Looking back now, she wondered if Mexico was a turning point. There had been an urgency in his pleas to her to stay with him—to put her husband ahead of her child. If Nina was so determined not to miss any school, he argued, why couldn't Kate hire a housekeeper to take care of her? Or if she didn't trust a stranger, let Nina stay with a friend, someone with boring, conventional parents who had steady jobs and led settled lives.

Contemplating the failure of her marriage, Kate was suddenly overcome with fatigue. She lay down on the couch, but when she closed her eyes, all she saw were images from the past. In hope of banishing them, she slipped a video cassette into the player—the movie Cliff had made in Mexico.

She was only half watching—it was not one of his best— when a young woman entered the shot, set a dish in front of the hero, and walked off again. Kate reached for the controls and rewound the film. And then she watched the entrance again. And then again.

The image of the young mother waving good-bye at the bus depot superimposed itself on the screen. Now Kate realized why Sharon had looked familiar. The memory was coming into focus. She was not an actress, but her husband had a sizable supporting role and she was living with him on location. Cliff had been rather taken with her and had given her a one-day, nonspeaking walk-on.

A wave of fear washed over Kate. It was a shock to realize that someone from her past, another wife like her who had been banking on her husband's career, could end up in the present in such desperate circumstances. Kate found herself having to acknowledge for the first time that like everyone she knew, she was only a crisis, an accident, a major illness away from having to sleep on the street. If it could happen to Sharon, it could happen to anyone. It could even happen to her.

"What are you doing in my study?" The voice was abrupt and accusing. Kate awoke with a start and saw her husband.

"Cliff! You're home!"

"Home? You still think of it as home? Even though you're trying to sell it out from under me?"

"I still think of it as home even though you left me to live in it alone. I warned you I wouldn't stay. Have you brought the papers?"

Cliff reached in his jacket pocket and handed a thick envelope to her. As Kate's fingers closed eagerly around it, Cliff's hand suddenly covered hers.

"It was a terrible mistake, Kate."

"What?"

"I should've taken you back with me at Christmas. You were all ready to go. I was a damn fool to leave you behind. And if you'd been with me, maybe things would've turned out differently." Letting go of her hand, he crossed to the shelf and stood looking at the mementos of his career. Bereft of words, he began to stroke the award he had won a few years earlier for a television film. "It's back to television for me," he said wearily. "I'll never get to direct another feature."

"What's happened, Cliff? Why have you come home?" Kate sat in the swivel chair behind the desk, the desk she had been using since she moved into this room, the desk she had begun to think of as hers once she had discovered all the secrets hidden inside its drawers. His actions—past, present, or future—no longer had the power to hurt her. The unfamiliar note of defeat in his voice drew her to him, but she was determined to resist.

"The picture's been shut down." He continued to stand across the room with his back to her.

"What? How can that be?"

"Our major investor got caught short in some commodities deal. He had to pull out and we couldn't find anybody to keep us going."

"But surely the picture has just been postponed? Till they raise more money?" Kate had counted on Cliff staying away till summer. The one thing she had not imagined when she was planning her next move was having him back in Los Angeles.

"I can't afford to wait around," Cliff said brusquely. "None of us were paid. I've got to get a job."

Kate forced herself to stay seated. Her stomach muscles began to knot with foreboding. "Where will you live?" she asked, trying to sound cool and collected. Waiting for his answer, she took the papers from the envelope. The spaces marked for his signature were blank.

"I'm in trouble, Kate. I need your help." He moved to the desk. His eyes, soft and pleading, caressed her.

Need! The word no woman can resist. She clutched the arms of her chair and remained entrenched behind the desk. "Why are you coming to me? As I recall, you're in love with someone else."

Cliff sank wearily onto the couch, stretching his long legs out in front of him and putting his arms behind him to cradle his head. Defenseless, he was at his most appealing, and he knew it. When all else failed, he could always count on candor. "It all came crashing down on me, Kate." He sighed bitterly. "Nothing was what it seemed at Christmas. The picture was not worth making. To tell you the truth, I was almost relieved when the money ran out. I'd fooled myself into believing that it had something to say and that someone who had loved me when I was young would help me find the way to say it. But there was nothing there, nothing anywhere." He put his hands in front of his face.

"So what happened? Did she kick you out when the picture shut down?" Kate asked coldly. She saw for the first time how old Cliff had become—or was she just comparing him to Ford?

Cliff stared at her. "You didn't use to be so hard, Kate."

"I don't want to be hurt again, Cliff. I told you when you left me at Christmas I wasn't going to live here alone. You gave me this house in return for letting you get away guilt-free. You can't go back on your promise."

"I don't blame you for being angry, Kate, but I have nowhere else to go. You have to give me time."

"There is no time." In spite of her resolve, Kate could feel the panic rising in her chest. All her plans depended on moving. There was no room in her future for this house—or for the husband with whom she had shared it. "I'm sorry, Cliff, it's out of my hands. The buyers are living in a hotel. They want to take possession as soon as possible. The realtor has already warned me that if there's any delay, the deal's off."

"Six months, Kate. That's all I ask. If you still want out by August, I won't give you an argument. Think of all the years we've invested in this marriage. Haven't they earned me a second chance?"

No, Kate wanted to shout. You forfeited all the credit in your account when you walked out on me! But the words stuck in her throat. She had never seen Cliff looking so helpless. Without the protective armor of a paid assignment, he seemed as lost as a child who had been abandoned by his parents.

Kate hated the feelings that were sweeping over her, but she couldn't help feeling sorry for him. During the nights she had slept alone in his study, playing his films over and over on the VCR, she had come to know the real Cliff—not the man, who could be petty and selfish, but the artist, who could frame life in a way that made you experience it for the first time. This was someone whose talent outstripped his credits. The best of him was in his work, but only in bits and pieces. He had yet to make the film that would establish him in the front rank of Hollywood directors, and now, in a business where only the profits of your last picture earned you the right to make another one, he might never get another chance. No wonder he had been so desperate to believe his last project would be the making of him—and so willing to sacrifice everything, including his wife, for the inspiration he felt he needed to make it. "You don't deserve what happened to you, Cliff," Kate said softly. "I've spent a lot of time with you while you've been away."

He gave her a puzzled look but waited for her to explain.

"I've been sleeping here in your study."

"So I hear," Cliff replied dryly. "Nina told me there wasn't a spare bed in the house."

Shelving the subject of who was sleeping where till later, Kate steered the conversation back to Cliff. She told him how much she had discovered about him that she never knew. There was a sensitivity, a compassion in his work that he seemed afraid to show in life. "When you left me, I wanted to hate you," she admitted. "It would've made everything much easier. All I had left of you was your work, but in watching it, I discovered things about you I never knew. You don't need me, Cliff. You don't need anyone. All you need is a camera and a script and you'll be fine.

You ought to think about writing your own. You're too good just to sit around waiting for someone to hire you. Your best movie is still locked somewhere inside you."

"I've never heard you talk like this, Kate. I always thought all you cared about was what happened in this house—between us. My work was just something I did to pay the bills."

"When I started feeling left out of it, I stopped paying attention," Kate confessed. "It was my loss."

"So what do we do now?" Cliff asked. "Can we start over? Nina's on her own now. It's just the two of us again."

Kate shook her head. "No, Cliff. Whatever we had—and I'm not sure it was ever enough—is finished. A couple is such a closed unit. I could never again be content to turn my back on the rest of the world and live here alone with you."

"What are you saying?"

"I'm leaving you."

"What about the house?"

"I can't sell it out from under you. If you want to continue living here, I can't stop you."

"I can't live here without you. I don't even know how to turn on the dishwasher."

"How romantic!"

"You know what I mean, Kate. You're part of everything that happens under this roof. Without you, this house is nothing but a lot of empty rooms. I'll go mad."

"Well, actually, there aren't a lot of empty rooms here at the moment," Kate began slowly, an idea taking shape in her head.

"Wait a minute, Kate. I'm not running a mission here. Nina told me about the family you've taken in. That's all very admirable, but you've been spending my money and you've got to stop. I'm out of a job—remember. It's going to take everything I've got in the bank to support my own family—I can't afford to take on a bunch of strangers."

"You don't have to worry about your own family. Nina's got a scholarship, and I'm prepared to take care of myself—though I was counting on the money from the sale of this house to carry out my plans. You said when you left I could have full title to it, but even if you go back on your promise, half this house is legally mine. If you don't want to sell it, you'll have to find some other way to pay me for it."

"Have you been talking to a lawyer? Do you want a divorce?"

"Not unless you do. I have no intention of getting married again, but I want what belongs to me. I may not have a career, but I've earned half this house."

"You've earned all of it, Kate. I admit it—but at the moment the point is academic. Because I just don't know where I'm going to get the money." The argument was getting out of hand. Cliff hardly knew how to deal with this new Kate. She was so calm, so sure of her ground. Everything that mattered to him was slipping away and he felt helpless to prevent it. "Until I can come up with it, I guess you'll have to stay here." Cliff was trying his best to sound sympathetic, but Kate could see a smile lurking at the corner of his lips. He was sure he had her where he wanted her.

"I don't know what I'm going to do now," she admitted. "I'm going to have to make some calls."

Cliff started for the door. "I'm too tired to think straight. I know it's going to take some time for you to forgive me, Kate. We don't have to decide anything right now."

Kate followed him into the front hall. His suitcases were piled at the bottom of the stairs. "You can unpack in the morning," she said quickly. "For now I guess you'll have to sleep in that little room off the kitchen."

"The maid's room? Are you crazy?" And he grabbed a suitcase in each hand and started up the stairs. "As long as I'm still making the mortgage payments on this house, I'll sleep in my own bed, thank you very much." He threw open the door to the master bedroom and stared in disbelief at the empty room. "What have you done?" he shouted. "Where's our bed? What happened to our room?"

"The same thing that happened to our marriage. It's been stripped bare. There's nothing there anymore."

"You gave away our bed, all our furniture?"

"No. Nothing has left the property. Ford just moved everything from this room into the garage apartment. He and his wife are living there now."

"For how long? I thought you were selling this house."

"The new owners have agreed to let them live there—rent-free—in return for looking after the house and garden."

"Whose idea was that?"

"Mine. I made it a condition of the sale. If you decide to keep the house, I'm sure they'll do the same for you. You won't miss me at all."

Cliff was pacing the room now, his emotions seesawing between confusion and anger. "I don't understand what's gotten into you, Kate. You're not the woman I left here at Christmas."

"No, I'm not. You might not have left the woman I am now." Kate was beginning to enjoy this exchange. She realized for the first time what an advantage her fear of losing Cliff had given him in past arguments.

"You can't do this to me." Cliff stumbled out of the room and down the stairs, defeated.

"I could be suing you for divorce. I've got the grounds. Then you'd be forced to sell the house to pay me my share. I'm willing to wait—to give you six months to decide what you're going to do with the rest of your life—even though it means losing the sale."

"You'll get another million by waiting," Cliff muttered.

"Maybe. Maybe not. I'm willing to risk it to help you. But I have plans and one way or another I'm going ahead with them. If you want to stay in this house, you'd better not stand in my way."

Just then the phone rang, putting an end to the argument. Kate hurried into the study to switch on the answering machine. "I don't want to talk to anybody," Cliff said gruffly, following her to the door.

"Neither do I. I always let the machine answer first."

Suddenly her recorded voice began to speak, giving only her phone number and asking the caller to leave a name and message.

"You erased my recording!" Cliff looked stunned, as if his territory has been violated. "Why would you do that?"

"It made the house sound empty." Kate mimicked his message. "This is Cliff Hart. I am currently filming on location and can be reached through my agent at the following number."

"It's important for people to know I'm working," he shouted.

"It's important for people to know I exist." For once Kate was determined not to let him outshout her.

He grabbed the phone. "Hello. This is Cliff Hart." Then a pause. "Oh, hello, Ruth. No, I'm home to stay." Like a man trying to get rid of a ticking bomb before it explodes, he handed the phone to Kate.

"Hi, Ruth."

At the sound of Kate's voice a torrent of words began to pour from Ruth. "Oh, Kate, I'm so glad you're still speaking to me. I couldn't live with myself if I thought I'd lost your friendship."

"It's all right, Ruth. Really. I had no right to judge you."

"I hate feeling I've failed you. But now that Cliff's home, you probably won't be available to house-sit anyway."

Kate stared at Cliff's retreating back as he left the study, closing the door behind him. "It's over, Ruth. Cliff has come home, but I'm not staying here with him."

"You're not?"

"He's finding it just as hard to believe as you do," Kate said with a laugh, "but I've never been more serious in my life. The only thing that's changed is that we're not selling the house—at least not for a while. I don't know where I'll go. I just know if there's one job for which I'm qualified after twenty-five years of homemaking, it's house-sitting!"

Kate laughed, but there was silence on the other end of the line. Finally Ruth spoke. "I hate you for the way you're making me feel, Kate," she said finally. "And I don't care what you say, this changes everything for me. What matters even more than what you think of me is what I think of myself. I've tried to be a good person. Henry and I support a foster child in Ethiopia and another one in Appalachia. I admit we don't tithe like my grandparents in Oklahoma did till the day they died, but the list of charities to which we contribute gets longer every year. And, yes,

I know how much they spend on overhead and advertising, and I don't like it any more than you do."

Her voice was rising now, swelling with emotion. "Damn it, Kate, I'm not going to let you make me feel guilty. You're living in a dream world. Do you realize the money you're spending on Ford and his family isn't even tax deductible? Please just calm down about all this. Now that Cliff is home, give yourself time to think things through. Try to figure out what you want to do with your own life before you get in over your head with other people's. What you need is some time alone, away from everybody, in a place that has no connection to your past. A place like my house. You'd be doing me a huge favor, I admit, but I'd also be doing you one. I'm not asking you to forget all your big ideas, just put them aside until you get your priorities straight. You have to take care of yourself first, Kate, then you can think about saving the world. You have time. You have the rest of your life."

"No, I don't, Ruth. Time's running out for all of us. If I'm going to make a difference, I have to start tomorrow. With or without your help."

"Then I guess this is good-bye," said Ruth, waiting for Kate to correct her.

"Good-bye, Ruth. Bon voyage."

"Bon voyage to you too, Kate. And good luck."

TWENTY-SEVEN

The sound of Ford backing his car out the driveway, taking his children to school, woke Kate, as it always did. As she walked toward the kitchen, she was startled to hear the sound of low voices. She pushed open the door and saw Teresa standing at the stove and Cliff seated at the breakfast table, awkwardly balancing her baby on his lap. The sight was so incongruous, Kate broke into peals of laughter.

"Well, I'm glad you think it's so funny," Cliff said. "I feel like a stranger in my own house. I need a directory to find out who's sleeping where."

"I'm sorry," Kate said, pouring herself a cup of coffee. "We had so many other things to talk about, I forgot to tell you Teresa and her baby were spending the night in Nina's room. But don't worry. I'm taking them with me today."

"Where are you going?"

"I spent several hours on the phone last night making plans. By noon you'll have the house to yourself."

"How many times do I have to tell you—I don't want this house to myself! I hate the idea of living here alone." As if giving voice to what Cliff was feeling, the baby began to cry. Kate set down her coffee mug and reached for him, but Teresa scooped him up quickly with one hand and with the other set a plate of scrambled eggs in front of Cliff. He smiled his thanks.

"How are you planning to support yourself if you leave home?" he asked, attacking his breakfast with relish. "You can't expect me to pay you housekeeping money to keep house somewhere else."

"I told you, Cliff, I expect nothing more from you than what you owe me under the law—my half of the current market value of this house, which by the most conservative estimate is worth two million dollars. So that means I'm entitled to a million. Now, I realize you can't come up with that kind of money without selling the house—which you don't want to do—so I'm willing to settle for twenty thousand as a down payment, then I'll give you six months to decide where you get the rest. If you're determined to keep the house, I guess you'll have to borrow against it to pay me my share. But that's for you to decide. I can't worry about it. By the same token, you don't have to worry about how I'm going to feed myself and anyone else I decide to take with me."

Barely containing his anger at this tirade, Cliff stalked to the sink and left his breakfast plate on the sideboard. "You're thinking like a child, Kate," he said. "You can't just live from day to day. You've got to plan ahead."

Kate glanced into the garden. Teresa was sitting on the grass, her back against a tree, nursing her baby and singing a lullaby in Spanish. Cliff followed the direction of her gaze. "You know," Kate said, turning to him with an unexpected smile, "you might consider letting Teresa stay on here—she could help look after you, fix your breakfast, do your laundry."

Cliff shook his head. "I don't know what your game is, Kate, but I'm not playing. I don't even speak Spanish. You don't know what I had to go through to get a plate of scrambled eggs for breakfast."

Kate brought the coffeepot to the table and refilled her cup.

Then, as an afterthought, she poured another cup for Cliff. "Thank you," he said. She gave him a surprised glance. "I know I should've said thank you a lot more often," he apologized. "I'm sorry."

Ignoring the apology, Kate walked toward the hallway. "Where are you planning to sleep when I leave?" she asked.

"I doubt if I'll sleep at all . . . I'm too upset."

"Then you don't care about moving back into the master bedroom?"

"And sleeping where? On the floor? You really haven't left me any choice. The study is the only room in the house that I still recognize." He moved behind her and slid his hands around her waist. "Why don't you come in there with me now and show me how to make a bed on the couch?" His hands cupped her breasts as he whispered in her ear, "Come with me, Kate. You know you're at your best in bed when you're not speaking to me."

Kate spun around and struck him across the mouth. "You bastard! I can't believe how easy I've made it for you all these years. And despite everything that's happened, you still think you can bring me around—a little sex, a little attention, a please here, a thank-you there, and I'll overlook anything, just like I always have. Well, my price has gotten higher—a hell of a lot higher—since you left. You can't afford me. You can't afford anybody! I can't believe the way you just left your plate beside the sink. Who did you think was going to wash it for you? Me? Teresa? If you think I'd leave her here to be your slave, you've got another think coming. It just amazes me that you can come home, after wrecking everything we had together, and still expect somebody else to do the dirty work around here!" And with that she slammed the door and took refuge in the study.

She was not coming back to this house if she could help it. Cliff was beyond redemption—a selfish, impossible man. Damn him for coming back into her life just as she was learning to live without him. And damn him again for wrecking her dreams. Fighting angry tears, Kate dragged the suitcases she had packed from the closet and flung them open. She had to make sure she had everything she would need to live the next six months in other people's houses. It was going to be a fight to get the money to buy another one.

Then she climbed the stairs to Nina's bedroom to gather up the few belongings Teresa had brought with her. The sooner she left this house and started her new life, the better.

A framed photograph on Nina's shelf drew her toward it. Kate could still remember the day it was taken. Nina was just learning to walk. Cliff held one hand and Kate the other, and Nina, smiling mischievously, was swinging on their arms, both legs in the air, postponing as long as possible the terrifying responsibility of standing on her own two feet.

"We were still a family then. Have you forgotten how happy we were?" Cliff was standing behind Kate, his voice gentled by the shared memory.

"No, I haven't forgotten," she said. "I don't want us to be enemies, Cliff. We can never go back to the way things were, but I'd like us to stay friends."

"I can't believe the way you're letting this family break apart," Cliff lamented. "You've always put your family first."

"I still do," Kate assured him. "My definition of family has just gotten broader in the last few weeks. Do you ever think about our son, Cliff? I do, all the time. Even though he's not related to us by blood and we'll probably never see him again. He'll always be part of our family. And we have a daughter— even though I didn't give birth to her. And I know she loves me as much and maybe even more than she loves you, the man who fathered her, and I know she loves me more than she loves her real mother, who, as it turns out, is not very good at loving anybody, even you."

Cliff turned away. "I wondered when we'd get to it. This is the real reason for what you're doing to me, isn't it?"

"Then you know I know."

"When Nina left L.A. last weekend, she flew straight to Toronto."

"To meet her mother?"

"No. To confront me. She's the reason I had the courage to come home. I knew the picture was about to shut down. Wenda had already walked out on me. I didn't know what I was going to do. Nina made me think I still had a chance with you. She's *our* daughter, Kate. She didn't want to hear anything about Wenda. You're her mother, the only mother she's ever known, the only mother she wants and needs. And you're my wife, Kate, the only wife I want. The only wife I need."

"Why didn't you tell me at the time Nina was your daughter?"

Cliff moved to the window seat, where Nina still kept the stuffed animals that had shared her bed when she was a child. He picked up a worn teddy bear and dug his fingers into it as if it contained all that remained of his family. "I was afraid you'd hold it against her." He paused, but Kate stood in silence with her back to him. "If you hadn't wanted a child so desperately, Nina would never have been born," he confessed in a low voice, looking out the window. "Her mother was not very happy about having a baby. She'd just gotten a divorce. She was afraid her husband would think it was his and make her come back to him. She hated the idea of family life. She still does. Especially when things start going wrong. Then she runs for her life."

Kate crossed to him and put her hands on his shoulders. "I'll always love you, Cliff—even though we'll probably never live in the same house again. But you're part of my family forever—just like that baby boy we'll never see again, just like Nina, whose own mother never wants to see her. A family is too complicated these days to be contained under one roof. What matters is that we care about each other. You still have a family, Cliff, and you can have an even bigger one if you're willing to fill all the empty rooms in this house."

Cliff laughed bitterly. "I may be out of work, Kate, but I'm not desperate enough to take in lodgers."

"The people I have in mind won't be able to pay you—but they won't cost you any more than the housekeeping money you've been paying me every month."

Cliff threw down the teddy bear and strode to the door, attempting to reassert his role as master of the house. "If it will make you happy, Kate, I'll let the woman with the baby stay. I need someone in this house to look after me."

"And she needs someone in this house to look after her," Kate stated firmly. "I wouldn't consider leaving her alone here for you to boss around. But I have a solution—providing you're willing to continue sleeping in the study."

"I already told you, I'm not setting foot in that bedroom without you," Cliff muttered. "But I don't want this house filled with strangers."

"There was a woman at the shelter yesterday that you knew," Kate said. "The wife of an actor you used in that movie you made in Mexico ten years ago. An attractive girl named Sharon—she lived with him on location. Do you remember?"

"Sharon? Yes, I do remember. She was quite striking. What was she doing at a shelter?"

"Her husband walked out on her when she gave birth to twins three years ago. Her mother was helping her, but then she died. Sharon has a weak heart, so she can't work. You know, I had the strongest impulse to bring her and her two boys home with me. I could've put them in the master bedroom—on sleeping bags. But they were headed for Florida, hoping her husband's mother would take them in. Next time I have an impulse to reach out to somebody, I'm going to do it. It's too late for me to help Sharon—but there are other Sharons. And other Teresas. Women with children who have no one to help them. Do you know what it would mean to them to live in a house like this? I know you're feeling out of luck now, Cliff, with the picture closing down and no job in sight and the women in your life running out on you, or at least that's how it must feel to you. But in spite of everything, you've been blessed. We both have. We've always had a house to live in and enough to eat. And you have a talent you can count on to earn a living. You'll get another job, Cliff, it's just a matter of time. And while you're waiting, you can start writing your own script. Who knows, there may turn out to be a story unfolding right here in front of you—you the only man in a house full of women and children. Don't tell me you haven't dreamed of living like that."

"Wait a minute, Kate," Cliff protested. "I haven't agreed to any of this yet."

The sound of a horn honking drew Kate to the window. "That's Ford," she said quietly. "Will you help me carry my suitcases to the car?"

"Is he going with you?"

"He's taking me to the place I'm going to be living for the next three months. A four-bedroom house in the Valley—which he's going to help me fill."

"Whose four-bedroom house?"

"Remember the makeup man on your last movie? His children are grown and his wife always travels with him. They spend more time on location than they do at home. They've been paying someone to stop by once a day to bring in the mail and water the plants. They were delighted when I offered to move in and do it for free."

"And they didn't object when you said you were bringing a crowd of vagrants with you?"

"I said I had some friends who were between houses—just as I was—and they said I was welcome to bring anyone I wanted. They said their house had survived five children and it would make them very happy to think that all the rooms were going to be full again."

· Kate moved down the stairs. Her suitcases stood packed and waiting by the study door. She picked up one in each hand and moved to the front door. Reluctantly Cliff picked up the remaining suitcase. "I don't want to be doing this, Kate," he said as she opened the door. "I don't want you to leave."

Ford got out of his car and started up the sidewalk toward her. Cliff suddenly slammed the door shut, locking the two of them inside, away from Ford. "What if I decide to stay here, Kate? If I don't sell the house and if I don't get another job, there's no way I can afford to pay your half. What will you do then? How will you live?"

Kate turned to face him. "I'll sue for divorce, Cliff. Then you'll have to sell the house. But in the meantime, do you know how many houses are standing empty in Los Angeles right this minute? Last night I started reading the trade papers you brought home. That's how I knew your makeup man was leaving town today. And I got six more names from *Daily Variety*—producers in New York, directors on location, actors on the road with plays. All of them leaving houses empty in Los Angeles. Last night before I went to sleep I called everyone I knew, offering my services whenever they leave town to forward mail, water plants, feed pets—no salary involved, just the right to fill the rooms. I can't imagine ever again needing—or even wanting—a house of my own."

She opened the front door quietly and handed her suitcases to Ford, who was standing patiently outside. The two men eyed each other, but no words were exchanged. Kate turned to Cliff, "So if you're free this morning, we could use your help."

"My help? How?"

"Ford has his car. I'll follow in mine. And you can follow me."

"Follow? Where?" Cliff looked at Ford, but he seemed as surprised by what Kate was saying as Cliff.

"Where are we going, Kate?" Ford asked, taking her other suitcase from Cliff.

"We're driving downtown to the shelter," she said. An excitement was building in her, pressing against her chest, filling the hollow spaces in her heart with a vision of peopling all the unused rooms in the city. "We're not selling this house, at least not for a while," she explained to Ford. "Cliff wants to stay here, but he's agreed to let you and your family continue living in the garage apartment. Teresa and the baby can have our daughter's bedroom, and since he'll be sleeping in the study, we're going to find someone for the master bedroom, preferably someone who can speak Spanish and look after Teresa."

Ford suddenly extended his hand to Cliff. "God bless you. You have as big a heart as Kate."

Cliff shook his head. "I hate what's happening here. But Kate's given me no choice. I've got to go along with her. At least for now. But, believe me, none of this was my idea."

Ford smiled in sympathy. "Not much of what's happened to

me in the past year was my idea either. Only faith has kept me going. And Kate."

Cliff shifted his weight from side to side. "Kate seems to be taking charge of all our lives. But she's made it pretty clear the only way I'm going to be able to stay in my own house is to share it with strangers." He glared at her. "Why do you need more than one car to drive downtown?"

Kate turned to him with a radiant smile. "We'll need your car for the people you bring back here—you've got the master bedroom to fill, plus the room off the kitchen. And now that Teresa is staying with you, I'll have three extra bedrooms in the house where I'll be living. And next week I know someone who's leaving for Rome . . . I'm not going to have any trouble at all finding room for everybody we can fit in our three cars today. So start your engines, gentlemen."

This time as Kate headed toward downtown, with Ford leading the way in his battered station wagon and Cliff following her reluctantly in his Jaguar, she laughed out loud as she turned onto the street called No. Hope.